SHEPPARD OF THE
ARGONNE

ALTERNATIVE HISTORY NAVAL BATTLES OF WWII

G. Wm. Weatherly

G. WILLIAM WEATHERLY

2ND EDITION

iUniverse LLC
Bloomington

SHEPPARD OF THE ARGONNE
ALTERNATIVE HISTORY NAVAL BATTLES OF WWII

iUniverse books may be ordered through booksellers or by contacting:

iUniverse
1663 Liberty Drive
Bloomington, IN 47403
www.iuniverse.com
1-800-Authors (1-800-288-4677)

Because of the dynamic nature of the Internet, any web addresses or links contained in this book may have changed since publication and may no longer be valid. The views expressed in this work are solely those of the author and do not necessarily reflect the views of the publisher, and the publisher hereby disclaims any responsibility for them.

Any people depicted in stock imagery provided by Thinkstock are models, and such images are being used for illustrative purposes only. Certain stock imagery © Thinkstock.

ISBN: 978-1-4917-3191-8 (sc)
ISBN: 978-1-4917-3192-5 (hc)
ISBN: 978-1-4917-3190-1 (e)

Library of Congress Control Number: 2014908620

Printed in the United States of America.

iUniverse rev. date: 8/7/2014

To all—past, present,
and future—who have
loved the ocean
and served
at sea

ACKNOWLEDGMENTS

Thank you
to my family and friends,
who endured drafts and rewrites
too numerous to count,
and to my patient editors
endlessly toiling
through my mistakes.

AUTHOR'S NOTE

Writing alternative history presents a plethora of choices. In this series of work, I chose to accelerate some technology development such as ship building, metallurgy, ordinance, and radar; while keeping others such as aircraft close to the actual timelines since that development was not restricted by treaty. Using fictional names for ships can be confusing where a ship of that name actually existed in the war. For American ships, I slavishly followed naming battle cruisers after famous American battles grouped by ships of the same design, aircraft carriers after sailing frigates, and cruisers after cities appropriate for their size. Battleships and destroyers are not named, but would follow historical traditions. Nation designators (USS, HMS, or KMS) are only used where the named ship actually existed as used in the novel. Names for allied and German warships followed their conventions to the best of my limited abilities.

To my several editors' frustrations, I have mostly followed naval usage and style from the early 1940's period, so please forgive the deviations from *The Chicago Manual of Style*. The spelling and usage of the rank and position of ship's captain as a reference or in conversation may have driven them to drink.

War in the twentieth century was dictated by technology. Presenting that without detracting from the battles and struggle of the protagonist, I hope leaves the reader with an understanding of why events can be shaped by the tools of war as much as by the men that controlled them.

PRELUDE

From November 1921 to February 1922, nine nations—the United States, Great Britain, Japan, China, France, Italy, Belgium, Netherlands, and Portugal—met in Washington DC as part of the Washington Naval Conference. The main goal of the conference was to come to an agreement on naval disarmament in the aftermath of the Great War, making it the first disarmament conference in history. By its end, the conference had produced three international treaties, including the historic Five-Power Treaty (a.k.a. the Washington Naval Treaty) that was signed by the United States, Great Britain, Japan, Italy, and France. The Five-Power Treaty strangled naval construction and limited ship and armament sizes, while flooding the world's scrap-metal markets with banned warships—all helping to avert a naval arms race among the great powers of that age for over a decade.

But what if the Washington Naval Conference hadn't transpired as history recorded it? What if one lone incident—an assassination, common in the politics of one participating nation—occurred and changed the conference ... thus irrevocably altering military history in the following years and ultimately World War II itself? What would history have looked like then?

What if ...?

Baron Tomosaburō Katō—Admiral of the Imperial Japanese Navy, Naval Minister, and head of his nation's delegation to the Washington Naval Conference—sat in his hotel room alone late on the evening of November 14, 1921. He listened to his favorite phonographic recording of traditional music while rereading staff notes on the position Japan would take for the conference's most-important second plenary session the next day. At that moment, someone knocked on the door, entered the room, and bowed. Two minutes later, Baron Katō lay on the floor in a pool of blood—dead. The murder remained unsolved, despite the unfettered efforts of the DC metropolitan police and all the resources the United States government could bring to bear.

Calling it an assassination and accusing the Americans of collusion, the remaining members of the Japanese delegation walked out of the conference, fearful for their own lives, since Baron Katō had been strongly in favor of a treaty limiting naval expansion, opposing his own militarists. Without Japanese agreement to stop the 8-8-8 building program enshrined in Japanese law, the United States continued the naval expansion it had begun with the 1916 and 1919 naval appropriations. Faced with growing Japanese and American fleets, Great Britain had no option but to continue her own construction programs of battle cruisers and battleships. Italy chose to restart the building of the *Caracciolo* class, sparking a renewed interest in the *Lyon* class by France. Finally, Germany renounced the Treaty of Versailles, collapsing the League of Nations. The former Allies acquiesced, unwilling to return to the trenches as Germany, too, began rearming.

Around the world, shipyards rang as riveters joined steel to hulls. New mines, mills, and factories sprang up to feed the growing demand for naval rearmament. Huge government arsenals continued the development of eighteen-inch and larger guns started in the Great War to defeat the thicker and better armor at longer and longer ranges. Industry hired more tradesmen to meet the endless government contracts. Laboratories accelerated the development of all manner of naval technology and metallurgy—perhaps at the expense of aviation, perhaps not. Flotillas of dredges slaved endlessly on shallow harbors; building ways were augmented by construction dry docks and expanding shipyards as warships grew too large for traditional launching methods, further bolstering civilian construction trades. Unfettered, warships grew ever larger, remaining immune to the weapons of all but their own breed.

The Roaring Twenties roared on with expanding work forces. Good paying jobs fueled consumerism and continued economic expansion avoiding the economic devastation of the Great Depression. Growing tax revenues satisfied the financial needs of the fleets' expansion. Plentiful jobs and rising living standards, as well as enhanced job opportunities in the growing navies, obviated the pressure on politicians for social programs. Empires flourished, although the Soviet Union's command economy lagged behind the other international powers. Still, Hitler, Stalin, Mussolini, and Hirohito all dreamed of and plotted greater empires, replacing the old order, until the world erupted once more in global conflict.

PROLOGUE

Like a predator, it had come again last night as he lay in a Norfolk BOQ room, stalking Sheppard McCloud in his sleep, feasting on his rest. But Evelyn, at home in San Diego, was not there to comfort and hold him. She could not tell Sheppard that it was just a bad dream—that he was safe with her in their bed.

But it was not just a dream. The pain in his shattered leg, the twinges from the shards of Japanese steel still in his body—they were real. Evelyn still had no idea that the dream had once been reality and that Sheppard often relived the events on the *Shenandoah* in his sleep. He loved her too much to share the horrors of exploding shells, screaming wounded, and the spray of blood, bone, and flesh peppering his face.

The Navy, too, was unaware of the dream. The nightmares had begun during the weeks of surgery, one operation after another at Balboa Naval Hospital to repair his leg and make him "fit for duty." And when Sheppard awoke during those weeks at the hospital— sweating, confused, wide-eyed, and rigid with fear—it was easy to blame the pain instead of the nightmares when nurses asked. Morphine dulled the reality of his horrific memories, but he had no morphine at home as he progressed from crutches to a cane and finally, now, to just a limp. Without narcotics, the dream grew sharper, clearer in the consequences of his decisions—his decisions, killing his men. Sheppard could not hide the dreams from Evelyn. He had never been able to hide anything from her. So he told her that it was indeed just a nightmare and that it would pass in time as his body healed. He could not tell if she believed him. He hoped she did, for her sake. It would make his return to war easier.

Sheppard feared that the dream would turn back into reality and he would have to live through it all again. Three months of reviewing his own decisions to find his mistakes and learn from them only left him frustrated. The logic for his actions appeared justifiable and sound, but his motivation ... what had it been—glory, ego, hubris? Before December 7th, Sheppard had been supremely confident, sure of his ability to lead his men, certain that he could not be beaten. He had been decisive, aggressive even, when he'd sought engagement with the Japanese carrier force. He had been so sure he had all the advantages: gunnery, radar, weather, a setting sun.

Now that his physical injuries were healing, the Navy assumed that Sheppard was still that confident leader—but they were wrong.

Norfolk Naval Base and Hampton Roads

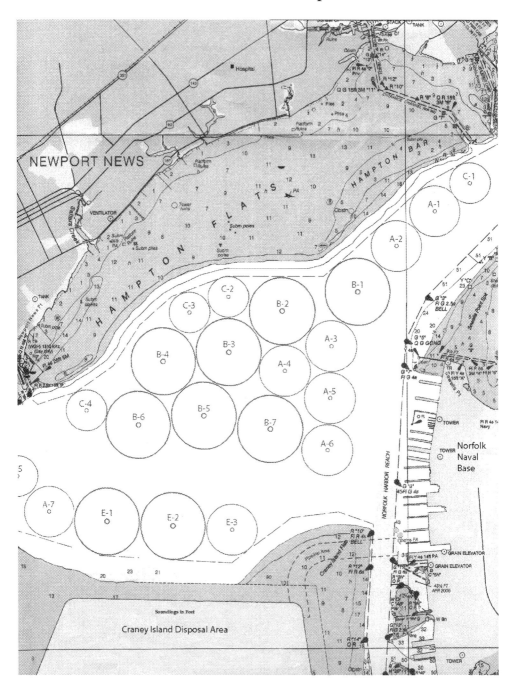

CHAPTER 1

RETURN TO DUTY

She waited, the loneliness of a crowd enveloping her, the activity of thousands lost to her in anticipation. What would he be like? Would he be firm, controlling her tantrums? She knew she was headstrong and impetuous in the self-confidence of her youth. Would he be gentle, subtly guiding her through the rocks and shoals of existence? Was he capable of demanding her best, knowing what she could achieve in her greatness? All she felt was the anxiety and hope of those around her that he would arrive today. Could he replace the first love of her life—the man who had raised her?

Vice Admiral Jonas Ingraham, Commander Scouting Forces Atlantic, knew the meaning of the rap on his varnished oak door. The guard at Atlantic Fleet Headquarters at Norfolk, Virginia, had already alerted the staff to the arrival of Captain Sheppard Jackson McCloud. At the call, Jonas's aide immediately hustled to meet the wounded warrior, hero of the Japanese raid on Pearl Harbor, to guide him to Jonas's office. Admiral Royal Ingersoll, Commander in Chief Atlantic Fleet and Jonas's boss, had made it unpleasantly but emphatically clear that Jonas would decide whether Sheppard was well enough—"fit for duty." Jonas also knew that the service desperately needed Sheppard now, not later when he'd fully recovered from his wounds.

"Enter," Jonas barked.

The two men stepped into his office. Both strode toward his mahogany desk framed by two stuffed leather chairs in front of the far wall. Alongside Jonas's aide, Sheppard stood, ramrod straight on the blue carpet, athletically trim. He was obviously in his best set of blues, the four gold stripes on each sleeve only lightly tarnished, with his white cover tucked under his left arm. His starched white shirt with black tie in the regulation four-in-hand knot reminded the admiral of their first meeting, over a decade ago. Jonas could not see Sheppard's black shoes but guessed they were spit-shined to a high gloss.

Jonas eyed his former gunnery officer critically: the square-set jaw and slightly bent nose, his face whiter than the usual dark tan of an officer comfortable with an open bridge and salt spray. There was a touch of gray at Sheppard's temples that had not appeared in his otherwise black hair the last time they'd met. Jonas also saw that something in his eyes had changed. They were different from when Sheppard, as a senior lieutenant commander, had made the service sit up and take notice. Perhaps it was the sense of mortality that came with serious injury in war. Jonas could not be sure, as his own service had not included the death, twisted steel, screaming wounded, and controlled chaos aboard a ship damaged in battle.

Jonas knew the details of the captain's medical record—the series of surgeries at Balboa Naval Hospital that had mostly removed the shrapnel and restored the bones and sinews of his left leg. However, the dispassionate official descriptions of his injuries aboard the battle cruiser *Shenandoah* did not provide insight into Sheppard's psyche.

The young lieutenant, sporting three rings on his aiguillette, stood on Sheppard's left, slightly behind the captain, where only the admiral could see him.

"Admiral," Jonas's aide said, "Captain Sheppard McCloud."

"Good morning, Sheppard. How's your leg?"

Vice Admiral Ingraham really did not care what Sheppard's answer was. He would form his own opinion, as Ingersoll had directed. The captain's limp had been barely noticeable when he'd entered the office. His weight now appeared equally supported on both legs. His gaze was steady; no narrowing of those pale blue eyes or flexing cheek muscles indicating grinding teeth that would betray hidden pain. Pausing, perhaps too long, but really only a few seconds, Jonas committed them both—and the Allied cause—to Sheppard's care.

With a nod to his aide, Jonas said, "Please have a seat."

"Better, Admiral; thank you for asking."

Sheppard thrust a telegram toward his old commanding officer from the *Ticonderoga*.

"My orders require me to report to you for duty or subsequent assignment as directed."

Jonas smiled. "I know."

He also knew his reputation as well as Sheppard did. Short-tempered and pugnacious, Jonas only delayed asking a subordinate to sit when he was not going to ask at all. Those meetings would be very unpleasant for the object of Jonas's ire as he raked a subordinate's incompetency with blistering invective. When he wished, Jonas could level his bushy brown eyebrows, seemingly out of place considering his snow-white hair, and deliver a bombastic tirade that would make the most seasoned boatswain cringe and believe he was in the presence of God almighty.

Sheppard sat, relaxed, and settled into the right-hand leather chair. Jonas's aide left, shutting the admiral's hallway door on the way out.

"Have you heard about Bill Leland?" Jonas asked.

It had been—what, eight? No,—nine years since the three of them had served together on the *Ticonderoga*. Leland and Sheppard had been integral parts of the team that had helped Jonas win the Battenberg Cup for the best capital ship in the fleet, with Leland's engineering department gaining consecutive red "*Es*" for efficiency, in the process matching the white ones of Sheppard's gunnery department.

"No, Admiral, the last I knew he was in command of the battle cruiser *Argonne*. How's Bill?"

"Dead!"

Clearly stunned, all Sheppard could say was, "When?"

"Early last month, heart attack, died on the bridge of his ship, returning to Norfolk following the *Argonne*'s post shakedown availability."

"Susan … The kids … How are they taking it?"

"Badly; moved back to her folks' place in Ohio." Jonas made a sweeping gesture with his gold-braided arm in the direction of the offices of Scouting Forces Atlantic. "Staff took care of everything." Leaning toward the captain, Jonas placed his forearms on his desk. "Look, Sheppard, time is short. I'm sending you to the *Argonne*. There is a 'situation' developing in the Atlantic. Do you know Ted Grabowski?"

"No, Admiral."

"He's a good officer, just too junior for command of a battle cruiser. Done a four-oh job in training the crew, keeping things together following the captain's death."

Jonas stood suddenly, frustrated that a fine officer like Leland was no longer available to the Navy in time of war. True to service etiquette, Sheppard rose in response—awkwardly on his one good leg.

"I should have known," Jonas said.

His lips tightened to a thin line, eyes glaring as he remembered how well Sheppard could hide pain. After all, he had won the intercollegiate light-heavyweight boxing championship while at the Academy, despite suffering a broken nose in the first round.

Feeling betrayed, Jonas flattened his eyebrows and growled, "Leg isn't well, is it?"

"No, Admiral, but it is good enough and getting better!"

Jonas looked at Sheppard, eyes afire with accusation and his own doubt on the decision he'd already set in motion. He stared into Sheppard's eyes, trying to plumb the depths of his soul. After what seemed like an eternity, Jonas softened, smiled, and relaxed.

"I'll take you at your word, Captain."

"Thank you, Admiral," was all Sheppard could muster in response.

"Your assignment to Dolf Hamilton's task force, anchored in the roadstead, is included with your orders to command," Jonas said. "My aide will give them to you on your way out. Good luck with the *Argonne*."

Jonas walked the few steps to the door with Sheppard, placing his left hand on the younger officer's back. If asked why he had done that, Jonas would not or could not say. All he knew was that it would likely be the last time he ever saw another officer he deeply respected.

— • —

Two hundred nautical miles to the east, Korvettenkapitän Hans Dieter Meier, holder of the Knight's Cross for gallantry and one of twelve U-boat aces with over one hundred thousand tons of shipping sent to the bottom, had to decide his next move for *U-179*. The morning trim dive to adjust his submarine's variable ballast, achieving exactly neutral buoyancy in the changed water conditions of his current location, was complete. If the Americans were as smart as the English, their air patrols would be arriving in the vicinity shortly. Normally, Meier would remain submerged and spend the daylight hours deep, running slowly on his battery and electric motors, avoiding all contact, as his orders directed. Regrettably, that course of action dictated his arrival at the mouth of the Chesapeake half a day later than he wished. Assigned one of the premier patrol areas, assuring a long list of kills before he was forced to return to France, Meier was eager to begin the hunt; unfortunately, his area was also the farthest from Le Havre.

He would be within his patrol area regardless, but Meier wanted the honor of the first kill. Gaining that distinction required knowledge of the shipping patterns the Americans were using, as well as understanding patrols in the vicinity. Meier knew there was little doubt of success. He had trained the *U-179*'s crew well. They had been together for almost a year, during which time he had scored one sinking after another. All he needed was to be on station early enough to gain the needed intelligence. Then Vizeadmiral Karl Dönitz—or "Uncle Karl," as all the German skippers referred to their commanding admiral—would congratulate him in a message every U-boat would read.

No, it would not be much of a gamble. The Americans had no reason to believe that German submarines were closing the East Coast to initiate Operation Beckenschlaege (Cymbal Crash). The lax Yankees would learn the same hard lessons as their English allies, while Vizeadmiral Dönitz's U-boats ravaged their unprotected shipping. With a little luck, Dönitz could end this war in six months without any assistance from the rest of the Kriegsmarine.

"Surface!" Meier ordered.

— —

Lieutenant John William Hamblen IV, USN, answered the 21MC "squawk box" report from the signal bridge with a curt, "Quarterdeck, aye." Lifting the sixteen-power long glass, symbolic of his position as the officer of the deck (in port), he focused on the signal halyards of the aircraft carrier *Sabine*. As the signal guard ship, she would repeat any flag hoist from the Norfolk Naval Operating Base signal tower to ships anchored farther out in the roadstead.

The light breeze from the west barely fluttered the five brightly colored flags and lone pennant that rose sharply to *Sabine*'s yardarm, making recognition difficult in the late-morning light. Yes, it was as the signal bridge had reported from their higher vantage point, just able to see the base's mast. "Charlie Charlie Four Nine" was *Argonne*'s hull number. What followed would be an order that Hamblen would be responsible for carrying out. "Easy, Pennant Six"—the call for the captain's gig—was what every man on board was anticipating.

Lowering the long glass, Hamblen turned to his boatswain's mate of the watch and said, "Boats, call away the gig."

Moving to the microphone for the ship's general announcing system (1MC), the petty officer placed the boatswain's pipe to his lips and piped, "*s*ˢ⁻ˢ⁻ˢˢˢˢˢˢˢ"—*Attention!*—using his lungs and hand position to make the staccato starts and stops of the notes, followed by, "Away the captain's gig, away."

Feeling pleased with himself, Hamblen took one more turn around the quarterdeck to ensure everything was squared away. Not a deck per se as it had been in the age of sail, the quarterdeck of *Argonne* was just an area of the starboard-side main deck adjacent the aft accommodation ladder and landing stage that was reserved for formal arrivals and departures. Located between the superstructure and the Number III main-battery eighteen-inch, three-gun turret, the deck was immaculate. A heavy steel locker jutted from the superstructure bulkhead nearby. An equally heavy armored cover, dogged shut when at sea, protected the communication instruments within from the muzzle blast of the guns. Now the cover hung open on its hinges, allowing access to the 1MC microphone, a ship's telephone, and the captain's command-announcing circuit (21MC), collision alarm, general alarm switches, and sound-powered telephone jacks inside. A snow-white decoratively braided lanyard dangling nearby led to the ship's bell three decks above. The only remaining item was a small portable desk, removed when the ship was at sea. Waist high and at the end of a stanchion decorated with coxcombing, the desk served as a place for the OOD to write the ship's log when in port.

Hamblen wished that the teak deck could have remained its normal peacetime holystoned off-white, but the dictates of war required that it now be painted a dull dark blue-gray, consistent with the Measure 12 (modified) camouflage scheme of all ships in the Atlantic Fleet.

— —

The bright flash startled Sheppard. He resisted the impulse to take cover, instinctively trying to avoid any outward sign of fear of the bursting shell as he directed the escape from the Japanese counterattack. The thick armor of *Shenandoah*'s command tower protected him; the hose teams extinguishing the blaze in the superstructure were not protected. They fell as if cut down by a scythe, shredded by the shrapnel and the explosion before Sheppard's eyes.

Why had he decided to attack the Japanese carrier force? The odds against him were overwhelming. Coldly calculating, he knew the weather was to his advantage. His new fire-control radar, just tested in the foul weather northwest of Oahu, allowed him to hide in the rainsqualls as his sixteen-inch guns sought revenge for the sneak attack on Pearl Harbor earlier in the day. He had thought he could get a few hits on the carriers before the heavy escorts closed within visual range in the fading gray light. Perhaps he could cripple or sink some of them. Supremely confident that the speed of his ship would safely allow him to escape, the "great" Captain McCloud, as he now sarcastically thought of himself, had not hesitated to engage. He had been so sure he could pull it off. Sheppard *had* always made the right decisions ...

"Captain? Captain! Does the captain require assistance?" The marine at the door stared at him.

Had anyone else seen him? Sheppard stood at the entrance of Atlantic Fleet Headquarters, his eyes adjusting to the bright wake-up call of a cloudless day, the brilliant sun in his face. He had to become the confident leader again for the sake of his new command. He knew that if he failed, the men would doubt him and more sailors—his sailors—again … would die.

As his vision returned, he steadied himself against the doorframe, for a moment fearing his left leg would betray him the way it had that Sunday evening when the *Shenandoah* had engaged the Japanese fleet. As a young officer, Sheppard had wondered why his captains clung so tenaciously to their commands. In his own first command—the destroyer *Rowan*—he had learned the answer: responsibility. The *Shenandoah* had taught him the dark side of that same responsibility.

"No, thank you," Sheppard answered.

Stepping out of the doorway, he exchanged salutes with the sentry, who cast an inquiring glance at the ribbons on his chest, stiffening to perfection as he noticed Sheppard's recently acquired red-white-and-blue ribbon of a Silver Star and the purple-and-white ribbon of a Purple Heart.

Vice Admiral Ingraham's heartening words assigning him to replace Leland—giving Sheppard another command, returning him to duty—were what he needed. What he hoped he needed.

——

An ocean away in Brest, France, Vizeadmiral Klaus Schröder walked across the gangway of his flagship, the *Graf Zeppelin*. As he stepped aboard Germany's first aircraft carrier, the pipe of the boatswain's mate twittered, and the first of fifteen guns fired in salute. A product of the Imperial Navy, Schröder gave the traditional naval salute rather than the Nazi stiff arm. Of course, he was a party member; all flag officers were required to join. But Hitler, that Bohemian corporal, was stupid and did not understand the nature of modern war at sea. Fortunately, Großadmiral Erich Raeder and his predecessors did, and they had prevailed in building an impressive navy that could tie down the British Home Fleet while barely retaining sufficient forces to strike at convoys.

The safe transit of those convoys was the only way for Great Britain to stay in the war. The *Graf Zeppelin* and her sister ship, the *Anton Fokker*, were the direct result of Raeder's efforts to educate the Führer in the new reality of war at sea—the necessity of air cover in all operations. With the final subjugation of France in the fall of 1941, all the French Atlantic and Mediterranean bases had become available to the Kriegsmarine, as had some units of the French fleet. Now Germany had a realistic chance of strangling Great Britain by cutting her supply lines.

The first foray of Schröder's fleet into the Atlantic via the Denmark Strait had been successful in not only sinking thirty-eight merchant ships and two armed merchant cruisers but also in destroying Admiral Tovey's cruisers patrolling the strait in the fog. Unfortunately, Schröder had not anticipated the heavy expenditure of fuel oil and gasoline necessary to maintain air cover in daylight hours, which he required to keep the British search planes from locating him. As a result, his fleet had to return to port sooner than he wanted. This deployment would be different; Schröder changed the mix of stores in his tanker supply ships in addition to acquiring several more. Little did the British know that the German supply ships were secretly operating from Spanish ports. Since they were not warships, they technically did not violate the sham of neutrality. This time Schröder was much closer to his operating areas, and the calmer waters of the southern latitudes would make it easier to replenish.

Schröder knew he could slip past the British airborne patrols in the Bay of Biscay at night during the April storms. Once he was clear, the British could not catch him before he began preying on the fat tankers and cargo ships vital to that island nation's existence. The German army might have failed in its invasion attempt when the Royal Navy sacrificed much of its destroyer strength to defeat the cross-channel assault. But the Kriegsmarine would not fail to humble the British lion and force Winston Churchill to accept Germany's terms, erasing forever the ignominy of the first war. The world would soon come to know German efficiency and discipline.

Unfortunately, the U-boats were reporting a high-pressure area to the west. His sortie would have to wait a few days for a low-pressure area and cold front to develop. In the meantime, the carrier's air squadrons, flying from the nearby French fields, would keep British forces at bay, preventing any damage to his ships while they remained at the ready in Brest.

As the last gun fired, Schröder dropped his salute and stepped aboard his flagship.

"Ah, Becker," he greeted the Captain of the *Graf Zeppelin*. "Your crew is well disciplined and executed the arrival ceremony well. I trust they are just as prepared when it comes to fighting."

— —

Boatswain's Mate Second Class Cruz was sitting in the aft starboard corner of the mess decks aboard *Argonne* with the rest of the gig's crew, enjoying a cup of thick navy coffee, when the 1MC call came. With the gig's crew wearing their best service dress blues, no officer could find fault with their current appearance (the Irish pennant on one of Fireman Russert's thirteen front trouser buttons that Cruz had found now corrected). Only four men were assigned to the gig. Cruz was the newest member, but as coxswain, he was in charge, since the bow hook, stern hook, and the engineman were all nonrated. Even though Cruz was a pay grade too senior, it had not deterred him from specifically requesting assignment to the captain's gig when he had reported aboard last month.

All four men had spent days shining brass, cleaning, varnishing, and spiffing the gig housed inside the *Argonne*'s hangar, where Cruz had convinced the aviation chief boatswain's mate to stow the launch awaiting the new captain's arrival. Out of the weather, the polishing, painting, and cleaning continued, unhindered by morning dew, salt spray, or passing squall.

"Okay, men," Cruz said, "it's show time. Goldstein, have Chief Bledsoe hoist the gig to the main deck starboard railing. I'll meet you guys there." Smiling, he added, "Don't leave without me."

Cruz was not worried. He knew that the three young men were already proud of their achievements and the importance of their assignment. He watched them disappear through the watertight door to the starboard-side passage before he turned, hustling past the tables and stools fixed to the deck until he came to the double ladder leading up to the main deck. He knew exactly what he was going to do, but service tradition and the chain-of-command dictated that he get his instructions from the officer of the deck.

— —

Sheppard kept surreptitiously glancing at Hampton Roads, hoping to see his new command, as Admiral Ingraham's sedan weaved its way toward the fleet landing. He knew *Argonne* was anchored out with her sister ship, *Belleau Wood*. Those two capital ships—in addition to the carriers *Raritan* and *Sabine*—would be the heart of the hastily assembled force his orders directed him to join. Beside the flattops and battle cruisers, the rest of the task force would include the armored cruisers *Quincy* and *Bethlehem*. Their designation was old, but the ships, with their speed, armor, and ten-inch guns, were really only smaller versions of the battle cruiser he would command. A light cruiser squadron for scouting, some of the new light antiaircraft cruisers, and two destroyer squadrons would complete the ships assigned to Rear Admiral Adolphus Hamilton.

Sheppard, though, would have to wait for his first glimpse of *Argonne*. The carriers anchored closer to the fleet landing, with their high flight decks and massive funnels, were blocking any view of the roadstead beyond. Crowded flight decks indicated they had already loaded their air groups at the carrier piers before returning to anchor.

Arriving at the landing, the admiral's driver braked to a halt and jumped out to open the right-rear passenger door for Sheppard. Yeoman Second Class Brewster, though, was not fast enough; the chief petty officer in charge at the fleet landing grabbed the door handle first.

"Good morning, Captain," the chief said.

Sheppard awkwardly climbed out of the sedan. "Good morning, Chief. I'm Captain McCloud."

"Yes, sir. Admiral Ingraham's aide called, saying you were en route. The *Argonne*'s gig should be here any minute."

"Thank you."

Sheppard believed the "Chiefs" were the glue that held the navy together. He had relied on them ever since Chief Stratton on the old battleship *New York* had kept him, as a young officer, from making fatal mistakes that would have cost him his career. Aboard *Shenandoah*, he had made it a point to visit the chief's quarters at least once a week for a meal and small talk, but only when invited.

When Sheppard was wounded, his executive officer Chris Baer's ready acceptance of the senior chief's first invitation was the last thing Sheppard had needed to cement his opinion—he then requested that Baer remain in command of the *Shenandoah* while battle damage was being repaired.

Yeoman Brewster returned from taking Sheppard's luggage to the landing.

"Captain," the yeoman asked, "is there anything else I can do for you before the *Argonne*'s gig arrives? Anything you need from the exchange?"

"No, thank you. I appreciate all you have done."

"Captain, if … if *Argonne* is in need of a yeoman before you sail, I know that Admiral Ingraham will let me go back to sea."

Sheppard turned and cocked an eyebrow at the yeoman. "Brewster, wouldn't that be short notice for your family?"

"No, sir. I am still single, and I'm coming to the end of my shore duty anyway."

"Very well. When I get aboard, I'll see how we are manned. I'll ask the chief of staff for your assignment if we have a billet open."

"Thank you, Captain!" With a crisp salute, Brewster was gone.

As the *Argonne*'s gig approached the landing, the coxswain's maneuvering seemed familiar. When the gig turned at the last second and backed down full to check its way, Sheppard knew why. The bow hook and stern hook, jumping to the pontoon, smartly made the gig fast to the landing and then hustled his baggage on board without a word, confirming what Sheppard suspected.

"Petty Officer Cruz," Sheppard said, "what are you doing here?"

"It's like this, Capt'n," Cruz said, saluting from the gig. "Capt'n Baer found out what happened to the *Argonne*'s first captain. He figured that your leg would just about be healed and the Navy would probably want you back in command. He asked if some of us would volunteer to transfer out of the shipyard. Give you a few familiar faces in your new ship. When Boatswain Reed called a friend in the Bureau and confirmed you might be going to the *Argonne* as soon as your convalescent leave was up, there was no shortage of volunteers.

"When I reported aboard, I told Commander Grabowski that I had been your coxswain before and volunteered to run the gig. It took me awhile to get Seaman Johansen, Seaman Goldstein, and Fireman Russert here trained up and the gig squared away, but we're getting there. Still have a lot of rope work to do."

With a suppressed smile at the fresh paint, varnish, and gleaming bright work, Sheppard returned Cruz's salute and stepped aboard, followed by the two seamen. Goldstein placed the shined brass ball at the top of the flagstaff, signaling to all ships and boats that a full captain had embarked. As Russert revved the engine in response to Cruz's order, Johansen and Goldstein synchronized a display of their boathooks, wordlessly impressing any observers. Cruz was clearly in charge; he had trained the gig's crew well. Wherever Sheppard went, he knew that he would be greeted with respect because of such a beautifully maintained and smartly run gig. Chris Baer had known that and made sure Cruz was one of the volunteers to go to the *Argonne*.

— • —

Meier watched the twin-engine aircraft closely with his Zeiss binoculars. Low on the horizon to the west, he knew he had the advantage of the sun behind him. He felt certain that it was a B-18, meaning it belonged to the US Army.

"Bah!" Meier muttered.

He dismissed the possibility that the plane's crew could spot, let alone recognize, his Type IXB U-boat at this range. His only concern was the white water of his wake.

Turning to his watch officer, Meier ordered, "Slow to five knots until the American disappears."

Meier did not expect a delay of more than a quarter hour. He smiled. He would still have plenty of time to observe the entrance to the Chesapeake before he would initiate the attack.

— —

Squadron Leader Rupert Wythe-Jones, RAF DFC, had already sunk one U-boat in this war, and Four-One-Five Squadron of Coastal Command had developed into a first-rate unit, equipped with Short Sunderland flying boats, under his command. But Rupert was not flying today. Finally, he had a chance to catch up on his paperwork.

A short man with neatly cut but rather long brown hair and mustache, Rupert was sitting behind his desk in his headquarters at RAF Pembroke Dock when the telephone rang, interrupting his thoughts of a quiet evening with his wife.

"Hello, Wythe-Jones here."

"Rupert, ol' boy, I thought I would ring you up with some good news."

Rupert grimaced. It was Air Commodore Andrew Blackstone, Commander of 19 Group, and a call from him was never good news.

"Sir," Rupert said, "I am working on my overdues as we speak and should have them posted in a day or two."

"Not to worry; I am sure you will get them done forthwith. I really called to give you the news that we are sending down some maintainers to install a new piece of kit in your Sunderlands. It should take less than a week and will give you a much better capability in bad weather. Until it is complete and your squadron trained in its use, you will be standing down. Two-Two-Eight Squadron will fill in for you out of Harnworthy. Any questions?"

Rupert said nothing, so the commodore quickly gave a "Cheerio!" and hung up. Rupert stared at the telephone receiver and wondered if the "kit" could be the new centimetric ASV III radar he had heard of. If so, his squadron would soon have an incredible advantage, not only in bad weather but also after dark. The U-boats crossing the Bay of Biscay would no longer be able to safely transit at night. They would be easy prey. *Dream on*, he thought. *At least I'll have these bloody reports done.*

— —

"*Argonne*'s coming into view, Captain."

"Thank you, Cruz."

Sheppard stood, steadying himself against the gig's motion in the light chop, accepting Cruz's offering of binoculars with a beautifully knotted white line lanyard.

Sheppard had met Cruz at captain's mast shortly after taking command of *Shenandoah*. While trying to decide on an appropriate punishment for a relatively minor offense under the "Articles for the Government of the United States Navy 1930", Sheppard had noticed something in Cruz's eyes: native intelligence, curiosity, defiance of authority … Sheppard wasn't sure, but he decided to spend more time than the routine formality of mast dictated.

It turned out that Raymondo DeJesus Cruz had grown up in a West Texas border town, where he had learned to use his fists, teeth, and a knife before his sixteenth birthday. His brother's death in a gang fight clarified his bleak future within a year. A judge had given him a choice between the service and reform school. Cruz had chosen the Navy only because he did not know anything about it.

From the day of mast forward, Sheppard had watched as Cruz developed into an exceptional petty officer. His street smarts stood him well when it came to understanding and motivating other troubled kids. As a boatswain's mate, more than a few of these kids could be found in the "deck gang" where Cruz served.

That was when the chiefs and other officers of the *Shenandoah* began to notice Cruz. As opportunities presented themselves, Cruz had taken them, never looking back. Sheppard suspected that Cruz looked at him as the loving father he'd never had and that he would do anything to please Sheppard. When the position became available, Sheppard requested that Cruz be his gig coxswain. On December 7th, it had been Cruz who dragged Sheppard out of the wreckage of *Shenandoah*'s bridge and carried him to the battle dressing station, saving both Sheppard's life and his shattered leg.

Sheppard stared, anxiously watching each new detail of his command slowly unmasked as the gig rounded the *Sabine*'s bow. There was no need for the binoculars. He took a seat lest his leg betray his emotions as he surveyed the battle cruiser before him.

She had to be a quarter of a mile in length, with a mountain of superstructure amidships. The two towering, massive funnels, spread far apart, were the visible indicators of an enormous machinery complex contained within her engineering spaces.

Sheppard knew she was part of the new concept for battle cruisers created by the US Navy's General Board. She was not a scout for the fleet but a long-range striking component with the ability to slow an enemy fleet by creating cripples. She was fast enough to control the battle range with any enemy or run down the fleetest cruiser. Tough armor shielded her vitals from opposing long-range gunfire, and she had an antiaircraft armament strong enough to destroy any aerial assault; these attributes created a ship that would give a good account in any fight, regardless of the odds. This he already knew intellectually, but the reality of wood and steel before him was greater than he had ever imagined.

He had heard rumors of this new class while he was out in the Pacific, but actually seeing one took his breath away. In addition to creating an image of overwhelming power, *Argonne*'s designer had achieved a balance and symmetry inadequately described as breathtaking; the only term that would do her justice was the Old Norse term *yar*.

Captain Sheppard McCloud surprised himself by whistling and saying, "So you're *Argonne*."

— —

Lieutenant Hamblen steadied the long glass against the awning stanchion, watching the bow of the *Sabine* with his bright-blue eyes for any indication of the returning gig. As the small craft came into view, he satisfied himself that he was looking at the correct gig by reading "CC-49," prominent on both sides of the bow.

"Messenger of the Watch, send my respects to Commander Grabowski and report that the captain's gig has just rounded the *Sabine*'s bow and should be alongside in ten minutes."

Replying with a sharp, "Aye, aye, sir," the messenger saluted and hustled off.

Hamblen lowered the long glass again, searching the quarterdeck and white canvas awning for anything that was less than perfect. From the first rumors of Captain McCloud's assignment to *Argonne,* every man aboard had anticipated this moment, trying their utmost to prepare *Argonne* for whatever the hero of Pearl Harbor might need them to perform in battle. The war that started in the Pacific had quickly spread to the Atlantic with both Hitler's and Mussolini's declarations. The United States now faced not one but three determined enemies and but one ally—a limping, if not demoralized, British Empire.

Raising the long glass, Hamblen tried to see the man that wardroom table talk credited with saving the West Coast from air attack. A single battle cruiser—the *Shenandoah*—supported by a lone destroyer had engaged a fleet of eight of the most modern Japanese aircraft carriers and four capital ships with other cruisers and destroyers in company. The fact that the guns of the *Shenandoah* had damaged several of the carriers before fleeing the escorts had saved some of the service's honor from the disaster at Pearl. Hamblen and his fellow junior officers were at a loss to explain how Captain McCloud had pulled it off, but they anticipated learning from the Navy's recent hero.

Hamblen was shocked out of his rumination by a cough of warning from the Boatswain's Mate of the Watch.

Hamblen waited a moment, as if contemplating the timing of his order, and then said, "Boatswain, pipe the side."

He tucked the long glass under his left arm just as Commander Grabowski and the captain's marine orderly arrived.

Coxswain Bergman keyed the general announcing system, piping *Attention*: "s^s-s-s-sssssss"—followed by "Now, muster four side boys on the quarterdeck."

Four designated seamen quickly appeared from the hatch. Chosen for their appearance and uniform height, they would make the first impression of *Argonne* in their dress blues. Bergman and Cruz had practiced their timing, and now it was Bergman's turn to pipe the *Alongside*—"_ssssssssss_s^sssssssss_s_ssssssssss_s^s"—a thirty-second call timed to end just as the gig arrived and touched the accommodation ladder.

— —

Captain McCloud heard the pipe as the gig approached *Argonne*. Something he hated was about to happen. The formal ceremonies of arrivals and departures had never made much sense to him. Sheppard always felt he was taking sailors away from far more important tasks than just meeting him or seeing him off.

Cruz pulled the gig alongside the *Argonne*'s accommodation ladder, backing full to check the gig's headway. This was not the two-deck climb Sheppard expected from his days on the *Shenandoah*. *Argonne*'s side was three decks high, and a moment of panic set in as he contemplated such a climb on his recovering left leg, with God knows how many officers and men of his crew watching him. He gritted his teeth. *I have to be the confident, fit leader in front of these men.*

Sheppard stepped to the stage of the accommodation ladder and began the climb. After ten feet, his left leg became dead weight. Just then, the boatswain's mate of the watch began piping *Over the Side*, similar to the *Alongside*, a low-high-low-high shrill of thirty seconds' duration. The boatswain would be trying to time his pipe to finish just as Sheppard saluted the officer of the deck, but that was *not* going to happen.

Sheppard managed another five feet before his left leg gave out. Fortunate to keep his knee locked, now he had to lead with his right leg for each step. That thirty-second pipe was going to have to last much longer. As Sheppard's head came level with the main deck, Bergman's lungs gave out, and the piping ended. Commander Grabowski and Lieutenant Hamblen glared; all Bergman could do was hold his salute and gasp. At least the side boys sensed what was going on and had the presence of mind to hold their salutes as well.

When Sheppard reached the top of the ladder, he saluted the Stars and Stripes fluttering at the stern. Turning toward Lieutenant Hamblen and Coxswain Bergman, Sheppard said, "Nice pipe, Boats," rather than the traditional request to the Officer of the Deck to come aboard. "I'm sorry my leg didn't cooperate with your timing."

An expression of relief washed over Coxswain Bergman. Then he sheepishly flashed Sheppard a grin.

Sheppard's face was flushed and sweaty, his hand shaking as he saluted, but he had reached the main deck. The climb was over.

"Commander Grabowski," Sheppard said, "I see you've assembled the department heads to greet me, and I thank you for that courtesy."

Sheppard could see surprise register on Grabowski's face, but the ship's executive officer did well to maintain his composure.

"If you don't mind," Sheppard continued, "I'd appreciate a few moments in my stateroom. Lieutenant Hamblen, well done on your quarterdeck ceremonies; you may carry on with the ship's routine. Mister Furlong, good to see you again! Corporal Pease, please show me to my quarters."

With that, Sheppard turned, limping after the departed marine as quickly as his injured leg would allow.

Sheppard knew he owed Cruz not just his life but now also the impression he had just made on the quarterdeck. It would remain their secret, but the list of the quarterdeck watchstanders and department heads that Cruz had slipped into his pocket when he'd stepped into the gig had given him all the information he needed. "You never get a second chance to make a first impression!" his mother had told Sheppard repeatedly. Her words had guided him many times in the past in the face of his father's inebriated abuse.

Recovering from his shock and not knowing what else to do, Lieutenant Hamblen purposefully strode over to the general announcing system microphone and passed the words, "*Argonne* arriving!"

— —

Corporal Pease held open the door to Sheppard's quarters. His in-port stateroom was an odd shape, with the barbette of the Number Six-Three six-inch, three-gun turret imposing a semicircular footprint in the outboard bulkhead. Sheppard located what he needed most and quickly sank into one of four overstuffed brown leather armchairs and rested his leg on a low coffee table, both of which were bolted to the deck. He had not been sitting for more than a minute when a sharp knock came at the door.

"Enter," Sheppard barked.

Corporal Pease opened the door. "Commander Grabowski requests to see the Captain."

Sheppard held back a smile at the familiar routine.

"In the future, Pease, please just knock and enter. It will save time. Please pass that on to all the orderlies."

A quick "Aye, aye, sir" and Pease was gone, shutting the door after Commander Grabowski had entered. Sheppard's executive officer looked to be a serious man; he was impeccably dressed in his blues, with receding reddish-brown hair topping the lean, pale face.

"Forgive me for not getting up, Ted," Sheppard said. "Please have a seat."

Taken aback, Grabowski walked over and sat in the chair opposite his Captain, obviously trying to keep his composure in the face of this new captain's unexpected actions.

"What is the schedule for today, Ted, and how can I help you?"

"Captain, your luggage is being brought up. As soon as it arrives, your steward will stow your gear. I have the department heads standing by in the wardroom to individually come and brief you on their status. Admiral Hamilton has called a meeting of all commanding officers on board the *Sabine* for 1400."

"I would prefer that you just make a schedule of briefing times for the department heads and inform them to come then. They can carry on with their routines, and we can all be more efficient. I'll have a working lunch here, with sandwiches for the briefers, so that we don't lose time. I would also like you to schedule in a meeting with the most senior chief petty officer on board. I shouldn't need more than five minutes with him, and please ask each department head to bring with him the standard form that he uses for his noon report at sea. Also, ask the chief engineer to bring a copy of the *Argonne*'s general arrangement plans that I may keep in my stateroom. Finally, does the duty officer know of the meeting with Admiral Hamilton and the need for the gig at 1330?"

"Yes, sir. As soon as I have the schedule typed, I'll give your orderly a copy for you. I am a little shorthanded in the ship's office, but it should only take about fifteen minutes."

"That reminds me: Admiral Ingraham's driver is a yeoman second class who wishes to return to sea duty on board *Argonne*. Please get me the details of *Argonne*'s manning shortfalls, and I'll see what I can do to help."

"Will there be anything else, sir?"

"Yes, Ted, please give yourself the last appointment and provide me with a list of all officers and chief petty officers assigned. I'll be discussing your impressions of their performance and qualifications with you. Do I have a yeoman assigned to me now?"

"Captain, I have assigned Yeoman Spence to be your writer from the ship's office."

"Good. I'll be returning him to you shortly, if I can get Petty Officer Brewster assigned. I'll take Brewster as the captain's yeoman. That will save you the trouble of having to train him into your routine, as I am sure you already have with Spence."

"Thank you, sir. Will there be anything else?"

"No. Thank you, XO."

After Grabowski had left, Sheppard got up, leg throbbing, and limped across the stateroom to his desk.

I have to stay busy.

As he rummaged through the desk looking for personal stationery with "USS *Argonne* (CC-49)" engraved on it, he was thankful that Ted had removed all of Bill Leland's belongings and mementos. When he found what he was looking for, Sheppard took out his fountain pen and wrote, thanking Admiral Ingraham and the staff for all their kindnesses and requesting Brewster's assignment to *Argonne* if convenient.

Corporal Pease knocked again, and another familiar face appeared in the door. Petty Officer George Washington Carver Jefferson, Commissary Steward First Class, entered with two other sailors in tow, carrying Sheppard's baggage. Nearly six feet tall and strong as an ox, Jefferson had grown up in the cotton fields of Alabama before escaping a life of poverty by lying about his age to join the service.

"Jefferson, you're a sight for sore eyes. Don't tell me Captain Baer shanghaied you, too," Sheppard said.

"No, sir, I ask'd to come to *Argonne*. I knews you would needs taken care of, but when Captain Baer said we's were shorthanded, I done wrote to your missus, 'cause I knews she was friends with Admiral Trotter's wife, and I figures if anyone could undo the cap'n's decision, it was her. I asked her to keeps it secret on account of I wanted to surprise you. When the admiral calls Captain Baer to send me, he yelled something fierce, but then he smiles and tells me to get out of there and takes good care of you."

Sheppard could only smile at the political acumen of his steward. "Well, I am delighted to see you, regardless of how you got here."

"Cap'n, when I's gets your things stowed, I'd be happy to makes you some of those toasted cheese and ham sandwiches you's love."

"That would be great, Jefferson, but you're going to have to make enough for several guests. It will be a working lunch."

"My pleasure, sir."

He had just finished speaking when Corporal Pease knocked and entered, announcing Commander Blankenship, *Argonne*'s medical department head. Sheppard gave the corporal the sealed envelope with instructions to have Petty Officer Spence deliver it to Captain Oldendorf at Scouting Force Headquarters.

"Captain, I am Hugh Blankenship. The XO thought I should see you first. If you don't mind, I would like to take a look at that leg of yours. I also took the liberty of bringing a bottle of aspirin for you. I am reluctant to prescribe anything stronger until I get a look at your medical record and read the surgeon's report on your leg."

"That won't be necessary, Doctor, but thank you for the aspirin."

With that, the briefings began. Sheppard felt that trying to take in all the information inundating him was like trying to take a drink from a fire hose.

— —

At 1330, Corporal Westbrook knocked, entered, and stated, "Sir, the gig is standing by to take the Captain to the *Sabine*."

Sheppard's leg was feeling better, and he managed the walk down the starboard main deck limping less than his earlier trip; the aspirin, no doubt, was helping. That walk past the numerous twin-gun mounts and five-inch ammunition handling rooms took longer than he had anticipated. Lieutenant (junior grade) Hughes was now the Officer of the Deck and clearly as determined as Lieutenant Hamblen had been to have a flawless quarterdeck ceremony. Sheppard decided that for the sake of *tradition* he was going to have to subject himself to these rituals aboard *Argonne* for the moment, even at the expense of time.

The ceremony was the same, just reversed, with a different order to the pipes *Over the Side* and *Alongside*. The moment that Hughes dropped his salute, the third-repeat pennant soared to the block on the port yardarm of *Argonne*'s foremast. Aboard the gig, Sheppard took a seat and propped up his leg. Cruz immediately called for full throttle by ringing the engine bell four times. On this trip, Cruz added an additional *ding* at the end, telling Fireman Russert to disengage the engine's governor for even higher rpm's. Cruz then headed directly to *Sabine*'s after-starboard accommodation ladder. As far as Sheppard knew, Cruz only used three speeds for the gig: maximum power ahead, maximum power astern, and stop—nothing else. It was a good thing, because Sheppard was running late. The two seaman synchronized their display of boathooks, and Sheppard settled down with the list of officers and chief petty officers that the XO had provided, beginning to memorize names.

Shortly, he heard the *Sabine*'s officer of the deck call out, "Boat ahoy!"

Cruz quickly answered with "*Argonne!*"

A perfect landing caught the *Sabine*'s quarterdeck watches by surprise, causing the boatswain's mate of the watch to swallow his last note of the *Alongside*. Sheppard stepped to the landing stage as smoothly as his injured leg would allow, cursing under his breath every aircraft carrier that ever sailed the sea. He would have to climb almost four decks to the level of her hangar. As he climbed, Sheppard noticed that he was not the last to arrive. Rear Admiral Raymond Calhoun, Commander Battle Cruiser Squadron Six, was still a few hundred yards off in his barge.

Another set of quarterdeck ceremonies later, Sheppard limped along after a marine lance corporal through the aft boat pocket that served as *Sabine*'s quarterdeck to "*Argonne,* arriving" on the carrier's general announcing system. They turned forward in the cavernous hangar filled with F4F-3 Wildcat fighters, SBD-3 Dauntless dive-bombers, TBD-1 Devastator torpedo planes, and a few odd utility aircraft. About three-quarters of the way forward in the hangar deck, the marine ducked through a starboard watertight door, through an open deck hatch, and proceeded down a ladder. When he reached the second deck, the lance corporal disappeared.

Now what? Sheppard thought as he limped down the ladder; surely he was going to be lost in this bird farm and die of starvation before anyone found him. Worse still, he would be late for the briefing, embarrassing himself and his ship in front of all these brown-shoe aviators.

"Hello, Sheppard," Admiral Calhoun said. "You look lost."

Sheppard had known Calhoun for years. The admiral's tanned and lined face confirmed his reputation as a seagoing officer. The ready smile and solicitous greeting softened his chiseled features and close-cropped gray hair.

"Yes, sir," Sheppard said sheepishly. "I am afraid I've never served on a carrier."

"You've crossed paths with Kevin Bailey, CO of *Belleau Wood*, haven't you?" Admiral Calhoun asked, glancing toward the pale, trim, and handsome captain with him.

"Yes, sir," Sheppard answered.

Sheppard gave a quick nod to Bailey, but it was without the customary smile. Sheppard knew more of the man than he wished to.

Crossed swords with him, is more like it, he thought.

They had both served in Washington DC in the mid-1930s when Sheppard had had the sixteen-inch gun desk at the Bureau of Ordnance.

Now, like then, Sheppard had little use for anyone he considered an ass-kissing, pompous incompetent. Bailey had spent most of his time at various headquarters and the Bureau of Navigation, as far from sea duty as possible. He was an ass-kisser—a paper pusher. Bailey probably viewed command of one of the Navy's latest battle cruisers as a just reward for attending numerous cocktail parties while escorting admiral's wives, just a short tour away from Washington to get his capital ship-command ticket punched. It did not help that Kevin had tried to have an affair with Sheppard's wife. Evelyn had thought it was hilarious, but that effort had branded Bailey as a special breed of pond scum in Sheppard's mind. Sheppard secretly suspected Ray Calhoun had picked the *Belleau Wood* as his flagship just to keep a watchful eye on Bailey's every move. After all, the nation was at war, and the *Belleau Wood* was a critical part of the fleet that remained operational after Pearl Harbor.

Sheppard followed the admiral into the wardroom, where all the senior officers of the task force had assembled. Charts of the North Atlantic, Mediterranean, and west coast of Africa hung on the forward bulkhead. As Sheppard sat, an officer's steward appeared and offered him a cup of coffee, which he gladly accepted.

Two commanders in aviation greens approached Sheppard. The leader was not that tall, though he was lean, with striking blue eyes. He had the air of a man who thoroughly knew every detail of his profession. The second commander was shorter and stockier; he had brown hair with a slight tinge of red and seemed too willing for the other to lead.

"Captain, please don't get up. My name is Bob Talbot. They call me 'Hawk'; I'm *Sabine*'s CAG. May I introduce Patrick Hernandez, *Raritan*'s CAG," he said, referring to the shorter officer. "He goes by 'Irish.'"

Aviators! Sheppard thought. *They all have to have their unique nicknames. Why can't they just be like the rest of the Navy?* But at least these two commanders were respectful.

"Pleased to meet you. I'm Sheppard McCloud."

"We know," Hawk said. "We've heard of you. My brother was wounded at Pearl and wrote me about how you took on the Japanese single-handed. I just wanted to say thank you."

Suddenly, one of the destroyer captains in the back of the wardroom shouted, "Attention on deck!" and Admiral Hamilton entered with his staff. Sheppard knew Hamilton, only by reputation, as a no-nonsense aviator. Tall and lean, Hamilton had proven his seamanship weathering a typhoon while in command of the carrier *United States*.

The admiral frowned, quickly commanding, "As you were!"

Sheppard was glad. His leg was not going to stand for rapid up-and-down movement. At the word, Hawk and Irish hustled off to the back of the wardroom, where the junior commanders were sitting.

"Gentleman," the admiral said as the wardroom clock struck four bells, "I trust you have all had a chance to meet each other and swap lies, but for those of you who may not have served in the Pacific recently, let me introduce Captain Sheppard McCloud,"—Sheppard almost choked on his coffee—"former commanding officer of the *Shenandoah*. His action engaging the Japanese striking force at Pearl Harbor was truly courageous."

Out of the corner of his eye, Sheppard could see Bailey squirming in his chair. As much as he hated being singled out by the admiral, Sheppard secretly reveled in Bailey's jealousy.

"The damage that he inflicted was the only real retaliation the United States managed to achieve on that 'Day of Infamy,'" Hamilton said. "The fact that he achieved anything in the face of overwhelming odds was exceptional. The additional fact that he brought *Shenandoah* back despite severe damage was even more remarkable and a testament to his leadership and foresight in training his crew. I am delighted that he has recovered from his wounds and will be with us in command of *Argonne*."

Sheppard blushed as his fellow officers stood, clapped, and offered their congratulations. This was an unexpected honor, and he wished he could share the moment with the families of the one hundred eighty-seven men of his crew who had paid the ultimate price. It might have eased their grief more than the simple letters he had written while on convalescent leave.

"Now," Hamilton continued, "for the task we've been assigned. I assume you are all familiar with the recent events of the war in Europe: Hitler's failed attempt to invade Great Britain and the huge sacrifices required of the Royal Navy to limit the landings in the face of the Luftwaffe. You are probably not aware that in conjunction with the attempt, Vice Admiral Schröder broke into the Atlantic with a force of two carriers, four battle cruisers, six scout cruisers, and a dozen destroyers. Before turning east, making for the port of Brest, they managed to sink Admiral Tovey's shadowing cruisers and devastate a convoy bound for England with critical war material. Luckily, the Fleet Air Arm inflicted some damage to the heavy units before they reached the safety of France. Most of those units have since completed repairs. The two German carrier air groups, operating from French airfields, have prevented further RAF attacks.

"The Brits are still trying to guard against additional breakouts as well as keep enough force to defeat Admiral Lütjens if he decides to seek a fleet engagement in the North Sea. Since they overran France, the Germans have been refitting the French units they captured for incorporation into the Kriegsmarine. Fortunately for us, the work mostly occurs in France. The French Resistance is both sabotaging the effort and keeping us abreast of progress. For their efforts, they are paying a heavy price; the Gestapo is rounding up suspects, and our sources of information are drying up."

Sheppard subconsciously hardened his facial muscles, his lips forming a thin line. This was all news to him, having just come from the Pacific.

Hamilton went on, "The newspapers have recently been reporting that there is heavy fighting between General Ritchie's Eighth Army and General Rommel's Afrika Korps. What you do not know is that Ritchie suffered a defeat, falling back to the east bank of the Suez at the direction of General Auchinleck, using that barrier to hold Palestine. If he is unsuccessful, it is likely that Turkey will enter the war as an Axis partner."

A low murmur of surprise and concern rose from the assembled officers.

Raising his voice to quiet the wardroom, Hamilton continued, "The British Mediterranean Fleet under Admiral Cunningham transitted the Suez Canal, just before the loss of Alexandria, to bases at Trincomalee and Aden. Churchill and the First Lord of the Admiralty have yet to decide whether Cunningham's fleet is to round the Cape of Good Hope and operate in the Atlantic or remain in the Indian Ocean trying to halt the Japanese advance on the Indian subcontinent. It appears that General Rommel is turning the bulk of his forces westward, leaving the defense of Egypt to the Italian army."

Turning to face the chart of the Mediterranean and African west coast, Hamilton swept his hand across Tunisia, Algeria, French Morocco, Mauritania, and Senegal.

"Intelligence estimates that the Germans are planning to take the French North and West African colonies as additional bases for the Kriegsmarine, outside the range of the Royal Air Force."

As Admiral Hamilton's words sank in, it was becoming clear to Sheppard that he was going to be in the Atlantic for some time. His revenge for *Shenandoah*'s dead would have to wait.

Hamilton paused, dropping his gold-braided arm from the chart of the west coast of Africa, looking dejected.

"There is precious little to stop them!"

Not a man in the wardroom of the *Sabine* stirred. Not a sound could be heard. It was clear that the Allies could soon be in an untenable strategic position.

"I am sure you are also not aware of the desperate state of the British. They're stretched to the limit. If Schröder breaks out of Brest, and we lose contact with him, there is no telling where he will go. The only thing we can be sure of is his objective: to raid the convoys. Any disruption and England will quickly run out of oil and gasoline. Food supplies are critically low, the population on subsistence rations. Even if only a few convoys are lost, Churchill will have no choice but to sue for peace. We are making contingency plans to move the British monarchy and the remnants of the Royal Navy to Puerto Rico. Perhaps then the British colonies will stay in the war."

Another low murmuring spread throughout the wardroom. It was becoming clear that Hitler's declaration of war against the United States was not simply his latest lunatic move but rather a logical step toward world domination by the Axis. If the US Atlantic Fleet focused on containing the Kriegsmarine too long, the Japanese would have a free hand in Asia, with the likely loss of Australia, New Zealand, and China. There was just not enough time to repair all the damage caused to the Pacific Fleet at Pearl. If the Allies lost those countries, Germany, operating in conjunction with the Japanese, could attack and defeat the Soviet Union. The Axis powers would not only own Europe and North Africa but Asia as well.

"Our task is simple," Hamilton shouted over the murmuring. "We must stop Schröder! God help us if he escapes into the Atlantic!

"My staff has a Top Secret package for each of you, containing detailed instructions for the operation."

Hamilton stiffened, his jaw set and his eyes ablaze with determination.

Sheppard knew that in Hamilton's chest beat the heart of a warrior, but he wondered: did he understand how little his carriers could do against Schröder's heavy ships?

A second later, Hamilton stepped toward the group of officers, his fists balled and voice rising in crescendo. "We sail in the morning!"

Abruptly, the admiral strode out of the *Sabine*'s wardroom, customary courtesies neglected. Everyone remained seated, too stunned to rise. What Sheppard had thought would be a routine operation was not routine at all—but rather one of vital strategic importance. He and Admiral Calhoun caught each other's eyes. In an instant, Sheppard knew it was not fortuitous timing that had landed him in command of *Argonne*. He had been picked! If Schröder was going to be stopped, Ray Calhoun and Sheppard were the ones who would have to do it.

Remembering their manners, Captain Jake Evans and the other officers of the flagship *Sabine* waited for Admiral Calhoun and Bailey to lead Sheppard out of the wardroom. Sheppard had known of Jake since the time that, as a young officer, Evans had won a Cleveland air race, reclaiming the Collier Trophy for the Navy. A distinguished flyer, Jake had gotten too senior to command a flying unit and was now serving in command at sea before what Sheppard surmised would be his inevitable selection for flag rank.

It was almost easy for Sheppard to retrace his steps to the *Sabine*'s aft starboard boat pocket. He came to attention and saluted as Admiral Calhoun received the required six side boys. The boatswain's pipe shrilled the *Over the Side* as the *Sabine*'s 1MC blared, "Battle Cruiser Squadron Six departing!" Since Bailey was riding in the admiral's barge, as the junior officer, he was required to board first. Whether by accident or design, he only received a perfunctory "*Belleau Wood* departing!" Sheppard smiled at the insult, musing that, somehow, sailors always knew.

Sheppard endured his own ceremony, not wishing to compound the fluster of the *Sabine*'s officer of the deck at muffing a ceremony while trying to keep all the ships and COs straight in seniority with the sequencing of their gigs. Cruz departed with his usual choice of speed. However, he had arranged a more intricate synchronized routine for the two boathooks, wordlessly impressing any observers near the flagship as they raced back to the *Argonne*.

— —

From high up in the shadows of the overhead, standing on the starboard wing of the flag bridge in the *Sabine*'s island superstructure with his chief of staff, Captain Henry Burke, Admiral Hamilton watched all the departures.

"You know, Henry," the admiral mused, "there is only one of them that I am certain will give a good account of himself and his ship in battle."

"I understand, sir. We were fortunate that the Bureau of Medicine and Surgery caved in to Admiral Ingersoll's demand for McCloud's assignment to command the *Argonne*. I understand he could only come up the accommodation ladder one step at a time."

"Yeah, Henry, he really needed another month or two to heal that leg, but Evelyn McCloud told Cindy Trotter that he was going nuts at home and should get back to sea. Well, she got her wish."

CHAPTER 2

FORGING A TEAM

What were Calhoun's plans for fighting the forces that *Argonne* and *Belleau Wood* would confront? Sheppard wished he'd had time to talk to the admiral before departing. But like every other captain, he had to begin preparations for getting underway as well as to review the packet of Top Secret orders. He knew that the fighting odds between ships of equal capability in which the only difference was the number of ships each side had was not a straight numerical ratio. Fredrick W. Lanchester's equations proved that if the ships were equal, then the odds for or against were actually the square of the numerical ratio. The brutal truth now confronting Sheppard was that if Schröder had four battle cruisers to Hamilton's two, the fighting odds were actually sixteen to four—four to one against the Americans. Their only hope would be that Hamilton's carriers could even the odds before *Argonne* and *Belleau Wood* engaged Schröder's heavy ships.

Lost in thought, Sheppard did not even notice when Cruz suddenly backed full for the landing. He looked up only when he saw the two seamen of his gig's crew attaching a lifting bridle to the ring bolts fore and aft on the gig.

Apparently recognizing the perplexed look on Sheppard's face, Cruz smiled. "Don't worry, Capt'n; I arranged things to be a little easier on your leg this trip."

With that, the gig magically rose at the end of a cable from the *Argonne*'s aircraft and boat crane. High above the main deck, the gig swung over the yawning mouth of the hangar and lowered to nest securely inside one of the fifty-foot launches. The bridle was unhooked as a ladder thudded up against the gig's gunwale.

Carefully descending the ladder to the hangar's deck, Sheppard had his first view of this cavernous space in *Argonne*'s stern, as well as the ship's boats and six OS2U-5 Kingfisher spotter planes stowed within. All had their wings folded or removed and stored on the bulkheads, making more room for handling the ship's boats in port. With the two aircraft resting on the catapults, he had twice the number of air assets that he'd had with the *Shenandoah*.

Sheppard actually liked coming aboard this way. Not only did it save his leg, but more importantly, there was no ceremony! At the base of the ladder, Commander Grabowski, Chief Hancock, and Corporal Henderson stood waiting for him.

"Commander, here are our orders and Admiral Hamilton's plans for this operation," Sheppard said. "Please get them to the communications officer for logging into the Top Secret control system. Also let the navigator know that they are here. Pass the word to all department heads that I need to have a short meeting with them in my stateroom at 1900. Please give them my apologies for the lateness of the hour. *Argonne* will be getting underway at 0845 tomorrow."

Like a coffin lid, the massive armored hatch over two decks above their heads slammed shut with a thunderous clang, sealing the hangar from the weather and protecting the fragile spotter aircraft from the crushing muzzle blast of the after turret's guns.

As the XO departed to complete the tasks assigned, Sheppard smiled. Now, with the hatch shut, there were no salutes. He turned to the *Argonne*'s senior chief petty officer, Chief Turret Captain Waldo John Hancock, captain of the Number II main-battery turret. Of average height and lean build, Hancock had wrinkled, tanned skin that made him appear older than his jet-black hair suggested.

"Good afternoon, Chief," Sheppard greeted him. "How may I help you?"

"Captain, from what I just heard, you are going to be a very busy man tonight, but I thought you might like to dine in the chief's quarters with us. I have already spoken to Jefferson to coordinate arrangements and let your yeoman—I think his name is Brewster—know where people can find you."

Sheppard smiled at the lightning-fast response to his request for Yeoman Second Class Brewster to be assigned to *Argonne*.

"Since it is getting close to 1600," Hancock continued, "I anticipated that you might like to come with me now and relax before supper. The chief's mess is actually close by, and it will save two extra trips for that leg of yours."

"Thank you, Chief Hancock, and if you have no objections, I would prefer to address you as Senior Chief Hancock in the future. It is a practice I started in my last ship as a special designation."

Visibly taken aback, Hancock lowered his gaze and voice. "Thank you for the honor, Captain."

"All right then, let's get on to the chief's quarters. If you don't mind leading, I am still unsure of how to get places on *Argonne*."

— ‒

Hancock led Sheppard through a series of ladders and watertight doors, leading the way first to the chief petty officer bunkrooms adjacent to the hangar bay. Sheppard noted that in every space Hancock took him the bunks were made, personal gear was stowed out of sight, and there were not distracting photographs of Hollywood starlets posted on the vertical surfaces—only tasteful photos of families and sweethearts, many in frames. They passed into a large open space with mess tables and stools fixed to the deck. Leather-covered benches with stuffed backs were attached to opposite outboard bulkheads for seating at the adjacent tables. Almost the entire aft bulkhead had a watch, quarter, and station bill for all the chiefs, showing their assignments for various evolutions. But those features weren't what held Sheppard's attention. His eyes glanced over the multitude of men, all in their blues, in the mess. There must have been over two hundred chief petty officers present. Sheppard guessed that Hancock had arranged to have all the chiefs off watch and available to meet the Captain as well as dine with him.

As they stepped into the mess, Hancock shouted, "Attention on deck!" Sheppard quickly countered with an "As you were."

He suspected that they were on *Argonne*'s third deck, probably walking on the thick armor steel aft of the Number III turret, but aboard a large ship, it was hard to keep track of where you were and even harder to determine how to get from one place to another.

As he glanced at each of the chiefs, Sheppard saw a few more of his former shipmates from *Shenandoah*. All had been key men for him before. He wondered whether this infusion of talented individuals was deliberate on the part of the service or just Chris Baer's desire to ensure Sheppard had some individuals he could rely on in crucial positions without having to watch their performance for weeks. He also began mentally checking off the roster of remaining personnel on *Shenandoah*. He certainly didn't want to benefit at the expense of Chris not having a successful yard period and a successful command when *Shenandoah* returned to service.

By the time introductions were finished, the mess cooks had brought the evening meal down in large stainless-steel pans that fit into the steam tables at the forward end of the compartment. At the first sight of food, the men quickly formed a line. Senior Chief Hancock led Sheppard to the head. At the start of the line, Sheppard picked up one of the stainless-steel mess trays with its six indentations, along with his knife, fork, and spoon, and then started down the line.

Hancock motioned Sheppard to follow him over to a table on the starboard side. The table quickly filled, with the older chiefs seizing the privilege of dining with the Captain. As the dinner conversation progressed, he learned that Chief Hancock was actually half Cherokee, which explained his jet-black hair without a fleck of gray, and that Chief Gunner's Mate Grazzi had a son at the Naval Academy. Sheppard told them about his wife, Evelyn, in San Diego, and about his three sons and two daughters. He described how his son Peter was in flight training and that David was an upperclassman at West Point. That prompted a few good-natured comments about treason and disowning the turncoat.

Dinner was almost over when Chief Watertender Peters asked how the war was going.

Sheppard knew that his answer would likely be immediate scuttlebutt, reaching every corner of *Argonne* before he returned to his stateroom.

"I really only have experienced two days of war, and you are familiar with the events of December 7th. The rest of my war consisted of sickbay, hospitals, and convalescent leave, except for today. One thing I will say is that I am certain from what I saw today that we are going to win, and I think the *Argonne* is going to have a major role to play. I am extremely pleased with what I've seen in how you have trained your men and the determination of everyone to perform their duties to the best of their ability."

That brought nods of agreement from the chiefs at his table and suddenly silenced the entire mess deck as everyone strained to hear his words.

Sheppard continued, somewhat self-consciously, "I have not had a chance to see the ship underway, at general quarters, or to see our gunnery performance," he said with a nod to Senior Chief Hancock, "but with the way the ship is functioning in port, I am confident her ability to fight will be just as good. From our briefing today, it is clear we will not have long to wait. My experience tells me that if everyone concentrates on maintaining their equipment and training their sailors to perform assigned tasks well, we will have an enviable combat record. More important than *Argonne* having a great record of accomplishments, though, is to keep in mind that as the Navy expands rapidly in the next few years, the men that will lead those new sailors are under your care now. We need to move them up the advancement and qualification ladder as quickly as they are able so that *Argonne*'s legacy is not just a brilliant combat record but a record that will allow many of the Navy's future leaders and veterans to proudly say, 'I served in *Argonne*!'"

The bulkhead clock chimed three bells in the first dogwatch—1730—and Sheppard decided he would have to make his exit if he was going to have any time with Commander Grabowski before the department head meeting. He hadn't had a chance yet to review the personnel status with him and go over the strengths and weaknesses of the wardroom. As he started to rise, Chief Hancock shouted, "Attention on deck!"

This time, Sheppard frowned at the interruption of the meal for the other chief petty officers, immediately ordering, "As you were!"

Sheppard did not initially notice, but no one sat down. They remained at attention while the senior chief escorted him to the aft starboard watertight door, where Corporal Pease was standing at attention. Somewhat flustered, Sheppard could only manage a weak, "Thank you," as he followed Pease out of the chief's mess. He was amazed at this show of respect—perhaps even of affection. He did not think he had said anything profound. He'd only meant to state what he thought was obvious. As they walked aft, he thought he heard the senior chief saying, "And I served under Captain ..." He did not know what he had done to deserve men like these.

— ▪ —

Not knowing—or, rather, not understanding—why his men responded to him in a manner foreign to her previous experience puzzled her. She had met many other officers. They had their quirks, their personality flaws, but this one was ... different. It was important to him to remain wary, measuring his words, controlling everything he said, and monitoring reactions of those around him. But why?

What were his fears?

What was he hiding from her?

More than anyone else, she would have to know him well and respond to his every desire—every caress.

— —

Sheppard followed Corporal Pease aft, through the labyrinth of compartments, up two ladders and watertight hatches, until they emerged in the starboard-quarter 40 mm gun tub aft of the Mark VII catapult with its Kingfisher perched aft. The canvas cowling covers had been removed in preparation for getting underway, though tie-downs were still in place.

Back on the main deck, Corporal Pease fell in slightly behind and to the left of Sheppard as they walked forward. It was going to be a beautiful evening. The sun was setting over Newport News. Clear skies and a light breeze reminded Sheppard of that Sunday evening before *Shenandoah* had left with the rest of the Pacific Fleet Scouting Force for an exercise. What quirk of fate had caused Admiral Trotter to install the new Mk 3 fire-control radar in Sheppard's ship instead of another battle cruiser of the Pacific Scouting Force? As more radars became available, the admiral wanted the new radar's capabilities tested at sea. Sheppard's ship had been chosen. Why? *Shenandoah* and a destroyer would detach before the other battle cruisers returned to Pearl on Friday, December 5th, to make it happen. It was Sheppard's decision to reposition farther to the northwest to include an investigation of the Mk 3's capabilities in bad weather. *Shenandoah*'s CXAM radar had provided the first detection of the Japanese air armada headed to Pearl, but like so many warnings, Sheppard's message had been lost in the lazy Sunday-morning ineptitude of Pearl Harbor's staffs.

Sheppard clenched his jaw, willing himself back to the present. He noticed that after two steps Corporal Pease was in perfect synchronization with him. Pease had adjusted his stride to match the still-awkward gait imposed by Sheppard's injured left leg. As they walked forward past the hangar hatch, Sheppard's mind again returned to the Pacific and that horrific day, now envisioning the boiling caldron of flame that *Shenandoah*'s hangar had become after the first Japanese shell had hit—the flames a beacon for the Japanese in the failing light. Unaccounted for in his planning, that blaze had nearly cost him his ship and crew.

No.

He was not going to allow it to happen again.

But … will I ever be free of these regrets?

Sheppard had to stay focused on the here and now. Dwelling on the past would put the safety of his current crew at risk.

Searching for something to command his attention, Sheppard's eyes tracked upward. The muzzles of the three eighteen-inch/55-caliber guns of Number III main-battery turret rose far above their heads, even though the guns were only elevated to the standard five-degree loading angle. Tied canvas muzzle covers, which the guns could shoot through, if need be, had already replaced the shined brass tampions normally used to keep rain and the salt air from rusting the rifling. Though it might have seemed odd to civilians, Sheppard knew that these massive pieces of steel—nearly a hundred feet long and weighing in excess of 150 tons each—required machining to the tolerances of a fine watch. They similarly required the same exceptional care to preserve them in a moisture-laden environment. Only with that kind of care would they be capable of reliably hurling their nearly two-ton projectiles more than twenty-five nautical miles with consistent accuracy when elevated to the maximum of forty-five degrees.

As Sheppard and Corporal Pease continued forward, they passed the left-side pointer's and trainer's sights, with their armored hoods poking out from the thick armor of the turret's side. Rising above their heads now was one "ear" of the fifty-five-foot coincidence rangefinder contained in the rear of the gun house. With that distance between its optics focused on the same point, measuring the small angular difference between the two ends would give an accurate estimate of the range to the target. Unfortunately, the great size and weight of the rangefinder restricted its height above the water, limiting the range to the horizon due to the earth's curvature. It could see much farther, though, by focusing on the uppermost superstructure and masts of a target "over the horizon." The target's vertical size thus controlled the total observable range. It was complicated to understand, but fundamentally, if a seaman wanted to see a long way, he had to be high up.

— —

U-179 arrived where Meier could begin his observation of the shipping patterns. He fully expected that the Cape Henry and Cape Charles lights would still be burning brightly.

Meier shook his head. *Stupid and undisciplined*, he thought.

Whatever advantages US merchant ships—likely already familiar with these waters—gained from the lights, this hardly compared with the help it gave German submariners, who were not. The Americans would eventually learn about these little things that influenced the tide of battle, but not until Meier had won his Knight's Cross with Swords. Leaning on the breakwater of the U-boat's conning tower, he imagined the ceremony in Hitler's presence as his eyes gazed on the curling water in his bow wave, a scarlet sunset beckoning his boat forward.

Even in war, there can be beauty.

Meier's control-room watch, searching with the higher periscope, reported a masthead bearing 285 degrees, not far from where he expected to see Cape Charles. If only he didn't have to wait, Meier thought. He could close the freighter and sink her with his deck gun after the remaining light faded. That would let the Americans not only see the flames of a burning ship but also hear the sound of German gunfire off their vaunted "invulnerable" coast.

No, orders were *orders*.

Knowing his watch officer would track the contact and search for more, Meier went below to the stench of rot and men, an odor he knew would pass as his nostrils acclimatized below. He would take a tour around his boat to ensure everything was in readiness for tomorrow.

— —

When Sheppard arrived at his stateroom with Corporal Pease, he found Jefferson, Brewster, and Commander Grabowski waiting for him. Corporal Pease took his customary post at Parade Rest, outside the door to the captain's quarters, as Sheppard entered.

Jefferson was the first to speak. "Cap'n, can I's gets you's anything?"

After exchanging amenities and serving coffee, Jefferson and Brewster left the two senior officers of *Argonne* alone.

"All right, Ted," Sheppard began, "let's sit at the table so you can spread out your papers and we can manage our coffee easily. Admiral Ingraham has already briefed me on your record and the good job you have done since Bill Leland's heart attack. If you had already been promoted to captain instead of waiting for your number, you might very well have kept *Argonne*, so let's review the department heads."

"Captain, let me start with the navigator. Commander Arthur Wesley Roberts, Naval Academy Class of 1923, has a wife and three children living here in a house they bought in Norfolk. His service has mostly been in large warships, beginning with the old *South Dakota* (BB-49). He served in the Bureau of Navigation for one tour. Before *Argonne*, Roberts was the flag secretary to Admiral Evans. He has yet to have a command of his own. I am not sure he wants one."

That caught Sheppard's attention. It was almost axiomatic that every line officer wanted command and would seek the first available opportunity in his career.

"Interesting," Sheppard interrupted. "How does he get on with his men and your wardroom?"

"He keeps his distance, maintaining formality at all times. I have not been able to bring him into the camaraderie of the wardroom, but his performance has never been anything but superlative."

"Have you met his wife and kids?"

"No, I haven't, Captain. When he made his arrival call on Captain Leland, his family was still in Charleston. They have not attended any of the dining-outs that the wardroom has had."

"I wonder. Do you know his wife's name?"

"Rachel, I believe, but I could be wrong."

Sheppard thought he understood. "Who's next?"

"Commander Charles—Chuck—Thurgood Williamson, Gunnery Officer, Naval Academy Class of 1924, has a wife, Kristen, but no children. They live in navy housing with three dogs. She is an accomplished member of the Virginia bar. Chuck has already had command of a destroyer and came to us from a tour at the Bureau of Ordnance in Dahlgren, where he did much of the development work on our new Bofors antiaircraft machine cannons. He is a good leader in the wardroom and with the men. He is in the mold of seeking forgiveness rather than permission."

"Any question about his reliability under stress?"

"If you don't mind, Captain, why do you ask?" Grabowski inquired, eyebrows arched.

"Ted, if things go the way I suspect, he and his people are going to have to perform against odds. I need to know how much direction versus guidance I am going to have to give him."

Even as he finished saying it, Sheppard regretted having brought up the subject at all. He had not intended to create doubt in Ted's mind, let alone his own. As an accomplished gunnery officer, Sheppard knew the responsibilities that Chuck had for the *Argonne*'s success in battle. He needed to be certain Chuck could control the guns and shift targets quickly as he directed. He was going to have to walk a fine line between getting Chuck to appreciate what he wanted and not appearing to be concerned about Williamson's performance or giving him too many rudder orders on how to run his department.

Changing the subject, Sheppard continued, "How is the chief engineer?"

"Captain, you are not going to find a better Engineer Officer. Commander Anderson Everett Scott, Massachusetts Institute of Technology Class of 1918 and Naval Academy Class of 1924, enlisted right after graduation from MIT, quickly getting an appointment to the Academy. You probably won't see much of him, since he spends most of his time in the engineering spaces in a pair of white coveralls. He has challenged his 'snipes' to keep those coveralls clean for a whole day by maintaining the boiler, engine rooms, and auxiliary machinery spaces spotless. He has been with the ship since well before commissioning. Andy knows every inch of *Argonne*. If I were ever fortunate enough to command a battle cruiser, I would want him above all others in my wardroom. He has had command of a minesweeper and a destroyer. He should be rotating off *Argonne* in a few months and will leave a huge hole to fill."

"Impressive, Ted. Has he indicated where he would like to go?"

"Captain, the only thing he has said is that his wife, Colleen, would like to stay near her family in Boston. He would like another command."

"Mmm, I'll see what I can arrange."

Sheppard knew that as much as he would like to keep his superstars, he needed to move them on as quickly as he could afford to, for their sake and the good of the service. The Navy was assigning senior commanders to command of the new light antiaircraft cruisers. Those ships would probably be in the thick of the fighting in the Pacific, and based upon the capabilities the Japanese had demonstrated at Pearl Harbor, antiaircraft was going to be one of the major factors in the fleet's survival. Sheppard knew what Brewster's first typing assignment was going to be.

"Well, Ted, I know our supply officer, Thaddeus Furlong, from *Ticonderoga*, and his early selection to lieutenant commander tells me he hasn't changed. I was impressed with the briefing Doctor Blankenship gave. I'm delighted that he is training the dentists and their assistants to do triage and uncomplicated surgery. If we take battle damage, that is going to pay tremendous dividends in keeping the fatalities down. Our surgeons can worry about the more severely wounded, saving some that otherwise would die."

A twinge of pain broke Sheppard's concentration on the present. Pensive for a moment, he had inadvertently reminded himself of *Shenandoah*—the other men lying in the battle dressing station as his overloaded medical staff triaged the dead and dying.

"Tell me about the head of our air department," Sheppard said, probably too quickly but desperate to not betray the emotions swirling in his mind. He fought to regain his focus on the task at hand.

"Yes, sir. Lieutenant Commander Bronco Billy Burdick—and that's not a nickname—is an aviator through and through. He always wears aviation greens in port and flaunts his brown shoes when he cannot. I think he would be at home as a fighter pilot and may be a little resentful with his assignment to a scout observation squadron. He is the natural leader of the junior officers in the wardroom and is always getting them into one scrape after another. It hasn't hurt any of them or us. Actually, I suspect his bravado has actually helped the ship's reputation. He is Naval Academy Class of 1932, our best pilot, and a bachelor."

Nodding, Sheppard massaged his leg, trying to relax the healing muscles from the torture of the day's events. It sounded as if Bronco was certainly a character. Sheppard could only imagine the impact his squadron commander had on the ladies ashore.

"What about the head of our marine detachment?"

"Major Morris Lofton Jenkins is good but has had an unusual career after graduating from the Naval Academy, Class of 1934. Following platoon-leader school, he specialized in infantry, and before the war he had embassy duty in Germany. He is fluent in German and French. He is married and an avid hunter. I can still remember the venison meal he provided the wardroom last fall.

"It might surprise you, but we have a full company of marines as part of the crew, including the heavy-weapons platoon. Major Jenkins has made an exceptional effort to have his marines integrated within the crew, completely manning two of our five-inch mounts. The major is the turret officer in our Number II main-battery turret. He also has four lieutenants and one marine captain as part of the detachment—all of them fully integrated into our battle-stations organization. In fact, his XO, Captain Puller, is in charge of the after main-battery plotting room."

"All right, I think that should cover it, Ted."

"Actually, Captain, we have another department you may not be familiar with. He did not get a chance to brief you because of time constraints earlier today. Lieutenant Commander Jonathan Schmitt Becker, our operations officer, is a department head in his own right."

Grabowski went on to explain that *Argonne* had something new called a Combat Information Center. With all the radars and the need to control aircraft, the General Board had incorporated a special space below the armor to serve as a clearinghouse for tactical information. It contains plotting tables and status boards displaying everything the radar operators, lookouts, and even the radio circuits provide with regard to the situation around the ship.

"Sifting through all that information and trying to make sense of it is Mister Becker's job. It takes a fair number of people to do the work, so the bureau decided to organize them with the signalmen, radar operators, and radiomen in their own department."

"Doesn't that leave the navigation department rather small?"

"Yes, sir. Roberts only has the quartermasters left to lead."

Sheppard wondered if perhaps this was another reason for Commander Roberts's attitude. Coming to a ship like *Argonne* expecting the traditional alignment of duties, only to find out he had no more than one division's worth of personnel to lead, could make even the strongest of officers a malcontent.

"What is Becker's background?"

"Sorry, Captain. He is a native of Minnesota. He graduated magna cum laude from Cal Tech in electrical engineering and was one of the first commissioned through the reserve officers' training program. He is very smart, a little odd, but there is no one I would rather have trying to maintain our radars and other electronic equipment. His men like him, though he may be too close to them. He is anything but formal."

Frowning, Sheppard leaned back, mulling over his approach to the next subject. "Any concerns with the rest of the wardroom?"

The XO stiffened, no doubt wondering what Sheppard might already know.

"We have our share of young ensigns making the usual mistakes of getting too close to their men and not mastering their equipment. Where I can, I have paired them with a seasoned chief petty officer."

Sheppard gave a small nod, remembering his own first assignment as a division officer on board the *New York* and how Chief Boatswain's Mate Mike Stratton had taught him the intricacies of a battleship's ground tackle.

Commander Grabowski's expression darkened. He lowering his head, breaking eye contact. "We do have one major problem, Captain."

So far, Grabowski had not told Sheppard anything that was out of the ordinary. As he watched his XO's face, Sheppard sensed his second-in-command's uneasiness. How Ted discussed this matter would be as important as the problem itself.

"When we were forming up the crew just before commissioning, Lieutenant Hamblen reported aboard, and the same day, Captain Leland got a call from Admiral Hamblen."

Sheppard's heart sank. When he had read Cruz's list of quarterdeck watchstanders, he had suspected the lieutenant was the son of the former most senior officer in the Navy, John William Hamblen, grandson of a hero at Santiago Bay and great-grandson of a Civil War naval legend, but he would never have suspected Hamblen could be a "weak sister." He anticipated where Grabowski was headed.

"Go on, Ted."

"The admiral told Captain Leland that he was concerned about his son and asked that he be placed in the gunner department in a position that would allow him to recover his reputation. We didn't know him or his reputation. Captain Leland could not refuse a request from CINCUSFLT. We assigned him as our main-battery fire-control officer, thinking that would be the best position. He's competent enough but easily frustrated to the point of paralysis when confronted with something new. Prior to December 7th, it didn't matter. Now, the fact that he's never faced combat frightens us. He might crumble like a house of cards in a pinch. Chuck Williamson has thought often about replacing him. That would end his career—and an angry four-star admiral, retired or not, could have a devastating effect on all of us."

Sheppard tried to freeze his expression. This was worse than anything he had experienced. Lieutenant Hamblen was not even in a location where a more senior officer could help him. Isolated 170 feet above the water in *Argonne*'s forward main-battery director, he was supported only by relatively junior enlisted men as pointer, trainer, cross-level operator, rangefinder operator, radar operator, and a phone talker in the confined armored Mark 38 director. Trying to replace him in the heat of battle would involve a long climb up the inside of the tower. If fear paralyzed him, there was no room inside the director to move him aside. How would Sheppard ever justify a reassignment now—either to Hamblen himself or the admiral—when he had not yet created a situation that called for such action? Sheppard leaned back, grasping his chin. He was in uncharted waters, without the benefit of experience, surprising himself in that he was unsure what to do.

— —

Sheppard's stateroom clock chimed two bells in the evening watch—1900—just as Corporal Pease knocked and appeared with the department heads. Andy Scott was not in his coveralls, and Bronco had changed to blues even though he still wore his brown shoes.

Sheppard offered them iced tea or coffee, pointedly complimenting Jefferson on his coffee being strong enough to stand a spoon. At this point, everyone regretted Secretary of the Navy Josephus Daniels's edict removing all alcoholic beverages from the United States Navy's ships. Almost unique among the world's combat fleets, the US Navy was dry.

"What I am about to tell you is Top Secret," Sheppard said to open the meeting, "and I do not want it to leave this stateroom until after the ship is underway."

The department heads stopped idly stirring their beverages and nodded their understanding.

"We almost certainly will be going into battle on this mission, with heavy odds against us. When I reported aboard this morning, I thought that the real war was in the Pacific and wished only to quickly conclude our expected assignment in the Atlantic and then take vengeance on the Japanese for their sneak attack without a civilized declaration of war or even an ultimatum. I suspect many of you share the same sentiments."

The nods of agreement indicated Sheppard had accurately judged his key men.

"Today, I am convinced I was wrong. The real war is in the Atlantic, and the Pacific will have to wait."

Spoons were set silently on the table. A few clinks sounded as coffee cups were returned to their saucers. *Argonne*'s senior officers stared at their Captain. Jefferson quietly shut the sliding serving door to the pantry, even though Sheppard trusted him not to repeat anything he heard.

Sheppard took a moment, measuring his words and the reactions that they'd created. He replayed the strategic situation and the disaster the British desert army had suffered.

"England is close to being starved into submission by the Germans. She must get every convoy at sea safely to her ports, with minimal losses, or she will not only starve but run out of fuel, restricting her fleet and the Royal Air Force. Churchill will have no alternative but surrender."

Now, only a stunned silence greeted Sheppard's words as he paused to catch his breath.

"England's fate, the fate of our only ally, is totally dependent on the war at sea in the Atlantic.

"That gets me to our current assignment. *Argonne* and *Belleau Wood* will be the heavy-gunfire component of the task force under Admiral Hamilton that you see assembled around us. There is a German admiral by the name of Schröder who commands a force of four battle cruisers, including two carriers equipped with Stukas and Bf 109s. He has cruisers and destroyers in support that are almost ready to leave Brest. His goal is clearly to slip out undetected and raid the convoys in the Atlantic. Our tasking is simple: we are going to find him and stop them."

Once more, only silence greeted his words. Had Sheppard presented too bleak a situation? He didn't want to give an overall assessment of eventual victory for these men as he had done for the chiefs—the department heads didn't need hopeful encouragement—but, at the same time, he was concerned that they might take too dim a view of the immediate future.

Chuck Williamson broke the silence. "Captain, I think it would be appropriate to let you know the advantages this ship will give you in a fight, as far as my department is concerned."

"Please continue, Chuck."

"Captain, as you know, the Bureau of Ordnance has been working for many years to reduce the erosion on the bore of heavy guns. Without changes, our eighteen-inch guns would wear out in as little as 125 rounds. Accuracy would degrade with every shot, and the muzzle velocity would fall off as the rifling deteriorated.

"The Bureau discovered a couple of years ago that if they add something called titanium dioxide, combined with wax in the form of a jacket around the powder charges, when the powder ignites, the jacket vaporizes, providing an insulating layer for the bore against the hot gases of the burning powder. It only lasts a few hundredths of a second, but it is long enough to reduce the erosion. The powder bags for our guns have those jackets. The eighteen-inch Mark IVs in our turrets were designed with this idea from the outset."

Sheppard gave a small nod. He had known of the effort to prolong the life of heavy guns, but Hawaii had been too far away to keep track of the latest developments. He was glad that his gunnery officer was willing to risk his ire by discussing such details. As an ordnance specialist himself, he should stay abreast of the latest developments. Not doing so could prove embarrassing.

"That is not all, Captain. When the Bureau of Ordnance realized what they had, it didn't make any sense to limit the ammunition carried on board to only 60 percent or so of the nominal life of the guns. We carry almost three hundred rounds for each eighteen-inch gun. There is no need to close the range to twenty thousand yards or so to sink an enemy before we run out of shells or wear out the guns. *Argonne* can stand off and slowly pound any enemy to the bottom. That also helps us in that the more steeply dropping trajectory of the armor-piercing shells allows easier penetration of the enemy's thinner deck armor. I am sure that is something that the Germans would not expect. But we have to control the range."

"Captain," Andy Scott interrupted, "I may be able to help us there. You may not know that we were never able to run the measured mile on sea trials, nor has any ship of this class. Designed to be fast, these ships are *really* fast. With our waterline length, we have a hull speed of almost fifty knots. No one knew for sure how much power it would take to reach the design goal of forty-five. The Bureau of Construction and Repair designed around the largest double-ended, double-reduction gear that Westinghouse could manufacture in order to transmit torque to the shafts. The resulting nominal of a half-million shaft horsepower should be more than enough to get us to our design speed. With the 20-percent overload that the Bureau of Steam Engineering has guaranteed in an emergency, we can make more. How much more is unknown.

"The only thing I caution about is the propellers. When we get above about thirty knots, small bubbles start to form on the trailing edges of the blades. The technical term is *cavitation*. This will get more severe as you go faster, to the point that above forty knots the propeller blades start eroding from the creation and implosion of these small steam bubbles. If we go much faster, I do not have faith that our bronze propellers will last much more than a few hours before we begin to lose speed. If you need the speed, *Argonne* will need a dry-docking to change them when we get back.

"I am sure you will also be surprised when I tell you that when we get underway tomorrow, I'll only have four boilers of our sixteen on line, with four more in hot standby. Those four will give you over thirty knots. The other four, which I can have on service in less than five minutes, will take you over forty. The original four will also give you all the steam that the main-engine astern rotors can handle."

Sheppard nodded and said, "I understand. Thank you."

"Captain," Williamson said in a subdued, almost conspiratorial voice, "I have a gunner's mate standing by with a demonstration, if you don't mind. It is extremely secret, and we are the only ship to have them."

Now there were smiles. His officers were leaning forward, no doubt all thinking of what they might contribute. Sheppard could feel the growing optimism from his department heads beginning to infect him. He was going to have to watch that. He knew that the safety of *Argonne* was going to depend on him making clear decisions, devoid of emotion. At least this discussion helped keep his demons at bay.

"Sure, Chuck," Sheppard said. "Let's see."

Commander Williamson rose and went to the door. Opening it, Williamson asked Corporal Pease to summon Gunner's Mate Third Class Tarbeau.

When he arrived, Tarbeau carried a five-inch shell on his shoulder, and at the gunnery officer's direction, he placed it in the center of the captain's table. Then he departed, closing the door behind him. From the painted colors—green overall body with a five-inch, brighter-green stripe just under the nose fuse-cap—the projectile was an antiaircraft common loaded with TNT as the explosive. The fuse-cap, a threaded bronze cup covering the nose of the shell, protected the sensitive fuse from damage caused by handling. The shells were stored like cordwood in *Argonne*'s magazines, requiring the cap to remain in place until the projectiles were hoisted to the gun mounts.

"Captain," Williamson began, "the first thing you probably noticed when you came aboard was that *Argonne*'s five-inch gun barrels are longer than *Shenandoah*'s. This class of battle cruisers is the first to be equipped with the new 54-caliber weapons. These guns have a significant range advantage over the old ones and pack a heavier punch. They don't fire quite as fast as the older five-inchers because of the heavier shell and powder charge that my crews have to manhandle. They can reach out thirteen miles and higher than any known aircraft can fly. But that is not what makes us unique or as devastating to aircraft as I think we can be."

As he talked, Williamson carefully unscrewed the fuse cap from the projectile to reveal something unexpected.

Sheppard leaned forward, not believing what he was looking at. The fuse was made of clear amber plastic. Not only that, but there were no lugs on the fuse to engage the fuse setter contained in the shell hoists. Sheppard raised an eyebrow. Without lugs, how would the fire-control system tell the shell when to explode?

Chuck continued in a hushed voice, "Captain, gentlemen, what you are looking at is the greatest advancement in antiaircraft gunnery since the introduction of the director. This plastic fuse is actually a small radio set. When the gun fires, a battery activates in the fuse during the first five hundred yards of flight; the fuse then begins transmitting radio waves continuously. As the shell flies, the fuse is listening for reflected radio waves from anything in its vicinity. When reflected waves become close enough to being in phase and of a high enough value, the fuse detonates the booster, and the shell explodes. The amplitude of the reflected-beat frequency was carefully selected to approximate a lethal burst for most aircraft.

"Not even my men or Morris's know what this is yet. It takes the multidimensional fire-control problem of trying to solve for an aircraft's course, speed, elevation, rate of climb or dive, and range, and it removes the hardest to accurately acquire—the range. We don't have to get everything exactly right to bring down an attacking aircraft with our five-inch guns. We only have to get this shell within about seventy-five feet of the aircraft sometime during its flight in order to badly damage, if not destroy, it. The fuse does have a problem: it will activate on anything, including the sea. As a result, it may not be very good against torpedo planes flying low, but the Germans don't have any on their carriers. Captain, I only have three thousand of these on board, and I am not allowed to shoot them where a dud could be recovered, but they should be about seven times as effective and will put a lot of German plane symbols on the sides of my directors."

Now Sheppard smiled, feeling the optimism rising again. He was beginning to think that they might have a chance against four-to-one odds.

— —

Thirty-three nautical miles to the east-northeast of Chesapeake Bay lighthouse, Korvettenkapitän Meier continued to monitor shipping off the entrance to the Chesapeake Bay. Admiral Dönitz had assembled a force of thirty-five U-boats to begin the attack on US shipping before the Americans had a chance to organize defenses. Dönitz had stripped the North and South Atlantic of U-boats, except for the shorter-ranged ones hunting English convoys near Europe and those doing "weather reconnaissance" for Schröder and Lütjens.

Right now, the fact that sinkings were way down for the month of March certainly was not going to please Uncle Karl or Großadmiral Raeder. Meier and his fellow U-boat captains were going to have to make it up this month, or the English would slowly start to replace their lost merchant ships. With every ton that the English managed to build in excess of what Vizeadmiral Dönitz was sinking, they would begin working Britain farther away from starvation. Germany had learned the lesson of starvation in the Great War, when the English blockade had broken the will of the German people to support the war. Even the army began refusing to fight. It had deteriorated to the point that, unthinkably, the spirit of some in the Imperial Navy had cracked and isolated mutinies had appeared in the High Seas Fleet.

This war was going to be different. This time it would be the English who starved while German families ate. Once the English capitulated, the Americans would be unable to hurt Germany. Yes, the soft, fat Americans with their cars and mansions would quickly lose interest in a war they could not win. Germany would then have a free hand in Europe and Africa to create *lebensraum*—living space—for the master race.

Who knew? Perhaps the Japanese might prove to be a worthy ally. Certainly they were better than the Italians. Between Germany and Japan, they could divide Asia, as well. The Japanese attack on Pearl Harbor had been masterfully executed, and their navy was proving it could fight in the Far East. Their army, too, was demonstrating that they knew how to conquer—using Chinese babies for bayonet practice. With that kind of approach, Stalin's Slavs would be chaff brushed aside by the Axis gale.

A faint red afterglow painted the western horizon as the expected faint loom of the Cape Charles Light materialized through Meier's periscope. *Stupid, lazy Americans*, he thought. This was going to be easier than he expected. He and the *U-179* were going to make Hitler, and all of Germany, proud.

— —

Sheppard's newfound optimism vanished when Arthur Roberts began to speak. "Captain, I do not think there is anything that can be done at this late hour, but tomorrow's underway will basically use the peacetime parade-of-ships method. That was fine before Germany declared war and could be sending their U-boats in our direction. Any day now they should start sinking ships off the US East Coast. I am sure a German U-boat skipper would like nothing better than to put some fish into *Sabine, Raritan, Belleau Wood,* or *Argonne.*"

Roberts was brutally correct. If even one of those ships sustained significant damage, the odds against the task force would become prohibitively worse. But every plebe learned the effect of changing direction after issuing initial orders. The phrase that went, *"Order, counterorder, disorder"* was dogma.

"I agree," Sheppard said. "The admiral's underway plan is too hard to change. We need a way to provide security for the fleet as it exits Thimble Shoal's cleared channel, until the destroyers deploy in an antisubmarine screen."

He looked around the table.

"Your suggestions, gentleman?"

Entrance to Chesapeake Bay

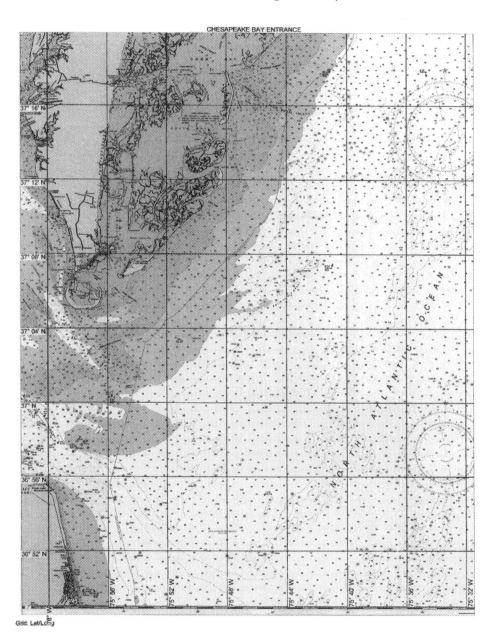

Grid: Lat/Long

CHAPTER 3

UNDERWAY

The department head meeting broke up about three bells into the evening watch—2130. Sheppard, though, wanted Art Roberts to stay behind for a moment. "Art, I'd like your insight into how *Argonne* handles. Ted tells me you are our best ship handler."

"Well, thank you, Captain. Despite her top speed, *Argonne* has a terrible horsepower-to-weight ratio. For all of Andy's pride in his engines, she will be slow to accelerate and slower to stop. That said, her twin rudders are large and located in the slipstream of the inboard screws. Her heading responds well when coupled with power going ahead. At sea, she is as nimble as a destroyer.

"In shallow water, though, the opposite is true. Her draft is almost fifty feet fully loaded. That leaves only a few feet of clearance to the channel bottom, not enough room for a good flow of water to the rudders. Without power to create a slipstream, she may not turn at all in response to the helm. You may have to twist her for significant course changes. The twin skegs aft make for a lot of deadwood that will make even twisting a slow process. At least her designers gave you an engine order telegraph for each shaft to help.

"I hope all of that is of assistance, Captain."

Sheppard gave a small nod. "What you tell me should make it interesting trying to control her when we make the turn past Fort Wool into Thimble Shoal Channel."

"Yes, sir. If the wind and tide are wrong, it will also make getting underway difficult. We may need a healthy twist to get her lined up fair in Hampton Roads."

Roberts paused. Sheppard wondered whether he was trying to guess what his Captain's reaction would be before he risked his next comment. Some captains prided themselves on their own ship-handling prowess, convinced they could park a battleship in a thimble with their eyes closed in a typhoon, any suggestion to the contrary immediately meeting with a tirade of invective.

"Captain, if you wish, I could … I could contact base operations and request several harbor tugs to stand by. I am reasonably certain that they will be there for *Belleau Wood* anyway, and it will do no harm to have them stand by for us, too."

"Good suggestion. Please see to it. Does she have any other faults?"

Roberts hesitated again. "Above thirty-five knots, if you use more than five degrees of rudder, the propeller wash from an outboard screw will affect the inboard prop. Trying to power her through turns will result in a devastating vibration aft. The only way to avoid it is to trail the inboard prop on the outside of the turn until you steady her on her new course. Doing that will require a little more rudder, but it will improve the reliability of the fire-control computers and radar sets."

Sheppard went cold, unsuccessfully trying to maintain his demeanor. Roberts could not know it, but he had just informed Sheppard why *Shenandoah* had gone blind while fighting the Japanese. It had been Sheppard's fault—his decision. No one else had deprived his ship of the ability to see what was around him in the fading light and squalls. No one else had caused the death of his men. One hundred eighty-seven officers and men had died because he had not understood what would happen and how to prevent it. His shoulders slumped, his eyes downcast, Sheppard suddenly felt like a different—defeated—man again.

Clearly sensing something, Roberts excused himself, leaving his Captain within the prison of his own thoughts.

Sheppard shook his head and sat up straight to clear his mind. "Concentrate on something," he whispered to himself. "Concentrate on anything."

Sheppard knew he was desperate. The distraction he so badly needed had to be something good—something he could do for his current men. He went to his desk, determined to refocus his mind. He took out a piece of paper, and began to write:

To: Chief of the Bureau of Navigation
From: Commanding Officer USS Argonne (CC-49)
Subject: Duty Assignment in the Case of Commander Anderson Evert Scott USN
1. *It is my pleasure to report on the exceptional performance of duty of Commander Scott onboard USS Argonne (CC-49)*

In the stilted language of official Navy correspondence, Sheppard continued, recommending that Andy be detached with assignment to command of a cruiser as soon as a suitable relief reported to *Argonne*. He needed to make certain that the letter's phrasing accurately reflected Andy's excellence. Too many commanding officers exaggerated an officer's performance in transfer recommendations, in order to remove someone they did not like. Sheppard had never tried to do that in the past, and he hoped his personal reputation for integrity would now help Andy.

As he was finishing, Westbrook knocked, and Petty Officer Brewster entered.

"Brewster," Sheppard said, "can you please make sure this letter is ready for my signature first thing in the morning? It has to go in the mail before we get underway."

Brewster smiled, took the letter with a crisp "Aye aye, sir," and departed. Then Sheppard took out a piece of his *Argonne* personal stationery to begin writing the letter that might get Andy the job he wanted.

Petty Officer Jefferson appeared at the pantry door carrying a special treat for Sheppard. Jefferson obviously knew his one great weakness and intended to keep his captain happy if it was within his power.

"Cap'n, when Senior Chief Hancock tells me he's going to invites you to dinner," Jefferson said, "I knews you's would accept. I's took a quick trip ashore to do's some shoppin' for your's favorites."

"How much do I owe you, Petty Officer Jefferson?" Sheppard intoned with an air of mock annoyance at the presumptive action on the part of his steward.

"Oh, noth'n for now, Cap'n. Missus McCloud gives me a sum before I's left. Missus done told me to makes sure you felts right to home on board so's you's wouldn't get into trouble on the beach."

In more ways than he would ever know, Evelyn conspired with his crews to both make him seem human and keep him mystified with her little intrusions into his professional life. He was sure that she knew every time she intruded, Sheppard loved her more for the wit she showed and the effect it had on his men.

With that, Jefferson produced a tall, cold glass of chocolate milk.

"Anything else, Cap'n?"

"No, thank you very much, Jefferson. If you don't mind, please make sure I am up at 0600. I'll see you in the morning."

"G'night, Cap'n."

Sheppard took out another piece of personal stationery and began to write again:

"My Dearest Evelyn …"

He chided her for arranging to have Jefferson assigned to *Argonne* without his knowledge and told her about the amazing size and power of his new command. He described the wonderful officers and the reception he had gotten in the chief petty officers' mess. He hoped that she, their daughters, Bonnie and Heather, and youngest son, Derek, were well and inquired about school progress and the other little details of family life. He told her he loved her more every day and described what Jefferson had told him when he had given him his chocolate milk. He asked whether she had heard from their two older sons, not expecting that she had. He said that, contrary to the way he'd felt when he left, he did not think he would be getting back to the Pacific anytime soon but that in war it was impossible to predict what would happen.

"My leg is getting stronger and not troubling me much," he wrote, knowing that she would suspect the truth anyway.

Closing, Sheppard described how Cruz had surprised him in his last coming aboard.

The clock was striking seven bells. His daily routine complete, Sheppard decided to spend a short time reviewing the general arrangement plans that Andy had left him. *Argonne*'s layout was similar to what he'd had on *Shenandoah*. She had a second mess deck and galley spaces forward in addition to the main ones near Number III turret. Her hangar was much larger than *Shenandoah*'s, with the mess decks close by, so he needed to ponder how to avoid the same devastating fire that had nearly cost him his last ship.

A little before midnight, he heard Corporal Henderson relieve Corporal Westbrook. Sheppard knew it was time to go to his cabin and try to sleep before getting underway tomorrow. Though he knew he had to get rest, sleep was something he was beginning to dread.

In his cabin, Jefferson had laid out his pajamas and neatly stowed all of his clothing. He took care to hang his best set of blues in the wardrobe. Sheppard opened the porthole to enjoy the cool sea air and then settled into his bed. That was something he was going to change if he ever got a shipyard period on *Argonne*. Beds belonged in houses. On a ship, he wanted the security, the tradition, of an officer's bunk, and he would have one installed at the first available opportunity.

— ▪ —

Sixty nautical miles to the east, Hans Meier lay under a wool blanket, waiting for sleep, in the small, unheated cubbyhole of a cabin aboard the *U-179*. Fully dressed with the exception of his shoes, he would be instantly able to respond to any emergency or alarm. Like many of his crew—clad in a wool sweater, now more gray than white, checkered shirt, and dark woolen pants—he hardly looked like a naval officer. His only badge of rank was an old service hat carelessly hung on a hook nearby. The dingy but still recognizably white cover told everyone in the Kriegsmarine that he was a commanding officer.

His first officer, Oberleutnant zur See Johann Schmitt, had the watch on the bridge. Meier knew that Schmitt would contact him immediately if anything significant were sighted. They had been together for almost a year, and Meier had grown to trust him implicitly. The night was clear, with good visibility. Only a gentle breeze caused the sea to rise in a slight chop, gently rocking the *U-179*; it was perfect weather to hide a periscope tomorrow, when Operation Beckenschlaeger would start at 1200 Greenwich Mean Time—0700 local.

As they always did just before sleep, Meier's thoughts turned to that day in Munich when his father had taken him to see Hitler and the SA march into the Bürgerbräukeller on November 8, 1923. Ultimately, the putsch Hitler started there with old General Ludendorff had led to success for the Nazi Party. After that fateful day, Meier and his father had attended every anniversary celebration near Munich, listening intently to the Führer railing against Germany's enemies both from within and without. Meier's blond hair and blue eyes, epitomizing the Aryan ideal, guaranteed their admittance and position near the front of the rallies. His fondest childhood memory was his fourteenth birthday, when he joined the Hitler Youth. A vision of Vizeadmiral Dönitz putting the Knight's Cross with Swords about his neck, as the Führer himself looked on, was always Meier's last conscious thought before the rumbling diesel engines lulled him to sleep. All he needed now was a little luck and some typical American stupidity.

—•—

Most slept, but she could not. She was intrigued by this man she had met. He could be the one. It was too soon to tell. As she tried to connect with his soul, there was darkness, a subterfuge. What was it that troubled him? Why did he feel so strongly the need to hide his pain within a portion of his mind inaccessible through the windows of his soul? It worried her and tormented her hopes.

Of course, she had her own secrets. She knew that he would learn them in time. She knew what others had done to her was wrong, and it affected her deeply. Certainly it would hurt them both—when he discovered the truth—but she could not tell him. She wished she could. More than anything she wanted to, but he was going to have to learn her faults on his own, no doubt when it would matter most. He needed to know all her secrets if their relationship were to grow and deepen, as she desired.

—

Sheppard awoke suddenly, dripping in sweat. He had to tell himself again that it was just a dream. It was a dream that had come to him many times before—too many times, he knew. Once again, Evelyn was not there to hold him and tell him that it was just a dream—that most of his men had lived; that Cruz and others had gotten them to sickbay, where his surgeons had performed miracles; that *Shenandoah* had survived and made it all the way back to San Diego.

Every time, the dream was so vivid. The "great" Captain McCloud had found the Japanese carrier fleet in the squalls north of Hawaii. The message—"Air raid, Pearl Harbor. This is no drill!"—had electrified his crew, every man determined to exact revenge. Plotting the returning aircraft radar echoes sent his battle cruiser racing to intercept. He would scout ahead for the ships leaving Pearl and shadow the Japanese until Admiral Trotter's Pacific Fleet Scouting Force could run them down, closing the carriers to engage. Then came stronger echoes from the search radar, allowing *Shenandoah*'s crew to plot what Sheppard believed was the Japanese formation, giving its course and speed—east at eighteen knots.

The enemy formation was the key for Sheppard. The Japs were not expecting a counterattack. What did the Japanese know that he did not? Why were they headed east? There was no time to wait for Trotter.

It had been his decision alone to attack with his sixteen-inch guns firing blind under radar control at the unseen enemy, trying to hit the eight large radar returns at the center of a cruising disposition. With less difficulty than he had anticipated, the radar operators and plotters coaxed the new Mark 3 fire-control radar onto the targets he designated.

First one, then another, and finally a third had slowed before the search radar went down from the shock of the guns. Sheppard felt blind. Turning quickly to what he hoped was a good course to disengage cost him the Mark 3 radar as well. When a Japanese cruiser appeared out of a squall, they exchanged salvos. He knew *Shenandoah* had little to fear from a cruiser, but the third enemy salvo set his hangar ablaze, giving the Japanese a bright target in the developing gloom. As his battle cruiser raced for the safety of another squall, more shells hit, and more fires started. His repair parties were responding; hoses snaked about his ship as men attempted to extinguish their most malevolent fear—*fire*.

Then it happened. Another shell burst nearby. He saw the shattered bulkheads, hose teams desperate to extinguish the blaze no longer there, replaced by crimson-stained water flowing toward the scuppers from the unseen horror that had once been *Shenandoah*'s chart house. That flash of an exploding shell had turned his hose teams into random bodies, piles of pulp and sprayed raw meat, everything dripping red. Transfixed by the horror of the pulverized bodies of his crew, the "great" Captain McCloud stopped thinking, planning his next course change—protecting his men. An unseen capital ship landed a salvo around his battle cruiser.

Barely cognizant of the horror he was witnessing, Sheppard vaguely remembered flying across the command tower … why? As a foggy consciousness returned, he was struggling to get up from the deck, but he could not. Why did his legs not respond? Was he wounded? Should he hope for death, absolved in its finality of his failures? This could not be happening. Not to him—he was too good a captain. He never made a mistake. The familiar items of *Shenandoah*'s command tower were suddenly and strangely out of place. Everywhere there was blood and pieces of flesh and bone. They had been his crew—men who had placed their faith in his abilities. It had all been so normal a moment earlier. He remembered that they had been in a battle. His beloved *Shenandoah* had been racing with everything she had toward a rainsquall. He had let himself believe that they might survive the battle he'd picked against the Japanese. It was all his fault—his fault. Would it happen again? Where his men going to die again? Would it all be his fault again?

His clock chimed two bells. Was it 0100 or 0500? Sheppard did not know.

— —

Vizeadmiral Schröder was up and wearing his blues. Impeccably dressed with a starched shirt and Windsor-knotted tie, he had his Iron Cross hanging from his neck. He relished the standards and traditions of the old German Imperial Navy. Tall by European standards, Schröder prided himself on his appearance. As he ate breakfast, monocle firmly held between right cheek and brow, he reviewed the messages received that night. There were the usual reports from Luftwaffe reconnaissance flights. The British Home Fleet was still in Scapa Flow. Tovey had gained another battleship that had completed repairs. Schröder grimaced. *That fool Lütjens had better make a move soon,* he thought, *or the British will once again be too strong for him.*

Admiral Hardy was still in port at Gibraltar with HMS *Ark Royal, Renown,* and *Repulse.* If Hardy so much as hiccupped, Germany's Spanish spies would keep him completely informed. There was nothing for him to fear from those ancient battle cruisers. The Italians, though, were afraid to force the strait and join the real fight in the Atlantic to eliminate Great Britain. They would not attempt it until something occurred to make the passage safer.

Fools, he mused. *With allies like them, who needs enemies?*

Well, it would only be a month or two before Rommel took the French North African colonies. Then the English defenses covering the south side of the strait could be eliminated.

Next Schröder read a report from the local Gestapo commander describing the latest roundup of French Jews and malcontent day laborers at the shipyard. At least the Gestapo knew enough not to execute the skilled workers that he needed to repair his ships. The sabotage, though, really was getting out of hand, and examples needed to be made. Perhaps the summary hangings would do some good, but Schröder doubted it. The decision to move some of Germany's skilled tradesmen to France was much more likely to allow progress on refitting the captured units of the French fleet. Raeder had already promised they would come under his command.

He studied the weather reports from the U-boats. Nothing of interest … only scattered reports from the Type VII boats in the eastern Atlantic. Soon, with the start of Operation Beckenschlaeger, he would also be getting reports from the Type IXs in the western Atlantic. Then he could plan in earnest.

Schröder was disappointed with the reports he read: no indication of a storm brewing, which he would need to hide him from the British air searches. He could always keep his fighters up, orbiting the fleet, but as he'd discovered when he broke out the first time, British flying boats were hard to shoot down and always radioed when under attack. The English knew there was only one explanation for Bf 109s at sea; an attacked search plane told almost as much as a contact report.

If this dragged on a few more days, the *Yorck* would complete her repairs and join his other battle cruisers *Scharnhorst, Gneisenau*, and *Blucher*. The *Yorck* would not be up to his standards of readiness, but he could use the operation to get her into fighting discipline. With a force of four, nothing that Hardy or the inept Americans could do would stop him. Besides, he was sure Dönitz's U-boats would exact a heavy toll on any American warships foolish enough to try to interfere. They were inexperienced at war, and the lessons that the U-boats would teach them would be painful, very painful.

━ ━

Sheppard swung his left leg out and massaged his thigh, at least what was left of it. It was sore and stiff from the exertion of yesterday. He stood and limped over to the bulkhead clock: 0505.

Might as well stay up, he thought, searching for the bottle of aspirin the doctor had left yesterday.

He took a quick navy shower: water on, get wet; water off, lather; water on, rinse; water off. It was always too cold or too hot, but if this was what his men were required to do, he would do so also. Fresh water was a precious commodity at sea. The boilers had the highest priority on output of the distillers. Men got only what was left—perhaps a few gallons a day.

Sheppard put on his blues, since officially they were still in port. Who knew what guest might unexpectedly come on board before they sailed? A clean shirt and tie, but today he would wear his number three set rather than the best that he had worn yesterday.

He decided to sit at his stateroom table and spend more time with the general arrangement plans. He wanted to learn how to get to the secondary conning station high up in *Argonne*'s forward tower mast, and the armored command tower with the bridge that wrapped around it. It intrigued him, this new combat information center. What communication channels were available there for him to contact other key stations? He wanted to see the CIC and have Jonathan explain how it worked. Perhaps, if it really was that good at presenting the true picture of what was happening, he should make that his battle station. For now, though, he would remain in the command tower, the way the ship's designers had intended.

Sheppard flipped through the sheaf of large blueprints until he came to the plan for the fourth deck—just under the armor. As he started looking for the CIC, he noticed two large, straight fore and aft passageways with intervening watertight doors. *Shenandoah* had featured only one. Why two, then? Would that give him some sort of advantage?

He finally found what he was looking for, but it was not much help. Yes, he could locate it now, directly under the forward tower—but the cryptic "to be provided" was all that the blueprint showed within its bulkheads.

Jefferson entered the stateroom, apparently expecting to find Sheppard asleep in his cabin. Taken aback for a moment, Jefferson recovered with, "Oh, morn'n, Cap'n. It's another fine Navy day."

That always brought a smile to Sheppard's lips. "That it is, Petty Officer Jefferson, and good morning to you, too."

Sheppard realized how much he had missed this morning ritual when he was convalescing. It was good to hear the familiar words.

— —

Fifty-five miles to the east, Hans Meier was eating his breakfast of fried sausage and toast, with a rare delicacy. The cook had managed to find one of the last remaining Spanish oranges on board and had saved it for the Kapitän in anticipation of the start of Operation Beckenschlaeger. Everyone knew that this operation might win the war for Germany. If only they could sink enough ships and light the night skies along the East Coast with burning tankers, perhaps the soft Americans would quit. Without America, the English could not survive.

Meier really did not care about the strategic situation. All he wanted was to sink heavily loaded American merchant ships and win his Knight's Cross with Swords.

He scratched his beard and ran his tongue over his teeth in a futile attempt to clean them. There was no fresh water onboard a U-boat for anything except cooking when necessary and the battery. Shaving, brushing his teeth, and a bath were things that had to wait until they returned to port and the palatial U-boat rest camps. En route to the bridge to see the sunrise and to gauge the sea and wind himself, he left the cubbyhole of a cabin and turned aft, through a watertight door and into the control room. From there, it was just a short climb up to the conning tower and then to the bridge. In some respects, he hated going to the bridge. He'd get used to the clean, sweet air, and it would prove painful to go below again, with its overpowering stench of sweat, rotting clothes, mold, diesel fuel, chlorine from the battery, and decaying food. There was a good reason they called submarines "pigboats."

— —

Finishing his breakfast of eggs (fried over hard, of course), bacon, toast, and coffee, Sheppard called out for Corporal Pease to summon Lieutenant Commander Becker. It was not long before Sheppard heard a knock on the cabin door. Expecting Becker, Sheppard was surprised to see his yeoman instead. Brewster placed an open folder on the table for Sheppard's signature. Recalling the letter he had given him the night before, Sheppard took out his fountain pen. Reading it over, he found no typographical errors.

"How many tries did it take you to get it perfect?" Sheppard casually asked as he signed the letter.

"Two, sir," Brewster answered.

"Very well, but I don't mind a typo or two on each page as long as you mark them with pencil so I can correct and initial them. That way we can both be more efficient."

Brewster stared in clear disbelief at his Captain. He had obviously never worked for an officer who was willing to have a typographical error on any page, let alone two.

"Captain, it really took me six tries. That typewriter you have is a little stiff."

Sheppard frowned. "Very well, Brewster; thank you for your truthfulness. But in the future, make it the norm."

"Aye aye, sir," Brewster answered.

Corporal Pease's knock interrupted any further recrimination, as the marine ushered Lieutenant Commander Jonathan Becker into the cabin.

"Brewster," Sheppard added. "There are two personal letters on the sideboard that I would appreciate being placed in the mail."

Another quick "Aye aye, sir," and Brewster left, surely thankful at escaping his Captain's displeasure.

Sheppard noticed that Becker had on khakis, rather than the blues appropriate when summoned to the captain's stateroom in port.

Becker's cheery, "Good morning, Captain," seemed out of place for the image standing—barely at attention—before Sheppard.

Taking in the blue eyes, rumpled uniform, and hair more than two weeks from a barber's chair, Sheppard could see the accuracy of Grabowski's assessment. At least he was clean-shaven—or did he even need to shave daily yet? Sheppard pondered whether he was going to have any better success at turning Becker into a naval officer than Bill Leland had had.

"Jonathan, I would like to see your combat information center before we get underway. I am sure my opportunities will be limited at sea."

"Ah. Yes, sir."

Becker just stood there, not recognizing that Sheppard meant he wanted to see it *now!*

Sheppard eyed him with a cold stare. "Unless you have something more urgent that—"

"I'd be happy to now, Captain."

Yes, it was going to be difficult trying to turn Mister Becker into an officer, Sheppard thought as he followed Jonathan aft to the passageway with Corporal Pease in tow. Turning outboard, they went down two ladders to the third deck. As they moved forward, they came to a trunk—a vertical laddered tunnel—and turned into it through a watertight door.

Sheppard stopped, feeling dumbfounded. There in front of him was the raised armored hatch that opened to a ladder leading to the fourth deck and the starboard passageway. That much he expected. What shocked him was the fact that it was a foot thick. Chuck had told him that conceptually these ships were to fight at long range, but he had not expected their armored deck to be as thick as *Ticonderoga*'s armored belt.

"Our designers changed the ratio of weights between the armor belt and the deck, giving us greater protection from plunging fire," Becker said. "The deck is also a new type of steel, much stronger and more resistant to penetration than the old STS decks you had on *Shenandoah*."

He may not be very military, Sheppard thought, *but he can be perceptive.*

They continued down the ladder and made their way forward to the combat information center.

Jonathan instantly began a rapid-fire explanation of the Sugar King radar's PPI displays.

"Slow down, Mister Becker," Sheppard said, only being familiar with A and B radar scans. "What is a PPI?"

"Sorry, Captain. A PPI is a plane position indicator. It is as if you were God looking down on the air and surface of the ocean."

The alphabet soup of SKs, SGs, DRIs, EM-logs, Mark this and Mark that, fade ranges, and PPIs was enough to make Sheppard's head hurt.

"Once the SKs detect an aircraft," Becker continued, "the range, bearing, and time of the contact are passed to this large clear-plastic plot. Some of my men learned to write backward so that they could write the information with a grease pencil on one side, and I can read it clearly from the other without anyone blocking my view. Since we have two radars, if one goes out of commission from vibration or shock—once we start firing the eighteen-inch guns—I can still give you a good picture."

"Who came up with this method?"

Becker gave him a sheepish look. "I did, Captain. I had the shipyard cut the plastic and install it in our post-shakedown yard period when the new radars were installed."

This kid is smart, Sheppard thought. "What do you do with this information?" he asked.

Becker continued as his petty officers busied themselves with pre-underway checks of all the equipment, unsuccessfully trying not to smile. "Besides telling you on the bridge, I can also send it to repeaters in the room forward, where one of my officers sits—one skilled at talking to aircraft. We can coax the F4Fs from *Sabine* or *Raritan* onto enemy aircraft before they ever see us. We just can't tell altitude."

"How do you tell our aircraft from enemy aircraft?"

"Captain, all of our aircraft have a new device called an IFF, for Identification Friend or Foe. When the aircraft detects a signal from the

SK radar, it transmits a signal on the same frequency as the radar, which then shows up on the radar PPI, letting the operator know whether that particular bright spot or blip is friendly, vice enemy, or unknown. The only hard parts are keeping track of which friendly group of fighters is which when you are trying to guide them to the enemy, not to mention knowing the altitude of the enemy."

"Can you do the same with ships?"

— —

Hans Meier had decided that they should close on the entrance to Chesapeake Bay. The water was shallow, only ten meters in most places, but he was determined to be the first to sink a merchant ship when Operation Beckenschlaeger officially began. He directed Wolfgang Brandt, his officer of the deck, to head west, and then he went below to study the chart and pick his spot.

As he studied the chart, Meier considered that he would have to submerge to attack in daylight, and for that he needed at least fifteen meters of water. He decided that that depth would be cutting it too close. He would need more to prevent an inadvertent bottoming when he sounded the alarm. Twenty meters was as far in as he would go. It would limit how close he could get to cover the two channels that exited the mouth of the bay. The one that rounded Cape Charles would be used by ships coming down the Chesapeake from Baltimore and Washington and then going up the coast to New York or out to sea. The other channel emptied close to Cape Henry on the south side of the entrance. Warships from the big American base at Norfolk, as well as the ships coming down the James River from Richmond or from the port of Newport News, would use that one. He was not concerned about the warships. If this were a British base, air patrols and small armed trawlers would be everywhere, but the Americans were too inexperienced, and they were not expecting Vizeadmiral Dönitz's new campaign.

It did not take long before Meier found what he hoped would be the best spot, twenty-five nautical miles due east of Cape Henry Light.

"Wolfgang!" Meier shouted up the bridge trunk. "Head for thirty-six degrees fifty-six minutes north, seventy-five degrees thirty-four minutes west. The quartermaster will give you the course."

"Jawohl, Herr Kapitän!"

"You should arrive in about an hour. Call me if you see anything."

— —

"Sort of, Captain," Becker answered in response to Sheppard's question about being able to identify ships in the same way as aircraft.

"Go on," Sheppard said.

"The Sugar George radars are designed for detecting surface ships, but they can only see out to about forty thousand yards, longer if the ship is large, but there is a problem with their waveguides at the higher frequencies."

"What's a waveguide?"

"Sorry, Captain. For the higher frequencies of radio waves, you cannot use a copper conductor; you have to guide them around inside a hollow conducting tube. We haven't quite figured out how to do that with the SG over more than a few tens of feet, so the radar sets have to be high up. The forward one is up by the secondary conning station in the fire-control tower. The after one doesn't work as well, because the waveguide is longer to the auxiliary conning station. The Bureau is working on getting us repeaters of the presentation from the radar, but we do not have them yet. I developed a work-around by having operators at both, with phone talkers to give us the information down here, which we will display on these plotting tables."

A better plan of how he could fight *Argonne* began to form in Sheppard's mind.

"What about IFF?" he asked Becker.

"It is not as good as for aircraft. Many of our ships are not IFF fitted yet. None of the Brits have any of this gear, so they will look like the enemy."

Sheppard suddenly noticed that Corporal Westbrook had replaced Corporal Pease. He needed to get to the bridge.

—•—

"Eric, how good of you to join me for lunch. Have you heard from your mother recently?"

Admiral Schröder got up from his desk to greet and hug his son. Klaus felt a justified pride in Eric. He had graduated well up in his class at the Flensburg Naval Academy. Eric, of course, had followed his father into the surface navy, being assigned to *Scharnhorst* for his first ship. Schröder tried to see his son often while in Brest and knew of his assignment as an antiaircraft battery officer. It was as good a place to start as any, particularly if his gunners could shoot well.

"I received a letter from her yesterday," Eric said. "She is well and so pleased that I was assigned to your command."

"Das ist gut."

Klaus smiled, not wishing to imply how he had pulled the strings that sent his eldest son to the battle cruiser *Scharnhorst*. If Anna, his wife, knew, she would never forgive him should anything happen.

"Tell me all about your ship, Eric. What duties have you been assigned? How soon will you be qualified as watch officer?"

"Please, Father, slow down. I love the ship. I am luckier than most of my academy classmates to be assigned to a battle cruiser, particularly one part of your raiding fleet. Did you have anything to do with that?"

"God only knows all the things that go into the Kriegsmarine's assignment of personnel."

"Father, they have made me the officer in charge of one of the divisions of light antiaircraft guns. I have almost fifty men, with responsibilities for both 20 mm and 37 mm guns."

"Tell me all about it as we eat. I especially want to hear about the discipline of your men and how you are training them to be good gunners."

—•—

Sheppard finished his exhausting eight-deck climb to the navigating bridge just in time for a greeting by Lieutenant Commander Joseph Archinbald, the assistant gunnery officer and the officer of the deck for the underway. Archinbald looked anxious. Sheppard hoped it was because they were within an hour of getting underway and because Joe had been unable to locate him. He did not want to consider that it might be his own appearance after his climb.

"Captain," Archinbald said in the formal language of the bridge, "request permission to station the special sea-and-anchor detail."

Sheppard had started a practice of saying exactly what he was giving permission for. Once, during his command of the *Rowan,* there had been two requests made close together. He meant to give permission for one and not the other, but his "permission granted" had prompted both actions.

"Very well," Sheppard said. "Station the special sea-and-anchor detail."

After Archinbald had relayed it to the boatswain's mate of the watch, he added, "Sorry I delayed your anticipated time line."

The boatswain's mate keyed the general announcing system and piped the call *All hands* "$s^{s\text{-}s\text{-}ssssssss}{}_s s^{sssssssss}s$"—which commanded silence and informing the crew that action would be required of everyone, followed by, "Now station the special sea-and-anchor detail!"

It was as if someone had hit a hornet's nest with a stick, as sailors and officers dashed to their assigned stations. Many of *Argonne*'s sailors were assigned in their blues and pea coats to "man the rails," a practice unique to warships and designed to impress everyone with the discipline and readiness of the crew. All other men had specific jobs to do and a chain of command to work through. Almost immediately, a flood of requests from them began inundating the bridge for Sheppard to act upon. The stationing of the special sea-and-anchor detail marked the official change from in-port routine, during which Sheppard had little to do directly, to the at-sea routine, where he controlled virtually everything through his direct representative, the officer of the deck—or

OOD. Rather than just issue orders to accomplish everything, Sheppard knew that waiting for a request was the best way to ensure that the chain of command and personnel who would execute the order were ready for it. This method only worked for routine evolutions; when unique events occurred, initiation came from the bridge, and the Captain's ability alone was tested. An old but true saying advised, *"In port the Captain is king, but at sea the Captain is God!"*

A torrent of orders and reports climaxed when the white-and-blue dovetailed flag "Able" was hauled halfway up—at the dip—on the port and starboard halyards, signaling other ships that all was in readiness. Lastly, engineering was directed to "Answer all bells. Answer all, stop." Then the officer of the deck or another officer who would actually control the movement of the ship—called a "conning officer"—standing near the OOD, directed the helmsman, "Rudder amidships."

— —

The *U-179* was on the surface, moving to the spot that Hans Meier hoped would be close enough to guard the approaches to Chesapeake Bay. The sun had risen well above the horizon to the east, which was part of his plan. Any lookout trying to spot them from the bay's entrance would have to look into the sun, and the reflection on the water would mask the U-boat's already small silhouette as they approached.

It was about 0805 when Brandt called him and reported smoke on the horizon, bearing 273 degrees. Almost due west, it was exactly where Meier expected detection for a fat merchant ship, careless with her boiler fires. He immediately went to the control room, up to the conning tower, and raised one of the two periscopes. The attack scope had the smallest possible head window and slimmest tube, so it was least detectable when closing in on a target to attack. Those advantages came with a price, though: poor light transmission and only limited magnification. Thus, Meier used the search periscope, which was designed not with detectability in mind but rather with optimum light transmission and as much magnification as German engineering and optics would allow in the periscope's barrel. Even with good binoculars, the OOD was only about four meters above the ocean surface, but the head window of the search periscope was almost ten, nearly doubling the distance that it could see. Even with the search periscope, Meier could only see smoke and perhaps a mast—or perhaps not.

"Wolfgang!" Meier shouted up to the bridge. "Come to course two-seven-three degrees. I want to close the smoke."

"Jawohl, Herr Kapitän."

Meier would close this target and see if it was worth one of his precious twelve torpedoes. He was not going to use his 10.5-centimeter deck gun in daylight. Even he was not that bold.

"Quartermaster," Meier ordered, "lay down a bearing of two-seven-three degrees on the chart marked with the time. Every two minutes, take another bearing to the smoke and see if it is moving to the right or the left."

If a bearing change became apparent, he would need to alter course and lead the target to prevent it from getting past him.

Meier smiled to himself. It was good to be back in the hunt after a month of inactivity transiting the Atlantic.

— —

Timing was critical, Sheppard knew. *Sabine* was already under way and the *Raritan* would be following her next. "Dolf"—a nickname from his days as a champion butterflier on the Academy swim team—Hamilton had ordered a separation of only one thousand yards between ships as they steamed out of Hampton Roads. With the slowness of *Argonne* to react to changes in speed, Sheppard needed to time his underway and acceleration with care to fall in exactly a thousand yards behind *Belleau Wood*. Third in line behind *Raritan, Belleau Wood* was beginning to raise her anchor. Sheppard could not do anything about Captain Bailey's timing in determining how well *Belleau Wood* maneuvered to her assigned station. His task was to be at the correct distance behind Bailey, regardless of where he was.

Sheppard's OOD sensed his uneasiness and helped with a, "Captain, request permission to raise anchor."

"Very well, raise the anchor."

In response to its massive electric motor driving through a hydraulic Waterbury speed gear, the wildcat began turning, grabbing each link in turn and hauling in the anchor chain. The 1JV circuit phone talker reported, "Anchor is up and down," meaning that they had pulled all the chain that could be taken in without lifting the anchor off the bottom.

Sheppard raised his binoculars to monitor the party of sailors stationed above the hawse pipe who were spraying the incoming chain with a high velocity stream of water from a fire hose, dislodging the mud picked up by the remaining chain.

"Anchor aweigh!"

Quickly the report came—"Anchor in sight"—as the starboard Baldt stockless anchor, one of two that *Argonne* carried, became visible to a boatswain's mate looking over the side.

The report of the anchor being visible prompted the conning officer to order, "All ahead one-third." The two lee helmsmen swung their enunciator arms quickly full travel and then positioned them to indicate the order to each of the four throttlemen. As those machinist mates spun open the ahead throttle valves, high-pressure super-heated steam rushed to the turbine blades of the main engines. The giant shafts, with their attached twenty-five-foot diameter propellers, slowly began to turn.

As the solid-bronze propellers rotated, a huge swirling mass of water majestically spread across the harbor from *Argonne*'s stern, an upwelling that smoothed the waves created by the morning breeze. Dozens of gulls appeared, feasting as the silversides and bay anchovies caught in the rising waters, first clean then tinged brown as mud too, reached the surface, drawn up and into the spreading acres of wash. Imperceptibly at first, the *Argonne* began to move forward.

The exhaust gases from the on-line boilers, rising up *Argonne*'s funnels, erupted in geysers of hot fumes as the water tenders cut in more oil sprayers, fueling the raging boiler fires, generating more heat, boiling more feed-water, and creating the steam to satisfy the ravenous thirst of the accelerating turbines. The watchstanders stationed at each boiler carefully monitored the color of the exhaust gases through periscopes and adjusted the airflow to the sprayers, anticipating if they could, reacting if they could not. Too much air would waste heat, with the boilers operating at less than their optimum efficiency in turning burning oil into steam. Too little air, and the oil would not completely burn, releasing clouds of black smoke and soot—fouling the boiler tubes, and limiting *Argonne*'s and the task force's endurance.

In war, enemies, if present, could see that rising black smoke at great distances.

— —

It had been twenty minutes since the first report of smoke, and *U-179* had closed almost six kilometers when Meier looked through the search periscope again. This time, he saw a mast and something that made his heart skip, then beat faster. Beside the two masts, he could now make out the four funnels of an old flush-decked American destroyer. Slowly swinging the search periscope around, pausing every five degrees to let every detail of the horizon make an impression on his retina, he spotted a second set of similar masts farther to the north on a bearing of 287 degrees—two contacts, probably both old four-pipers.

Why would the Americans have two museum pieces out here at the entrance to the Chesapeake? Neither one was worth a torpedo, but if they were patrols, they were not being very effective. Their motions did not indicate that they were the screen for a convoy.

"Wolfgang, slow to minimum steerage way," Meier yelled up at his watch officer.

"Jawohl, Herr Kapitän! Dead slow ahead both."

"These contacts are old destroyers. Keep pointing them until we can determine their search patterns."

These ships could hurt him. It would be inconsistent with what the Americans had demonstrated so far for them to be aggressive or attentive to their searches. Their crews were likely just counting the hours until they could return to port and the pleasures that lonely sailors find ashore.

Yet, why are they here? Meier wondered.

— —

Sheppard was studying *Belleau Wood* as she approached the turn past Fort Wool into Thimble Shoal Channel. He had his binoculars focused on the water at her stern to gauge the rudder orders and engine orders that Bailey applied to his sister ship. Perhaps Sheppard could learn something from *Belleau Wood*'s maneuvers. Every three minutes, the navigator, Commander Art Roberts, was reporting their position from the bearings that he took on Old Point Comfort Light, the signal tower, and Fort Wool. Each bearing, when drawn on the chart, created a "line of position." A second crossing line created a position "fix" of exactly where *Argonne* was at that moment. Like all prudent navigators, Roberts took a third bearing as a check.

The navigator then reported to the OOD that they were "on track" or the precise number of yards right or left of track. Commander Roberts had laid out the track that *Argonne* should follow, including turns of the standard fifteen-hundred-yard diameter ending in the center of all of the channels, where the methodical Army Corp of Engineers' dredges had excavated the deepest trench. Staying centered in the channel was not just to prevent touching the bottom; it also assisted in maneuvering the ship with a better flow of water to the propellers and rudders.

Suddenly, a swirl of white water and spray burst up on *Belleau Wood*'s starboard side as she tried to make the last turn into Thimble Shoal channel. Bailey must have been backing hard on the starboard propellers to swing his battle cruiser onto the correct heading. Sheppard guessed that he had mistimed the turn and now had to take a more drastic action to line up fair in the channel. Lowering his binoculars, Sheppard saw that one of *Belleau Wood*'s watchstanders had not been paying attention, and a huge mushrooming cloud of black smoke shot up from her after funnel.

— —

Aboard *U-179*, forty miles to the east, Wolfgang Brandt called to Meier, "Herr Kapitän, more smoke on a bearing of two-seven-zero degrees."

Meier raced to the conning tower, painfully scraping his back on the hatch coaming as he climbed for a look through the search periscope. It was an immense sooty cloud, low hanging, and already slowly dissipating in the morning breeze. Meier swung the periscope slowly to the right. In turn, he sighted each of the American four-pipers, noting the relative bearings from the foundation ring above the periscope, before a quick glance at the gyro repeater to convert the relative to true bearings in his head.

The two Americans were continuing to lazily steam in racetrack patterns. They were clearly on some type of patrol, perhaps making certain that the entrance to the Chesapeake was clear before a convoy of merchant ships, or perhaps a large warship, departed the port.

Swinging the periscope again, he took note of the sky, angle of the sun, direction of the sea and, finally, the wind-driven ripples—all to gauge the environment for his attack. Though climbing, the sun would still be behind him if either of the destroyers looked in his direction. After over two years of war, Meier—even at only twenty-six years old—had developed a fine sense for the tactical advantages that careful observation of nature could give.

He decided to close another kilometer, risking detection by the crow's nest lookouts on those destroyers. Something was coming out of that channel close to Cape Henry Light. What was it called? *Oh yes.* He remembered. *Thimble Shoal.* A strange name, but Meier was determined to find out what was now approaching.

He sensed his own emotions—that developing degree of anticipation, the heightened awareness, a slowing of time, his own pounding heartbeat. These all told him of an impending kill. He decided to wake up Oberfunkmaat Cuyler, his man with the most experience on the underwater sound gear, to listen in that area for any propeller noises.

Meier went to the bridge. He wanted to relish this moment in the hunt. The anticipation of the kill—perhaps the first of Operation Beckenschlaeger, perhaps a major warship—and with it a Knight's Cross with Swords. The clean, sweet air and warm sun on his neck did not distract him from informing Brandt of his desire to attack.

— —

Argonne completed the series of turns more easily than *Belleau Wood*. Sheppard had discussed his observations with Joe Archinbald and the conning officer. When the turn bearing for the last big turn into Thimble Shoal Channel was marked, the conning officer executed their plan. Masterfully, by only using the outboard starboard engine going astern, they achieved not only the benefit of "twisting" *Argonne* but also maintained a smooth flow of water past both rudders, assisting the turn. As they approached the correct course for Thimble Shoal Channel, the conning officer issued his orders.

"Steady course one-zero-eight," John Hamblen called to the helm. Then, to the starboard lee helmsman, "Number three main engine, ahead one-third."

Joe Archinbald was using the stadimeter to take the range to *Belleau Wood*. It used the same trigonometry that a rangefinder used, but instead of a long-base focusing on one point, it used one point to focus on a known distance. Lining up the split image, he called off the range. "One-zero-two-zero yards."

Sheppard smiled. The task force was now lined up in the channel and proceeding to sea at eight knots. The light cruisers and destroyer squadrons were not yet turning into Thimble Shoal Channel when Admiral Hamilton ordered a speed increase to twelve knots.

— —

Meier's sound operator strained to comprehend what he heard. The look of intensity etched in his bearded face demanded Meier's rapt attention. They had not seen any more smoke for almost thirty minutes. The two oblivious four-piped destroyers were not changing their racetrack patterns, obvious from Meier's periodic observations with the search periscope.

For the last ten minutes, the oberfunkmaat had started to move his finger in silent counting of the propeller beats he alone could hear, only to stop in apparent frustration. Suddenly, the sound operator's eyes lit up.

"Herr Kapitän," he exclaimed at discovering the cause of his frustration, "there are several sets of heavy propellers. There are too many for me to count, but at least five ships with multiple screws, bearing two-seven-three degrees true."

"Das ist gut," Meier said, a wry smile spreading beneath his blond beard. He turned to his first officer. "Johann, wake the crew. See that they are well fed, for today we make history."

Meier turned back to the soundman and asked, "What about escorts?"

"Herr Kapitän, that is what I do not understand. I do not hear any."

Korvettenkapitän Hans Meier's smile broadened. The stupid Americans were presenting him the opportunity of a lifetime; it would guarantee his Knight's Cross with Swords. Perhaps the Führer himself would present it!

CHAPTER 4

SURPRISES

Hans Meier ascended into the conning tower, raised the search periscope, and intently studied the bearing that he had gotten from his soundman, but he saw … nothing. Making a thorough full-circle search, he checked for other contacts, taking observations on the old destroyers for his quartermaster to put on the chart as he went. Those American four-pipe destroyers were still maintaining their racetrack patrols.

"Wolfgang, keep a sharp lookout for aircraft. I suspect something important is coming out of the Chesapeake Bay," he shouted up to his OOD over the growl of the idling diesel engines.

That, too, was a fortuitous omen, as his batteries were at peak charge. *U-179* could not be in a better position for the start of Operation Beckenschlaeger.

The sun was climbing into a cloudless sky, but there was still a fresh breeze, raising a good chop to hide his periscope from attentive lookouts. *Should one exist*, he thought, chuckling to himself.

No sign of aircraft. As he came to a bearing of 270 degrees, something caught his eye—mastheads, several of them. Meier was ecstatic. The first two ships only had one mast each, which was puzzling, but the next groups of mastheads were on two larger ships with two masts each. The appearance of each masthead kept changing as he watched. Why? What could be moving at their tops? From the orientation and short spacing between masts, he knew he was to the north side, just off the track that they would follow toward his location. Following the two larger contacts were two more single masts, again barely discernable, but they appeared to be much smaller, and he knew that he might only be seeing the tallest of theirs.

Perfect!

All he had to do was wait for the Americans to come to him like ducks in a shooting gallery. As he studied the masts, he began to see what looked like the forward tower of a battleship on the third contact, the arms of her rangefinder jutting above the dark-blue horizon. Meier lowered the periscope, dropped into the control room, and checked the chart—eighteen meters. It would have to do.

"Alarm!" Meier shouted.

— —

Argonne was approaching Lynnhaven Inlet on her starboard side. Sheppard had discussed the department head's plan with Joe Archinbald, and the OOD had been issuing the necessary orders for the last twenty minutes.

To further test John Hamblen's abilities, Sheppard decided to let him work out the true wind. It was a simple procedure, but its importance to the ship and safety of his airmen could fluster an unsure officer. Using readings taken on the wind speed and direction from the anemometers on the ends of *Argonne*'s forward yardarms provided information on the relative wind—with the indicated speed and direction from them plotted on a "maneuvering board," starting at an arrow representing *Argonne*'s course and speed. The true wind direction was the line from the tail of *Argonne*'s arrow to the tip of the anemometer arrow, and the wind's speed was the length of that resultant, using the same proportion as the other two. Hamblen completed it quickly and correctly, further confirming Ted Grabowski's observations.

When he had finished, the computation was passed via a phone talker and provided updates for the CIC, gunnery, and the air department. The latter needed the information so that they would know how the air was moving relative to the ocean that *Argonne* was operating in. Without the true wind to adjust their dead reckoning, they would not know where to find *Argonne* if they flew out of her sight. That same moving ocean of air affected the flight of *Argonne*'s projectiles and was an input into the fire-control computers. As a result, every hour the true wind determination was of considerable importance to accomplishing the battle cruiser's mission.

— —

Every crewmember on board *U-179* sprang into action. Those off watch, always in their clothes, instantly awoke and ran to their posts. Mechanics standing beside the thundering diesels shut down the engines on the first sound of the alarm. Another watchstander shifted propulsion to the electric motors and batteries. The huge air inlet valves for the engines clanged shut, as did the equally large diesel exhaust valves. Lieutenant Brandt and the lookout literally dropped into the cramped conning tower with Brandt, slamming the hatch shut behind him. The lookout spun the hand wheel to seal the hatch shut in the event of depth charges. Once closed, the higher pressure of the water on the outside would hold it firmly in place except in the case of the shock of an explosion. The main vents opened, letting the air trapped in the ballast tanks escape and quickly filling the tanks with water from the huge openings in the bottom of the thin plating. The system that kept them on the surface was like an inverted glass in the water. As long as the air could not escape, the U-boat was light enough to stay afloat, but when the air escaped, the additional weight of water in the ballast tanks allowed submergence.

Two-thirds speed, ordered on the enunciator, caused electricians aft to adjust the port and starboard motors, increasing the boat's speed and thereby giving the diving planes greater bite in the sea and controlling the depth of the submarine. Most sailors think a submarine submerged is like a blimp, but it is not. Unlike a blimp, it is unstable. If it starts to rise, it will continue, as the hull expands from lower sea pressure. The submarine will rise uncontrollably until it comes to the surface. Similarly, if it starts down, the increasing pressure compresses the hull, continuing a fatal descent to the bottom and crushing it when it reaches its "collapse depth," if it is in the deep ocean. It is a slow process to adjust the U-boat's weight by using the trim pump to remove water or a small valve to bring more water aboard into trim tanks. But any use of the pump takes its toll on the battery and creates noise for listening destroyers.

When the boat is submerged, an officer supervises the two "planesmen" and the operator of the trim system, as well as a petty officer controlling the use of the high-pressure air. That "diving" officer must do whatever is necessary to get on the ordered depth and stay there.

Meier ordered "Twelve meters!"—the depth measured from the keel of *U-179* to the surface.

— —

The reports had been coming to the bridge that all of the orders had been completed, meaning that it was time for Sheppard to issue the next order himself. This evolution, by its nature, was dangerous to his men. He made certain, by looking aft, that everything was in readiness. He turned to the OOD.

"Launch aircraft," Sheppard ordered.

The phone talkers relayed the order to Bronco's men aft at the Mk-VII catapults. Rotated so that they faced into the relative wind, the tie-downs on the Kingfisher scout-observation planes had already been slacked and removed. Firing gunpowder starting cartridges brought the Pratt and Whitney radial engines to a pleasant roar. When these were warmed up, all preparations for launching were ready, prompting Sheppard's order. Now the aviation boatswain's mate in charge of the port catapult pulled a lanyard on the trigger. The gunpowder charge—a five-inch-diameter cartridge—fired, and the Kingfisher accelerated down the track into the air. After the port catapult fired and its Kingfisher cleared, the starboard hurled Bronco and his radioman across the armored hatch, just clearing the safety lines at the port gunwale.

As the two Kingfishers climbed for altitude, Archinbald ordered two more OS2U-5s prepared for launching. The catapults were trained to their normal stowed positions. The armored deck hatch opened. In turn, two Kingfishers, on trolleys, were trundled under the dangling hook of the crane by the collective pushes and tugs of nearly all the V-1 Division's men. Hoisted and swung onto the forward ends of the catapults, the loaded cars then withdrew aft on their rails to launch positions at the aft ends. Once in place, wings were unfolded and locked, depth charges loaded, and the aircraft fueled. The risks of volatile aviation gasoline were too great to tempt an explosion or fire in the confines of the hangar, except in extreme circumstances. Bronco had forced his men to practice repeatedly until they could reliably perform the difficult evolutions in the darkest night or foulest weather.

— —

While the first Kingfisher was climbing away from the *Argonne,* a surface lookout on board *Sabine* reported, "*Argonne* launching aircraft." A phone talker relayed the report to *Sabine*'s OOD, who relayed it to his captain and to the flag plot, where Admiral Hamilton had just ordered a signal flag hoist. Fluttering up the carrier's signal halyards, the pennants read "Corpen one-three-seven," which translated to "Prepare for a sequential turn to starboard on a new course." The launch of Kingfishers was not part of Admiral Hamilton's air plan. His surprise lasted only a second before he turned, scowling, to a staff officer.

"Make to *Argonne*: 'Interrogative aircraft launch.'"

Picking up a sound-powered telephone handset, the lieutenant relayed the order to the signal bridge. Almost immediately, the *Sabine*'s twenty-four-inch signal lamp began clattering out the Morse code.

— —

On *Argonne*'s signal bridge, Chief Signalman Evan Bryce noticed that the flagship was signaling. Over twenty years of service had taught him to watch the admiral's ship continuously when underway. Bryce reported to the officer of the deck, "Flagship signaling"—even as he began reading the Morse code. His signalmen were bending on the flags for "Corpen one-three-seven," clipping them in turn from the steel signal bags and then hauling the hoist halfway up the halyards on both the port and starboard yardarms. Chief Bryce noted with satisfaction that his signal gang got the signal "to the dip" before *Belleau Wood* or *Raritan*. On such small things, a ship's—and captain's—reputation depended.

The flashing light read, To: "NMAT", which was the visual call sign for *Argonne*, From: "CTF 48", which was the call for Commander Task Force Forty-Eight Admiral Hamilton, and finally the message itself: "Interrogative aircraft launch."

After each word, Chief Bryce would flash back a long dash to indicate *Argonne* had received the word and understood it. Having served with Sheppard on the *Shenandoah*, the chief smiled at the completed message. He knew that this was the Navy's polite way of asking, "What the hell are you doing?" Chief Bryce knew his captain well enough to know that the answer would be a good one, one which the admiral surely had not thought of.

— —

As the *Sabine*'s signal lamp was flashing, Sheppard absentmindedly started reading it. Like many naval officers over the course of his career, he had gotten quite good at reading Morse code. As he read the message, he knew exactly what it said and began phrasing his reply before the signalman arrived with the written-out message and holding a signal pad to record Sheppard's response.

He dictated quickly. "To: CTF Forty-Eight, From *Argonne*: 'Additional short-range antisubmarine patrol.'" Every external communication that left any navy ship had to be released for transmission by the captain or the admiral on board.

A slight smile crossed Sheppard's face as the signalman ran off to get the message to Chief Bryce.

Sheppard hoped this would satisfy the Admiral without offending him based on the fact that Sheppard had considered Hamilton's patrol of the two old destroyers inadequate. Sheppard knew—and Hamilton should, as well—that if you forced a submarine to submerge in response to an air patrol, its mobility would be severely restricted, along with the distance that its men could see with the periscope. You changed him from a surface ship stalking you at eighteen knots to a floating mine at two. Sheppard also knew that the Admiral's plan included SBD-3 Dauntless antisubmarine patrols around the task force being launched from the carriers. However, the carriers had to be free to maneuver and head into the wind to launch; they had to be well out to sea to do that. Sheppard and *Argonne* did not.

— —

U-179 dove in about thirty-five seconds. Not as fast as the smaller Type VII boats, but Meier was satisfied. As soon as they were at twelve meters and Schmitt had control of the boat, he slowed to three knots, letting his second in command trim the boat to within ten kilos of perfectly neutral buoyancy. Only then did Meier return to the conning tower, confident in his ability to control the exposure of his periscope.

The conning tower could only hold two or three people at the most; it sat on top of the main pressure hull of the submarine. Designed to get the periscopes as high as possible, the conning tower sat directly above the control room. The periscopes were not long enough to remove the conning tower from the danger of collision with a merchant ship or escort trying to ram the U-boat. The U-boat, however, could survive if the conning tower was rammed and flooded, as long as the hatch between the conning tower and the control room remained shut.

In Meier's wake, Schmitt moved to the base of the ladder in order to hear his Captain's orders clearly and also to pass on any comments on what he saw through the periscopes.

"Both ahead slow," Meier ordered.

When the underwater log read two knots, he raised the search periscope. He started his look in the direction the soundman was reporting the heavy screws and rotated slowly clockwise. He could still see the tops of mastheads where the old destroyers continued their lackadaisical patrols, and he reported their bearings to the plotters as he passed.

He knew that, once submerged at slow speed, he had nothing to fear from aircraft. The dark gray, almost black, paint on all topside surfaces of the U-boat made him invisible to their downward glances. On his second periscope rotation past the bearing to the sound contacts, he detected two mastheads. They looked to be in the same orientation, and the spacing was consistent with the two lead ships, but closer.

"Johann, bearing two-six-three degrees, estimated range twelve thousand meters; second contact, bearing two-six-eight degrees, estimated range fourteen thousand meters."

Meier lowered the scope and slid down into the control room, nearly crashing into his first officer as Schmitt was relaying the reports to the quartermaster.

"Good, they are still on the same track as before," Meier said. "What is the distance to the track?"

"Fifteen hundred meters, Herr Kapitän," the quartermaster responded.

Meier smiled. Quartermaster Lehmann had been with him for ten months and knew exactly what he wanted almost before he asked.

"Left full rudder, come to course one-five-zero."

This is almost too easy.

—•—

The flag hoist for the sequential turn of the long column of ships to course 137 degrees had made its way to the last destroyer in the line. When that ship's captain and officer of the deck understood the meaning of the signal, the OOD ordered his signalman to raise the flag hoist to the top of the halyard at the level of the yardarm. This raising of the hoist "to the block"—commonly referred to as "two blocked"—was a signal of understanding to the ship ahead. If the signal was understood by them, then they also "two blocked" it and so on until the *Raritan* raised her hoist to the block, informing Admiral Hamilton that his task force was ready to execute the ordered course change. Every signalman's eye was now glued on *Sabine* for the execute signal, marking the spot of the turn.

Hamilton had timed it well, and within two minutes, *Sabine* reached the point that he wished the task force to use as the turning point. He ordered the "execute," and the flag hoist "Corpen one-three-seven" was dropped by the flagship's signalmen as fast as they could haul it down. Every ship in the line did the same as soon as they saw it occur on the flagship or any ship ahead of them. It was not a surprise that Chief Bryce's signalmen were the quickest.

— —

"Herr Kapitän, the target's course is changing," Oberfunkmaat Cuyler reported.

Surprised, Meier leaped up into the conning tower and raised the search periscope. His heart sank at what he saw. The mast and its yardarm had changed orientation, with the yardarm less visible. That meant the target had turned so that he was looking more at her beam than her bow. The second thing he saw was the top of her funnel. It was huge. He looked at the second ship and saw that she had the same type of funnel aft of her mast also, but this funnel appeared very narrow. He knew that only one type of ship had a single mast and long narrow funnel.

Aircraft carriers!

The second ship was turning now also, and Meier guessed that they were still in a column executing a turn to a new course. That did not matter. On their new course, he could not get into a firing position before they were well past him.

Lowering the periscope, he leaned over the open hatch and barked, "Left full rudder, steer course one-eight-zero. Fifteen meters, both ahead full."

Every second counted. He wanted to go faster, but if he went his maximum speed of 7.7 knots, the battery would last less than an hour. No, a little less than seven knots would have to do. At least at that speed he could run for an hour and still have half of his battery capacity left.

— —

Lieutenant Barry Jensen busied himself raising the lead Kingfisher's flaps, leaning back the mixture of his Pratt & Whitney Wasp Junior engine, and trimming the aircraft as he climbed out to 750 feet. He never really got over the thrill of a catapult launch: the bone-crushing jar as the gunpowder charge of the catapult fired, throwing him back against the armored backrest, and then the elation of flying, skimming the waves as the Kingfisher gained airspeed.

A quick check on the intercom. "Emerson, you okay?"

"Fine, Mister Jensen. It's great flying again."

Jensen took the reply as confirmation that his radioman-gunner was none the worse for his jolt and that his single flexible .30-caliber Browning machine gun had survived in good shape. Jensen banked his OS2U to a course of zero-eight-zero degrees for the fifty-mile outbound leg of his assigned search pattern. Both he and Emerson had their heads moving, searching for any anomalies in wave patterns or color. When he got to the end of his outbound leg, he would turn right ninety degrees and fly five miles before heading back to the ship. He knew that Bronco was doing the same thing except on an initial course of one-zero-zero degrees. Between the two Kingfisher pilots and the two radiomen, they stood a good chance of detecting any U-boats that might be lurking off the VACAPES. Even if they did not detect the submarines, the Kingfishers would force them to dive.

As he trimmed, the feel of the aircraft confirmed for him that two 325-pound depth charges still hung securely beneath the wings. By setting the fuse of one at fifty feet of water depth and the other at twenty-five, he hoped to ensure that their explosions would bracket a diving submarine if he spotted one. A kill would depend on how close

Jensen could drop his charges to the swirl of the diving submarine or its periscope. He secretly hoped that this time he might actually get a chance to practice his bombing. Even though he was the second-best pilot in the squadron—nobody was as good as Bronco—Jensen possessed that burning desire to be better. A U-boat kill this early in the cruise would be the talk of the wardroom for days.

— —

Admiral Hamilton had grunted an acknowledgment when his flag lieutenant relayed Sheppard's reply. No one was going to know that he admired McCloud's initiative in adding something he had not thought of—no one, that is, except his chief of staff, Henry Burke, who gave the admiral a wry smile.

Now Hamilton busied the staff with a flurry of signals to the task group, ordering the destroyer and light cruiser squadrons to break column formation and proceed ahead, taking up a bent-line antisubmarine screen as well as a scouting line ahead of the task force, respectively. A blizzard of multicolor flag hoists and flashing signal lights caused puffs of black smoke from destroyer stacks as they increased speed to thirty knots, racing to their assigned stations. Mindful of the collision risk, squadron and division commanders kept the sixteen destroyers in columns of divisions until well clear of the heavy ships.

Hamilton knew that only the carriers and large cruisers were still constrained to the trench off Cape Henry on course 137 degrees true.

— —

U-179 had been running to the south for almost forty minutes. Oberfunkmaat Cuyler kept reporting bearings to the heavy screws of the carriers and the battleships following them. The bearings to all his targets were drawing to the left, and Meier was sure that these ships would get past him, depriving him of the opportunity of a lifetime.

Suddenly Cuyler's eyes widened and his voice cracked. "Herr Kapitän, many high-speed screws bearing between two-eight-zero degrees and two-nine-five degrees!"

Those, Meier assumed, had to be the escorts finally coming out to screen the larger ships. *Not surprising*, Meier thought, but Cuyler then reported that bearings to the carriers were now steady. That could mean just one thing: he was staying up with them and they would not get past him. He had to look and look *now!*

"Both one-third ahead, thirteen meters!" Meier shouted.

He bounded back into the conning tower and waited. As soon as Johann reported the speed was down to two knots, he could look.

"Six … five … four … three knots," his first officer called out from the underwater log as Meier waited. Finally he heard, "Two knots, Herr Kapitän!"

He raised the attack periscope this time, rapidly swinging it to the last bearing that the soundman had reported for the lead ship.

Meier bellowed out target classifications and bearings so all in the control room could hear. "Aircraft carrier, *Brandywine* class, bearing two-one-zero degrees true; second carrier, *Brandywine* class, bearing two-one-seven degrees true. Battle cruiser, *Antietam* class, bearing two-two-three degrees true; second battle cruiser, *Antietam* class, bearing two-two-nine degrees true. Armored cruiser, *Quincy* class, bearing two-three-five degrees true; second armored cruiser, *Quincy* class, bearing two-three-nine degrees true."

He did some quick mental calculations of the range to the targets, using the scribe marks in the periscope at specific angle measurements and the known masthead heights of the targets memorized long ago from his reference publications. His mind racing faster than ever, Meier calculated the battle cruisers were closer to him than the carriers, with a height from the waterline to the top of their forward director of forty-three meters. The carriers were just outside the range at which he knew he could make a successful attack. His distance to the track of the battle cruisers was less, meaning he had a good chance of hitting them.

Meier slapped the outstretched handles up, lowered the periscope, and looked down into the control room. Catching Schmitt's eye, he ordered, "Make ready tubes one through four! Open bow doors!"

He was ready to attack, finally—ready to kill.

"Three thousand meters to the track," Lehmann called out.

Too far—Meier was too far! He was at the outer limit of the range wherein he had any real chance for success. He had to close more!

"Both full ahead!" Meier yelled.

He had to close the track at least another five hundred meters.

— —

The signal flags flew up *Sabine's* halyards again. Hamilton's flagship was finally clear of the shoal to the east and free to take a course toward the deep water with the core of his task force. Eight more minutes and he could maneuver into a circular formation, with his destroyers out in front for protection. Once they reached their stations, they would slow and commence their sonar searches.

Eight more minutes ... and the danger that McCloud had rightfully recognized would be behind them all. The admiral looked at his chief of staff, a thin wisp of cigarette smoke rising from the end of the Lucky Strike held between the first two fingers of his right hand.

"Henry, I think we will get away with it. I doubt the Germans could have made it all the way across the Atlantic without Naval Intelligence knowing about it."

— —

Time for another look ...

Meier was slowing *U-179* when Cuyler surprised him again.

"Herr Kapitän, the lead ship is maneuvering!"

"Three knots ... two knots," Schmitt called out.

Meier raised the attack periscope and could not believe his eyes. The leading carrier had turned toward him. Meier began shouting bearings and ranges interspersed with staccato orders of course and depth. The gods of war were on his side; he was in the perfect position to attack. Not only that, but now he saw the blue flag with the two white stars—an admiral's flag.

The flagship!

Her flight deck was crowded with aircraft, all undoubtedly fueled and armed. He lowered the periscope.

"Attack procedures!"

All he had to do was make one more observation. Then he could launch his torpedoes—electric, slow, but wakeless. The Americans would be clueless when their lead ship erupted with underwater explosions. Were they from torpedoes or mines? That ambiguity might ensure a safe escape, hugging the bottom at minimum speed to fool the echo-ranging of the escorts.

— —

When the nor'easter had come up the East Coast of the United States three days earlier, it had slammed into the shallows of Chesapeake Bay and its approaches. The waters of the Chesapeake rose, angry at the intrusion, with large white-capped waves churning the sand and silt of the bay's bottom. Normally, the nutrient-rich top layer of the Chesapeake was a dark green when viewed from the air, meaning that the German U-boat's black paint would blend well with that dark algae background. But the passing storms that had churned the bottom, frustrating the Army Corps of Engineers dredge captains, had changed the background to a lighter, more sandy, shade of green. Now, with the sun high in a spring sky, and against the lighter background, a submarine's shape might be visible from above—that is, to the discerning eye of an airman flying above the calmer sea.

— —

Lieutenant Commander Bronco Billy Burdick might have been many things—ladies' man, squadron commander, egotist, frustrated fighter pilot—but more than anything, he was a great aviator. And like all great pilots, his head stayed on a swivel, constantly moving while he was flying. His men thought he was a character with the white silk Navy scarf that he always wore while flying, but the reality was that it kept his neck from chafing from the constant motion. His radiomen were always amazed that he could fly so smoothly and effortlessly with his head in constant motion.

Today was no different from any other day as far as Bronco was concerned: more flight hours for his logbook, and another chance to excel, was the way he looked at every launch. He had deliberately assigned himself to the more difficult "cross-deck" launch from *Argonne* for the simple reason that he was her best pilot. Bronco knew that opinion was emphatically shared by the other pilots in his squadron.

During the infancy of VHF voice radio, for identification and without giving away tactical information, aircraft squadrons and ships received a unique noun. They were supposed to be meaningless and not connected to the real identity of the unit. *Supposed to*, however, was a relative term. Somehow, Bronco had arranged to have the word *Mustang* assigned to Scout-Observation Squadron Sixty-Eight on board the *Argonne*. Bronco was Mustang Zero-One and Barry Jensen was flying Mustang Zero-Five. The *Argonne*'s voice call was Jaguar. Voice-radio phrasing always used the station called as an alerting word, followed by the station calling. The message then followed, with everyone listening on the circuit certain of who was talking to whom.

High above the water, Bronco's head stopped swiveling, and he reached for his radio.

"Jaguar; Mustang Zero-One."

— —

Sheppard ordered the starboard anchor housed and secured for sea, since they were reaching water where the *Argonne* would not need it to suddenly aid in stopping should a rudder failure occur. On the fo'castle, Chief Boatswain's Mate Jack Donnelly had tightened the chain as far as he could. His men were installing pelican hooks to hold the chain and anchor securely against its bolster when they shut down the motor that turned the wildcat and loosened the band brake on the wildcat drum.

Suddenly, the speaker on the bulkhead next to Sheppard blared,

"Jaguar, Mustang Zero-One; submarine bearing zero-six-five degrees, range five thousand yards from you—attacking!"

Sheppard was surprised—stunned was more like it—but only for an instant. His orders flowed quickly. "Man battle stations, hoist the submarine alarm on the port yardarm, ready aircraft for immediate launch!"

If the *Argonne* had looked like a stirred-up hornet's nest earlier when they'd stationed the special sea-and-anchor detail, now the hornets appeared incensed. Sailors were scrambling in the controlled chaos of manning battle stations as fast as they could run. As all the assigned crew reached their compartments, the watertight doors and hatches slammed shut and were hurriedly dogged, sealing men in over a thousand separate watertight compartments. Ventilation fans stopped, and the bulkhead isolation flappers clanged shut, except for electronic facilities and the engineering spaces. One would think that all the hustling about would result in collisions, broken bones, and bruises. Not so. The Navy had a simple rule: if you wanted to move forward or up in the ship, you did it on the starboard side; down or aft you did it on port.

Thus, from above, *Argonne* looked like an ant colony with all the ants racing counterclockwise.

— —

Admiral Hamilton was chiding his air operations officer for not considering the use of the cruiser floatplanes in the task-group orders. A master at removing the sting from a criticism, Hamilton knew that the twinkle was returning to his brown eyes as the possible danger of an attack faded with each passing second.

Hunched over the chart table, his close-cropped gray hair was directly below the voice-radio speaker in flag plot when Bronco's report blared out.

The admiral grabbed the VHF radio microphone. "Dog-patch, this is Labrador. Immediate execute, emergency turn nine, maneuver independently as channel permits. Emergency speed two-five!"

He had to turn *Sabine* and *Raritan* immediately; *Belleau Wood* and *Argonne* would have to wait until they got more sea room. *Quincy* and

Baltimore could turn away from the submarine now. His light cruisers and destroyers were already proceeding independently to assigned stations ahead on his track. He could only trust their captains to avoid collisions with his larger ships. He would lose complete control of his task force for the moment, but he had to preserve his heavy units.

— —

With dreams of success flooding his mind, Korvettenkapitän Meier grabbed the hoist lever for the attack periscope. Without a word from Schmitt, he knew to the second how long it would take his crew to execute his previous orders. They would be ready now.

"Final bearing and shoot," Meier ordered. "Johann, we will spread the torpedoes along the length of the carrier with gyro offsets of left nine degrees, left three degrees, right three degrees, and right nine degrees. Stand by!"

He raised the attack periscope and saw heavy black smoke pouring from the funnel of the ship in his immediate view. He was looking close to her beam, so the fact that she was turning was lost in his lust for glory; however, she was exactly where he had expected to see her. It was going to be a perfect shot. There wasn't anything the stupid American captain could do about it.

He ordered, "Torpedoes *los*."

In rapid succession, compressed air escaped into the aft end of torpedo tubes one through four. The electric G7e torpedoes, each with a three-hundred-kilogram explosive charge, were on their way to getting Kapitän Meier his Knight's Cross with Swords. As each tube fired, poppet valves opened as the torpedo exited the tube and gulped back the compressed air so that no large air bubble fountains would reveal his location. "Well, Captain," he smirked, "Are those explosions sinking your ship torpedoes or mines? You won't know, will you? That mistake will ensure my escape."

— —

It had been five years since Bronco had served in a bombing squadron. He knew he might be a little rusty in predicting the flight path of bombs, judging his release point, anticipating the real location of the moving submarine, and trying not to hit the refracted image quickly growing in his windshield. His mind raced to calculate the needed impact points of his depth charges as he instinctively flew the Kingfisher, applying stick and rudder to compensate for the breeze raising waves on the surface and the shadow that was his target. Focused on the attack, it never dawned on him that he was making the first attack on a U-boat in American waters.

Now!

Bronco pulled the bomb-release levers with his gloved left hand, and the Kingfisher jumped as the two 325-pound Mark 17 depth bombs fell away. Wires, attached to the Kingfisher, pulled out of the hydrostatic fuses arming the bombs only a few feet from the floatplane's wings. Bronco had to be high enough on his pull-out that the blast of an instantaneous detonation on water impact would not down the Kingfisher, killing him and his radioman-gunner. He slammed the stick back into his belly with his right hand as he firewalled the throttle with his left, and the Kingfisher made a gut wrenching, high-G pullout less than two hundred feet from the waves of the Chesapeake.

Despite all the variables in timing his release, Bronco managed to get his two depth charges close. The first one to detonate, the one set at twenty-five feet, landed close to the starboard side of the U-boat, amidships. The second one, with the fifty-foot setting, landed closer to the bow but farther away. It also exploded. With each detonation, the sea first boiled and frothed in response to the shock wave reaching the surface in less than a hundredth of a second. Then the expanding bubble from the explosion gases followed, creating towering white mounds of spray nearly a hundred feet high. The two columns of water that climbed high into the sky left no doubt in anyone's mind as to the location of the submarine—too close—directly on the beam of the flagship.

— —

Barry Jensen, flying over in Bronco's direction from about five miles away, had heard his report to *Argonne*. Not the cold, experienced professional that his squadron commander was, Jensen felt his heart racing at the import of Bronco's words. He was much younger—less than three years out of Annapolis—and his high-pitched voice and baby face had required him to work that much harder to gain his wings and learn to lead his men. Barry idolized Bronco and would do anything to help. Now he saw the frothy white columns of water rise and fall in sequence, erupting in turn to ten-story domed splashes, white as new-fallen snow. As the columns fell back into the sea, the white froth became sprinkled with floating fish—some stunned, most dead. He also saw something else: an expanding pool of iridescent diesel fuel staining the ocean at the site of a damaged submarine.

"Emerson, will you look at that!"

"Yeah, Mr. Jensen; looks like Commander Burdick got a kill."

The spotter VHF radio interrupted their conversation. "Mustang zero-five, this is zero-one. Drop your bombs on the oil slick to make sure that Kraut is dead."

"This is zero-five, roger."

"Well, Emerson, it looks like we get to practice our bombing. You keep watch for Bronco and anyone else, so we don't collide while I concentrate on my run."

— —

U-179 was grievously hurt. The first depth charge had thrown Hans Meier against the periscope eyepiece, stunning him. The starboard side of the conning tower dished inward from the explosion, and a welded seam ruptured. The attack periscope, still raised, whipped to port, bending at the top support on the bridge. The packing glands on both periscopes failed, spraying more water into the conning tower. A seam on one of the fuel ballast tanks ruptured, and diesel fuel began gushing out.

"Kapitän ... Kapitän!" Schmitt yelled as the seawater from the conning tower poured over him, a torrential herald of their coming deaths.

Meier, barely conscious, did not hear and—did not answer.

With no time to waste and a muttered, "Sorry, mein Kapitän," Schmitt pulled the lanyard on the lower hatch, slamming it shut to stop the inrushing torrent from flooding the control room and sending them all to a watery grave—and sealing Meier in the conning tower. The water, rising quickly, condemned Meier to a cold, wet tomb.

As the hull whipped from the detonating depth charge forward, piping ruptured, men screamed unheard as a valve in the high-pressure air system blew apart, killing the petty officer at the air station and creating a roar of unimaginable intensity that deafened everyone in the control room. The din prevented anyone from hearing the orders Schmitt screamed as he tried to control the damage.

Seawater flanges in the engine room failed and light bulbs shattered, momentarily plunging the crew into total darkness. Then emergency flashlights were reached, to provide waving wands of illumination reflected from an atmosphere filled with dust and paint chips. Water rose there also, but the watchstanders were able to find the valves and stem the flood before more than half a meter had accumulated in the bilge.

The second depth charge, exploding near the bow had also forced open the inner door on torpedo tube number three, rapidly flooding the compartment through its 53.3-centimeter-diameter hole. Stationed between the tubes, a torpedoman, reacting more than thinking managed to shut the outer doors, despite blood flowing from a head wound—before the compartment had filled more than two meters deep.

The sudden added weight from the tsunami of water overwhelmed the ability of the planesmen to hold the boat either level or on depth. *U-179* nosed down and struck the bottom, settling in the soft sand and mud at a depth of twenty meters. Had she been in the open sea, she would have continued down to her eternal grave when the sea pressure crushed the hull like a stomped tin can, killing everyone aboard.

—▪—

Jensen might not have been as good a pilot as Bronco, but he was happy for the chance to drop live ordnance on an enemy, especially since his brother had been badly wounded at Pearl.

"Zero-five, this is zero-one, watch your air speed."

"Zero-five, roger." *What did Bronco mean by that? I need to get to that point of the oil slick as fast as I can before that U-boat has time to move off at high speed.*

"Zero-five, watch your angle of attack! Drop to hit the source of the oil; the wind is spreading the slick to the south."

"This is zero-five, roger," *What is he talking about? I am already committed. I am going to put these bombs right on that slick.*

"Drop, drop," Barry told himself as he pulled the bomb-release levers, certain the bombs would fall in the middle of that oil slick. He yanked back on the stick, subjecting Emerson to a gut-wrenching pull-out to escape the explosions.

"Sorry, Emerson! I should have warned you."

"I am okay, but I am afraid we missed."

Jensen's heart sank. He noticed two small splashes in the oil slick where his depth bombs had skipped off the water. A hundred yards further on, the sea boiled as his bombs sank and detonated. As he leveled off, Jensen morosely thought that the squadron would now be subjected to long hours of bombing lectures and practice because he had missed. There was nothing more to do except circle the site of the oil slick, hoping for more evidence of Bronco's attack.

— —

An explosion—in the direction of his target! Meier cheered his own success as he tried to shake away the blackness that enveloped him. His head throbbed, and he could taste the trickle of blood running down his nose from his forehead, which had been lacerated by the periscope eyepiece. He was certain his first torpedo had struck home.

Another explosion—his second torpedo!

He could see Hitler now. "Congratulations, Kapitän!" the Führer would say. "All of Germany salutes your success."

Meier saw the flags and cheering crowds of loyal Nazis as he rode with the Führer, Großadmiral Eric Raeder, and Vizeadmiral Karl Dönitz through the streets of Berlin, the Knights Cross with Swords hanging from his neck.

He blinked and returned to reality. He was wet. Standing up, he felt the seawater up to his thighs. "What?" he muttered. Why was he wet?

Korvettenkapitän Hans Meier suddenly realized that the lower conning tower hatch was shut—*he was trapped!*

The seawater was rising. There was no hope of getting out.

— —

Captain Jake Evans, the aviation pioneer and commanding officer of the *Sabine,* had put his rudder hard right as soon as he had heard Bronco's initial report on the voice-radio speaker on his bridge, deliberately risking jamming the rudder machinery in order to turn as quickly as possible.

"All ahead flank!" had immediately followed.

In an instant, he realized that the reported position of the submarine was forward of his port beam, about twelve hundred yards away. German torpedoes were wakeless but slow at only thirty knots. If he could just get around and his engineers could get power to the shafts fast enough, he had a chance to outrun them. Because the torpedoes were wakeless, though, he could not see them and thus maneuver to comb the wakes, as was the standard tactic in the First World War.

He called down to his engineer in main control on the 21MC. "Give me everything you got, *now!*"

He sounded the general alarm and the collision alarm. That would shut watertight doors and hatches as quickly as possible. But there was nothing he could do about the fueled and armed dive-bombers on his flight deck awaiting launch. He silently prayed they would not slide to port as his carrier heeled in response to his orders; if they did, they would likely hit one another, spilling the flammable aviation gasoline and starting a deadly fire. Despite her nearly thousand-foot length, *Sabine* and her sisters benefitted from the maneuverability lessons learned from the Navy's first aircraft carriers; they were as agile as a young girl escaping a sailor's embrace on a park bench.

Evans needed to shave every inch possible off her tactical diameter if his ship was to escape. He prayed that he could just pull *Sabine*'s stick back into his gut, risking a blackout as he had done in the Cleveland air race while turning faster than anyone else. But all he could do was go out on his port bridge wing, stare at the circling Kingfishers, and anticipate the explosions, columns of oil-filled water, inevitable reports of dead and injured sailors, fires, and damage to his ship.

— —

Sheppard had just finished looking aft to verify the reports that two more Kingfisher scout-observation planes were ready for launching. Art Roberts was in the process of taking over the OOD duties from Joe Archinbald, so he directed his order, "Launch aircraft," in their general direction and got an acknowledgment from Joe. Archinbald passed on the order, and two more OS2U-5s accelerated down the catapults, thundering skyward. Sheppard knew that if they had found one submarine off the mouth of the most important naval base on the East Coast there were likely more. It was time for him to make his way to his own battle station inside the armored command tower, where Joe and Art were still relieving.

Argonne's command tower was a full two feet thick of face-hardened armored steel, the best that money or American industry could produce. However, from Sheppard's perspective, the two-foot thickness and the outward bevel of the top, bottom, and sides of the small oval access were an obstacle that he had not figured out how to enter. *Shenandoah*'s had only been sixteen inches thick, and there had been a hand grab on the inside. Knowing his injured left leg would not support him if he lifted his right through first, he put his damaged left leg through instead and sat straddling the inner doorframe until he could find something to grab and pull himself into the tower with his arms. It was a good plan that failed miserably.

There was nothing to hang onto, and when he tried to use his left leg in that awkward position, it collapsed on him. Unceremoniously, he entered the hub of all power and control for one of the mightiest battle cruisers in the world as a heap in the port aft corner of the command tower—the same place he had landed when wounded on *Shenandoah*.

His men rushed to his side. "Captain," his OOD shouted, "are you all right?"

As Sheppard sat up and looked at the nerve center of *Argonne*, he saw blood, flesh, and bone fragments peppering the smooth gray inner surface of the armor. There was a crater, jagged and stark steel gray, in the opposite curved wall next to where he had been standing viewing the horror of *Shenandoah*'s superstructure. Lifeless men and parts of men, with the visceral smells of shredded abdomens and quiet moans of the dying, flooded his senses. Sheppard's face drained and he grew woozy, detaching from the scene before him as he fought the darkness trying to envelop him. He lowered his head, looking down at his left leg. It wasn't abnormally bent. It did not feel wet.

"Get me out of here," he gasped, barely audible to the men gently lifting him.

His orderly Corporal Pease, the messenger of the watch, and the boatswain's mate of the watch, Petty Officer Bergman, all tenderly lifted Sheppard, carefully passing him back out the port armored access door.

"Set me down against the bulkhead," Sheppard whispered, struggling with the confusion over what was real and what was not.

It did not take long for him to regain his strength—and sanity. But Sheppard knew that if he was going to be able to fight *Argonne* effectively, damaged leg or not, he could never venture inside the armored protection of the command tower again.

— —

Suddenly alert in the morning sun, she knew something was terribly wrong. What had happened to her? What was happening to him? Would he be okay? What could she do to help? Could she will her strength into his struggling body? So many questions, but no one could help her understand. She knew enough about him to know that he would never tell her, could never tell her enough to ease what was troubling him so. She had to suffer though this bond of love that they had begun to develop alone.

She sensed that those around him would care for her love, but could they do anything about his troubled psyche? If she could not help him, could anyone? What was to become of them all, when danger hunted them ... when fate stalked them in the guise of war?

— —

Commander Kenneth Radisson, *Sabine's Cheng*, or chief engineer, had a master's degree in mechanical engineering from Rensselear, and he genuinely loved the power and complexity of the *Sabine's* machinery. Years ago, when assigned in the Bureau of Steam Engineering, he had helped in the design, though not in a big way. He was one of the few engineers on board who really understood thermodynamics. When Captain Evans ordered him to provide everything that he had, he knew just how to do it.

Radisson grabbed the microphone for the engineer's announcing system—2MC—and began barking orders like a pit bull in attack mode:

"Throttlemen, open the ahead throttles wide!"

"Standby boilers, open your steam stops now!"

He knew his only hope to get more boilers on line was to catch them "on the fly," just at the moment when the steam header pressure, dropping as steam rushed into the thirsty turbines through opening throttle valves, matched the pressure in the boilers already heated in anticipation of the task force increasing speed.

"Boilermen, cut in all burners and open the air supply wide—smoke be damned! Raise blower speed to maximum!"

"Main control, boiler room four, there are high-speed screws and intermittent knocking on the port side."

"Main control, roger." That must be one or more of the German torpedoes bouncing along the hull.

"Water tenders, open feed valves. Raise turbine feed-pump speed to twenty-four hundred rpm."

Commander Radisson was using the hot metal in the engineering plant to make and superheat the steam, much as New Englanders used hot rocks for clam and lobster bakes. He knew he was hitting his engineering system with the maximum thermal shock possible and would have to deal with dozens of steam and feed-water leaks later, but he understood the details of the metallurgy and fatigue characteristics of the high-tensile steel. He was almost certain—well, nearly sure—that *Sabine*'s engineering plant would hold together. It was a gamble, but it might pay off.

In less than a minute, *Sabine*'s main engines were providing the maximum torque they could with the twelve boilers available. Propellers were beating her wake into a maelstrom of churning water as the carrier slowly—too slowly—accelerated. That was when a German torpedo detonated aft.

— —

Shaking off the effects of his concussion, Meier felt the sharp shudder of the third explosion, the sudden punch of the water rising against his lungs. He heard the quick report echoing off the bottom and surface, stretching sound waves and amplifying them—the sounds of expanding gases pushing against the seawater and rising until the bubble pushed a mountain of ocean a hundred meters into the sky. Finally, he recognized the sound of hundreds of tons of water raining back into the sea. Perhaps wishfully, perhaps due to his dazed consciousness, the sound matched the two previous detonations he'd heard.

Three hits—nearly a thousand kilograms of Hexanite, Meier thought, congratulating himself. *With a little luck, those aircraft will burn, and that carrier will be mine.*

But when a fourth detonation did not immediately follow, he suspected that one torpedo had missed, yet he did not know whether it was the first or the last. It didn't matter. He was certain of the three hits and equally certain that three well-spaced hits in one side of a carrier would create enough damage to cripple, if not capsize and sink, the ship. Aircraft carriers were floating ammunition dumps loaded with bombs, bullets, and torpedoes, not to mention hundreds of thousands of liters of the high-octane, highly inflammable aviation gasoline in the ship's tanks and in the fragile aircraft stored on board.

Meier smiled. Whichever way he looked at it, he would end up with the award he'd coveted, even if it was at the expense of his U-boat. Germany would trade a thousand-ton U-boat for a fifty-five-thousand-ton carrier anytime.

He had to live!

A posthumous Knight's Cross with Swords was not in his plans.

CHAPTER 5

ASSESSMENT

Everyone in the open in Task Force Forty-Eight saw the ugly column of dirty water and mud rise over three hundred feet at *Sabine*'s stern. Her stern visibly lifted and shook.

Jake Evans grabbed the windscreen of the port bridge wing, fighting the bucking and pitching of the *Sabine*'s agony. His head inadvertently followed the rising column of water on the starboard side of his stern until it merged with the boiling black river of smoke from his boiler fires. The crack and whoosh of the underwater explosion, an instant later, assaulted his ears. His mind raced. Had he done everything he could to prevent this disaster?

Captain Evans began to receive the damage reports from his chief engineer and DCA almost immediately:

"Main engines one and three shut down due to loss of lubricating oil—"

"Fire on the hangar deck—"

"Flooding in the shaft alleys—"

The helmsman reported that *Sabine*'s rudder was not responding to his orders and was jammed at right full. The safety valves from half of the boilers lifted, sending plumes of steam out the top of *Sabine*'s funnel, creating a cacophony of noise and making it difficult to hear or speak on her bridge. Ominously, smoke began to pour from the aft elevator opening in the flight deck. Reports of broken legs, cuts, and contusions were flowing in from the after-battle dressing stations. *Sabine* was hurt, the extent of damage yet to be determined.

— —

The water level in *U-179*'s conning tower had stopped rising, the spray around the periscope packing glands now a trickle in the beam of a flashlight. Kapitän Meier shook the last of the cobwebs from his brain, the cold seawater shocking him awake, and he thought he could hear screaming and the roar of high-pressure air escaping in the control room below him. He imagined he had felt, more unconsciously than consciously, the U-boat hit the bottom and the stern falling until it was level again.

We must be on the bottom.

With the ruptured hull seam in the conning tower, the only way he could get out was for the *U-179* to surface and get that weld seam above the water. Only then could they drain the water and open either of the hatches to the conning tower. But that was impossible with the American fleet above them. Surfacing would mean immediate destruction by American gunfire; his crew would not even get on deck, let alone escape.

If his men were alive, they would have to wait until the ships left before they could surface. Darkness was almost eight hours away. Could the air left in the conning tower last that long? His mind raced.

But the water level had not stopped rising. It continued to creep up the inwardly sloping hull of the conning tower. Suddenly, the rush of high-pressure air from below in the control room stopped. His men were alive—thank God! If they lived, they would find a way to save his boat. But could they save him? His Breitling Kriegsmarine wristwatch still worked, and with its luminous dial, Meier began to time the inexorable rise of water against the conning tower bulkheads.

— —

Bronco's head was again on a swivel despite having more than enough justification to stare at his victory. The head of Bronco's radioman-gunner, Jim Miller, also twisted back and forth, searching. Neither expected another sub in their immediate vicinity, but you never knew. Bronco had ordered the two additional Kingfishers to search out fifty miles on a pattern centered on bearing zero-six-three degrees, but he kept Barry Jensen as a wingman circling on the opposite side of the racetrack pattern they flew. That way, one of them would always be looking down-sun on this clear April morning.

"Mister Burdick," Miller said on the intercom, "that oil slick is growing. Do you think it is moving?"

Bronco looked down. What were there now, maybe a thousand gallons in that slick? The oil was smoothing the waves and reflecting the sun with every color in the rainbow.

There is a certain beauty in enemy oil slicks, Bronco thought.

"No," Bronco finally replied. "The wind and sea are spreading the slick slowly to the south-southwest. I don't think that Kraut is trying to move to the north-northeast, toward our destroyers."

Bronco was really not sure whether the submarine was moving or not. It did not make much difference; he could not do anything about it with both of his depth bombs dropped. Bronco decided he would continue to circle and watch for any sign of motion or danger to the task force.

"Miller, watch that slick for any sign of a periscope."

"Roger, Skipper."

At least they could serve as lookouts with a ringside seat.

— —

As soon as the helmsman reported the rudder was not answering, Captain Evans ordered the breakdown flag hoisted. A signal to all the other ships that *Sabine* was not under control and a significant hazard for a collision, the yellow flag with a blue St. Andrew's cross warned everyone else to keep clear as she circled uncontrollably. Everyone could keep their distance except the two bigger ships, *Belleau Wood* and *Argonne*, who were both still confined to the trench off Virginia Beach.

Evans's mind filled with possibilities. Was the rudder flat flooded too? Were the machinist mates stationed in emergency steering dead—drowned—or had they abandoned their post, risking further flooding by opening a hatch to escape? Should he slow, making it easier for *Raritan* and the battle cruisers to avoid him? German subs had four bow tubes, so what of the other torpedoes? His carrier was too big, too inviting a target not to fire four. No, he needed all the power his port engines could put out for a few more minutes.

— —

Sheppard's left leg throbbed. He didn't think he had broken it, but the stabbing pain he first felt worried him. Had he damaged the surgeons' repairs? There was only one way to tell; he gingerly got to his feet, using the conning tower armored bulkhead for support. Slowly putting weight on his leg, he was ecstatic when it held.

Sheppard was standing just as Commander Blankenship arrived. "Captain, what happened?" he asked, peering intently into Sheppard's face.

"I slipped and fell in the conning tower, Doc," Sheppard answered, trying to make light of it and send the doctor on his way.

"The report I received requesting I come to the bridge indicated that you nearly fainted and had to be carried out of the command tower."

"Nonsense, Doctor. I am fine now. See for yourself," Sheppard emphasized as he hopped on his right leg.

"Be that as it may, I still want to check you out. I still haven't had a look at that leg of yours, and reading your medical record, it's a wonder they didn't amputate. This new episode has me concerned."

"Commander, my planes just attacked a submarine. The task force flagship was torpedoed. I'm in the middle of an engagement, and you want to check me out!"

Sheppard had to smile at how ludicrous this sounded even to him. But the ship's surgeon was clearly not going to take no for an answer.

"All right, Doctor, as soon as we secure from general quarters, I'll see you in my sea cabin."

"Captain, I am not leaving until you at least let me check your eyes."

"Very well."

Sheppard acquiesced and let the doctor flick a flashlight back and forth in front of each eye.

"I will see you in your sea cabin immediately after general quarters secures, Captain."

Seeing the breakdown flag, Sheppard turned back to the command tower, where Art Roberts had taken over the OOD duties from Joe Archinbald.

"Slow to one-third and back down if *Sabine* appears to be a danger," Sheppard ordered. "And make sure the quartermasters are plotting fixes frequently!"

— —

Meier's teeth began to chatter in the dark. How long would it take for hypothermia to dull his mind? Meier again timed the rise of water in the conning tower, checking his watch, perhaps too frequently. In less than an hour, he would drown. So, the question was, would he drown or drift off from the cold? Which would occur first? The latter was certainly preferable, but he had to find a way to survive. He took a breath of air, dove, and felt for the hull rupture. It was barely five centimeters wide; there was no way out through the hull seam. The lower hatch had the pressure of the sea keeping it shut. That left the upper hatch as the only way out.

Wunderbar! It came to him. With that size of a hull split, pressure inside the conning tower was the same as sea pressure. That explained why the water was rising so slowly now. The air inside the conning tower must be leaking out through those periscope packing glands.

Unfortunately, the water was up to his neck. If he didn't find a way out of the conning tower soon, he would die. He looked around, searching his memory for something to stop the loss of air. He saw nothing, but then the thought came to him that the spray shield, designed to prevent a leaking upper hatch from spraying on the periscopes, might hold air. The thin sheet metal would provide enough of a barrier to keep an air pocket in the conning tower, at least for a few moments, if he could just get the hatch open. He could then duck under the shield and swim to the surface. What were they—eighteen, twenty meters beneath the surface? He could swim that easily. He had to remember to exhale the pressurized air as he swam upward; otherwise, his lungs would rupture. The water was at the level of the spray shield and rising. It was time to try!

Hans undogged the hatch and tried to open it—failure. A differential pressure had to still exist, since the air was leaking out. He took a deep breath, ducked underwater, put his back against the hatch, and pushed with every ounce of strength he had. If he failed, his crew would find his body when they surfaced, cold and lifeless, his lungs filled with seawater. He had to succeed. He told himself he would succeed—just as his Führer had—but again he didn't.

Two more deep breaths of air, already becoming stale, and he ducked under the spray shield again. He pushed with everything he had, his back against the hatch, feet firmly planted on the ladder rungs, and it finally gave and opened. Hans returned to the conning tower, gasping in the rapidly diminishing air pocket. He took a few deep breaths, holding the last one. Pulling himself under the spray shield, he swam for the surface, exhaling through his mouth, releasing the expanding air from his lungs the whole way—rising toward the light.

— —

Bronco spotted the man immediately when he broke the surface.

Survivors! Bronco thought. *At least one, anyway.*

"Jaguar; Mustang Zero-One; I have a survivor swimming in the oil slick."

That ended any concern about the U-boat posing a further threat to the task force. Bronco could see the Kraut was trying to swim and needed help. That enemy, Bronco knew, might give up valuable information about the boat or their mission. It would take time for an escort to slow and launch a whaleboat for rescue. The sea was reasonably calm. Landing his floatplane would be the only chance to retrieve a live enemy.

Bronco circled low over the *Sabine,* turned back to the north, lowered his flaps, and idled the engine. He touched down 650 yards south of the oil slick. He had lost sight of the German submariner while he was circling, but as he coasted up to the iridescent patch, he spotted him again. The light chop was washing over his head, oil fouling his blond hair and beard. The man's sodden gray sweater made it difficult for him to lift his arms, so much so that the man could no longer swim. He was clearly desperate.

"God only knows what he has gone through to escape," Bronco muttered.

— —

Hans Meier, former captain of the *U-179,* had swallowed a combination of seawater and diesel fuel when he broke the surface. The chop of the Chesapeake Bay entrance limited what he could see, but the mast of his carrier and the rising smoke from a huge fire heartened him. He had scored a great victory for the fatherland. All he had to do was survive.

How? He knew his strength was fading fast. He felt so cold. Shaking uncontrollably, Meier feared he would break his rotting teeth from the chattering. He couldn't swim another stroke. He didn't have an inflatable life belt. The waves and oil kept washing over his head. Meier finally had to admit it—he was dying.

Retching, he barely noticed the float seaplane's approach until it bumped his shoulder. He tried to reach for the grab rail on the float, but he was unable to lift an arm from the sea. More diesel oil, more seawater—he was drifting into unconsciousness, until he was grabbed by an American. Meier's eyes burned from the fuel; everything was a blur. He did not have enough strength left to climb up onto the float and finally passed out before he was lifted to the fuselage.

On the edge of death, he shook violently. Korvettenkapitän Meier never noticed that the American ships were intact. His target was not listing or down by the stern, and it had stopped burning.

— —

Bronco taxied over toward the German, being careful to stay downwind. He wanted to keep pointing into the breeze, allowing him to use the engine and rudder to hold the Kingfisher stationary relative to the man in the water. Demonstrating that he was the best pilot in the squadron, Bronco gently nudged the survivor with the Kingfisher's main float. As the man slowly turned to see what had hit him, Bronco looked into vacant eyes as the survivor struggled unsuccessfully to grasp the handrail on the float.

"Miller, get down on the float and get that man aboard!" Bronco ordered.

"Roger, Skipper."

Miller rushed to unbuckle his shoulder harness, disconnect his intercom, remove his cloth helmet and flight jacket, and then climb out of the rear cockpit, being careful to walk on the port wing, where he could hold on. Gingerly, he lowered himself to the main float, nearly losing his footing on the wet slick aluminum.

"Don't do anything stupid!" Bronco yelled, well aware that Miller could not swim.

"Skipper, this guy is in bad shape," Miller shouted over the noise of the Pratt & Whitney engine.

Bronco dangled the end of the hook-on cable for Miller to grab. "Tie this to him with your belt under his arms, and I'll help pull him up."

"Roger, Skipper."

Lying crossways on the main float, Miller began working his belt under the man's arms and through the eye of the cable as a wave with wind-blown spray washed over both of them. He had let go of the grab rail to use both hands, and Miller flailed as the wave crashed him into the forward strut of the Kingfisher.

Seeing his friend wrapped around the strut, Bronco called out, "Miller, are you okay?"

"Yeah, Skipper, just a little wet!" he said.

On the second try, Miller put his belt through the cable before the man could slip away. Finally getting the cable secure, Miller shouted, "Ready, Skipper!"

Bronco kept the Kingfisher pointed into the wind with the rudder pedals alone, and then, between Bronco pulling on the cable and Miller lifting, they managed to get the survivor halfway onto the port wing, just as the man drifted into unconsciousness. It was all Bronco could do to hold on while Miller climbed up the starboard side of the OS2U, crossed over the middle cockpit, and lifted the dead weight the remaining distance. Miller propped him against the fuselage, unfastened his belt, got a grip under his arms, and then lifted the smaller German and lowered him into the middle by the fuel tank. The gunner, showing the agility of a ballerina, returned to his rear-facing seat near the tail. He was wet but ecstatic that he had not fallen in.

"Skipper, everything is secure," he reported on the intercom once he'd buckled up.

Lieutenant Commander Burdick revved the engine, taxiing as quickly as the sea state would allow, and headed in *Argonne*'s direction with the first German prisoner of the war.

— —

Jake Evans's diminutive size, perfectly suited to the tight cockpits of air racers, failed to affect the command in his voice or determination in his mannerisms. He stared at his JA phone talker as the young seaman began to speak. "DCA reports that the hangar-deck sprinkler system and fire curtains have been activated."

Evans had to think, not as a world-renowned aviator but as a ship captain trying to minimize the effects of the damage *Sabine* had suffered. "To the flight-deck control officer: lower the aft elevator." That should ventilate the fire and prevent heat buildup from causing more damage and personnel casualties as the fire parties fought to extinguish the blaze.

Evans barked at a phone talker, "JA talker: 'CAG, break the spot and get all your people pushing the aircraft on deck forward away from the fire.'" He needed to get control of *Sabine*'s heading if he was going to keep the smoke and flames away from his air group.

Turning to another phone talker Evans shouted, "IJV talker: 'Engineer report status!'" He needed two things: propulsion and control of the huge barn door that was the rudder, which was actually larger than a whole barn. Without either, the fire in the hangar would gut the life out of his carrier.

"Captain,"—it was his JA talker—"the DCA reports the rudder flat is dry and the circuit breakers for the rudder hydraulic pumps have been reset. The rudder should be back in commission."

"Roger." Turning to his helmsman, Jake ordered, "Left full rudder," as *Raritan*'s broadside slid across his bow. *I guess this is the same as pulling the stick into your stomach when you are in command of a ship*, he thought. *Sabine*'s bow passed her sister ship's stern by mere yards.

Now he needed to worry about what that idiot Kevin Bailey was doing with *Belleau Wood* and about the distance to shoal water.

"Navigator, get a fix and report the nearest shoal water!"

He wasn't worried at all about McCloud; he could already see *Argonne* was backing to kill her headway, giving him more room to maneuver and opening the distance between the two battle cruisers. *Quincy* and *Bethlehem* were already well clear.

The 21MC demanded his attention. "Bridge, answering bells on main engines two and four. Shafts one and three stopped and locked due to loss of lube oil. Engine and boiler rooms secure with no—repeat no—flooding."

That was good news. So what had happened with that explosion?

It was his JA talker again. "CAG reports the hangar fire is out; assessing damage."

"What the hell is CAG doing fighting the hangar fire!" Jake bellowed to no one in particular. He scowled and spoke into his JA talker. "CAG, report to the bridge."

— —

Meanwhile, Commander Radisson was coping with the engineering casualties in *Sabine*'s main control. He knew that tripping of main engines caused the safety valves to lift. As soon as his water tenders shut down the oil sprayers feeding the fires in those boilers, the valves would shut, and that problem would be over.

The main engines were a different story. Radisson had to find out whether they were damaged or the propeller shafts bent. Stopping and locking both shafts quickly was the only way to prevent more damage. Without oil flow from the failed lube-oil systems, the bearings in the turbines and reduction gears would quickly be beyond repair as the slipstream spun the propellers. He turned to his 1JV talker. "Engine rooms one and three, inspect all lube-oil strainers and report."

Shortly, his 1JV talker reported, "Lieutenant Chisholm reports that the lube oil to number three main engine has been restored by resetting the circuit breakers to the standby pump and placing the steam reducer back on service for the main pump. Inspection of the oil strainers shows only dirt and minor debris, no evidence of bearing damage."

"Engine room three, unlock the shaft and test the main engine in the ahead and astern direction." That should reveal any hidden problems outboard of the hull.

It was the 1JV talker again. "Number three main engine tested; test satisfactory; ready to answer bells."

Using his engineering announcing system, he passed on the 2MC. "Number three engine room, answer the ordered bell." That would be enough to alert his water tenders and boilermen that there would be a large increase in steam demand.

He grabbed the mike for the 21MC and announced, "Bridge, answering bells on three main engines. Number one remains stopped and locked."

Now what was happening with number one main engine? There had been enough time for a preliminary report.

— —

Sheppard had watched through his binoculars as Bronco and radioman Miller rescued the survivor. The moment they started taxiing toward *Argonne*, he turned to the command tower door and ordered, "Officer of the Deck, prepare to recover aircraft using the astern method."

There were three methods to recover the Kingfishers—simply put: alongside to port, alongside to starboard, or astern. Each had its advantages relative to the speed *Argonne* could make during recovery (relevant in the first two) or the simplicity of the rig (relevant to the last). Port or starboard in the alongside method was dictated by the wind and sea conditions. The fastest to rig was the astern method, making Sheppard's choice easy with Bronco already en route and a survivor clearly needing medical assistance.

Any of the methods required *Argonne*'s Kingfishers to taxi up to a towed woven-wire rope sled, where a spur on the main pontoon could grab the steel-wire mesh. When verified by slowing the aircraft's engine, the Pratt & Whitney could be stopped, as the Kingfisher was now being towed by *Argonne*. The radioman-gunner then had the hardest job. Leaving his cockpit, he had to take the lifting bridle from the pilot and place it over the hook of the aircraft and boat crane dangling above them. This was always the most dangerous part, and Sheppard watched from the bridge, ready to instantly respond to a man overboard.

Once hoisted aboard, the OS2Us would be stowed or refueled and readied for launch. Certainly not as fast as landing on a carrier, it was "reasonably" safe, since losses were still within the ability of the Chance Vought factory to replace. Once they were on board, it was infinitely easier to transfer personnel off the aircraft.

— —

Commander "Hawk" Talbot arrived on the bridge of *Sabine*, wet and sooty, where Admiral Hamilton had joined Captain Evans.

"We got the fire out in the hangar before it did any real damage," he reported to Captain Evans.

"I know. Any damage to your air group?'

"No, Captain. We were lucky."

Captain Evans frowned at Hawk's appearance. "Did you lead the fire party yourself in the hangar?"

"Yes, sir," the air-group commander answered, well aware that it had been the wrong thing for an "airedale" to do.

"Hawk, I need you fit to lead my strikes, not recovering in sickbay."

"Captain, I was in the aft end of the hangar when the torpedo hit, and as the senior officer present, I had to take charge," Hawk said in an attempt to assuage his captain's justified anger. It wasn't the first time that he had been criticized for jumping into situations himself, and it certainly wouldn't be the last.

"Okay, Hawk, get yourself cleaned up and see to defueling and spotting of the aircraft on deck."

"Yes, sir."

Hawk turned to leave, well aware that his mentor was more concerned for his health than critical of his actions.

— —

Convinced that Hans Meier was dead in the flooded conning tower, Johann Schmitt assumed command of the *U-179*. It would be hours until they could surface, if ever. Reports from the engine room confirmed that the flooding had been isolated, but an inspection revealed that the starboard engine had three cracked cylinders. It would take days to repair, if it was even possible. The seawater lines and air valve would only take a few hours, once they could make noise. The torpedo room was half full of water but otherwise intact and functional. Schmitt suspected that the submarine was leaking oil; it was inevitable with this much damage. He had one dead, besides the captain, two men with broken bones, and almost everyone suffering from cuts and bruises. The challenge would be convincing the Americans that they all were dead, to avoid further attacks.

A bold gambit might work. Time was running out before the Americans would suspect a ruse. His dead sailor, Machinist Petty Officer Karl Huygens, would be loaded into a torpedo tube with mattresses, some food, and any debris from the depth-charging that would float. He would eject that out of the torpedo tubes and release more oil to mimic the destruction of the U-boat. After that, he would lie still and silent until the Americans left. To know when that occurred, he needed his soundman, but it would take time before anyone in the control room would hear well again. Once Schmitt knew they had left, he would pump out what water he could, using the drain pump. After dark, he would use the air he had left to surface.

"Carry Huygens forward, put an inflated life belt on him, and load him into number two torpedo tube.

"Torpedo room: load mattresses, clothing and anything that will float into number four torpedo tube.

"Engine room: all personnel bang as hard as you can on the hull, but when you hear the tubes fire, stop immediately."

"Engineer: when we fire the tubes, release five hundred liters of fuel!"

In less than two minutes, he shot the load of remains, flotsam, and jetsam to the surface, overriding the poppet valves and releasing the impulse air. Then he ordered the crew to lie down and conserve oxygen in the absolute silence of a tomb.

— —

Barry Jensen had taken sole responsibility for circling around the dead U-boat, watching for any additional survivors while waiting his turn to land and be hoisted on board *Argonne*. Suddenly, he saw an eruption of a huge foaming air bubble, with lots of oil, junk, and perhaps another survivor amidst the oil slick.

"Jaguar, Mustang Zero-Five, I have a second possible survivor, more oil, and debris in sight; landing to investigate."

Jensen was less experienced than Bronco at bombing, but he was his equal at open-ocean landings. In no time, he taxied up to the floating man.

"Billy Ray, get that man onto the float," Jensen ordered to his radioman-gunner.

"Roger, Mister Jensen."

Emerson quickly stripped off his gear and dove into the cold Chesapeake. He was an excellent swimmer and former lifeguard, and before long he and Jensen had the remains of the dead German lifted onto the Kingfisher, along with samples of everything else that came to the surface. Thoroughly chilled and shaking, Radioman Third Class Emerson then thankfully climbed back next to his .30-caliber Browning.

The moment Emerson reported on the intercom that he was back in his cockpit, Jensen taxied over to the *Argonne* to await his turn for recovery.

— —

Commander Radisson had to make this report in person. The hangar damage was relatively superficial. An aviation fueling cart had overturned when the stern had leaped in response to the explosion. Ignited by a spark of steel on steel, the intense flames were confined to the after end, fortunately away from any of the aircraft. But the burning paint, damaged electrical cabling, and melting spare wings had taken time to completely extinguish and cool. The air department would have a huge cleanup job. *Sabine* would have to go on "water hours" until all the wetted aircraft had been washed down with freshwater. Little real damage had been done.

The DCA reported that the flooding in the shaft alley had been caused by damaged shaft seals. Tightening the emergency flax packing slowed the leaks to a trickle. Repair parties were in the process of pumping out the water.

Number one main engine was a different story. An inspection of the lubricating-oil system strainers showed a heavy accumulation of Babbitt metal, indicative of badly damaged bearings, but the engineer did not know which ones. He suspected, based on the location of the explosion, that it was the thrust bearing. To be sure, he had to open the reduction gear and disassemble all the bearings. That was going to create a problem.

The shaft-locking device could only hold the shaft against the forces created by the propeller up to twenty knots. If *Sabine* exceeded that while the bearings were being inspected and replaced, the shaft would turn. Rotating the reduction gear and thrust bearing while they were open and locked could damage them beyond repair. That speed limit meant that *Sabine* would probably not be able to operate aircraft, as launch or recovery required a thirty-knot wind over the deck.

The long climb from the engine room to the bridge gave Radisson an eternity to contemplate being the bearer of bad news. Once informed, Captain Evans would need to tell Admiral Hamilton. The Admiral would have to decide whether the task force could afford to nurse a cripple for five or six days, or whether *Sabine* should be sent back to Norfolk, which was his recommendation; in that case they would lose her completely to the mission.

— —

Sheppard called for Major Jenkins. There was no need to keep him inside Number II turret. Senior Chief Hancock was more than capable of handling things until his return.

"How many of your men speak German?" Sheppard asked when Jenkins appeared on the bridge.

The question seemed to take Jenkins aback. He thought for a minute and answered, "Beside myself, two officers and eight of my marines."

"Great. We just captured two Germans, and I want you to use those marines as their guards in the brig. Rotate them frequently, because I want them to listen to everything said but not to react in any way. I don't want the prisoners to think they understand German. I also want you to question them, but do it in French or English. Don't let on that you are fluent, and don't react to something that they may say in German."

Jenkins smiled. Sheppard knew that his marine commander was going to enjoy trying to outwit the Krauts.

"Get eight of your marines in full battle dress, with fixed bayonets, to greet the Kingfishers," Sheppard continued. "Each has a prisoner."

Soon enough, though, Sheppard realized there were two problems with his plan. When Bronco had shut down his engine on Mustang Zero-One, the German prisoner had been unconscious and near death. Instead of escorting the German to the brig, the marines served as stretcher bearers, taking the Stokes litter with the prisoner inside to sickbay. Once there, Doctor Blankenship quickly diagnosed a severe case of hypothermia and ordered the man wrapped in heated blankets to raise his body temperature. His condition was grave, the doctor opined, but he would recover. The prisoner was placed in the empty isolation ward and handcuffed to a bed flanked by two marine guards. His war was over, though he did not know it yet.

The second problem was simpler. The other prisoner was also carried to sickbay. Doctor Blankenship examined him and pronounced his demise.

— —

When Commander Radisson reached *Sabine*'s bridge, he found Captain Evans and Admiral Hamilton in discussion. His arrival silenced them both.

Radisson began, "Captain, it appears that German torpedo detonated on the bottom. Shaft number one took the worst of the blow, and I am also worried about what might have happened to the rudder. That explosion should have been just about abreast of the rudder, based on where the water column and mud were thrown up and the resulting mud and damage to the flight deck galleries there. I must recommend we go into dry dock immediately to assess damage and effect repairs. Even if we just return to port and send divers down to inspect, I would feel a lot better about *Sabine*'s continued operation."

Captain Evans replied, "Engineer, I understand, but she is answering her helm well and we have power on three shafts."

Admiral Hamilton interjected, "I don't need to remind you that this flight deck and air group are vital to successfully completing our mission—or do I?"

Chastened, Commander Radisson stood silent.

Jake Evans asked the critical question. "If you assume, as you suspect, that the thrust bearing on number one shaft is wiped and that has jammed the thrust collar, do you have all the parts you need to repair the damage?"

Avoiding Admiral Hamilton's stare, Radisson answered, "Captain I have everything I need except a new thrust-collar shaft. That piece would have to be specifically manufactured by GE or Westinghouse and would take months. Even if I can't repair the reduction gear, I can still guarantee you twenty knots with that shaft locked."

Admiral Hamilton spoke. "That settles it. I'll take that risk!"

CHAPTER 6

TRANSIT

Sheppard made his decision. He shouted through the command tower's open port armored door, "Officer of the Deck, relieve the conning officer. I am taking him and my orderly up to the secondary conning station in the forward tower. Call down to CIC and give my compliments to Mister Becker. Request he send a good phone talker up there to man the captain's battle circuit. Send my compliments to Commander Grabowski and ask him to arrange for a helmsman and two lee helmsmen for the conning station also."

Art Roberts looked at Sheppard quizzically. "Captain, with the exception of the conning officer and your orderly, those individuals are already there."

Sheppard stifled a frown. He hated looking foolish. "Sorry, Commander, I didn't know that. I want to leave you here in the command tower, with the officer-of-the-deck function. As the navigator, you have the authority to relieve the conn immediately if we become casualties in the tower. I am going up to the conning station now for a clear view. I understand there's an SG radar up there that I can use directly for the surface picture. My intention is to fight *Argonne* from that location. Let Commander Grabowski know of my intentions and location."

"Yes, sir," Roberts said.

"When you are ready, you may secure from battle stations, set condition yoke below the second deck, and set the regular underway watch."

Smiling inwardly at the fact that Art Roberts had actually corrected him and trusted his Captain enough to not take offense, Sheppard turned on his heel and headed aft, dreading a seven-deck climb. There was one redeeming feature in this, though: if the doctor wanted to examine him, Commander Blankenship would have to climb fifteen decks from sickbay to do it. That brought a smile to Sheppard's face as he reached the first ladder, with Corporal Pease in tow.

— —

Johann Schmitt and his soundman were listening to the propeller beats growing fainter and fainter. Sweat running down their faces glistened in the faint light. Even without activity, Schmitt was breathing hard, laboring to get enough oxygen out of the depleted air.

From the reports of explosions by men in the torpedo room, Schmitt was certain they had hit the carrier with three torpedoes. The absence of any continuing activity in their vicinity convinced him she had been sunk, probably capsizing from the hits on her port side. That made the conditions of cold and stale air they were breathing almost bearable.

Their gambit must have paid off; the stupid Americans were leaving. If they had been English, it never would have worked. The last bubbles, oil, and the body of poor Huygens had not followed immediately after exploding depth charges, and the water was much too shallow for them to have been crushed. The English would have known it was a ruse.

— —

His tanned face grinning from ear to ear and white silk scarf hanging loosely around his neck, Bronco was talking to his aviation chief boatswain's mate about painting a symbol for the submarine kill on the sides of Mustang Zero-One. It couldn't be the standard German swastika flag for an air-to-air kill. It had to be something special. Bronco wanted it in white with a black crooked cross superimposed, to be located on both sides directly under the sliding canopy adjacent to the pilot's seat, proclaiming to the world the success that Bronco had achieved. He wanted to pose next to it in his khaki flight suit and fleece-lined brown leather jacket and send a photo to his folks back in Kansas. After a discussion, Bronco agreed that the best answer was a contest within the squadron's personnel.

When that conversation was through, Bronco knew he had to get on to the business of teaching his pilots how to estimate the trajectory of their depth charges—having seen how badly Jensen had missed with his follow-up attack. Or had *he?* As gratified as he was with his own success, Bronco knew that his measure of success as a squadron commander would be how well all of his men performed. They, too, needed to gain kills. The troops were doing their part in maintaining the Kingfishers.

— —

Completely winded, Sheppard—and his not-even-breathing-hard orderly—finally reached the secondary conning station. There, Sheppard had found just the essentials: helm, binnacle, gyro compass repeater, enunciators for the engines, chart table, and communication circuits. A dozen or more watchstanders crowded into the small space. Forward, slightly to starboard, was what he needed most: a high-backed swivel chair. The precious SG radar with its operator and phone talker were in an anteroom to port.

When he stepped out on the wraparound platform with its high windscreen, he had a phenomenal view: everything on board his ship and the sky above. This was where he would fight *Argonne*. But what he liked most was that immediately aft of the conning station, through a joiner door to starboard, he found a small enclosed cabin, with a fold-up desk, small head, and—an honest-to-goodness bunk!

Sheppard was checking out the small cabin when Doctor Blankenship arrived, similarly winded. Sheppard could not resist smiling and asking him if he was feeling all right.

"Sure you don't want to lie down, Doctor?"

"Perhaps I will need to do a rectal exam on you after all, just to be safe."

Sheppard gave him a look of mock surrender before enduring the poking and prodding with indignant stoicism. When the doctor finished, he asked the time-honored medical question, "How are you feeling?"

Sheppard answered that he felt good, considering his leg had been shredded by a Japanese shell three months earlier. He admitted to himself that he was growing fond of the doctor.

But he would never tell him of the dreams.

— —

Gradually, Hans Meier came to, his teeth no longer chattering. Trying to wipe his eyes, he discovered the handcuffs lashing him to the bunk he now lay upon. They had removed his wet clothing, and now he felt the cool cotton sheets next to his skin. They must have also bathed him, for he only smelled the gently moving, sweet, clean air. Awkwardly, he lifted his head and shoulders, glancing around at a small white bunkroom. He saw three other double-decked bunks beside his, but no other patients. The overhead had huge bolt heads projecting downward. Meier figured that he must be under a heavy armored deck. That meant he was on one of the battle cruisers. Looking farther, he noticed that two men in helmets, with olive-drab shirts and pants and wearing web belts containing ammunition pouches, stood each side of the only door he could see. Each man held a rifle, bayonet fixed, and wore a determined expression.

He had no idea which battle cruiser was his jail. It must have aircraft, because he remembered that a floatplane had bumped into him before he passed out. A sailor in white bell-bottom pants and a white T-shirt came through the door and checked his pulse. The sailor then stuck a thermometer under his tongue and took his temperature. He went to the foot of his bunk, opened a metal clipboard, and scribbled something inside. Then he left without a word. Meier guessed he was in a sickbay.

— —

It had been over an hour since the soundman had heard anything that sounded like a ship, and Johann Schmitt decided it was safe to start trying to repair the damage. He issued the orders and his men—yes, they were *his* men now—responded quickly. First, he would try to pump out the torpedo room. If that proved unsuccessful, it would be pointless to try anything else.

His machinists began the difficult task of disassembling the starboard diesel to get at the three cracked cylinder liners. Johann cautioned them to make sure the large pieces would not move about when they tried to surface. They started the pump with the valves of the drain system arranged to remove water from the torpedo room.

Slowly, the water level started to drop. As it did, morale rose. The air-system valve that had killed Machinist Huygens looked as if it would be repaired before the pumping was even finished. Schmitt mumbled a short prayer of thanks that none of the seawater had seeped into the battery compartment. The resulting chlorine gas—the first gas ever used as a weapon, in the Great War—would have burned everyone's lungs, resulting in an agonizing slow death as the lungs filled with the body's own fluids.

— —

Squadron Leader Rupert Wythe-Jones had enjoyed another quiet evening at home in his rented flat on Tremeyrick Street, Pembroke Dock in Wales, with his wife Lois. The maintainers and a few aircraft artificers had arrived yesterday from 19 Group Headquarters. Rupert was delighted to learn that it was the new ASV III radar that required his stand-down. Soon, the abilities of his Sunderlands to detect U-boats would be unmatched in Coastal Command. What made the day, though, was the fact that he had finished his over-dues and posted them to RAF Headquarters. He hated writing performance reports on his officers. In war, it seemed so pointless. If you survived, numbers meant you were promoted. If you did not, what was the point of a bloody report that said how good you were? You obviously had not been good enough.

The leading sergeant responsible for the installs had assured Wythe-Jones upon arrival that they would be completed in three days. Rupert had smiled and told him not to rush. He was going home to his wife. The sergeant winked at his mates, assuring the squadron leader that at the very earliest, the installs couldn't be completed before late the next morning.

— —

The bulkhead clock was chiming eight bells; Sheppard had been silently observing the subsequent watches relieve each other. Ted Grabowski had made the long climb up to the secondary conning station. Hardly winded, he was obviously in much better shape than Sheppard or the doctor. The two light cruisers had just finished taking their stations between the two battle cruisers a thousand yards ahead of *Sabine*. They were fine-looking ships, with four 6-inch triple turrets—two each fore and aft. Perched on their stern were two catapults, with floatplanes and a sliding hatch between. Little extra room remained on their fantails for the single crane arcing over them. He guessed there could not be much room in the hangar for more than two additional floatplanes, as the cruisers would have to stow all four in the event of a storm.

Sheppard swiveled his chair as the XO approached. "Ted, I am going to fight *Argonne* from up here." he informed him.

Grabowski paused, his facial muscles tightening, his lips pursing. "Captain, I must strongly disagree. The command tower protects not only you but also all the functions that need to be coordinated in battle. Up here, you are isolated without the armored communications circuits."

"Ted, I may not have all of them, but there are more than enough for me to be effective. Besides, the tower is a small target, with the communication circuits protected to the same degree as the main-battery director cabling. If you assign two more phone talkers, it may be a little crowded, but we will be fine."

"Captain, this pilot house only has one-inch plating for protection. That won't even stop machine cannon shells like our 40 millimeters."

"It is more than enough to stop shrapnel. Besides, you are going to be in the after-conning station, and I am leaving Art Roberts in the command tower as OOD. Chuck Williamson is in the gunnery control station just above him. There is nothing that those two can't take care of without me. If anything happens up here, they'll see it and take over until you get forward."

"Captain, please, you need to be behind heavy armor!"

"My mind is made up. This is where I am going to be." Sheppard smiled. "Besides, look at it as a golden opportunity to get your own battle cruiser."

Sheppard rotated his chair forward and raised his binoculars, inwardly pleased and amazed that his officers were willing to disagree with him and state their opinions forcefully. That was how the best decisions were made.

— —

Meier watched as the two guards suddenly snapped to attention at the arrival of a man dressed in khaki shirt and pants. Meier guessed he must be an officer, as he wore metal pieces that looked like gold on his collar. Raising his head farther, Meier saw shoes polished like black mirrors.

"What is your name?" the man snapped in English.

Meier decided he might be better off if they did not know he spoke English. He just looked at the officer with a questioning frown as if he were trying to understand. The officer shifted to French and asked the same question.

Meier replied with the name of one of his torpedomen. "Fritz Otto Mueller."

The officer continued in French, "What is your rank and specialty?"

Again Hans lied, "Torpedo mechanic third class."

"What is your service number?"

"One-seven-four-two-nine-six," Meier replied, using his own number so that Germany would know the truth when the International Red Cross reported it.

Meier knew he was not obligated to say anything more, but then again, an enlisted man might not be as quick to cite the Geneva Convention and go silent.

His interrogator continued in French, "We picked up another survivor, but I regret we could not save his life. He never regained consciousness. Would you be able to identify him for us?"

Meier kept himself from showing an emotion. If someone else had tried to escape, had his submarine been destroyed? And would there be any report of his great victory to the Führer? Would another boat get credit for his kill while he languished as a POW?

"Yes, I knew everyone on board," Meier said.

The officer produced the key to his handcuffs. "Are you well enough to stand and walk?"

"Yes, I think so."

The officer barked orders in English for a hospital corpsman to bring a set of "dungarees" and summoned a "Doctor Blankenship." The officer spoke to the doctor in a low whisper that Meier could not make out while he donned the clothing provided.

Standing, he staggered slightly. He felt the blood draining from his face, but he managed to walk across a passageway to another, larger, white room, where a shape was lying, covered with a white cotton sheet. There was only one table the size of a bunk in the center, and large lights hung fixed to the overhead. Meier blinked at the sudden brilliance, noting the bulkheads lined with cabinets and strange equipment that he suspected to be medically related. The doctor pulled back the sheet to reveal the head and shoulders. Meier saw no obvious wounds and suspected the man had drowned, recalling his own miraculous escape.

Meier answered truthfully, in a hoarse, halting voice, "His name is Karl Huygens. He was a mechanic."

The officer politely said in French, "Thank you for identifying him. We will bury him with full military honors."

Two additional guards arrived, with rifles and fixed bayonets. The officer produced a blindfold and covered Meier's eyes. The men led him through winding passages and down ladders until they stopped. His blindfold removed, he was unceremoniously thrust into a cell. The barred door clanged shut and was locked. The officer turned and left. The key to his cell door had been placed on a hook out of reach on the far bulkhead. It didn't matter anyway; those two guards with gleaming bayonets stood between his tiny cell and the key.

— —

The crew of the *U-179* had finished repairing the air valve and had pumped out both the torpedo room and the engine room. Schmitt had tried to drain the conning tower, but the pressure clearly indicated that it was open to the sea. They would have to surface blind. Once on the surface, they could use the forward hatch to get men on deck for a view of what awaited them there. The English would have left a patrol boat, lying still, that could easily sink them with gunfire. Were those old four-pipe destroyers still patrolling? Though unsure how he could shoot without a periscope, Schmitt ordered the bow torpedo tubes reloaded. If nothing else, it would make more room for his sailors who had to sleep there and would also convince his crew that they stood a chance at defending themselves.

The sun set over an hour before they finished their preparations. As more water was pumped out of the trimming tanks, the bow started to lift off the bottom. Schmitt ordered the trim pump stopped and lined up to pump the aft tank to the forward tank until the submarine again rested on a level keel. He continued pumping and trimming until, finally, the submarine rose evenly from the bottom. Slowly, he allowed the U-boat to rise.

"Both motors ahead two-thirds," Schmitt ordered when the propellers had cleared the bottom.

"Fifteen meters."

As the speed climbed to three knots, his planesmen were able to maintain depth and trim.

"Left full rudder."

Schmitt planned to swing *U-179* in a complete circle, while his soundman listened carefully for any indication of machinery noise or propellers.

As the circle came to completion, the soundman reported, "No contacts!"

For better or worse, it was time to order the main ballast tanks blown with the remaining high-pressure air. *U-179* surfaced, and as air gushed out from a ruptured starboard ballast tank, the boat quickly listed. Fortunately, the sea was calm. Schmitt left Brandt in charge in the control room with orders to submerge immediately if he heard gunfire. Then he and a lookout went forward to the torpedo room, cracked open the hatch as rushing air equalized the pressure, and climbed on deck.

No contacts.

He and the lookout climbed to the bridge. What Schmitt saw made his heart sink—the upper conning tower hatch was open.

— —

Sheppard had enjoyed the sunset. The beautiful hues of red and gold from the developing high cloud cover had created a setting made to order for a gifted marine artist. Interspersed on the horizon, the silent black shapes of warships were the only reminder of man and his machines. The gentle roll of *Argonne* in the swell was in stark contrast to the gyrations of the destroyer masts that Sheppard could see; the swish of the bow wave was the only break from the lulling hum of the forced draft blowers; the clean, sweet smell of the sea—it was hard to believe that the world was at war and men had died here today. He said a silent prayer for the German officers and men of the U-boat that his Kingfishers had destroyed. Like him, they were just professional seamen carrying out the orders of their government. Unlike the Japanese, Sheppard could not hate them, for they fought by the rules of the Geneva Convention.

Interrupting his thoughts, Petty Officer Jefferson arrived with a tray loaded with plates of beef stew, mashed potatoes, corn, salad, and apple pie.

"Jefferson, did you carry that all the way up here?" Sheppard asked.

"Well, Cap'n, yes sir and no sir," he answered with a big grin, the faint red light shining off his teeth. "Bos'n Bergman done made me the Jim dandiest carrying rig you ever done seen. Once I gots to your sea cabin, I done took the plates out, put 'em on the tray, easy as that. So, you see, I really didn't carries it up all the way."

Sheppard suspected that it was Jefferson who had sought out the boatswain's mate and told Bergman exactly what he wanted.

As he mused over his steward's inventiveness, it dawned on Sheppard how hungry he was. In all the excitement, he had completely missed lunch.

"Thank you, Jefferson. That sure smells good."

"Cap'n, while you are eating, I's goin' to bring up your khakis, your foul-weather gear, and your night things so you's feels right to home. I suspects you're goin' to stay up here likes on *Shenandoah*."

The simple hushed thank-you seemed inadequate.

Taking in the view from the secondary conning station, Jefferson nodded and said, "It's sure a purty end to a fine Navy day. Mister Burdick's men havin' a contest, who can draw the best broke sub. The winner gets to paint Mister Burdick's Kingfisher. It's good she done got her fust kill today."

Sheppard smiled at Jefferson's comment. If Jefferson took advantage of the opportunities to sightsee when he finished the climb from his pantry, Sheppard would never deny him that small compensation.

"Yes, Jefferson, it was a fine navy day."

As he was finishing his meal, balancing the tray on his lap, Sheppard noted Major Jenkins standing at parade rest by the passage door.

"Yes, Major—how did your questioning go?"

Morris looked surprised that Sheppard had guessed why he'd come. "Captain, the man has lied about who he is. Though he claimed being enlisted, his clothing didn't match the clothes on the other sailor. He identified that sailor as a machinist, Karl Huygens. From the calluses on that man's hands, I believe that statement. This prisoner has no calluses and is wearing a Hitler Youth ring. That tells me he was well connected and more than the torpedoman he claims to be. Based on my experience in Germany, if he understands French, he is also likely to be educated—and likely to know English, too. I believe he is an officer, and by his age, he may well be the commanding officer of the U-boat."

"Excellent work. Well done, Major! We'll continue with our plan and see what this prisoner lets slip. Try to see him once or twice a day, and make sure your men don't let on they know German."

Sheppard could not be happier. If he had the commanding officer, surely the U-boat now lay destroyed on the seabed, with the task force's sailing unreported to German high command.

— —

Admiral Hamilton had a dilemma. The light had faded before he'd been able to implement a zigzag plan. Designed to change the course of all his ships simultaneously about a base course at different intervals of time, zigzagging was effective in making submarine attacks slightly less successful. Hamilton needed daylight to implement it by flag hoist. Directional flashing light could not send the execute signal to everyone at the same instant. He did not want to use the VHF radio Talk Between Ships, or TBS as it was called, either, as a German submarine might be on the surface now and within its range. That left him with no options other than to pursue a straight course tonight.

He had also seen the red sunset. The old saying, "Red sky at night, sailors' delight; red sky at morning, sailors take warning," only applied in more southerly latitudes. Off Norfolk, this developing cloud cover portended foul weather. A front was strengthening and moving eastward. He summoned the staff meteorologist, directing him to come to flag plot via the weather decks. At least Hamilton could force his "weather guesser" to look outside the confines of *Sabine*'s meteorology office.

— —

Nine decks below and aft of the admiral, Commander Radisson was inspecting the reduction gear of the number one main engine with his leading chief machinist and Main Propulsion Assistant.

"What do you think chief?" he asked.

"Well, sir, there are a few new scratches in the bearing Babbitt, but nothing that I would say is anything to worry about. The journals themselves are in good shape."

"MPA, what about the gear teeth? How do they compare to the last time you inspected them?"

"Cheng, they look 'bout the same. There are no indications of any large particles going through the meshing. The fine scratches on the contact surfaces are the same as the last inspection." Lieutenant MacLiesh was a mustang who had worked his way up through the ranks. Radisson knew that if anything were even slightly amiss, he would say so.

"Well so far so good," Radisson intoned, "but it means we will have to lift the gear cover, the pinions, and quill shafts to get at the thrust bearing."

With a clear sense of the magnitude of the task ahead all three men resigned themselves to a job none had ever attempted outside a shipyard.

The first step would be lifting the top half of the reduction gear case. Without a word, their machinist's mates were gathering the tools in preparation for lifting the cover to gain access to the entire reduction gear complex. The huge cover, weighing a dozen tons or more, would have to remain suspended by chain hoists after carefully maneuvering it off to one side above the gear. That was the only way that the pinions and quill shafts could be lifted out with other chain hoists. There was simply no area large enough to put it down in the engineroom.

Radisson said a silent prayer for good weather. If that cover fell, it would take *Sabine* a year in the shipyard to recover, if a new bull gear even existed.

—●—

The crew of the *U-179* finished draining the conning tower, and Schmitt took the opportunity to inspect the damage. The split hull seam was impossible to repair; it prevented them from submerging without grave risk of sinking. The bent periscope was a further danger. It was designed to rest on the keel when lowered. If they did dive deep enough to evade an English attack, sea pressure would push it into the hull until the bend created a large opening in not only the conning tower but also the control room, sinking them all.

No, unable to submerge for attack or escape, Schmitt could not continue with their mission. *U-179* had to return to port. Johann had long ago lost any desire for glory.

Damn war—it is all for what? he thought. *Meier was the zealot, not me. My only duty is to my men. They deserve to live.*

He ordered a course of zero-five-two degrees true, heading for their home port of Saint-Nazaire, France, at *U-179*'s maximum speed of thirteen knots on one diesel engine. He had to get out of range of any air patrols before dawn.

What had happened to Meier seemed a mystery to Schmitt. If he had escaped, he was most certainly a prisoner. Johann had been loyal, probably to a fault, but the time for loyalty was over. Now his duty was to report the action and what his captain had seen through the periscope. It was necessary to file a midnight weather report, including his location, to Uncle Karl, now that Beckenschlaeger had begun. He left the watch in Brandt's capable hands and went below to compose the messages for encoding.

— —

Art Roberts sat in the charthouse of *Argonne*, composing the night orders. Besides the usual entries of the formation—which ship was the guide, the currently ordered course and speed—the night orders also included any anticipated evolutions and required preparations for the dawn message drop of Hamilton's revised orders. Hamilton had sent them to *Argonne* by flashing light just before sunset, tasking them to copy and distribute them to the task force. Bronco's airedales would be awake early readying both OS2Us for launch at first light.

The night orders contained Robert's calculation of the time of first light and sunrise, based on his best guess of *Argonne*'s eastward progress. The farther they went, the earlier the time, so if he were off by forty miles, his times would be off by almost five minutes. These items were normal, even in peacetime. However, this was war; and there were extra items. Captain McCloud had told him to have two of the antiaircraft directors—called Sky-One and Sky-Eight—continuously manned, as well as several of the five-inch mounts. Any aircraft or surfaced submarine deemed hostile coming from any direction could be immediately engaged before the *Argonne*'s crew arrived at battle stations.

McCloud directed that the crew be called and battle stations manned by first light. As the eastern horizon developed a glow, it might reveal an enemy silhouetted against the dawn. Any enemy to the west might see *Argonne* well before anyone aboard *Argonne* could see them. With battle stations manned, *Argonne* would be in the best possible position to respond, and she would also be buttoned up, with almost every watertight door or hatch shut and dogged tight.

Finishing the orders, Roberts made the long climb to where the Captain was located. Sheppard reviewed the night-order book, made a few corrections, and signed them. A messenger hand-carried the book to the XO and department heads for their initials. Chuck Williamson had to set up a watch bill to rotate the crews of his five-inch mounts and directors through those designated so that all could get some sleep.

Noting the required speeds and anticipated evolutions, Andy Scott would write his own set of night orders for his engineers, specifying the boiler and engine status as well as any auxiliary equipment needed to keep *Argonne* ready.

Then the messenger would route the book back to the OOD, who would execute every order as directed.

Only then would Sheppard dare to sleep.

—▪—

Vizeadmiral Klaus Schröder had awakened at his usual time—dawn. After dressing in blues, he called his steward for his usual breakfast of sausages and eggs in the flag quarters on board *Graf Zeppelin*. He directed his messenger to have the staff communications officer bring him the morning message boards. He wanted to see the weather observations that the Beckenschlaeger U-boats should have reported during the night.

He finished his breakfast before the young officer arrived and impatiently walked over to his porthole, cursing another beautiful day. Schröder would make sure the lieutenant was aware of his displeasure and not repeat the delay again. Finally, Oberleutnant zur See Schenker showed up with the boards.

"I am sorry, Herr Admiral, for the delay," Schenker said. "There was a long message from *U-179* that I had to finish decoding. When you called for the boards, I had already realized its importance and knew you would want to see it immediately."

"Very well, Schenker, but in the future, allow enough time so that you are not late again. You are dismissed."

A chastened Schenker left, and Schröder began to read. Finally, good news. High clouds were developing all along the East Coast of the United States, and the barometer was dropping, indicating the likely arrival of a weather front. The low-pressure area would bring the storms he needed to evade the English.

Moving on to other reports, Schröder saw that Schenker had indeed been correct about the message from *U-179*. It seemed the captain had been lost in an engagement with an American fleet leaving Norfolk. The first officer managed an excellent contact report, despite severe damage. Schröder was delighted at the fact that they had managed to sink one of the two *Brandywine*-class carriers. With only one remaining aircraft carrier and the two *Antietam*-class battle cruisers, Schröder was more than a match for them, this despite the fact that the American air group was about the same size as the combined total he had on both of his carriers. Two Civil-War-class capital ships, with their sixteen-inch guns, were no match for his four battle cruisers and their 45-centimeter guns. His ships could outrange the Americans and also had thicker belt armor. He would close and devastate them with his superior firepower. The two armored cruisers were inconsequential, armed with just ten-inch guns. The only hard part would be finding them.

It would take the Americans seven days to arrive. So he only had a week to wait—until he could hunt them down for destruction.

— —

At 0430 on the dot, Sheppard heard a knock on his cabin door.

"Captain, it is another fine Navy day!"

"That it is, Petty Officer Jefferson, and good morning to you, too!" Sheppard responded in their customary exchange.

"Captain, I's be back shortly with your breakfast. Would you's likes it here or the conning station?"

"I'll take it on the conn, if you don't mind, Jefferson."

Sheppard shaved and brushed his teeth in the small sink in the adjoining head. Then he quickly dressed in his khaki shirt with the eagles of his rank on the collars, along with a black tie, long khaki pants, black socks, and black shoes. He put on a brown sweater and crossed onto the conning station immediately forward of his cabin, where he was greeted with a loud, "Captain is on the conn!" by the boatswain's mate of the watch.

Sheppard took a seat in his high-backed swivel chair that allowed him to see the horizon over the windscreen. When action might be imminent, he would probably live in this chair, catnapping as he could, only leaving the conn to attend to the calls of nature that could not be avoided even by captains.

"Captain," his OOD said, "request permission to man battle stations."

"Permission granted to man battle stations."

Sheppard pulled a stopwatch from his pocket. He wanted to know how long it would take before he would be fully ready to engage an enemy.

The boatswain's mate of the watch stepped to the microphone and piped the call *All Hands*—"$s^{s\text{-}s\text{-}ssssssss}$ $s^{sssssssss}s$—Man battle stations." Then he rang the general alarm, with its *bong-bong-bong*, fourteen times—each bong heightening a sense of urgency—followed by another "Man battle stations."

Sheppard started his stopwatch with the sounding of the general alarm. The hornet's nest erupted in its counterclockwise pattern, with sailors scurrying while simultaneously donning clothing, life jackets, and steel helmets. He could hear the pounding of feet on the ladders leading up the forward tower as men ran to their sky lookout stations on the uppermost open deck. Immediately below them were the surface lookouts, somewhat protected by thin "splinter shields." Above them all, with the best view of the horizon, Lieutenant Hamblen, his pointer, trainer, phone talker, cross-level operator, rangefinder operator, and radar operator hurried to man the MK 38 director.

The supervising stations maintained a check-off to ensure everyone reported "manned." When every sailor who needed to pass through had, the watertight doors and hatches were shut and dogged. Damage-control parties broke out and the men donned their specialized equipment. Shells and gunpowder filled the ammunition hoists. All the boilers were either placed on service or heated to hot standby, with fires lit. Additional turbine generators were paralleled into the electric grid, and the grid was split to prevent one fault from taking down the entire power distribution system.

As the equipment was readied, additional reports of "ready" were made. In the command tower, Art Roberts kept track of all the incoming reports. When every department had reported, he directed the JA phone talker to relay to the captain, "Battle stations manned and ready." This assured Sheppard that *Argonne* was ready for anything and that every one of his sailors was accounted for. None had fallen overboard in the night, unnoticed by the after lookouts stationed to watch and listen for screams.

Sheppard stopped his watch: five minutes, thirty-eight seconds. Gazing through his binoculars, he scanned the surface. The first hint of dawn was making the eastern horizon distinct.

Good, he thought.

On the *Belleau Wood* and *Sabine*, sailors were still running.

Sheppard walked out onto the open platform and looked aft to verify that his Kingfishers were ready to take Admiral Hamilton's revised air plan, using the light cruiser floatplanes for inner ASW patrols to the ships of the task force. The plan had been transmitted by flashing light from *Sabine* last night; it was now his responsibility to deliver it by "bean bag" to each ship.

The wind had strengthened and now blew from the northeast. This would make it more difficult to land the floatplanes, but he judged conditions still safe.

Returning to the conning station, he ordered, "Officer of the Deck, launch aircraft!"

Passed quickly by phones, Art Roberts ordered, "Launch aircraft."

A moment later, the first catapult fired, sending Barry Jensen and his radioman winging into the dark dawn. Less than fifteen seconds later the second fired, catapulting Lieutenant (junior grade) Charles "Chip" Petite and his radioman off in Mustang Zero-Three.

Even this routine operation presented a training opportunity. Sheppard ordered Chuck Williamson to track the two Kingfishers. In response, the portside MK 37 directors slewed onto the bearing, and their Mark 4 radars tilted to follow the aircraft aloft. Williamson was too good a gunnery officer not to practice handing off targets from one director and Ford computer to another as the aircraft weaved around the task force. As for Bronco, he was seizing this chance as a training evolution to develop the bombing skills of his pilots. The ballistics might not have been identical to depth charges, but the weighted soft bags would help his junior pilots develop their estimating abilities. He had made certain that they carried more weighted bags than they needed in case they missed a ship completely.

— —

From his flag bridge on *Sabine,* Admiral Hamilton watched the cloud cover reflecting the red glow of the sun and felt the breeze from the northeast. Why couldn't he shake the notion that the fiery sky portended ill? Carriers and flying were all he had experienced. More than most, Hamilton recognized the fragile nature of aircraft at sea. His carrier crews would work tirelessly to ready one massive strike, but the second would be half that strength. Would he launch first to catch Schröder napping? Would his carriers damage nothing with a misdirected strike? Alone, with no one to share his thoughts, he paced, gray-haired head lowered as his aide watched from the open watertight door.

That was in the future, Hamilton knew, and he had decisions to make now. Would the weather be satisfactory to recover a dawn search and antisubmarine patrol by *Raritan*'s Dauntless aircraft four hours hence? Should he implement a zigzag plan or make as much progress as possible toward the position where he intended to wait for Schröder? Should he continue the planned launch of Kingfishers by his light cruisers, or would the sea be too rough for them to recover? There was no possibility of replacing lost aircraft. Flying them this far from Europe was a balance between maintaining his pilot's proficiency and risking their lives.

"Make to *Colchester* and *Burlington*," Hamilton said. "Do not—repeat, do not—launch today's inner antisubmarine patrol."

"Aye aye, Admiral," the young lieutenant said as he hurried to flag plot. The aide would return shortly, but it really did not affect Hamilton's loneliness.

The dawn search and patrol was another decision. Landing on a carrier would be much easier if the weather were marginal. *Raritan* was a larger ship, turning into the wind and seas for recovery. Returning briskly to flag plot, he directed his operations officer to order *Raritan* to prepare to launch her searches, reporting back when ready. It should only take her ten minutes to move the pilots and gunners from their ready rooms, man their aircraft, start the engines, and warm them. When *Raritan* reported ready, he would turn the task force into the wind, and she would launch.

Scouting Squadron Ten's search would cover half the compass centered about the track of zero-six-five degrees out to a radius of 250 nautical miles. Each SBD was armed with a five-hundred-pound general-purpose bomb—"just in case." Bombing Ten's Dauntlesses, armed with two 325-pound depth charges, were far more likely to see action. Hamilton decided against a combat air patrol. The narrow track of the F4F's landing gear was unforgiving in the best of conditions. Those young fighter pilots would be facing German combat veterans in Bf 109s. Their only advantage lay in numbers.

— —

His khaki uniform stained with oil spots, Commander Kenny Radisson had catnapped on the deck plates of his number one engine room all night. He wanted to be instantly available whenever his men had a question or found the source of the bearing material. The questions had been numerous, the source elusive.

"Engineer … Engineer," an insistent voice called out, startling him back to consciousness. Radisson turned.

"We finished rolling out the journal bearings," Chief Towers said.

"Okay, let's have a look."

With a powerful light, Radisson inspected the cylindrical surfaces for telltale signs of metal-to-metal contact. Although not as shiny as they were when new, the surfaces showed no evidence of recent damage.

Radisson shrugged his shoulders. His stubbled cheeks were hollow from lack of sleep, and there were dark circles under his eyes. When had he last eaten—yesterday? Or had it been the day before?

"Well, Chief, the journals look good; that leaves only the thrust bearing."

"Yes, sir. We'll need to build a crib for the casing to set on off to port. We don't have enough chain falls to leave it suspended. When we lift the pinions and first reduction gears, we'll have enough room to move them off to starboard. It's the only way we can get at the thrust bearing."

"I'll get the carpenters and shoring timber."

Unlike the journal bearings and caps, these elements were not small, that is, within the capability of his men to lift by hand safely. The work would be slow with chain falls, but he remained confident—pretty confident—that he could complete it within the estimate provided to Captain Evans and the admiral.

— —

Vice Admiral Sir Bruce Jennings Hardy—RN, VC, KBE—was sitting in his flag quarters aboard the battle cruiser HMS *Renown*. The First Lord of the Admiralty had only recently posted him to command of Force H. Young for this assignment, Hardy knew of the service rumors that had more senior officers rejecting it as suicidal. However, he had been promised additional forces as soon as Lütjens could be cut down to size. Unfortunately, that did not ease his current dilemma. Spies in Spain were reporting that the German tankers in A Coruña, Ferrol, Port Gijón, and Bilbao were loading 15 cm ammunition, gasoline, and fuel oil. That could only mean that Schröder was planning to break out of Brest, and soon.

Hardy's main force included HMS *Ark Royal*, with seventy-two aircraft equally divided between the venerable Swordfish torpedo bombers and Fulmar fighters. Neither aircraft was any match for the German Bf 109s. If he were going to be able to use them at all, it would have to be at night. Besides *Renown*, he also had HMS *Repulse*—both dated from the First World War and slower than Schröder's ships. At least they had been modernized, with a good antiaircraft fit of 4.5-inch dual-purpose guns, 40 mm pom-pom mounts, and Oerlikons. He had one light cruiser and a flotilla of eight destroyers. Not much, but with his experienced crews, it would have to be enough.

What he desperately needed was more cruisers to hunt down the supply ships before they scattered too widely. The only ones he thought the Admiralty might give him were in the South Atlantic, patrolling for German auxiliary cruisers. Nothing more than armed cargo ships, they were disguised as innocent merchants. After sneaking up on an unsuspecting steamer, they would drop the disguise, run up the German naval ensign, and sink or take as a prize the fooled ship. There had not been any reported for over a month. Hardy thought there was no harm in asking for the cruisers.

As long as he was asking for additional forces, Sir Bruce decided that a squadron of long-range Catalina flying boats would be invaluable if Schröder decided to head south. The only British base in the eastern Atlantic was Gibraltar, and flying from the harbor would extend his surveillance almost an additional thousand miles. Intent on procuring the Catalinas, he sent off an insistent message to the Admiralty.

— —

The seas were building. It was going to be difficult to get his Kingfishers back on board. Battle stations having long since been secured, Sheppard needed to station special watches for recovering aircraft.

"Prepare to recover aircraft on the starboard side," he ordered to his OOD.

That would set the wheels in motion. When they were ready, he would use *Argonne*'s size and power to calm a strip of ocean heading into the wind, allowing the OS2Us to land safely. Once down, they could taxi alongside in *Argonne*'s lee until he was ready to lift them aboard. The first task would be easy; the second would take time.

He directed the conning officer to open the range to *Sabine* to three thousand yards but maintain her on the same relative bearing. Raising the white flag with the red diamond "Fox" to the dip on both yardarms would inform Admiral Hamilton that he was preparing to operate aircraft. When the OOD reported, "Ready to recover aircraft," Sheppard took the conn himself.

"All ahead full, left full rudder."

As *Argonne* accelerated, the churning propellers thrust the seas away from her stern. As she turned left, the flow of water under her hull rose on the port side aft, creating smoothness in the otherwise overly rough sea. Art Roberts had been correct about the vibration. As Sheppard felt it start, he ordered the starboard inboard shaft stopped. When *Argonne* was pointing *Sabine*—surely to Admiral Hamilton's chagrin—Sheppard ordered, "Shift your rudder. Number one main engine ahead full. Number two main engine stop."

The helmsman spun the wheel to right full and *Argonne* now flattened another section of the sea.

A final set of orders came from Sheppard. "Steady course zero-six-five, all ahead standard," and *Argonne* coasted nicely back to her station, trailed by a broad, smooth swath of ocean pointing the wind.

Both Kingfishers immediately landed there before the smoothness dissipated, and they taxied into the lee on her starboard quarter. Mustang Zero-Three engaged the landing mat first and was hoisted aboard. The aircraft settled on top of the armored hatch, where she had her fuel tanks drained and wings folded. The aircraft and boat crane then lifted the Kingfisher again, the hatch opened, and one aircraft was safely stored in the hangar. Then it was Mustang Zero-Five's turn as Sheppard watched from the conning station starboard pelorus stand. The wind and sea were rising, and his section of flattened ocean had long since dissipated and been left far behind. If disaster occurred, he was well aware that the sea was too rough to launch a boat for recovery of personnel.

— —

Just in time, Radioman Third Class Emerson slipped the eye of the hoisting bridle for the Kingfisher over the hook of the aircraft and boat crane.

"Hang on, Emerson!" Barry Jensen screamed over the roar of the wind and sea.

Emerson grabbed wildly for the cable as the Mustang Zero-Five yawed to starboard.

"I can't hold it," Barry cried to no one in particular as the left wingtip float submerged.

"Damn it! Haul away, Smitty!" Chief Bledsoe yelled at his crane operator.

Things were going from bad to worse as the left wing of Mustang Zero-Five dove under a wave—crumpling the float and outboard section.

"You men with the hold-off poles, brace yourselves," Bledsoe shouted. "That plane is going to swing your way."

Eyes wide as silver dollars, Jensen and his radioman were helpless onlookers as their plane was dragged from the clutches of the sea by the prompt action of Aviation Chief Boatswain's Mate Bledsoe. Swinging toward *Argonne*, the forward hold-off pole, caught between the Kingfisher and the starboard catapult, snapped, sending splinters the size of baseball bats flying, while crushing the cowling of the Pratt & Whitney engine. Without the hold-off pole, the left wing crashed into the hull, crushing the thin aluminum. By the time the OS2U was resting on the armored hatch, both soggy men were shaking but thankful they hadn't had to swim for their lives.

"You boys okay?" the chief asked.

"Yes, I think so," Jensen answered, "but look at my plane."

"Don't worry, Mister Jensen, we've got a spare wing on the hangar bulkhead. We'll have her good as new in a few days."

— —

Admiral Hamilton's morning search and antisubmarine patrol were returning. It was time to turn the task force into the wind and recover the SBDs. The seas were much rougher than when they had launched. He signaled to *Raritan,* canceling the follow-on patrols. It took a few minutes for her to respot her flight deck, bringing the readied replacement antisubmarine patrol below to the hangar. The admiral watched the *Raritan*'s progress through his binoculars. When the last SBD had started the descent on the forward elevator, he ordered a simultaneous course change into the wind.

As soon as the carrier had steadied on the new heading, the SBDs began landing at thirty-second intervals. *Raritan*'s fight deck crew could put any Broadway show to shame with the intricate choreography necessary. In eleven minutes, every SBD had safely landed. It was a wise decision for Hamilton to suspend flying. The wind and seas continued building.

Eastern North Atlantic from England to Spain

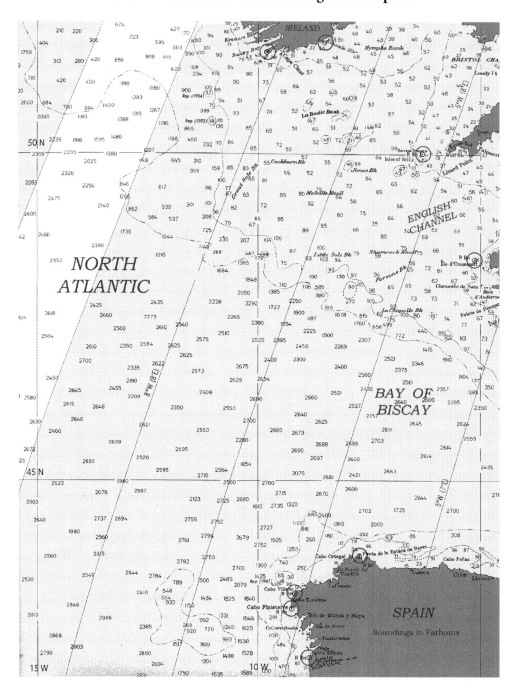

CHAPTER 7

CHESS MOVES

*T*he certitude of their bond comforted her, encouraging her to look deeper into this man she was growing to love more intensely with every passing day. His face intrigued her. Was it the slight bend of his aquiline nose away from the faint scar? What had caused his injury? How had it happened, and when—long ago in his youth, or as a man? Had he been a fighter? She thought it consistent with his character. He did not shy from danger, but was he reckless? Intelligent, perhaps, but it was too soon to determine the depth of his intellect.

His care for those around him was obvious, but who cared for him? Would that be her role—nurturing this man, enveloping him with her love, providing him a haven from his burdens and a respite from his responsibilities for others? His first name suited him: the strong protector of others—the guide to a greater good.

—

The seas were rough and the wind howled through the signal halyards aft of the flag bridge of *Sabine*. A full gale had developed, making it impossible for Dolf Hamilton to launch searches. It seemed that his task force was keeping pace with the storm as it crossed the Atlantic. His staff meteorologist tried to assure the admiral that it would end soon—perhaps in a day or two. Weather reports from the US East Coast already reported clearing, with pleasant forecasts.

The war news, though, was not. There was a sustained submarine assault on East Coast shipping. Every night, US citizens witnessed the spectacle of burning ships, followed at dawn by spreading oil slicks, the bloated corpses of seamen, and flotsam washing ashore on the formerly pristine beaches of peacetime. Commander in Chief Atlantic, Admiral Royal Ingersoll was scraping into service every available ship capable of outfitting as a patrol boat—even large yachts; few U-boats had been sunk or damaged and those mostly by aircraft when the weather cleared. His staff was desperately trying to develop a convoy plan at the urging of their British allies. Every oceangoing merchant ship sunk off the East Coast was one less available to carry food, fuel, and materiel to Great Britain. Emergency programs were being put in place to shift as much of America's transportation needs as possible to the railroads, new pipelines, or the intracoastal waterway, in the hopes of reducing the need for shipping and losses to submarines. Henry Kaiser, California Shipbuilding Corporation, the Bechtel/McCone Company, as well as giant Bethlehem Steel, were building a host of new shipyards, but the effort, like the plan to put together convoys, would take time.

Those were the president's problems; Hamilton needed to focus on dealing with Schröder. The task force continued resolutely toward Cape Finisterre, off the northwest corner of Spain. In this bad weather, the wizened American admiral was guessing that Schröder would use the storm to get as far away from the English air patrols as possible. That could only mean a course of south by southwest until he cleared the Spanish coast, where his movements would become less predictable. Hamilton's plan was to wait near forty-three degrees north, eleven degrees west, and conduct thorough air searches to the northeast, weather permitting.

— —

The *Argonne* had fallen into a routine: dawn battle stations, followed by breakfast for the crew, followed by training evolutions for all hands. Every move and coordination required between the members of the five-inch-mount crews was practiced repeatedly and then practiced again to get the loading time down to Sheppard's goal of five seconds. By practicing for a full thirty minutes, the mount's loaders improved to the point that they could fight off a sustained air attack while manhandling the seventy-pound shells and thirty-five-pound powder cases.

Sheppard's director and plotting room crews practiced for hours a day, tracking the *Colchester* and *Burlington* as they weaved about in front of the task force. Sheppard demanded that they have the ability to shift the control of main battery turrets between both of the Mark 38 directors, as well as with the two Mark 34s nominally assigned to the six-inch-gun battery. His five-inch directors could not practice against aircraft, but they practiced tracking the destroyers and cruisers in the task force as well.

Art Roberts's lookouts worked on identifying enemy warships to cut the time from detection to classification. The signalmen practiced sending each other messages with small Aldis lamps as well as by semaphore, using just their hands. Chief Signalman Evan Bryce promised special liberty at the next port to any man who could send or receive faster than he. No one could.

The *Argonne*'s damage control assistant tirelessly worked his repair parties at controlling and extinguishing simulated fires in every space imaginable. He held timed blindfold races to improve his men's ability to grope their way through smoke-filled compartments. They practiced plugging holes and shoring up watertight bulkheads. They lugged portable pumps and hoses in races from one end of the ship to the other. They practiced with the new Oxygen Breathing Apparatus, and there was also specialized training for the electricians and firecontrol men in rewiring power around damaged cables or jumpering electrical signals for the directors and the analog firecontrol computers.

Unlike the secondary batteries, there was no easy way to practice with the eighteen-inch guns, though some of the component parts of loading—parbuckling the 3,850-pound projectiles and manhandling

110-pound powder bags—were practiced. There had been no opportunities to actually fire any of the guns or engage a target.

— —

Johann Schmitt had survived for five days. The weather had been a godsend to everyone except his machinists trying to repair the cylinders on the starboard diesel engine. Repairs had suffered as a result, and he would need at least another day to complete them. Then *U-179* would be able to increase speed to eighteen knots and, with luck and bad weather, make Saint-Nazaire in five more days. The crew's morale improved with each passing day and the conviction that they now had a chance to get home. Perhaps even the Luftwaffe would provide air cover in the Bay of Biscay against the British air patrols.

Dutifully every night, Schmitt had radioed his position and the weather to Uncle Karl. Little did Schmitt know that he was providing the key information for Vizeadmiral Schröder's decision-making process on when to sail. *U-179*'s reports were the only source of mid-Atlantic weather information. With the storm now approaching the French coast, the reports gave the German admiral a vital perspective on how large and how long it would last.

— —

Schröder, it seemed, was getting nothing but good news. *Yorck* had completed repairs yesterday and had even managed to get in a quick sea trial outside the breakwater, verifying the restoration of her machinery. All of his ships had been topped up with bunker oil. He now had his full squadron of battle cruisers easily able to sweep aside Hardy's relics and the American vessels, even if they joined forces. Once he had finished with them, there was nothing to stop him from raiding the Atlantic convoys for months. If the Americans thought they were losing ships now, wait until he showed them the real meaning of losses. Dönitz would never be able to match what his ships would accomplish as he slaughtered whole convoys at a time.

Schröder had ordered his supply ships to sail yesterday, carrying more than enough fuel and ammunition to keep him at sea until England starved. He only had to conserve the heavy shells for his battle cruisers and the bombs for his Stukas. Both were too large and heavy for transferring at sea. That would not be much of a problem. His ships could match the forty knots of the American heavy ships, and they would make short work of the even slower British ships with their pitiful armor.

It suddenly struck Schröder that he'd find more glory commanding his fleet in a battle cruiser rather than in the carrier where he was currently embarked. If the battle went as he expected, he calculated that he should lead it from the bridge of *Scharnhorst*, not watch it from a distance on the *Graf Zeppelin*. If he stayed on the carrier, Konteradmiral Eisner, commanding the battle cruiser squadron, might be the hero. As fleet commander, Schröder would not get the accolades he would be justly due. Everything had been set for days, with his staff comfortably settled into *Graf Zeppelin*. Designed to house a fleet commander, she had every facility they could want, and a last-minute change might create confusion. But what about the glory?

— ◆ —

The knock on his cabin door awoke Major Jenkins. It had been a long day of drilling his turret crew, inspecting, and instructing his marines.

"Enter," Jenkins barked.

"Major," a young marine reported, "the prisoner mumbled, 'That carrier got me my Knight's Cross with Swords' just before he fell asleep."

"Thank you, Corporal. Dismissed."

Finally, here was proof of the prisoner's lies and of his true rank. The occasional babbling about the "stupid Americans" and how easy it was to fool them had been inconclusive. Even the wondering if the attack on the carrier was the first blow of the so-called Operation Beckenschlaeger could have been ascribed to any crew member. But this—the mention of a sunken carrier and a Knight's Cross with Swords—this was conclusive.

Fool, thought Jenkins. *That can only mean he already has the Knight's Cross with Oak Leaves.* No enlisted submariner would hold that high a medal in Nazi Germany.

Only a U-boat ace would hold that award. So, he had to be the captain—and his true rank must be korvettenkapitän.

A wry smile crossed Jenkins's taut features. His brown eyes twinkled in delight at a plan forming in his mind, but he would need Captain McCloud's permission to execute it—an appropriate word, *execute.*

——

Squadron Leader Rupert Wythe-Jones sat at his desk, idly running a hand through his brown hair. Longer than the RAF desired, his hair was one of the few concessions he made to his wife, Lois, who detested the cropped length regulations required. Thinking of his wife, he knew he must ring her up.

"Hello," came back the angelic voice that had won his heart a decade earlier.

"Dearest, I fear I will not be home tonight. Must make a flight, but I will see you in the morning," he lied, knowing full well that if his test of the new ASV radar lived up to expectations he would probably not see her for days. What made it worse, though, was that Rupert knew Lois would see right through his deceptions but still love him more for it.

He assembled his crew in their flying clothes and briefed them on his intent. Then he informed 19 Group, getting clearance for his flight. The last thing he wanted was the Chain Home radar system reporting him as unidentified, prompting interference by nosey Spitfires or antiaircraft batteries. He planned to head into the developing weather front to the west, locate a convoy, and see how this bit of kit performed in bad weather with real contacts. With luck, he would be back before sunrise and could brief his men on the morrow.

——

The clock chimed seven bells, waking Sheppard. He had slept for almost twenty minutes. Lieutenant Commander Burdick was the first seeking his attention.

"Yes, Mister Burdick, what can I do for you?" Sheppard said, yawning and stretching his arms to the heavens as he shook the fog from his head.

"The repairs to Mustang Zero-Five have been finished, Captain. That project in the hangar looks like hell, but we've just about got it cleaned up. I've been working with my pilots on their bombing and am confident we will do better if we spot another U-boat."

"Good work, Bronco. By the way, do you think your pilots are well enough trained to be catapulted at night?"

"There are four beside myself that I would trust with a night launch. You're not thinking of asking us to land at night, are you?"

"No, Bronco." Sheppard smiled at the implication that all black-shoes were crazy when it came to risking aviator's lives.

"I am not sure exactly what is possible," Sheppard said. "What could you do from the air if we spotted a German capital ship?"

"That is an interesting question, Captain. Let me talk it over with my pilots, and I'll get back to you, if that is acceptable?"

"Please get back to me tomorrow."

Sheppard smiled again. It was clear that he had sparked an idea in the leader of his air department that might help even the odds a little. Seeing someone else waiting to speak with him, Sheppard swiveled his chair further to face his marine company commander directly.

"Major Jenkins, how are you today? How is our guest?"

Morris had given up trying to decipher how the Captain always knew the subject he wanted to talk about. "Sir, request permission to confront our prisoner."

As Jenkins elaborated on his idea, Sheppard thought it was brilliant, but he would have to tell Admiral Hamilton. That way Hamilton would not try to interfere in the events as they unfolded on *Argonne*'s signal bridge. Sheppard grabbed a signal pad and furiously composed a message for the admiral.

— —

Commander Radisson, Engineer Officer of the *Sabine*, looked like hell. Besides the five-day growth of whiskers and besides the dark circles under his brown eyes, his khaki uniform was stained with sweat, blotches of lube oil, and grease—but he had finally found the source of the bearing material in the number one main-engine oil system, as well as the reason for the shaft not windmilling. That was the good news.

The rest was all bad. The torpedo explosion immediately aft of the number one propeller had pushed the shaft forward, wiping the bearing material off the thrust shoes. The bearing material had then jammed the thrust collar, preventing the shaft from rotating and possibly warping the collar. Radisson did not have the precision equipment or the ability to rotate the shaft in order to find out. He hoped that, since Babbitt metal was very soft and the thrust collar was hardened steel—if the friction had not heated it too hot—it might be okay. Other than a new thrust collar shaft, he had all the replacement parts needed. Radisson would just have to hope for the best as he reassembled the reduction gear. Worst case, it should last for a day or two.

However, for now *Sabine* was still a cripple. The heavy seas had caused the reduction gear cover to sway ominously despite all his attempts to constrain it. One tie-down strap had chafed through from the swaying. The cover had shifted enough to bend seven studs used to bolt it down to the reduction gear casing. It had taken Radisson's men the better part of two days to remove the damaged studs and manufacture new ones in *Sabine*'s machine shop. He was just starting to put the reduction gear back together.

— —

Admiral Sir Bruce Hardy had a dilemma. If he left Gibraltar too soon, he might need to return before making contact with Schröder. His destroyers only had a nominal four-thousand-mile range at cruising speed. Despite his objections, his fleet oilers were now carrying bunker oil from Aruba to the United Kingdom. If he waited until Schröder sailed, he might miss the German fleet altogether. Looking at the chart of the eastern North Atlantic, he had decided that the optimum place to intercept the Germans was off Cape Finisterre, at forty-three degrees north latitude, eleven degrees west longitude. That meant Force H had farther to steam than Schröder did. If he tried to compensate by running at the maximum speed of his heavy ships, the destroyers were certain to run out of fuel.

There was also the matter of the Italian Battle Fleet in La Spezia and Naples. Heading out into the Atlantic would leave the Straits of Gibraltar unguarded, with the possibility that they might try breaking out, joining Schröder. Hardy could not be in both places at once. Worse, he knew that Spaniards sympathetic to the Germans would quickly report whatever he did. He had to deceive both. As a devilish smile crossed his weather-beaten face, he ordered Force H to raise steam immediately. His fleet would sail at 1800 Greenwich Mean Time.

—▪—

The prisoner should have lost complete track of time by now. His watch had been taken when he was unconscious in sickbay; the lights remained on in his cell twenty-four hours a day; meals varied in time and type of food, but without any pattern detectable; and the guards changed at random intervals, never longer than two hours. He was never allowed to sleep more than twenty minutes at a time, yet every time he was awakened, a new set of guards were on duty. Everything possible had been done to leave him confused, exhausted, and bewildered.

Major Jenkins, though, was running out of time. If they were to get useful intelligence from this man, he had to act today. The guards continued their routine of reporting every time the prisoner started sleeping. Jenkins decided to act on the most recent report.

Dressing quickly, Jenkins descended deep into the bowels of *Argonne* to the brig and briefed the oncoming guards on their roles in the most epic drama of the prisoner's life. Now all he needed was a sign that the submariner might be dreaming.

The major did not have long to wait as he focused on his prisoner's moving eyelids. With a nod to the guards from Jenkins, the larger of the two shouted in German, "Herr Kapitän, tanker bearing one-seven-five degrees!"

The prisoner heard the report. He jumped out of his bed and ran to look—smashing headlong into the steel bars of his cell with a monumental thud. Stunned but still conscious, he fell back onto his aluminum-framed, mattress-covered rack.

Major Jenkins now shouted in German, "You lied to us! You are no torpedoman! Your rank is korvettenkapitän! You were the commanding officer of the U-boat!"

Blinking as if trying to focus through the pain and fatigue, the prisoner could only nod.

Jenkins continued slowly, allowing his words to sink in. "You lied, and because you did not tell the truth about your name, … your rank, …. or your service number …—you are a spy!"

The color, what there was of it, drained from the German's face, the dark circles under his eyes growing coal gray, the reddening pattern of the bars on his forehead fading, while his lips began to quiver almost in synchronization with his shaking hands. His shoulders slumped, and his midsection collapsed like a toy balloon with the air let out of it. Jenkins fought to control his own elation.

Again, slowly, as if a judge pronouncing sentence, the major added, "In accordance with the Geneva Convention, you will be executed!"

Jenkins, relishing his success, turned to leave, hiding the involuntary delight in his eyes.

In English, a weak "Wait," gurgled up from the prisoner.

Jenkins turned as if an afterthought had come at him. Confronting the smaller man, but still only a few inches from his bearded face, he snarled in English, "Oh, by the way, you will be hung at dawn. A firing squad is for honorable men."

"No!" the prisoner screamed. "I am Korvettenkapitän Hans Dieter Meier, commanding officer of the *U-179,* service number one-seven-four-two-nine-six. I tell you the truth; I swear it!"

With a sneer, Jenkins stared into the sunken eyes. "More lies. You are a spy, and we hang spies! The Geneva Convention requires combatants to tell the truth when captured, and you didn't."

With that, Jenkins turned and left.

When the major was safely out of earshot, the larger of the two marines—the one who had shouted the report of a tanker—snickered and said in German, "Stupid, arrogant Kraut!"

Both marines bore wicked smiles.

— —

Admiral Hardy's destroyers led the way out through the south entrance of the mole in Gibraltar Harbor. To the south of the entrance, his second carrier, *Splendid,* was sitting on the blocks in the Prince of Wales dry dock. He would miss her additional squadrons, but there was nothing that could be done to speed the repairs from the submarine torpedo that had damaged her starboard side. In a way, he was lucky he had managed to get her back to port.

High above, on the top of the rock, the 9.2 inch gun turret looked out on the strait. The admiral could see both the Moroccan coast and the Spanish town of Algeciras. Admiral Hardy was counting on the German spies in Algeciras to be watching every move he made. He was certain he would not be disappointed.

His light cruiser *Leonidas* cleared the mole, followed by *Renown,* *Repulse,* and *Ark Royal;* then they turned south in column. The sun was just beginning to set, and he knew he had timed his sailing perfectly. His destroyers formed an antisubmarine screen as the light was beginning to fade. Still visible, he turned his fleet east as if to embark on some mission against the Italians. Having him loose in "Mare Nostrum," as Mussolini referred to the Mediterranean, should be enough to convince the timid

Italian admirals to keep their battle fleet close to home. If they did not, Hardy had another surprise in store for the Italians.

— —

The conning station clock chimed four bells. The messenger of the watch began the same report that had been given since before the Civil War. "Captain, the officer of the deck sends his respects and reports the hour of twenty hundred."

Then he handed Sheppard the navigator's position report with the best estimate of the geographic location of *Argonne*. The position report included the latitude and longitude, but it also contained the ship's course and speed, as well as the basis for the estimated position. The last fixed position, or *fix*, was five days old, and they could be twenty or more nautical miles from the estimate.

Sheppard looked up to see his marine commander.

"Good evening, Major," Sheppard said. "How did the confrontation go?"

"My marines played their parts well, Captain. As I left, he was screaming his name, rank, and service number in English. Turns out he was indeed the commanding officer of the *U-179*."

"Well done, Major. We'll see if the next phase of your plan loosens his tongue even more."

— —

Admiral Hamilton was concerned. His staff navigator was standing in front of him explaining how he'd arrived at his estimated position. Hamilton could not find fault with the process, but something told him to be careful. His navigator was frank in the assessment of how far off he could be. It was all reasonable: the expanding circles he used to account for unknown currents, errors in the initial fix, and errors in the measurement of *Sabine*'s speed and gyrocompass course steered. His uneasiness stemmed from the size of the resulting error circle. His task force could be anywhere within that fifty-three-nautical-mile radius. It was probably not as bad as that in the east-west direction. Exact sunrise and set were not observable, but they appeared to be close to the predicted time, which meant his longitude estimate was not more than thirty or so miles off. There wasn't anything either of them could think of doing, other than praying for a break in the clouds to get a sun line or star sights.

— —

Sunderland "Don Yoke Charlie" danced to the buffeting of the full gale as Rupert Wythe-Jones attempted, unsuccessfully, to keep his cup of hot cocoa from spilling onto his flight suit.

"Suh, Sparks got something on radar!"

"Roger, Dawes; thank you!" Wythe-Jones shouted over the roar of the four Pegasus radial engines while stowing his mug in the gyrating "wardroom" under the flight deck.

He ricocheted from one piece of aircraft to the next as he lurched forward to the radar displays. It had taken him longer to find a convoy than he had planned; however, there laid out in neat columns on the scope in front of his face was the convoy. He could see every merchant and escort as a distinct white blip. He also saw something that made his blood run cold: another blip ten miles or so behind the last ship in one of the starboard columns of merchants. It did not seem to be trying to hurry back to station as an escort would if it were returning after having held down a submarine. No, this was smaller than the blips he took to be escorts—it was just shadowing the convoy, like … *a U-boat, calling the wolf pack together.*

Returning to the flight deck and the Sunderland's controls, Wythe-Jones first plugged in his throat microphone.

"Pilot to crew, we've found a convoy, but Gerry's found it too. Dawes, load depth bombs on both tracks and run them out, double quick."

"Roger, suh." Dawes said and then turned to his mates. "Double quick, right! Bloody officers, you'd think they'd bloody well know how long it bloody takes."

Those tracks ran out under the wings of the Sunderland to drop positions. A unique feature for these flying boats, it allowed complete selection of weapons from stores without either a leaky hull opening or air drag, but it was mostly hard manual work.

"Pilot to crew: we'll circle and come at Gerry from astern. Sparks, as we close, count down the range. If we can't see the U-boat, I'll drop when we should be over him."

There was little light; the new moon cycle would start on the fifteenth. Wythe-Jones would just have to trust Sparks to count down accurately and hope he sighted the wake or the sub itself. An attack would at least force the U-boat to dive, allowing the convoy to break contact.

Squadron Leader Wythe-Jones flew down the convoy's port side, hopefully far enough from the escorts to prevent the lookouts from detecting his engine noise—more importantly, outside the antiaircraft gun range of the warships. After all, mistakes had been made; if things went awry, this would not be the first time he had received "friendly" fire. Banking left and dropping to three hundred feet, he could just make out the white-capped waves on the ocean as he turned again to the convoy's course. His radar operator was calling the range down. "One thousand … eight hundred … six hundred … four hundred … lost contact!"

There it was: the swirl and stern of a diving U-boat. Wythe-Jones pickled off his bombs just before Sparks should have said zero. He had no idea whether he had hit it or missed, but as he climbed back up for altitude and turned to look, the blip was gone. He circled for a complete sweep with his radar and flew up to the starboard wing escort, flashing the day's recognition signal with his hand-held Aldis lamp. When the escort answered, he flashed a Morse message conveying what had transpired. He bid them Godspeed, as his fuel state demanded that the Sunderland turn for home.

He would enjoy waking Air Commodore Blackstone when he got back, to inform him how wonderfully this new centimeter radar performed.

— —

Johann Schmitt rubbed his black beard, trying to alleviate the itching. He ran his tongue over his yellowing teeth in a vain attempt to clean them. Perhaps he would use his newfound privacy to sneak a little water and brush them.

No, a captain must lead by example as much as by direction.

Schmitt paused, struck by the discipline that responsibility imposed on him at a time when he was the supreme authority on *U-179*. Regulations and traditions held him, but even more, he found himself constrained by a moral compass to do what was right.

Despite the contradiction, Schmitt was beginning to enjoy command. Morale was continuing to climb as they got ever closer to France. The machinist's mates were making as much progress as the U-boat's corkscrewing motion in this wretched weather allowed. Perhaps two more days would see completion of the diesel engine repairs. Yesterday, he had actually heard the men in the forward torpedo room singing. With luck, they might actually make Saint-Nazaire.

He had finally decided to inventory Meier's belongings, package them, and store them. The hardest part was that he did not know his captain's fate. Was he dead? It seemed likely. The water had only been about fifteen degrees Celsius. At that temperature, in two hours Meier would have died of hypothermia. It seemed unlikely that the Americans would see him, let alone rescue him, when one of their aircraft carriers was sinking. Schmitt said a prayer for his dead captain and lay down in the captain's bunk—yes, it was *his* bunk now—for a nap.

— —

As was his habit, Vizeadmiral Schröder awoke at what should have been the crack of dawn.

"What, still dark! Has the weather front finally arrived?"

As he stumbled to the starboard side of his cabin, the porthole beckoned. He peered at what should have been familiar shapes, barely outlined from the deeper gloom of the bulkhead. His ships—his fleet was all but invisible! What he could see of the *Graf Zeppelin* glistened from a passing squall.

"Wunderbar!"

Quickly dressing, he called for his chief of staff.

Fregattenkapitän Bodermann poked his head in the doorway.

"Ah, Fritz," Schröder said. "It is a gloriously bad day, is it not?"

"Yes, Herr Admiral, there is a solid overcast already, and the cloud layer is dropping. It should start raining continuously by 1600. Do you wish me to set the sailing time at 1500?"

"That would be good. I am concerned about our flagship, though. When we engage the Americans, everything will depend on aggressively closing the range and finishing them off quickly."

Fritz looked momentarily confused. "That is true, Herr Admiral; our limited ammunition supply for the heavy guns requires it."

"Konteradmiral Eisner might not pursue the Americans vigorously enough to prevent wasting shells. Perhaps we should transfer the flag to *Scharnhorst* and lead the battle cruisers ourselves."

"I must strongly protest, Admiral. *Scharnhorst* lacks the command facilities of *Graf Zeppelin*. Besides, before there can be a surface engagement, we must gain contact. Using the carriers for long-range searches should gain us that advantage. You need to be here to use that information quickly. Sending the scouting reports from our carriers to the battle cruisers will take time. That may make all the difference to which side launches the first air strike. What we learned from the Americans before the war confirmed that if one side can disable the other's carriers and keep their own operational, that side will win."

Schröder laughed. "Naïve Americans! They always feel compelled to write about their tactical discoveries. Very well, Fritz, we will stay on the *Graf Zeppelin*, but I want to keep the carriers close enough to maintain control of any surface battle."

"Jawohl, Herr Admiral." A faint expression of relief crossed the chief of staff's face.

"Fritz, why don't you join me for breakfast and send for the messages?"

"Thank you, Herr Admiral. I will call for them now."

—-—

Two burly marines grabbed Meier by the arms, yanking him awake as they roughly stood him before his accuser. Shaking his head to clear the last vestiges of sleep, Meier stared up at the muscular officer before him.

"On your feet, spy! It is time for your execution!" the officer shouted in German.

There were four marines in total, two with rifles fixed with wicked-looking long bayonets. The other two were holding Meier firmly, their strong grip biting into his arms as they tied his hands behind his back. A blindfold quickly followed, and they pushed him out of his cell.

Meier began to realize that they really were going to execute him. Well, at least he would get his Knight's Cross with Swords posthumously. He might not be there, but his parents, extended family—and yes, all of Germany—would know the glory of his achievement in sinking the American carrier. This war couldn't last much longer before the United States, alone and weakened, would sue for peace. Even if the *U-179* had been lost, the truth would come out, and he would be a hero of the Third Reich. His name, the name Hans Dieter Meier, would live on in glory for a thousand years.

The two marines holding his arms dragged him up one deck after another. It was hard to keep track of the number—perhaps seven. His guards appeared to make certain he fell frequently, stumbling on every obstruction. He banged his head on every hatch combing they went through. By the time they stopped climbing, Meier, bruised and in pain, had a trickle of blood running down his forehead.

Well, he thought, *a Knight's Cross with Swords must be earned*. If he had to suffer in the process, so be it.

When they finally stopped moving, the officer ripped the blindfold off. There, staring Meier in the face, was a noose with thirteen wraps to the knot. He looked around—this was no *Antietam*-class battle cruiser. There were too many antiaircraft mounts. He saw triple turrets abreast the bridge. No, this ship was much bigger. There were men everywhere, manning antiaircraft mounts. He had been wrong in his classification of the battle cruiser.

"I am never wrong! I am the best in the Kriegsmarine," Meier said aloud in German.

The two marines holding his arms then spun him around to face forward. As they did, Meier focused his eyes first on the *Raritan* and then the *Sabine*.

— —

As soon as they had manned battle stations, Bronco realized they were not going to be flying again today. He and his fellow pilots had spent most of the night going over the Kingfisher's characteristics and the ordnance on board *Argonne*. Bronco was not the type to admit defeat, but this time, he thought as he made his way up to the conning station, they had only one option, and it was dismal. He would have to temper his message to the Captain with the grim assessment that his only prospect was impossible—that against the antiaircraft defenses of the German battle cruisers, his squadron was powerless.

"Good morning, Mister Burdick, and how are you this fine Navy day?" McCloud asked, mimicking the now widely known routine greeting of the Captain's steward.

"Fine, thank you, Captain, but I haven't got any good news for you. My pilots and I hashed out the problem you gave me, and the only answer we came up with would be suicide if we tried it."

"What's your idea?" McCloud asked.

"Captain, the only bombs we have aboard are one-hundred pounders. They will just bounce off the main deck of any capital ship, perhaps damaging some AA mounts, but that would be it. The only other thing we have is depth charges. We thought that if we set them to twenty-five feet and dropped them next to the rudders or propellers, we might slow the Germans or cripple them. To get that good a placement, though, we would have to fly directly up to the target at low altitude, skipping the bombs off the water until they hit the ship's hull. With the antiaircraft armament those capital ships have, that would be suicide. We would never get close enough to drop."

"Flying with both depth charges set to twenty-five feet would not interfere with your ability to spot the fall of shells or scout would it?"

"Of course not, Captain. The only change from our normal procedures would be that both charges are set to the same depth."

"Very well, then set both depth charges to twenty-five feet, and let me think about the antiaircraft defenses. Perhaps I can come up with something."

With that, McCloud left his chair, walking out onto the open wraparound walkway to watch the theater developing on *Argonne*'s port signal bridge.

— —

By the time Rupert Wythe-Jones returned to RAF Pembroke Dock, debriefed his mission, and woke up Air Commodore Blackstone, it was too late to think about going home. He rang up Lois and apologized, even though he still was not sure what the plans were for the morning. Blackstone had said that Four-One-Five Squadron would be going back on operations soon and had told them that they would get a telex with the orders.

Even though annoyed by the early call, Blackstone was nonetheless delighted to hear how well the new centimeter ASV radar had worked. He promised to look into how the convoy had made out with Western Approaches Command to satisfy Wythe-Jones's curiosity, sharing Rupert's pessimism with the results of the attack. Blackstone promised to get RAF Headquarters working on the problem of illumination during night attacks, something the new radar had clearly made possible.

It did not take long before the telex started clattering away. Wythe-Jones's squadron was back on operations, with orders to take off and patrol the Bay of Biscay and western approaches at 1400. Unlike the normal wording, though, it directed that if his squadron detected a surface force, his Sunderlands were to stand off and continuously shadow. Just one problem: the weather was going to be horrid.

— —

Meier could not believe his eyes. There in front of him was the target that he had hit three times with G7e torpedoes. Each hit had been an explosion of three hundred kilograms of mostly TNT. Yet, there steamed his target—not listing, not burned, and certainly not deeper in the water.

His heart sank—so much for his dreams of immortal glory in the thousand-year Reich. No Knight's Cross with Swords would ever grace his neck. There would never be a ceremony, posthumous or otherwise, and certainly not in the presence of the Führer. Hitler would never even hear his name. Worst of all, he was now going to die at the end of a rope, like a common criminal, on the port yardarm. The black hood suddenly placed over his head left him alone with his thoughts. The noose was carefully but roughly placed around his neck and tightened with the knot behind his left ear.

"Any last words, spy?" the officer said in German, disgust dripping from every word.

"I am not a spy! I am Korvettenkapitän Hans Dieter Meier of the Kriegsmarine, serial number one-seven-four-two-nine-six. I am the commanding officer of the Type IX-B *U-179*, homeported in Saint-Nazaire, France. I am not a spy. I was in the uniform of the Kriegsmarine U-boat arm when captured. I lied to conceal my identity."

"Why should we believe you now? You are probably lying to try and save yourself." The officer continued in only a slightly less disdainful tone, "If you are not lying, tell me something only the captain would know."

"*U-179* left France on March 15 under radio silence. Our orders were to patrol off the entrance to the Chesapeake Bay and begin sinking merchant ships at twelve hundred Greenwich Mean Time on April 7 as part of Operation Beckenschlaeger," Meier said, trying to control the whimper in his voice.

"Any crewman would have known that."

"No, only the captain would know that there were thirty-four other boats assigned to the operation. All the Type IXs Admiral Dönitz could get together received assignments as part of Beckenschlaeger. Only the

Type IIs and Type VIIs remained behind to attack the convoys in the Atlantic. Vizeadmiral Schröder will sortie to raid the convoys while the U-boats attack the East Coast. You must believe me!"

"I will see if you are lying. We will let you live—for now—until we can check this preposterous story."

The noose was lifted from around Meier's neck and the black hood removed from his head. The marine guards then replaced the blindfold and manhandled him back deep into the bowels of the battle cruiser, slamming the cell door behind him without bothering to untie his hands. How long would they let him live? Meier could only guess.

— —

It had been all Major Jenkins could do to keep his composure and convince the German that he really was going to be hung. Jenkins knew the Geneva Convention required that as long as Meier was in uniform, any German uniform, when captured, he had to be treated as a prisoner of war, regardless of whether he told the truth or not. Meier clearly had not.

Jenkins took the five decks of ladders to the conning station two steps at a time—racing like a schoolboy, elated at the success of his ruse.

McCloud was waiting for Jenkins when he got to the conning station. "I watched from the windscreen. What did he say?"

"Captain, he told about the disposition of the U-boats in the Atlantic and the fact that Schröder is about to sortie. He gave up the boat's home port, when they sailed, and some of the details of an Operation Beckenschlaeger."

"Well done, Major! I don't know whether to put you in for a medal or an Academy Award. Please write down for me exactly what he said so that I can send it over to Admiral Hamilton. It will be his decision whether to break radio silence or not. Please also give me a list of all of your men who played a part in our charade. I want to write each one a letter of commendation."

— —

Admiral Hamilton had watched the mock execution through his binoculars. When the marine major had put the hood and noose on the prisoner, Hamilton wasn't sure whether he would have to convene a general court-martial and try Sheppard for murder or not. Soon after, though, the signal light on *Argonne* had started flashing with the best news he had received in days. Now the horns of a dilemma beckoned. If he broke radio silence to send what he believed to be vital intelligence, the German high-frequency, direction-finding network would surely pinpoint his location. If he did not, Admiral Ingersoll and the British Admiralty would not have Meier's revelation about Operation Beckenschlaeger and the redeployment of U-boats.

Hamilton was much too far out to send the information in one of his utility aircraft, even if the weather wasn't making such a launch risky. Not knowing his position could easily land his pilot in Ireland or over France, where the Luftwaffe would gain an easy kill. No, if he could not launch or recover a search, which was more important to him, he would not risk a launch to send information.

His task force was still a day away from where he wanted to intercept Schröder. It was a big ocean, and his ships could be anywhere within four hundred nautical miles of his located position by the time he arrived there. He had not provided any other locations to the German RDF network; Sheppard's intelligence meant no patrolling U-boats could have sighted him; and, hopefully, the Germans might not assume it was him. From what he knew, it seemed like the correct call to send the message.

Admiral Hamilton called his staff communications officer to start encoding the message.

— —

Vizeadmiral Schröder was ecstatic. The afternoon messages included reports from the German Embassy in Spain that Force H had left port yesterday afternoon and headed into the Mediterranean Sea. It could not have been a deception, since Schröder's fleet had not yet sailed. Admiral

Hardy would have to double back to engage him, and that would take too long. His fleet would be well into the Atlantic, raiding convoys, before those ancient battle cruisers and the *Ark Royal* could be within range of his forces.

Even better was the news that the inexperienced Americans had broken radio silence, and the efficient German listening posts had located their fleet five hundred miles south by west of Cape Finisterre. Now he knew where to find them. He outnumbered them two to one in every important category. Schröder would teach them a hard lesson. He would sail southwest toward Cape Finisterre and then northwest to attack the Americans from behind. They might be brave, but taking on his four superior battle cruisers and experienced air groups would be a fatal mistake.

It was time to go to his flag bridge and watch his fleet get underway. They needed to clear land by sunset, at which point he would change course from northwest to southwest. With luck, he would engage the Americans on the morning of the day after tomorrow.

— —

Four-One-Five Squadron assembled for briefing on the upcoming mission; rows of chairs were filled with men in sheepskin flying clothes in front of portable blackboards covered with the details. First up, the meteorologist began, not because his knowledge was more important, but for the simple reason that everyone would immediately pay attention. There were the typical grumblings about the bloody fools at 19 Group doing nothing to help their men find their way back to Pembroke Dock in the dismal weather expected before dawn. They also grumbled about the late takeoff. Common among all the various complaints voiced in the briefing hall was this question: exactly how effective a search did headquarters think possible at night in bad weather?

Then Wythe-Jones stood. As squadron leader and a pilot who led by example, he commanded instant respect. Silence followed as he began describing the mission and the vital importance of finding

Schröder's ships. With everyone's rapt attention, he began describing the new centimeter radar, pointing out how his crew was able to "see" the convoy laid out in front of them. He described the different sizes of blips between escorts and merchant ships and explained that the radar had even been able to distinguish the small blip of what he took to be a U-boat at almost forty miles. Wythe-Jones went into detail on coordinating the attack with the radar operator, not trying to imply that he had sunk the shadower; he only claimed to have driven him down. Hopefully, that would have been enough for the submarine to lose contact and allow the convoy's escape.

There were many questions, which took time to answer, but Wythe-Jones knew his squadron's success tonight depended on answering them all. When the questions finished, he added the best news of all: on the return to RAF Pembroke Dock, the radar had painted the southwest coast of Wales, not like a map, but clearly enough. Personally, he was not concerned about returning home.

Four-One-Five Squadron was late leaving for their patrol, but every man now understood the mission's importance and the advantages the new radar provided. Wythe-Jones decided to hold back two crews in reserve, thinning the coverage, but still enabling contact past the endurance of the first sorties, just in case they did manage to find Schröder's ships. If the weather were horrid, at least his boys would not have to worry about the Messerschmitts. Once the weather cleared, it would be a different story.

——

As Commander Kenny Radisson tried to straighten, several vertebrae popped—the inevitable result of catnapping on the steel deck plates of *Sabine*'s number one engine room for six whole days. He could not remember the last time he'd showered or brushed his teeth. Finally, though, everything was back together. At least, he and his men thought it was all back together through the fog of their caffeine-soaked senses. He ordered his men to start up the lubricating-oil system for the main engine and reduction gear. After a half hour, he shifted the oil strainers and had his machinists show them to him. There were some small pieces of bearing material, but not enough to stop his plan.

He next ordered the strainers reinstalled with fine muslin bags. The extra filtration was impossible while running the engine. However, just running the oil system with them in place would remove any dirt particles that might have entered the system while it was open. After four hours of carefully monitoring all sight-flow indicators and differential pressures, he again inspected the bags personally.

So far, so good, Radisson thought as he made the long climb to *Sabine*'s bridge.

It was after 2000 when he finally faced Captain Evans with a status report. He tried to convey to him that he would need to hold the shaft stationary with steam while his men removed the shaft-locking device. He was confident that the shaft could then windmill at the current eighteen knots. That would be the first test for any undetected misalignment of the tail shaft outside the hull. If it did rotate, he needed to let the engine freewheel for at least an hour with gland-sealing steam applied to unbow the turbine rotors. If the shaft did not rotate, the locking device would be reinstalled; there would be nothing more he could do to repair the engine. *Sabine* would remain a cripple, constrained to less than twenty knots, as any more speed could break the lock and risk flooding the engineering spaces as the rotating warped shaft tore open the seals that kept out the ocean.

— —

Sheppard couldn't remember the last time he had stretched. He had been living in the conning station chair except for the occasional head call, which he always followed with a shave and change of uniform. It seemed his leg was bothering him more now, and he rubbed it through his khaki pants. Doc Blankenship's aspirin wasn't touching the pain. A built-in barometer, the wounded leg seemed to react to every passing weather front, bringing agony in his left thigh. Would that ever change?

Since the weather had been bad, this latest pain must mean it would improve, though he could not tell this by scanning the sea. Tomorrow would bring a new moon, and the night was nearly absolute black. No stars, so it still had to be overcast.

The hourly true wind determinations also showed both a drop in the northeast wind's speed and a veering to the east. That would be good for gunfire and bad for air attacks. With the wind coming from the east, the carriers obviously would have to take that course into the wind in order to launch. If any enemy were suddenly discovered in that direction, the carriers would have to run directly at the danger when they were at their most vulnerable, with fueled and armed aircraft on deck. One shell exploding on the flight deck was all it would take to turn *Raritan* or *Sabine* into a cauldron of flame and exploding aircraft ordnance.

Conversely, the wind would clear the hot funnel exhaust and smokeless powder gases from the enemy's direction when *Belleau Wood* or *Argonne* fired. The distortion caused by the hot gas, like the heat waves rising from a radiator in winter, would bend the image, moving the target's apparent location from its true line of sight. It was enough to create another error. That could make the difference between a hit and a near miss at long range.

Sheppard was just about to doze off in his conning station chair when an idea hit him. He sent his orderly to wake Commander Roberts and request the latest copy of *Jane's Fighting Ships*, as well as the Office of Naval Intelligence publication on the characteristics of the German ships. If what he believed concerning the antiaircraft mounts of the *Scharnhorst* class of battle cruisers was true, he might have just thought of a way to solve Bronco's problem.

— —

Admiral Sir Bruce Hardy had reversed course as soon as the last light faded in the developing storm over the Straits of Gibraltar. He cleared Cape Saint Vincent before dawn, well outside the range of any land-based prying eyes even if the weather weren't awful. He was still not sure how he would deal with Schröder, and more than anyone else in his force, he knew England's fate hung in the balance.

Once clear of the towering cliffs of Europe's southeastern tip, Sir Bruce had been driving north all day along the Portuguese coast, but well outside visual range, at his destroyers' most efficient speed. Squalls and near-continuous rain had prevented the launch of any air reconnaissance, but it had also hidden him from the German Fw 200 Condors. One report from the French Resistance told him that Schröder had sailed with all four of his battle cruisers headed northwest at about 1600. Though probably accurate, the Admiral suspected Schröder was playing the same game he had. Northwest only took the Germans closer to the Home Fleet and the RAF. No, Schröder would turn to the southwest, with an intercept likely planned for the morrow.

Hardy knew his only real hope lay with the Swordfish biplanes on HMS *Ark Royal*. They did not pack much of a punch with their eighteen-inch torpedoes, but he just might get lucky and damage some of Schröder's ships badly enough that he would turn back.

He noted, too, that the wind was veering to the east. To be successful, he needed to stay well outside Spanish territorial waters. When he reached forty-three degrees north latitude, he would have to open the distance from Spain by heading west until he could turn *Ark Royal* and the rest of Force H into the wind for launching a search to the northeast. As much as he wanted to set up a patrol line east-west, this wind was going to keep him almost stationary as he ran east to launch and then west to open the coast. At the end of the air search or combat air patrol's endurance, he would have to turn back to the east and again run into the wind to recover aircraft.

The obvious answer was to divide his small force into two parts. That, however, would leave *Ark Royal* defenseless against even a destroyer's attack. No, he would keep his force together and protect the carrier. His battle cruisers were too badly outgunned to accomplish anything useful by themselves.

Wythe-Jones decided to keep the most dangerous search sector for himself. His crew was rested enough to be safe, and if judgment of risk versus reward was necessary, he wanted to make those decisions himself. His Sunderland "Don Yoke Charlie" had taken off at about 1700 hours GMT, flying southwest until passing Land's End and then turning south. The new ASV radar gained contact on the French coast at about 1830, quickly followed by the Île D'Ouessant. He wanted to stay more than sixty miles offshore, out of range of the German Freya radar network. As briefed, the weather was atrocious.

About 1900, his radar operator began reporting multiple contacts. Wythe-Jones turned over the flight controls to his copilot, wanting to have a look for himself. He saw six large contacts in a column, with twelve smaller ones in a semicircular pattern about a mile and a half ahead of the leading ship—probably escorts. Farther away were six contacts fanning out to the east southeast.

Scouting cruisers?

These contacts had to be the German surface fleet they were after. Wythe-Jones directed his radio operator to begin enciphering a contact report. "Six large contacts in column, eighteen smaller in vicinity forty-eight degrees thirty minutes north latitude, five degrees thirty-five minutes west latitude, at 1910 hours; course southwest, speed eighteen knots."

As soon as it was ready, he sent it off to 19 Group Headquarters. Another message to RAF Pembroke Dock alerted one of his standby crews for a dawn takeoff and rendezvous in Schröder's vicinity. Wythe-Jones was determined to maintain contact even if it meant losses to the Bf 109s when the weather improved.

It took three attempts before 19 Group Headquarters received the message clearly. They deciphered it and telexed it to RAF Headquarters near London and then, after a slight delay, the RAF sent it to the Admiralty. Enciphering with a different code held by the Royal Navy took time before retransmission by high-frequency radio to the fleet. That transmission did not happen until about 0400, by which time Schröder had moved over 125 nautical miles.

—◼—

At some point, the Admiralty, figuring the Americans might want this information, sent a copy to the naval attaché at the American embassy. Recognizing its importance immediately, the attaché whisked it to the embassy coding room at 0900 GMT. Then it went by transatlantic cable to the State Department in Washington. The State Department received it at about 0515 local, where decoding took more time; then they waited for a naval liaison officer to arrive. Also recognizing its importance, that lieutenant promptly sent it by teletype to Naval Headquarters Washington, where it was encoded and sent out on a fleet broadcast at 1015 Washington time—1515 GMT. Twenty hours' time late, it was utterly useless to Admiral Hamilton.

CHAPTER 8

CONTACT

Commander Kenny Radisson had finished his report to Captain Evans and received a heartfelt "Well done!" The testing of the number one shaft had gone as well as anyone with a technical background could have expected. In engine room number one, every machinist mate—although tired, grimy, and unshaven—cheered when Radisson called the bridge on the 21MC. "Ready to answer bells on all main engines!"

Sabine, as far as anyone knew, was no longer a cripple. There was a slight vibration aft with the application of power to number one shaft that Radisson recognized as new, probably related to the torpedo damage and probably in the number one propeller or tail shaft. His professional opinion, as he had relayed to the Captain, was that *Sabine* needed to go into dry dock, but he was confident that the tail-shaft bearing would last for a few weeks, which should get them back to Norfolk.

The only problem was that everyone he'd met in the passageways leading to his stateroom had wrinkled their noses and looked at his week-old beard with disgust. Now it was time to go to his cabin and solve those problems with a Hollywood shower, shave, and clean uniform. No, he was going to get some sleep in his own bunk, between sheets, after the shave. The clean uniform could wait until morning general quarters.

—-—

Alone in his sea cabin aft of the flag bridge, Admiral Hamilton was having a sleepless night. He shouldn't have been, though, as he knew *Sabine*'s repairs were complete. As soon as the weather permitted, she would be launching a combat air patrol in addition to a search by Scouting Squadron Eleven out to 250 miles. It certainly appeared that the weather was improving. The wind had veered to the east, dropping to only about twenty knots. The fuel state of his destroyers, unfortunately, still weighed heavily on his mind. With the bad weather, he had been unable to arrange refilling their tanks from his heavy ships. They were down to only a third of their capacity from yesterday's noon fuel reports. His carriers had hardly used any aviation gasoline or ordnance. Task Force Forty-Eight had not engaged a German force, so his magazines remained filled with powder and shells.

Aside from the fuel issue, he could not explain to himself the source of his unease, but it was there nonetheless as he tossed and turned the night away. Every hour brought them nearer his planned interception point—but were the Germans moving faster than he had expected?

— —

Sheppard had found what he was looking for. Both the unclassified *Jane's Fighting Ships* and the classified Office on Naval Intelligence report on German warships had listed the heavy antiaircraft armament of the *Scharnhorst*-class battle cruisers as twenty-four 10.5 cm/65 SK C/33. What that meant to Sheppard was twelve open mounts with the gun crews unprotected by shields. The 15 cm twin mounts were a different story. Though armored, they were not a threat to aircraft. The two publications differed in the numbers and types of light antiaircraft guns; however, they too were all open, as expected. He had only been concerned about the possibility of protection to the heavy antiaircraft mounts.

A slow smile formed on Sheppard's face. He was sure he had the answer to Bronco's problem. Whether they would ever need it was a different matter.

— —

Sir Bruce had the reports from both the French Resistance and Four-One-Five Squadron. The staff navigator plotted them and projected Schröder's advance through noon. The German carriers and battle cruisers would still be too far away for any kind of a night attack in the few remaining hours of darkness. Besides, it was new moon—too dark for the plane handlers and pilots to safely spot aircraft on *Ark Royal*'s flight deck and then fly off.

At dawn, he could launch the Swordfish fitted with long-range tanks, but if the weather was good enough for that, it was good enough for Schröder to have a combat air patrol of Bf 109s. The only word to describe what would happen to his aircrews then would be *slaughter*. He could launch his Fulmar fighters with the Swordfish, but their range was more limited. The Fulmars were also no match for the Messerschmitts. Sacrificing his fighter aircraft would at best create a diversion that might allow some Swordfish to launch their torpedoes before eventual destruction. Without his Fulmars, it was inevitable that Force H would be discovered by the Focke-Wulf Condors. Schröder's Stukas would then make short work of *Ark Royal* and his battle cruisers.

Admiral Hardy needed to preserve his force. If the Italians forced the Straits of Gibraltar and joined with the French and Germans, on paper they had the force needed to defeat the Home Fleet. Without his small force, there was nothing to stop that. It was clear that he could not stop Schröder directly.

Perhaps maintaining contact would be enough. His radar was better. He could vector his Fulmars to intercept any German searches. It would not be enough for Schröder to know that he was in the vicinity to initiate a strike of Stukas. Keeping track of Schröder would allow the Admiralty to reroute convoys with sufficient foreknowledge. The flaw in that plan was Schröder's scouting line. Those scout cruisers created too broad a front to miss a slow-moving convoy.

If he were Schröder, what would he do with his Bf 109s—cover everything weakly or cover his main force in strength?

—-—

Sheppard had dozed off in the conning station chair again. He was back in *Shenandoah*'s command tower, where Quartermaster Jacob's lifeless body sprawled on the deck, a pool of red spreading from beneath his tattered dungarees. The pulsing stream of blood from the boatswain's mate's arm socket splashed against the inner curved bulkhead of the armor. The ship's wheel, helm, and binnacle were a mangled maze of shined brass, bronze, and steel. Severed electrical cabling dangled from the overhead. His left leg—

"Captain, Captain!" Joe Archinbald cried, shaking his arm to get his attention.

Sheppard sat bolt upright, rubbing his eyes while he cleared his senses. Had he said anything? Would Archinbald suspect?

"Captain, the phone talker reported that the SK radar has detected a bogey bearing zero-one-zero degrees true, range 128 nautical miles."

"What time is it?" Sheppard said, still in the grip of his nightmare.

"Captain, zero-four-twenty-six," Archinbald answered without a hint of concern for a dream that might have been terrifying his Captain.

"Does CIC have a plot on what this bogey is doing?" Sheppard asked, rising to his feet and heading toward the chart table, only to realize that it would not contain the plotted information.

"Captain, the contact approached from the northeast, turned right, and now is flying on a course of two-nine-five at a speed of about a hundred and fifty knots."

"Has the bogey been reported to CTF Forty-Eight?"

"No, sir. I wanted to tell you first."

"Very well."

Sheppard grabbed a signal pad and dashed off a report. He handed it to the messenger of the watch, looked at the bulkhead clock, and directed Archinbald to man battle stations.

— —

Admiral Schröder had every reason to be pleased. The intermittent squalls and low clouds were prefect for concealing him from the British air patrols in the Bay of Biscay. There were no indications of British radar on his intercept receivers. The squalls had even allowed him to escape the Royal Navy submarines that he had rightfully suspected were positioned off Brest, waiting for a chance to cripple one of his heavy ships. The weather was too foul for flight operations from his carriers yet, but he had arranged with the Luftwaffe to send out an augmented patrol of long-range Focke-Wulf Fw 200s. These modified prewar airliners had a combat radius of over a thousand miles and a cruising speed of about two hundred miles per hour. With any luck and a few breaks in the clouds, they would help him find the convoys.

Even without the help of the Condors, he had his scouting line. He had sent them ahead on a hundred-kilometer front to find the American fleet. With Force H safely occupied in the Mediterranean, that lone American carrier and two battle cruisers were the only ships that could interfere with his plans. All he had to do was find them, and he would quickly brush them aside.

— —

Admiral Hamilton was being snooped. Even though *Sabine*'s CXAM air-search radar had not detected it yet, the air contact reported by *Argonne* had to be a Luftwaffe search out of France. The weather was marginal at best for flight operations, but the staff meteorologist had predicted that the cloud ceiling was going to rise as the morning wore on, with improving visibility. Hamilton decided to order both carriers to ready a CAP of F4Fs and *Sabine* a search by eighteen SBDs. This time, he was not going to arm them with five-hundred-pound general-purpose bombs; cloud cover would preclude any dive-bombing. He did not want to tempt his pilots into a heroic but stupid action that would only have the effect of losing contact. He needed intelligence of Schröder's location more than anything else.

Colchester's signal lamp began urgently flashing a message for the flagship.

— —

Squadron Leader Wythe-Jones and his crew had been lazily carving figure eights in and out of the rainsqualls north-northeast of Schröder for almost eight hours. The constant turbulence was more tiring than the need to keep a lookout. Flying the Sunderland in the soup while relying almost exclusively on instruments was exhausting. At least the weather prevented the carriers he was shadowing from launching any fighters now that the sun was beginning to reflect off the higher clouds.

How wonderful it would be when the next Sunderland relieved him in an hour, taking over shadowing duties. Would Lois understand if he went straight to bed once he got home?

A tap on the arm alerted him, yanking him back to reality. "Suh, Sunderland Apple-Freddy reports another group of ships," his radio operator shouted above the roar of the four engines.

"Thanks, Sparks," Wythe-Jones yelled back as he took the decoded message.

"Six large ships with many others heading zero-nine-zero at eighteen knots, forty-three degrees thirty minutes north, fifteen degrees twelve minutes west."

It could not be a convoy, Rupert thought. It was heading east at well over a convoy's maximum speed of eleven knots. Perhaps it was Force H returning from a sweep in the Atlantic for German raiders. The Admiralty never did let Coastal Command know where the fleet was.

— —

Dolf Hamilton had to act fast. *Colchester* was reporting skunks (unknown surface contacts) bearing zero-six-eight degrees true from her at a range of forty-two thousand yards. Task Force Forty-Eight was heading almost directly at them at eighteen knots, while both of his tender aircraft carriers were readying planes on their flight decks. He had to get them away to safety and get his heavy ships detached to deal with the contacts.

Grabbing the TBS radio microphone, Hamilton began issuing orders, foremost directing *Colchester* to shadow the contacts and not close any farther. If he could maintain the element of surprise, the growing light on the eastern horizon would silhouette his enemy on the skyline, giving his optics a priceless advantage.

He'd direct Admiral Ray Calhoun to take control of *Belleau Wood, Argonne,* the four light cruisers, and Destroyer Squadron Thirty. Those ships should be sufficient for Calhoun to counter any threat to the task force. Hamilton could trust Admiral Calhoun to extricate his ships from the formation in the dark without causing collisions. Until those ships were clear, Hamilton dared not issue an order for his carriers, cruisers, or the remaining destroyer squadron to reverse course and reform. The only thing he could do was slow down.

I have to keep my carriers clear!

— —

Ray Calhoun was leisurely drinking a second cup of coffee (black and bitter, of course) in flag plot on the *Belleau Wood* when Admiral Hamilton's voice, issuing orders, boomed over the TBS speaker. *Belleau Wood*'s signalmen had not alerted Calhoun to the flashing light signal from the *Colchester*. Calhoun was clueless as to where the threat was or what it was. *Belleau Wood*'s radar operators weren't reporting any contacts. Speed of action, though, was critical.

He lunged, grabbing his communications officer. "Make to *Argonne*: 'Follow me!'" he barked, knowing full well that McCloud would do the right thing. At least he would have both battle cruisers together for whatever it was he would have to accomplish. Then he yanked the TBS microphone from its overhead mount. "Interrogative skunks?"— assuming that Admiral Hamilton's sudden direction could only be caused by the appearance of surface contacts just as Admiral Hamilton ordered the task force to slow.

The single voice-radio circuit made a hash out of both transmissions. No one could understand the gibberish broadcast into every command space in the task force. Both admirals recognized what had happened to the voice radio, and both tried to pass their message again, with the same devastatingly confusing result. Admiral Calhoun gave up. Admiral Hamilton did not.

— —

Sheppard knew exactly what was happening, from the time he had watched *Colchester*'s signal lamp to the point of listening to the two admirals step on each other's radio transmissions. He heard Admiral Hamilton's final order to slow to ten knots but surmised it did not apply to Admiral Calhoun's forces. Reading the flashing-light message from *Belleau Wood* that directed him to follow her—but, thankfully, not specifying a distance to maintain—Sheppard instinctively formed a battle plan. Calhoun's order suited him just fine. The greater the tactical freedom he had, the better. He would not immediately turn toward *Belleau Wood* until *Sabine* had dropped behind.

As he watched, *Colchester* turned to starboard. Barely visible against the faintest of horizons, she started signaling again. Much longer this time, the message read, "Four large skunks in column heading west, bearing zero-six-five, range four-zero-five-hundred yards, smaller contacts in formation." This could only be Schröder's battle cruisers. Having reached Cape Finisterre, they had turned west to break out into the Atlantic. Schröder must be keeping his carriers behind the battle cruisers for protection.

Sheppard turned to his JA phone talker and ordered, "Guns, Captain, load armor piercing. Target bears vicinity zero-six-zero degrees true, range in excess of five-zero-thousand yards."

With that one order to Chuck Williamson, every JA talker on *Argonne* let the watchstanders in their vicinity know that this battle stations was different.

Next, Sheppard turned to his 1JV phone talker. "Engineering, Captain, light-off all boilers. Prepare for maximum speed."

Now everyone in the boiler rooms, engine rooms, and auxiliary machinery spaces knew that *Argonne* was preparing for a fight.

Finally, Sheppard turned back to the JA talker. "Officer of the Deck, Captain, antiaircraft gun crews forward of the bridge and aft of the superstructure lay below the third deck."

If he did not get them under cover before the eighteen-inch guns fired, they would be roasted alive.

— —

No longer trusting the TBS, Ray Calhoun was firing off flashing-light messages as fast as his staff officers could write and relay them to *Belleau Wood*'s signal bridge. The next message went to *Burlington* to form on *Colchester*, a thousand yards astern of her. Calhoun wanted those two cruisers to shadow the enemy from the enemy's southern flank. Until *Belleau Wood* and *Argonne* gained contact themselves, those two light cruisers were the only way he was going to get any information on the enemy course, speed, or disposition. If his light cruisers were discovered and engaged, Admiral Calhoun had to have another method of maintaining contact. It was still too dark to launch aircraft.

Well, light cruisers are expendable.

Hopefully, he could engage before the Germans sank them.

His other two cruisers, *Sioux City* and *Bellingham,* were less than fifteen hundred yards from his battle cruisers. Calhoun had to clear them out of the way to enable his big ships freedom of maneuver. Another message directed *Bellingham* to form a column behind *Sioux City* and proceed to the northern flank of the enemy at "best speed." An overall plan of engagement was forming in his mind. With a little luck, once on station, his two groups of light cruisers could stay with the enemy formation, shadowing by radar—if their captains were intelligent— regardless of what direction the enemy turned, while remaining invisible with the dark western horizon behind them.

That left the eight destroyers of DESRON 30. With his cruisers running at high speed, he wouldn't have to be concerned about U-boats. More importantly, Calhoun had to keep the destroyers close to counter any torpedo attack by the German light forces. Another consideration was not having the destroyers' funnel gases in the line of sight between his battle cruisers and the enemy. Those swirling clouds of superheated gas would create distortions, degrading his gunnery. Admiral Calhoun directed the squadron commander to split into divisions and keep both on the disengaged bow of *Belleau Wood*. If the admiral needed them to repel an attack or make one of their own, they would be immediately available.

Barely discernible, *Bellingham*'s stern sank lower as a phosphorescent glow in her wake marked her acceleration. Calhoun had a moment to think about exactly how he intended to fight an enemy that outnumbered him. He had the element of surprise, yes. His enemy was in a column, coming at him with ships armed with four twin turrets—two forward and two aft. If he took *Belleau Wood* and *Argonne* across the front of the enemy column, Schröder would only have his forward turrets to fight with until the German admiral turned. Keeping his broadside facing Schröder, Calhoun would have six triple eighteen-inch turrets facing Schröder's eight twins. Initially, he would have the advantage in firepower. Concentrating on the leading enemy battle cruiser, *Belleau Wood* and *Argonne* might be able to disable it before Schröder turned. Then the odds would be three to two for the slugfest. All he needed to do was send one more message to Sheppard. "Concentrate fire on leading enemy battle cruiser until disabled!"

— ·—

High above Sheppard, with his head outside the hatch of the main battery director, Lieutenant John Hamblen had the best view of anyone for the unfolding action. From a height of 172 feet above the water, he could see the horizon nearly thirty thousand yards away. If his target had a height of more than one hundred feet, then Hamblen could see it when it was fifty-two thousand yards away. The only problem was that the optics in the Mark 38 director could not gather enough light to see mastheads in the predawn twilight. Hamblen had discovered this during the dawn battle stations as they were coming across the Atlantic and brought something better with him to his current perch.

Using the sixteen-power long glass, he could make out the mastheads of four contacts as he stood on his seat looking out of the director, supporting the telescope with his elbows on the armored hatch.

"Guns, Spot One, four mastheads in sight," he called into his sound-powered phones for Chuck Williamson in the armored conning tower.

This was no different from all the practices that he had been involved with. Barely audible above the wind was the soft whirring of the radar-antenna drive motors shifting the phases of the transmitting polyrods back and forth. It was all so familiar, comforting, and reassuring that he had done this successfully dozens of times before.

But it *was* different. These were real ships with real crews. How many men ate and slept beneath those mastheads? How many would die when *Argonne*'s two-ton shells crashed into their spaces, exploding in a rain of red-hot fragments? His gut began to churn with a sudden urge to find a head.

— —

Senior Chief Hancock had received all the reports that turret II was manned and ready. His 1JC (weapons control) phone talker had passed the order from gunnery to load armor-piercing shells. Below the senior chief's location on the shell decks and magazines, over a hundred men slaved, parbuckling the two-ton shells into hoists and sweating as they carried 110-pound bags of smokeless nitro-cellulose powder across the powder-handling rooms deep in *Argonne*'s bowels to feed the insatiable powder hoists.

With the shell and powder hoists filled, it was now time for Major Jenkins to command, "Load!"

Spanning trays were lowered into alignment with breeches and rammers thrust shells with the force of a locomotive, seating the shells in the rifling of the nine eighteen-inch barrels with a clang heard by every man aboard. *Hell's bells!* defined the thoughts of more than a few. How many of them would die? they wondered, certain in the knowledge that German bells were ringing as well. With rammers withdrawn, four bags of powder were rolled into the spanning tray, spread apart so that four more could roll, and then all eight were delicately pushed by the rammer into the breech. Pushing too fast or hard could ignite the black-powder patch on the bag ends, which would incinerate every man in the gun chamber and destroy the turret.

Withdrawing rammers signaled the raising of spanning trays, and breech plugs swung upward, rotating into locked position. Gun captains signaled ready, allowing the fire-control system to take dominion over each of the two-hundred-ton wielders of death.

— —

Sheppard was the only man on board who did not have a specific task to occupy himself. Over three thousand others were busy. He watched from his chair, alone with his thoughts, idly watching the turrets swing in the enemy's direction. It all seemed so familiar, with the clang of shot seated in bore further reminding him of the last time he had heard the nine bells of a battle cruiser readying for a fight. Like fingers seeking to touch objects in the dark, barrels rose, quickening it seemed, seeking the distant enemy. Sequentially they settled together, aligned and ready. Events were rushing toward inevitable violence. Only he had the luxury of time to think through the next action: What could go wrong? How would he react under fire?

He was also one of the few men on board who knew the answer to the last question. He had felt the gnawing fear of the enemy, listened to the supersonic boom and whoosh of shells passing close by, been drenched by the mountainous columns of water thrown up by near misses, seen the blood, and heard the screams of men amid the rending steel of hits. Almost everyone else on board had yet to experience those horrors.

Sheppard envied his men their innocence.

— —

Admiral Hamilton raced up to the flag bridge of *Sabine* in time to see *Belleau Wood* turn to port. *Argonne* was also turning and accelerating to fall in astern of her sister ship. Both *Sioux City* and *Bellingham* were ahead of *Belleau Wood* and opening from her as their speed continued to increase. Barely discernible in the predawn light, *Argonne*'s main battery turrets swung to starboard as she turned and the big guns elevated. Hamilton was gaining confidence that he would save his tender carriers, which would be able to launch in less than a half hour.

Hamilton knew enough about a surface action to realize that half an hour was an eternity. Thirty or more salvos could decide the fate of England. If Calhoun failed, then what? He would have to run back at the Germans to launch. A strike group to damage the enemy would take an hour at least to prepare.

Too long …

Those Germans would run him down. His carriers would be flaming wrecks before any of his dive-bombers or torpedo planes left their decks. No, it all depended on Calhoun and Sheppard.

It was time to turn his carriers away from the threat and run!

— —

Argonne's surface lookouts, located two decks below Hamblen, were reporting mastheads bearing zero-six-eight. The SG radar operator adjacent to the conning station reported skunks on the same bearing, at a range of 47,500 yards. CIC designated the ships of the enemy column as skunks "Able," "Baker," "Charlie," and "Dog."

Sheppard felt they had enough light to support one more action, so he called Art Roberts on the 21MC.

"Prepare to launch aircraft," he ordered.

The two Kingfishers on the catapults had to be either launched or jettisoned. They were too great a fire hazard to remain on board unless all their fuel was drained and ordnance removed. Even then, if the situation dictated turret III firing in their direction, the gun blast and heat would turn them into scrap. Loath to waste the aircraft, Sheppard took Bronco at his word and decided to launch with only the faintest of horizon visible.

Bronco must have anticipated the decision. Almost immediately, Sheppard heard the starting cartridges fire and the cough and roar of the Pratt & Whitney engines over the increasing moan of the air parting around *Argonne*'s tower as she accelerated.

Chuck Williamson called on the 21MC, "Tracking Skunk Able!" he said, indicating that he was ready to open fire, politely goading Sheppard to give the order.

The JA phone talker relayed, "Ready to launch aircraft," which was quickly followed by the same report from Art Roberts on the 21MC. Without direction from Admiral Calhoun, Sheppard took it on himself to order the Kingfishers aloft.

First Mustang Zero-One and then Mustang Zero-Five shot off the catapults, engines screaming, clawing the heavy predawn air to gain flying speed. Both flashed past the secondary conning station, blue flames visible in the predawn light from the exhaust pipes of their Wasp Junior radial engines.

Sheppard went to the TBS microphone and passed a message using Admiral Calhoun's call sign. "Buccaneer, this is Panther. Request permission to open fire."

— —

Try as he could without rudder orders, Ray Calhoun had been unable to convince Kevin Bailey to rely on his people to do their jobs. Even though he rode aboard *Belleau Wood* and Bailey knew his orders before *Argonne* even received the messages, Bailey's meddling in detail caused his flagship to lag far behind her sister ship in executing his orders. There was nothing more Calhoun could do about it now. His coaching while they crossed the Atlantic had made little difference, as Bailey continued his micromanagement and his crew remained obstinate laggards near the point of insubordination.

Admiral Calhoun was inside the flag level of *Belleau Wood*'s armored command tower, with a 330-degree panoramic view, when he heard Sheppard McCloud's request. *Belleau Wood*'s turrets were just beginning to train to starboard as her eighteen-inch guns elevated in no particular order—haphazard in a stunning display of training inconsistencies.

For better or worse, he had to concentrate on his own duties. Calhoun knew that in the dim light, no one could see the color of the shell splashes in the distance. Each of the two battle cruisers had an assigned dye loaded into the windscreens of the armor-piercing projectiles. *Argonne*'s splashes would look red; *Belleau Wood*'s green. Without the ability to see the color, it made sense to spread the salvos of his battle cruisers in time. That way, each could differentiate theirs from the salvo splashes of their sister ship. If the gunnery officers confused the sets of splashes, they would keep imposing more errors in the target solution rather than removing them. The shells of each succeeding salvo would land farther away instead of closer.

Calhoun figured that it should take less than a minute for Kevin Bailey to be ready. He estimated the flight time of the shells to the target as ninety seconds at this range. If the salvos from his ships landed more than thirty seconds apart, it would be easy for the main-battery director officers to "spot" the fall of their own shells and not their sister ship's.

He went to the TBS microphone. "This is Buccaneer. Commence firing!"

— —

What had been the result of the earlier confusion on the TBS? Would his commanding officers be able to recognize whose voice belonged to which admiral? Dolf Hamilton heard the order to commence firing and decided that Ray Calhoun should not need the voice-radio circuit in the immediate future. He waited what seemed like an eternity, but actually no more than thirty seconds, to be sure before grabbing the microphone.

The first order to his remaining ships was, "Immediate execute, turn one-seven-zero."

That would turn them all at once to a course away from Schröder's battle cruisers. Could he get far enough to the south to avoid detection by Schröder as Calhoun led to the north, if his heavy ships failed to stop the Germans? His next order was to increase speed to twenty-seven knots, opening the distance as quickly as he could yet leaving a margin of excess speed for his antiaircraft cruisers and destroyers to take station on *Sabine* and *Raritan*.

Sabine, designated as the formation guide, hoisted the "zero" flag—white with five blue crosses—to indicate she was on station. *Raritan* took station three thousand yards astern. Both carriers would thus have some freedom of maneuver and sufficient air space for flight operations. He ordered a formation axis of 180 degrees so that when he turned the formation into the east wind for launching aircraft, the carriers would be on each other's beam with clear areas for the air groups to form. He positioned his two armored cruisers between the two carriers so that the four ships formed a diamond. The four antiaircraft light cruisers he positioned fifteen hundred yards on the beams of his carriers. Finally, he put Destroyer Squadron Twenty-Eight in a circle of five thousand yards radius from the center of the square. They would have to deal with the scout cruisers until his armored cruisers could close. He was moving much too fast for a sonar search but not fast enough to avoid a lucky submarine. It was a risk he would have to take until everyone was on station to increase speed further.

Had he forgotten something? It was a new feeling, this notion of real death and destruction; yet, though he was in as much danger as the others—the staff and crew of *Sabine*—only his orders or lack of foresight would kill or maim them all.

With his immediate plan in motion, he silently prayed for Calhoun to impose a quick and devastating victory.

—•—

The echo from Calhoun's order had not even died away. "Guns, Captain: commence firing!" Sheppard passed on the 21MC to Chuck Williamson in the armored command tower.

"Guns, roger," Commander Williamson acknowledged and turned to his 1JC phone talker, passing the order to the assistant gunnery officer in the main-battery plotting room located beneath CIC, ten decks below him.

Joe Archinbald heard that order from his phone talker and ordered, "Commence firing" to the fire controlman standing at the Mark 41 Stable Vertical. The petty officer closed the salvo-firing key to alert all turret personnel to the impending blast. Then he closed the automatic firing key. Shaped like a pistol grip with a trigger, it signaled the Mark 1 Ford analog computer to fire the guns.

Sheppard heard the firing alarm just in time to shut his eyes. Like a giant photographer's flash, only much longer, the night was turned to day in *Argonne*'s vicinity. Sheppard was caught off guard by the duration of the flash; it was much longer than that from the sixteen-inch on *Shenandoah*. Great clouds of white-hot incandescent gases exploded from the muzzles of all nine eighteen-inch guns, formed first into a spray, then expanding mushrooms, as each turret's merged into a rising, swirling mass of flame. The water beneath the flash boiled and frothed from the shock wave as the blast overpressure touched the sea. Sheppard could only imagine what everyone else in the open could feel: the heat on their faces from the expanding propellant gases as three sets of three dull red dots arced away, the heated bases of the projectiles and lit tracers making them visible in the predawn. The noise was more of a deafening, long, exaggerated, whoosh than the sharp crack of a rifle. Personnel on the weather decks could hear the sonic boom from the shells echo off the sea and *Belleau Wood*.

As quickly as the light had come, it was gone, replaced by the acrid smell of smokeless powder, steam from the ocean's surface, and the burned oil that had coated the gun barrels before they were fired. No sooner had the blast dissipated than the great guns started to drop as quickly as the elevation lead screws could turn, until the guns reached their loading angle. Barely visible in the predawn, an innocuous white puff of smoke appeared at each muzzle as the bore-clearing air blast removed any remaining embers of powder bags. The clang of new shells ramming home replaced the eerie silence imposed on deafened ears as gun captains raced to reload.

At that moment, John Hamblen, still looking out of the armored hatch of the forward main-battery director screamed "No-o-o-o!" into his 1JC sound-powered phone. The shout was loud enough that even Sheppard heard him, recognizing his voice four decks below as he stood at the starboard windscreen of the conning station.

— —

Off to the south-west, a climbing aircraft caught the morning light peeking beneath the cloud cover. Immediately, a sharp-eyed lookout on the second ship in the column called out, "Aircraft bearing red one-five."

The officers on the open compass platform lifted their binoculars to look at the aircraft that had appeared with no warning from the radars. It was obviously a floatplane, not a flying boat like a British Walrus. It only had one central float, unlike the twin floats of a German Arado 196. That left the officers puzzled, until the aircraft turned away from the ships. The thirteen horizontal stripes alternating red and white on the moveable part of the vertical stabilizer, with the large white stars containing a red circle and an overall blue background on wings and fuselage, identified the aircraft as American.

"Flash bearing red two-zero," one of the lookouts sang out.

Had the Americans made contact with Schröder? Was he farther to the west than Sir Bruce Hardy had anticipated?

Turning to his flag lieutenant, Hardy ordered, "Flags, make to *Leonidas*, 'Investigate flash bearing two-five-zero.'"

Nine mountains of white water began to rise more or less around the light cruiser *Leonidas* a thousand yards ahead. As splashes climbed ever higher and wider, Admiral Hardy and his flag captain stood stunned when the sonic booms of the arriving shells reached their ears—all nine merged into a single extended crunching sound. Then the boom of the distant guns could be faintly heard. The splashes continued to grow and touched the sun's rays, where they turned from dull white to red. Over five hundred feet high, they marked the impact points of what both officers believed must be eighteen-inch or larger guns. The solid spray slowly dissipated, replaced by transparent pink mist.

They were under attack by those bloody colonials!

— —

I knew it! Chuck Williamson thought.

He should never have put John Hamblen in the forward main-battery director. Hamblen's nerve had broken in the first real engagement that *Argonne* had fought. It would take time to get anyone up there to replace him. Williamson should have insisted that they not put a "weak sister" in such a demanding position, even if he was the son of CINCUSFLT. Captain Leland had caved in to the four-star admiral's pressure, and now they were all going to pay dearly for it.

Williamson had to act now to minimize the damage. "Plot shift directors to spot-three," he ordered Archinbald in the forward main-battery plotting room. He then called the officer in the forward Mark 34 director, "Spot Three, Track skunk Able."

He could only pray that Spot Three would be able to see the fall of the first salvo either visually or on their Mark 8 radar. Without that observation, their first salvo would be wasted, and with it the advantage of initial surprise would be lost. There was nothing else he could do. He had to wait until the Ford computer "fall of shot" signal sounded to indicate his salvo's splashes.

— —

"Corporal Pease, do you have your forty-five?"

Sheppard entertained the idea of sending his marine orderly to the forward director and having Hamblen summarily shot. However, as Sheppard thought about it, he realized that that course of action would leave Hamblen's body obstructing everything. The cramped director would become slippery with blood and probably only further unnerve the seven sailors inside manning the instruments. He needed that director to function well. He needed to get Lieutenant Hamblen to come down under his own power.

Belleau Wood's starboard side erupted in flame and froth as her first salvo interrupted his thoughts. Swirling clouds of expanding and cooling gases lit the scene white and then red, destroying what was left of Sheppard's night vision. A resonant boom filled the air as the thunder of an eighteen-inch broadside reached his ears, followed by the tearing sound of the projectiles arcing toward the enemy. The sonic booms echoing off the ocean were more pronounced as the flash subsided, replaced by the growing light of dawn.

The "fall of shot" signal sounded, and Sheppard lifted his binoculars to judge his gunners' accuracy. Nine mountains of water were climbing skyward. Nine meant there were no hits. That was expected from the first salvo. There were so many variables in determining where the shells would actually land: the wind at higher altitudes, the exact enemy course speed and range, the humidity aloft …

However, the water columns should have been close to each other—but they weren't! There must have been much more than a thousand yards between the right- and left-most splashes.

Argonne's second salvo sundered the night as Sheppard's heart sank. His beloved battle cruiser, the best that American technology and industry could produce, could not hit the broadside of a barn! He was committed to battle without hope of exploiting his greatest asset: effective long-range fire from his main battery. Worse, he had led his men unknowingly into a suicidal situation against overwhelming odds. Visions of *Shenandoah*'s damaged superstructure and deranged command tower danced before his eyes. Sheppard was certain most of his men would die. His only hope, *actually a prayer*, was that he would quickly be among the dead.

— —

Lieutenant Hamblen was fourth-generation navy. He had grown up in one navy port after another. San Diego, Norfolk, Charleston, Pearl

Harbor, Bremerton, San Francisco, even London—all had been home at one time or another. When most boys were collecting baseball cards and memorizing Ruth's or Gehrig's statistics, he was watching ships. He memorized their appearance and could recognize them even as a mother could pick her own child out of a crowd. He knew the way designers thought and the look that each nation inadvertently had achieved. The stolid upright look of the British, the haphazard piling of one superstructure level on another of the Japanese, the elegant flow and hint of speed achieved by the Italians, the businesslike efficiency of the Germans—these were almost inbred into his subconscious mind.

As the superstructure of the second ship in the enemy column had risen above the horizon, he'd noted the squared-off appearance without a noticeable command tower. That ship wasn't German—it was British!

They were shooting at an ally. He had screamed, "No-o-o-o!" But he knew that report was useless.

Now he spoke more slowly and clearly, with less emotion at the surprise of *Argonne*'s actions and his own part in the imminent death of friends. "Guns, Spot One, targets are classified as British warships!"

But he wasn't in time to stop *Argonne*'s second salvo.

— —

"Incompetent colonials!" said Captain Kelley.

"God save us from our friends!" another officer muttered.

Admiral Sir Bruce Hardy was not a man who feared combat. His Victoria Cross, won taking command of a destroyer in the First World War, proved that. As the senior officer on HMS *Renown*'s compass platform, the niceties of civility did not apply to his emotions. He was also a man who could not abide stupidity. His first reaction to the realization that his allies were trying to sink him was unprintable and cast serious aspersions on the lineage of everyone in Admiral Hamilton's task force, not to mention President Roosevelt and every admiral who ever served the United States. His comments, which took less than a minute to deliver, would have made any boatswain's mate blush.

Immediately, he turned to his staff officer and shouted, "Flags, emergency turn to port together!"

Turning to his flag captain, he said, "Captain Kelley, turn immediately, if you will."

Hardy next grabbed a signal pad and began writing furiously as the young lieutenant ordered the hoist and Kelley shouted down a voice pipe to the helmsman. Hardy tore off the sheet, giving it to his flag lieutenant just as *Belleau Wood*'s first salvo arrived.

— —

Convinced that Hamblen was mentally unhinged, Chuck Williamson was on the horns of a dilemma. His clear, concise report of the target classification should have been easy to ignore, but what if he was correct? What if he were shooting at allies? What if his second salvo, already en route to the target, did not miss?

If the targets were German, *Argonne* and *Belleau Wood* were outnumbered four to two. If he stopped shooting, he would forfeit whatever advantage he had from the element of surprise. Could he afford to stop shooting? None of Williamson's other director officers had as clear a look at the targets as Hamblen had. At this moment, he regretted his decision to go to the Naval Academy instead of following the family tradition of West Point.

"Check fire!" Williamson said, addressing his 1JC phone talker.

It was the hardest decision he'd ever made. He knew it might very well cost every man aboard *Argonne* his life. Now he had to tell his Captain.

He stepped over to the 21MC. "Captain, Guns: checked fire on targets classified as British warships," he reported.

It was his decision, not Hamblen's. He had chosen to believe the report. There was no point in trying to lay his action at the feet of the young lieutenant. That was not the way he had been trained to act as an officer.

— —

Of all the officers on board *Argonne,* Sheppard actually had the next-best view to John Hamblen's. He was looking at the enemy when they started to turn to port. He saw *Belleau Wood*'s first salvo arrive. Her pattern was tighter than *Argonne*'s had been. Gauging from the nine splashes, Sheppard saw *Belleau Wood* was only slightly off in train. He thought she must have been using her radars, trying to measure the bearing to the target as well as the range. The growing distinctness of the eastern horizon did not give *Belleau Wood* as good a background as *Argonne*. So, why had his pattern been so large? If closer to the accepted standard of five hundred yards at this range, he could devastate any target. With careful bore sighting and by removing all the lost motion in the synchros, it was possible to reduce pattern sizes even further. Aboard *Ticonderoga,* he had reduced his to 375 yards at a range of forty thousand.

Sheppard heard Williamson's report of "Check fire" come from the 21MC speaker, overtones of alarm and dread heavy in the transmission. Had Williamson lost his mind too? Sheppard had long known that the first taste of combat sometimes did strange things to a person, but Commander Williamson was much older and more experienced than Hamblen. What did he know that Sheppard did not?

Through his binoculars, he studied his targets as they turned. The second ship in the column was starting to send a flashing-light message. She did not look like the *Scharnhorst*-class battle cruiser he had studied only a few hours earlier in the manuals. He acknowledged his guns officer's report with a curt "Very well" and continued to read the message.

"Treaty of Ghent ratified by your Congress February 16, ended hostilities …"

"in 1815 …"

"Obviously you were not informed."

He had to let Admiral Calhoun know! The mountains of water from his last salvo began shooting up into the sky. Sheppard could not turn away until he knew the results. Chuck Williamson had made a good correction from the first set of splashes. With the second salvo, *Argonne* was dead on in both range and bearing. He recounted to be sure, but only eight towers of spray were visible.

Sheppard had to get Admiral Calhoun to stop *Belleau Wood* before an even greater tragedy occurred.

"Turn one-seven-zero. Speed two-seven." The TBS was still blaring out Admiral Hamilton's formation orders to the rest of the Task Force. It was pointless to try the voice radio to get an urgent message through.

— —

Admiral Calhoun was still in the lowest level of *Belleau Wood*'s armored command tower. His horizon was only eighteen thousand yards away. He could not see the flashing light from the enemy's leading battle cruiser. Calhoun could see the shell splashes as they rose into the air but had no idea of their location relative to the targets.

Inside the armored tower, just above Calhoun, Kevin Bailey also had no idea of what was happening or how well *Belleau Wood* was shooting. His gunnery officer in the top level couldn't see the message from Admiral Hardy, either. The only officer on *Belleau Wood* who could see it clearly was the forward main-battery director officer, but he was unable to read Morse code that quickly. Making an adjustment for the fall of *Belleau Wood*'s first salvo, he was too distracted to care what the enemy might be signaling.

— —

The only thing Sheppard could do was send a flashing-light signal. He jumped to the 21MC box. "Signal Bridge, Captain, make to *Belleau Wood!*" he shouted. *"Cease fire! Targets British! Cease fire!"*

He could hear the signal lamp begin to clatter out his message. He could see the acknowledging long dashes. But Captain Sheppard McCloud was not in time to stop *Belleau Wood*'s next salvo—corrected for all errors in range and bearing.

— —

Admiral Hardy had done what he could. His turn and speed increase would hopefully degrade the American fire-control solution. It would all depend on how much time he had bought in comparison to how long it took his message to make its way to the American admiral. The first two American salvos had errors in range and bearing, as expected. The first salvo was also extremely large. No self-respecting British gunnery officer would have ever allowed such alignment errors to develop in his system.

The third salvo was again very large, but accurately centered on his cruiser *Leonidas*. He was grateful for the size of the pattern, as *Leonidas* was not hit. However, as Hardy picked himself up from his compass platform's heaving deck, he realized that the pattern was so large that *Renown* had not escaped. There was still a splash nearby, but not large. The projectile must have hit the water only a few feet from the B starboard boiler room. As her ancient hull protested with creaks and groans, it whipped up and down as well as side to side. Her topmast above him swayed, snapping a few stays. He wondered if her ancient rivets, hammered on the Clyde nearly thirty years ago, would hold. Hardy knew his flagship had been hurt, but how badly? Small as the splash might seem in comparison, it still added insult to injury by drenching everyone on the compass platform, including Sir Bruce himself.

Regaining his feet, wet and dripping, Hardy waited for the reports of the damage to come to his flag captain, Sir Phillip Kelley.

"Flooding in starboard outboard voids—"

"Number one turbo-generator off line—"

"Water rising in B boiler room—"

Captain Kelley relayed the information to Admiral Hardy as the reports came in, acting on those items he could do something about and ignoring those he could leave to his men.

Admiral Hardy noted with optimistic satisfaction that *Renown* was still answering her helm and accelerating in response to his order.

—•—

Trying to tell one set of splashes from another in the predawn light, but unable to pass a meaningful correction to *Argonne*, Bronco felt useless flying around with his wingman, Lieutenant Barry Jensen. The third salvo, which he knew was *Argonne*'s, had unleashed an oil slick in the wake of the first big ship in the enemy's formation. Unsure what the American battle cruisers might know or not know about their targets, he decided that he at least could give them that information. After all, he had the best seat in the house.

"Panther, Mustang Zero-One. Second ship is trailing oil."

He continued to scan the area, thinking about anything else that might be useful, since he could not spot fall of shot.

"Panther, Mustang Zero-One, leading ship of enemy formation is a four-turreted light cruiser, next two ships are three-turreted battle cruisers, and trailing ship is an aircraft carrier."

— —

"God, no!"

Admiral Calhoun heard Bronco's report to *Argonne* on the aircraft-spotting net radio. The hair on the back of his neck stood up as he scrambled toward the 21MC. He knew immediately on hearing the report that he was shooting at Britain's Force H. Would history judge him as the man that lost the war? Even if Vizeadmiral Schröder had split his force into two equal groups, Schröder did not have any three-turreted heavy ships.

Desperate, he shouted, "Cease fire!" into the microphone, thankfully in time to stop *Belleau Wood*'s third salvo. That left everyone praying that her second salvo would be a miss.

— —

Admiral Hardy coolly watched the Americans' last salvo land with the detached professionalism of a former gunnery specialist. The pattern of the falling shells he estimated at five hundred yards in diameter. As the mountains of water and spray rose, he also saw it was well placed. If

Leonidas had not turned as she accelerated, she would have been exactly where the American had aimed. As it was, her turn took her to the left edge of the pattern but not far enough to avoid it. His light cruiser was lost in the mountains of water.

"One … two … three …" Hardy counted the seconds, waiting for the water columns to drop, trying not to think of his cruiser's fate.

Almighty God, may I see her again whole and afloat, he silently prayed.

No light cruiser could stand up to a broadside salvo from a capital ship. These heavy shells were clearly coming from two. In the growing light of dawn, this last salvo was tinted green, whereas the one that had hit *Renown* had looked reddish. Too slowly, the splashes were turning to a thinning mist.

— —

"How can a gunnery officer possibly make errors this big in his alignment?" Sheppard muttered to himself as he began to pace inside the conning station.

Williamson seemed like a good officer; he certainly knew what he was talking about in the wardroom, he thought.

Sheppard was shaking his head as his pace quickened, and he ignored the pain in his leg. As if on cue, his conning officer and the watchstanders in his vicinity surreptitiously moved away from their captain, leaving him alone with his thoughts and muttering only to himself.

The Navy's procedures for aligning guns within the turret to the turret centerline and the turret to the fire-control system clearly defined everything required. He himself had used them on the old *Ticonderoga* during a shipyard availability, while his ship was getting her hull cleaned and painted. An acceptable pattern size was only dependent on doing the procedure correctly, as written out. If your goal was true excellence, then you had to take more time and get all the lost motion out of the system by approaching the aim point from the same direction with every component that you adjusted.

He had to admit to himself, though, that God worked in mysterious ways: *Better to shoot and miss at allies than enemies—learning early of the problem.* Perhaps he would yet find the error and be able to do something about it.

———

John Hamblen could not anticipate what was going to happen to him. After all, he knew he was personally responsible for the performance of his director and crew. It was up to him to ensure the proper target classification. What had he done wrong to allow this disaster to occur? It was going to be just like his first ship: he would be blamed for everything.

He had watched *Argonne*'s last salvo land, perhaps hitting the second ship in the British column—a remodeled *Renown*-class battle cruiser. He knew the modified armor of those ships was no match for the eighteen-inch superheavy projectiles that *Argonne* was shooting. He could spout off the thicknesses and extent of coverage from memory as if he had *Jane's Fighting Ships* in front of him. At best, the British ships were little more than modern armored cruisers, slower than most but more heavily armed.

"God, please do not let anyone be hurt by my mistake," he prayed.

As Hamblen continued to watch, he saw *Belleau Wood*'s last salvo land, bracketing the leading light cruiser. He silently counted the splashes—six, seven, eight. Had he missed one?

It really did not matter. He was already responsible for whatever death and destruction had occurred on that second ship.

———

"Mister Burdick, what's goin' on?" Bronco heard over the Kingfisher's intercom.

"Damned if I know," Bronco replied to Radioman First Class Miller.

One good thing about flying with an open cockpit was no one could hear you if you didn't cue a mike.

"Goddamn black-shoes!" Bronco muttered—without cueing the mike. "They expect you to spot and search, defend against U-boats, even rescue; but no one tells you anything. Now they stopped shooting. What do they want me to do up here, go over and get shot down?"

He had no idea that he was a hero for the second time today. Neither did he know that when he had banked, it had caused the British to realize his American identity; nor was he aware that his report, leading to the cease-fire, had prevented any serious additional damage.

After a few minutes, Bronco decided that he might as well serve as an antisubmarine screen while he waited on daylight and *Argonne*'s readiness to recover aircraft.

"Mustang Zero-Five, this is Zero-One. Search for submarines on Panther's starboard side; I'll take port. Stay within ten miles."

— —

Admiral Hamilton was only aware that his ships had stopped firing. For whatever reason, clearly Ray Calhoun no longer believed there was a threat to the east. In that case, then, as soon as his ships were on station, he could turn them together and launch both his dawn search by Scouting Squadron Eleven and the combat air patrol from both carriers. Accordingly, he sent word to *Sabine*'s signal bridge.

"Make to *Raritan*: 'Prepare to launch aircraft.'" He then passed the same message from flag plot to the *Sabine*'s bridge watch.

In both carriers, the pilots, lounging in the fighter-squadron ready rooms waiting for something to happen, began briefings to the effect that eight of them from each squadron would be launching to form a CAP. It took longer to alert and brief pilots in Scouting Squadron Eleven's ready room and the enlisted radio operators/rear gunners for an impending launch. Pilots hastily drew the search patterns to the northeast and their assigned individual sectors on their chart boards. The carrier's meteorologist updated them on weather conditions, including the vitally important wind speed and direction, and how the wind might vary at higher altitudes—along with cloud cover and a best estimate of how things might change during the next six hours. Blackboards in each ready room prominently displayed the most important piece of information: where they would most likely find their carrier again at the end of their wedge-shaped search pattern—vital, if for any reason the carrier's homing beacon or their receivers failed. Unfortunately, point "option" represented little more than Admiral Hamilton's best guess of what would happen in the next four hours. At sea, predicting the future was a risky business.

It was but a few minutes before the carriers' announcing systems blared out, "Pilots, man your planes!"

The young men grabbed their navigation boards and cloth helmets and scrambled up one level to the flight deck where their aircraft were waiting. Fully fueled and armed but with only machine-gun ammunition for the search, each aircraft had a plane captain who had supervised the fueling and loading. The plane captain personally made a thorough inspection, ensuring the aircraft had no loose access panels, foreign objects, or leaking fluids. He helped each pilot strap into the cockpit while briefing him on the fuel load and readiness of the aircraft for flight. There was a unique bond between plane captains and pilots, for the pilots did not have the time to make such checks themselves. Pilots trusted the plane captains with their lives.

—•—

It was only by luck or divine intervention that a disaster had been avoided. Regardless, Admiral Hardy was truly thankful. *Leonidas* had emerged unscathed from the mountains of seawater, only listing slightly as the tons of seawater cascaded off her weather decks. Reports from the crew of *Renown* confirmed only minor damage. His flagship's only real problem was a slight list, which was quickly corrected. The oil slick in Force H's wake would make him more vulnerable to visual detection by aircraft, but nothing could be done about it. The continued leakage would not last long, as the tank would eventually empty.

A slow smile crept across Sir Bruce's face as he began to recognize the advantage that the Americans represented: those two American ships could not stand up to Schröder's by themselves, but they might be able to make some cripples that the timid German would use as an excuse to return to port. Perhaps they would even slow the Germans enough for a night torpedo attack by his destroyers. Now, that would really do the trick.

"Flags, make to all: 'Come to course three-one-zero, speed twenty.'"

Vice Admiral Hardy reformed his column and adjusted his course to intercept the leading American capital ship. He was most concerned now with coordinating with the Americans. Together they might have a chance against Schröder. The German admiral should be less than two hundred miles to the northeast.

CHAPTER 9

SEARCH

She knew all his secrets, listening intently as he muttered in his sleep. The more she learned, the greater her love. As she watched him, she knew his men shared her belief in his abilities. She had seen them defer to his comments and had observed his consideration of their viewpoints. More than anything, she wished to take away his pain, but she knew she was contributing to it. By any standard, he had done all he could and did not deserve his own scorn.

As she wrapped herself around him, enveloping him in her affection, somehow she knew that he would see them through the adversities fate might hold for them both. Never again would she hide her past from him as she had before, which now seemed like an eternity ago.

———

Raritan's signal light was flashing, reporting her readiness to launch aircraft. She had finished warming the eight F4F-3 Wildcat fighters aligned on her flight deck. The pilots throttled back to idle the Twin Wasp fourteen-cylinder radial engines, saving gas for what they expected would be a long and boring flight as they waited for the carrier to turn into the wind. It took a few more minutes for Captain Evans of the *Sabine* to report his readiness. In addition to Wildcats, his flight deck also arrayed the spinning propellers of eighteen SBD-3 dive-bombers. Their nine-cylinder Wright Cyclone engines were not as powerful as those on the Wildcats. With only nine cylinders and no superchargers, they were also not as complex.

Admiral Hamilton intently surveyed her flight deck and the horizon from *Sabine*'s flag bridge. He wanted to be sure that there was enough light for the aircrew's safety. Without bombs, the SBD-3s should have plenty of extra power for takeoff. Similarly, with only twenty-six aircraft spotted for launching, they would have a long deck run into the wind. As it was still too dark for communication by flag hoist, he used the TBS. "Dog-patch, this is Labrador. Immediate execute, zero-nine-zero turn."

Every ship in his formation put her helm over to left standard rudder. Hamilton also ordered the two destroyers closest to his two carriers to assume plane-guard duties. At times like this, he sometimes regretted his decision to leave destroyers and go to flight school.

Each of the two captains ordered thirty-two knots. Quick puffs of black smoke signaled that watchstanders in their boiler rooms were cutting in more sprayers to make more steam for the higher speed. The destroyers heeled outboard, turning toward their new positions, a huge white curling wave at each bow. Their sterns sank lower as the increased power spun their screws faster, pushing ever harder in a losing attempt to climb the pressure wave ahead. Wakes climbing above the levels of their main decks would give any sailor a thrill. Here was the reason that ambitious young officers gravitated to destroyers: the chance to control a "greyhound of the sea" at a young age, executing difficult maneuvers in tight quarters.

Almost as quickly as they had accelerated, the two destroyers turned into their new stations and slowed five hundred yards astern of each carrier. Everything was in readiness.

"Launch aircraft!" Admiral Hamilton ordered.

The flight-deck officer in his cloth helmet spun his small flag in rapid circles above his head, ordering the leading fighter pilot to maximize his engine speed and power. Satisfied with the ensuing roar, he glanced over his shoulder to judge the rise and fall of the bow in the long ocean swells left by the storm. Timing things so that when the fighter reached the end of the flight deck *Sabine*'s bow would be at its highest, he dropped his flag and pointed it to the bow, his legs bent and body leaning forward. The pilot released his brakes. No sooner had the first plane started its deck run than more enlisted plane handlers in dungarees and yellow cloth helmets were coaxing the next aircraft into launch position with hand signals that would make any traffic cop hang his head in shame. The flight-deck officer began his dance again. Every fifteen to twenty seconds another aircraft started its run into the predawn light. No other navy did this as well or as rapidly.

No sooner had the last SBDs left than Admiral Hamilton, having checked the completion of *Raritan*'s launch with his binoculars, ordered another turn to a course of zero-eight-zero, and the two destroyers returned to their screening positions. He wanted to maintain the weather gauge, hopefully remaining upwind of Schröder. Only in that way could he turn into the wind for flight operations without risking his carriers to gunfire by closing the enemy.

— —

Vizeadmiral Schröder stood on the flag bridge of the *Graf Zeppelin,* watching the gathering dawn. White-capped waves were just becoming visible in the dim light. For a moment, he thought that *Graf Zeppelin* might be racing them to some unseen destiny. He had come almost two hundred nautical miles since turning to the southwest. A low ceiling completely covered the sky. Intermittent rain had recently washed the deck of his flag bridge. With the help of the U-boat weather reports, his meteorologist was sure that the passing squalls would stop soon. The cloud ceiling, predicted to rise, should support flight operations in an hour or two. Schröder decided to have the Bf 109s brought up on the flight decks of his two carriers and readied. They did not have much endurance, and he would need them all to maintain an adequate combat air patrol. Until the weather improved, he would rely on the Condors for searching. The Stukas could stay in the hangars.

Schröder did not like having to rely on the Luftwaffe for reconnaissance, but his other options were even less attractive. If he used his Stukas, he would reduce the number he had to sink the American carrier once located. The battle cruiser floatplanes had similar disadvantages. The Arado 196s had a good range and endurance, but he only had sixteen in total. Any he sent off on searches would not be available to spot the fall of shot in a surface engagement at long range. The white-capped waves also made landing and recovery risky, if not impossible. If Schröder launched the floatplanes, he had to slow his ships to create landing slicks and give the pilots the best chance of safely recovering the aircraft. Of course, he could always direct them to fly to Spain, but he would need them later with the convoys.

What Vizeadmiral Schröder did not know was that the staff meteorologists at Luftflotte Three had concluded the weather was too poor for the Condors to start their searches. Not privy to the U-boat weather reports, that officer had a much more pessimistic forecast. Without clear weather, the risk to the delicate Fw 200s did not balance the potential gain. Luftflotte Three issued orders to the two *staffel* (squadrons) to keep the Condors on the runways until the weather improved.

— —

Sheppard watched as the developing light illuminated the horizon in all directions. It was time to give his crew breakfast and return to underway watches. A word to his JA phone talker was all it took to get the watch relief in motion. He glanced up at the Mk 38 main-battery director turning back toward its normally stowed position; the rangefinder arms spread athwartships like the wings of a bird of prey, the sight shutters closing for the raptor's slumber. Sheppard knew he had to deal with Lieutenant Hamblen, but not yet. The director rangefinder might remind him of a bird of prey, but this bird had no talons. He turned to his marine orderly with a scowl.

"Corporal, please send my compliments to Commander Williamson and request he lay to the conning station with the alignment data for the main battery."

Sheppard knew what to look for. If it were repairable, he would find it.

— —

Admiral Hardy had managed to slip below into his flag quarters, dry off, and change his uniform, leaving the immediate task of returning Force H to a north-westerly course to his equally drenched flag captain. By the time he returned to the compass platform, it was almost sunrise. Mornings were the times he enjoyed most on the open platform, cluttered with watchstanders, voice tubes, the pelorus, and a panoramic view sheltered only by a windscreen. Having spent so many years standing on this basic Royal Navy platform, he had to say it felt like home. When Hardy left for sea at fourteen as a midshipman, he had known already that his destiny lay far from his ancestral home at Portesham House in Dorset.

There were reports of aircraft to the west, no doubt a morning search by the Americans. As the sun rose, the fire-control towers and funnels of two large warships took shape on the western horizon. Their look confirmed they were American. These ships must have been responsible for the salvos that had nearly crippled his force. He was not sure what he was going to tell this admiral who had tried to kill him, but now those two ships represented his best hope of defeating Schröder.

In his absence, *Renown* had been set to right. All the minor casualties caused by the shell's detonation under her keel had been corrected. The list caused by the two holes in the starboard antitorpedo bulge had been removed by pumping fuel oil to port-side tanks. Except for the diminishing oil slick, there was no apparent damage to his flagship.

If Sir Bruce wanted to communicate with his American opposite number, he would need to take a more northerly course. He had learned forty years earlier that if you wanted to intercept another ship, you had to take a course that resulted in an unchanging bearing to the object. These American ships were drawing to the right.

"Flags, order 'Column turn to three-one-five, speed twenty-four,' if you please."

Hardy implicitly trusted his flag lieutenant, Masterson, to direct his force as commanded. While his young lieutenant was busy with flag hoists, he concentrated on developing a plan that would work whether the sky cleared or not.

— —

Sheppard was sitting on his perch in the conning station when a sheepish Chuck Williamson arrived, trailed by Lieutenant Commander Burton Forbes, Senior Chief Hancock, and Chief Gunner's Mate Smith, all carrying ordnance publications and notebooks of data. *Argonne* was pulling up to her assigned station fifteen hundred yards astern of *Belleau Wood*. The sun rising above the eastern horizon obscured a clear view of the British ships in the glare as they closed on Admiral Calhoun's formation. As much as he might wish otherwise, Sheppard would have to forgo his usual eavesdropping on the flashing-light communications he suspected would determine his future course of action. Getting his guns to hit the target was far more important.

"Captain, I don't know what to tell you," Commander Williamson began. "I brought along my experts to help explain what we did on the last alignment."

Sheppard flexed his jaw muscles, pale blue eyes narrowing without saying a word—riveting Williamson in place with a pause palpable to everyone on the conning station. It was only a moment, but Sheppard had learned the value of that stare in separating the devious from the incompetent.

"Very well, let's spread out in my sea cabin so we do not disturb the watch."

There wasn't much room in Sheppard's sea cabin, but the bunk would do to spread out the alignment data books and various publications. With the chair moved to the head, they had enough room for everyone to stand around Sheppard as his inquisition began.

Sheppard knew the alignment procedure by heart, but for something this important, he wanted his people to recognize that you always referred to the latest revision of the written word. Williamson had brought the requisite manuals, bookmarked and dog-eared to the relevant pages. At every step, Sheppard had a simple command. "Show me your recorded data."

After an hour and a half of investigation, the data that Chuck had shown him supported a rather thorough batten bar alignment of the entire system. Uncomprehending, Sheppard could not find anything wrong in the data. *But … there has to be a cause!*

Chuck might have appeared to complete the procedure correctly, but something had to be wrong. "Commander, when was this alignment of the system accomplished?" Sheppard asked.

"The last ten days of January of this year, during our postshakedown availability at New York Shipbuilding in Camden," Williamson answered.

"Why was it done?"

"Captain, during our shakedown cruise our long-range firings were not as good as I had hoped. Our pattern sizes were about six hundred yards at forty thousand yards. All the technical experts agreed the patterns should be smaller, but New York Shipbuilding did not want to redo the full alignment, claiming that they were only contractually obligated to do it once. That was completed during construction, well before anyone in my department arrived. They wanted a ton of money to conduct another one.

"Captain Leland was not able to get either the Bureau of Ordnance or the Bureau of Construction and Repair to fund a new one. He finally browbeat the supervisor of shipbuilding at New York Ship to use his discretionary money and rent the equipment, allowing my people to conduct it on our own." Williamson paused, as if weighing his next words.

"Captain," Williamson continued, "we even bribed some of the shipyard foremen to watch us and make sure we used their equipment correctly."

The only thing Sheppard could say was, "Mmm!"

The cause of the large pattern remained a mystery. Even more troubling was the fact that the patterns had not been as large as they were now. There had to be an explanation.

"Very well," Sheppard said. "Thank you, Mister Forbes, Senior Chief, and Chief Smith."

Taking their cue to leave, the men recognized that Sheppard wanted to talk to Commander Williamson in private. Every member of the United States Navy was well versed in John Paul Jones's dictum: *"Praise in public, admonish in private."*

Sheppard eyed Williamson. "Commander Williamson, how did you know that the targets you were firing at were British?"

"John Hamblen in Spot One identified them as British. I wasn't sure that he was right, but I decided not to risk shooting any more salvos at an ally. Captain, to be honest, I just didn't know—but … it was my decision, not his."

"All I heard from Hamblen was a loud *no*. What else did you hear?"

"My 1JC phone talker told me about the shouted no, but soon after, he reported that Lieutenant Hamblen had stated, 'Targets are classified as British warships.' I felt that if he had the presence of mind to use correct procedures, then there was probably truth in what he said. But I want to reiterate the decision to check fire was mine and mine alone."

"Thank you, Chuck. Let me think on the alignment, and I'll get back to you later."

A quick "Yes, sir," and he was out the cabin door.

Two hours had passed, and Sheppard was no closer to finding the cause of *Argonne*'s huge pattern. He would have to let it go for the moment. The clock in the conning station struck two bells. As if on cue, Petty Officer Jefferson arrived with his carrying rig and Sheppard's belated breakfast. How Jefferson managed to deliver it way up there and still keep it hot would forever be a mystery to Captain McCloud.

— —

While Sheppard was in his sea cabin, Admiral Hamilton had been busy. From the prewar carrier exercises, he knew that the carriers that launched a strike first were most likely to win the day. If that strike could arrive before the enemy launched, the victory would be lopsided.

Accordingly, as soon as the last SBD had left *Sabine*'s deck, her blinker light had begun clattering out the orders to *Raritan*. The Admiral's staff sent the same order directly to *Sabine* to prepare a maximum strike with all the remaining aircraft. Only sixteen fighters, designated for a replacement combat air patrol along with the sixteen orbiting, would remain with the task force.

In less than a minute, the large rectangles of the carriers' elevators disappeared from the flight decks. The automatic guardrails rose to create a barrier and prevent an inattentive individual from falling three or more decks into the yawning chasm. As quickly as the elevator left, it returned to the flight deck, this time supporting a TBD-1 Devastator torpedo plane, wings folded. Dozens of dungaree-clad men, some with blue jackets zipped against the cold, rushed up and began pushing the aircraft to a spot at the aft end of the flight deck. Ordnance handlers wheeling dollies carrying Mk 13 aerial torpedoes stopped precisely under each Devastator and began loading it. Armed with four hundred pounds of high explosive, each aircraft became a lethal threat to any ship it attacked. Other enlisted personnel filled the Devastators' tanks with volatile aviation gasoline, while more ordnance men loaded machine-gun ammunition for the fixed and flexible mounts.

Soon, all eighteen TBDs were in position, and it was time to load the SBD-3s of the two bombing squadrons onto the elevators and bring them to the flight deck. Again, the huge elevators cycled up and down, but the smaller aircraft, without folding wings, snuggly fit each platform. Once they were raised, men pushed and pulled the smaller Dauntlesses into position. This time, the ordnance men used their dollies to bring thousand-pound semi-armor-piercing bombs up the bomb hoists adjacent to the island. Similarly fueled and armed, the SBDs were soon ready to go.

Raritan now had more work to do than *Sabine*, with an additional squadron of SBDs still on board, but her shrinking takeoff run only allowed loading of quarter-ton bombs.

Lastly, it was time for both carriers to bring up eight Wildcats. Hamilton wanted them in the front. Should the task force detect an inbound enemy strike group before the American attack launched, the fighters could be launched immediately, contributing to the defense of the fleet. Striking second was not Admiral Hamilton's plan. He intended those fighters to escort his strike and clear the air of any defending Messerschmitts.

— —

The SBDs of Scouting Squadron Eleven flew outward from their launch point like the spokes of a wagon wheel. Staying just under the cloud ceiling, each Dauntless's crew was enjoying the cool, clean air that follows a spring rain. Inactivity had weighed heavily on the young men itching to get at an enemy. Now they were on a real operation— no more training flights. Their briefing officers had emphasized the importance of the mission to locate the German ships, thus enabling an early and crippling blow by the waiting bombers and torpedo planes. The pilots were paying particular attention to navigation, as the critical information would be *where* the enemy was located. To a man, their thoughts were focused on finding Schröder and wondering how they would react under fire.

As they flew, the cloud ceiling was gradually lowering, forcing the search planes to descend with it. Flying at a lower altitude restricted the range of what they could see, and gaps formed in the coverage between adjacent spokes of the wheel. Worse, the farther they flew, the stronger the wind became, creating errors in dead-reckoning of their positions and raising more whitecaps on the seas below. It was not long before every wave looked like a ship's wake. Soon, the fatigue of battling the wind gusts just under the cloud layer began affecting their concentration and the effectiveness of the search. It would be a miracle if they found anything in these conditions.

On the outbound leg of the search, the radioman/gunner of aircraft 11-S-11 managed to spot a cruiser of the German scouting line.

Following orders, the pilot, a young lieutenant junior grade, circled his contact, ducking in and out of the clouds and attempting to remain hidden from the German lookouts below. He radioed his position and the course and speed of his contact. Unknowingly, had he continued, he would have passed directly over Schröder's battle cruisers—certainly finding the prize.

— —

Almost as soon as he returned to the conning station, Sheppard heard the contact report and directed the quartermaster of the watch to put the position on the chart, laying down a DR for the contact. Located a hundred nautical miles away, the position gave Sheppard a clear idea of when he might spot the contact or what he would have to do to intercept it. Suddenly, he remembered there was something else he had to do.

He turned to his orderly. "Corporal Pease, send my compliments to Lieutenant Hamblen and request that he lay to the conning station to meet with the Captain."

Soon John Hamblen arrived, out of breath, uncharacteristically dressed in blues as if he were expecting the worst. His choice of uniform convinced Sheppard that there was more to John Hamblen than first met the eye.

"Lieutenant, please accompany me into my sea cabin so that we can talk."

Once inside, Sheppard asked Hamblen to close the cabin door. "What happened in the director this morning?" Sheppard asked. "Why did you shout *no*?"

"Captain, when I realized that we were shooting at British ships, I couldn't immediately think of a standard Navy phrase to convey the urgency of stopping. I didn't know what else to say."

"Why did you think you needed a standard phrase?"

Hamblen looked dumbfounded. "I—I was criticized every time I failed to use standard language on my first ship. I—I was taught that you could only use standard phrases."

"Who on earth told you that?" Sheppard was beginning to understand Hamblen's problem, but he would have to ask more questions after he got the answer to this one.

"Captain Smith on the destroyer *Boone*," Hamblen said, with a questioning look in his eyes.

As much as he wanted to, Sheppard knew he could not tell a junior officer the sad truth about a higher-ranking officer. Norman Ulysses Morgan Smith was still on active duty and still held the rank of commander. His rank and uniform deserved respect, even if the man did not. Norm—or Numb Nuts, as senior officers referred to him behind his back—would never have another command. He would never again be in a position to ruin junior officers with his own insecurities.

"How did you get assigned to the *Boone*, anyway, John?"

"To be honest, Captain, when I graduated from the Academy, my father wanted to control my assignment. He was always trying to arrange things for me—control everything that I did. When I found out, I tried to stand up to him and told him that if I were going to make it in life or the service, I would do it on my own. I was dating a girl from Norfolk my last year at the Academy. I wanted to continue seeing her. The *Boone* was the only Norfolk destroyer left on the list when it was my turn to pick."

Sheppard understood; he had met Evelyn just before graduation but had not made Hamblen's mistake. Evelyn must have known they were destined for each other long before the idea crossed Sheppard's mind. She had maintained a faithful correspondence with him. As the months dragged on, Sheppard began to realize what a find she was and arranged a transfer back to the East Coast. The day they were married six months later was the happiest of his life. She had never asked him for any consideration with respect to his career other than to do "what will make you happiest." He could think of nothing better than to spend the rest of his life with her.

"Did your father try to dissuade you from going to the *Boone*?"

"Yes sir, but I thought he just didn't approve of my girl. Her family was Jewish."

Sheppard confirmed in his own mind the course of action needed for Hamblen. He had to rebuild the young officer's self-confidence and initiative to turn him around. It was clear that Hamblen did not know about his father's call to Bill Leland. That needed to remain a secret.

"John, your decision to stop our third salvo by whatever means you thought would work was appropriate. Standard phraseology is important but not at the expense of accomplishing the action needed. I expect you to continue to think and act accordingly. Do that, and I will always back you up, even if you are wrong!"

"Thank you, Captain," Hamblen said, a look of astonishment on his face.

"One other thing, John. How did you know they were British ships?"

"Captain, when I was growing up, the only way I got to see my father was meeting him on the waterfront or riding in his barge. He was proud of his ability to tell one ship from another. I guess I picked it up from him and would try to outdo him with the foreign ships we saw together."

"Very well, John," Sheppard said, convinced not to change Hamblen's battle stations assignment.

Taking a cue to leave, Hamblen opened the door to Sheppard's sea cabin and began descending the ladder. After Hamblen left, Sheppard was suddenly struck with something else to check for the main-battery alignment.

— —

John William Hamblen IV slid down the railings from the forward tower his hands alone touching the brass railings a smile from ear to ear illuminating his face until he reached the landing of the next deck. He turned and slide down that ladder. Landing, slide, landing, slide ... continued until he reached the second deck of the superstructure. He turned to port and walked aft in the passage way passing the ladder to the wardroom and the port side showers. Turning into the second alcove he unlocked and opened his stateroom door.

Hamblen went immediately to his desk, pulled out a piece of personal stationary and began writing as fast as his penmanship would allow:

"Father,

"Today we nearly fought our allies. All the years we spent learning ship silhouettes paid off. I was able to recognize HMS *Renown* with only the top of her superstructure and stacks visible and stopped *Argonne* before we fired our third salvo.

"Dad that is not the most important thing I wanted to write about. I have finally seen an officer that matched your descriptions of what I should be. Our Captain didn't criticize me for non-standard phraseology. He did not caution me about further action or failure to identify our target earlier. Dad, he told me that as long as I tried to do the right thing he would always back me up. I can't tell you more, but I now know that the Navy does contain leaders in the mold of the Academy ideals we were taught.

"You are probably aware of the critical mission we have been assigned. I hope this letter eventually finds you regardless of the outcome.

Your son,
John"

He sealed the envelope with a prayer that it would be delivered before any notification of his death or injury.

— —

While writing a letter to his son Eric, Vizeadmiral Schröder had received the message from the *Fellbach* reporting an American dive-bomber at their position. It was clear to him that the American carrier was close enough to have launched a search and that they had found at least one of his scout cruisers. Surely the American admiral would not be foolish enough to waste his strike on a single small cruiser. On the other hand, perhaps he would indeed launch, hoping that his search planes could find Schröder's battle cruisers and carriers before the strike got to the *Fellbach*. The Americans might think of redirecting the strike en route.

If their strike groups arrived without warning, they stood a good chance of crippling his big ships before his carriers could launch defending fighters. He had to find the Americans!

Schröder couldn't understand what had happened to the Condors. He had personally traveled to Luftflotte 3 headquarters in Paris to discuss the need for long-range reconnaissance. They had assured him they understood, yet here he was, about to engage an American carrier task force without any knowledge of their location. This was unacceptable. He did not want to waste any of his limited number of Stukas searching. Reluctantly, he contemplated ordering his battle cruisers to ready eight Arado 196s. The seas were too rough for their recovery, but he had to find his enemy.

Schröder also decided to prepare his Messerschmitt Bf 109s for launch. He would keep them on deck warmed and ready. If an attack developed, he would launch them all. His flight decks would then be clear for bringing up the Stukas from the hangar deck. Schröder called for his staff. They had to devise a method for regaining the initiative.

— —

Back in the conning station, Sheppard issued a quick order to Pease. "Corporal, send my compliments to Commander Roberts and request he bring the deck logs for the month of January to the conning station."

Sheppard wanted to look at the midnight entries for the period during which the *Argonne* had been conducting the main-battery alignment.

Only a few minutes later, Art Roberts arrived. "Here are the logs, Captain. Is there something specific I can help you find?"

Sheppard led the way into his sea cabin, and Art spread the logs sequentially out on his bunk. "I want to see the midnight entries for the last ten days of January, Art," said Sheppard.

Roberts lay the logs out on the bunk and found the requested one. "Here is the log for the twentieth, Captain," he said, placing the legal-size piece of paper in front of Sheppard.

The entry began, *"Moored as before ..."*

"Where is the log for the twenty-first?"

"Here, Captain."

It read, *"Moored as before using standard mooring lines doubled to the south side of the pier, berth thirty-seven at New York Shipbuilding and Dry Dock Company, Camden, New Jersey."*

Now Sheppard thought he knew the answer. With Roberts's help, he confirmed that every midnight entry for the remainder of the month began the same way. What those words meant was that *Argonne* had been afloat, tied to a pier in the shipyard. In all probability, stiff pontoons—a.k.a. "camels"—had held the ship away from the pilings but with sufficient slack in the lines to accommodate changes in the Delaware River's water level.

"Thank you, Commander," was all Sheppard said before returning to the conning station.

He arrived just in time to hear additional contact reports from Scouting Squadron Eleven.

"Corporal Pease, one more trip. Please send my compliments to Commander Williamson and request he see the Captain on the conning station."

— —

Admiral Hamilton looked at the bulkhead clock. Scouting Squadron Eleven should have completed their outbound leg, right turn, and be on the return leg of their search. Why hadn't they found Schröder? He knew the weather to the northeast was probably worse, fatiguing his pilots. He had only one contact report on a scout cruiser. *Where the hell were the carriers?*

The bulkhead speaker from the voice-radio net blared out, "Contact, one ship, probably a scout cruiser, forty-five degrees fifteen minutes north, zero nine thirty-nine west." It was 11-S-6, west of the center of his search.

Another scout cruiser, Hamilton thought.

Two more scouting reports quickly followed. He'd found Schröder's scouting line. Well, at least four of them. But he had not found his task force. The four ships that the SBDs had located formed a clear line with about equal space between them. There were two scout cruisers missing from the intelligence report. But were the missing two on the west end of the plotted contacts or to the east?

— —

Commander Williamson was standing in the open joiner door to the conning station as Captain McCloud and the quartermaster of the watch finished plotting the new contact reports. With a quick order to the quartermaster to lay down DRs, Sheppard turned to Williamson. "Let's go into my sea cabin. I have a few more questions," he said.

Williamson followed McCloud into the small cabin and shut the door behind them. Williamson's face showed his suspicions that this meeting was not going to end as pleasantly as the last.

"Chuck, was your last alignment done with *Argonne* afloat?"

"Yes, sir. Why do you ask?"

"Where were the batten beams positioned while you were doing the alignment?"

"Captain, they were on the pier. Why do you ask?"

Sheppard's eyes narrowed and his lips pursed as he asked, "Why didn't you put them on board *Argonne*?"

Williamson felt his stomach turn. "Captain, there was no room. We were installing the 20 mm and some extra 40 mm mounts forward of Turrets I and II as well as aft of turret III. The shipyard said that if we cleared the deck to set up the batten beams, they would charge millions of dollars in 'delay and disruption fees.' I didn't think we had a choice, Captain."

"Chuck, did it ever cross your mind that the procedure specifies doing the alignment in dry dock for a reason and what that reason might be?"

"I knew that, Captain, but the Supervisor of Shipbuilding said that New York Ship had always been allowed to do the alignments waterborne. They only had two dry docks large enough for *Argonne*.

Both contained new battle cruisers under construction. Rear Admiral Troutman said that, contractually, it fell into what he called 'previously accepted practice' on the part of the Navy. If the Navy wanted to change it, there would be huge and costly changes to every contract in the yard."

"I can understand all that. What I am having difficulty with is the fact that by having *Argonne* floating alongside a pier and the batten beams on land, any change in the wind, current, water height, or *Argonne*'s loading would cause an alignment error from one gun to the next in each turret. You as a gunnery professional should have recognized that danger and *not done the alignment!*"

— —

Commander Williamson felt two inches tall. The blood drained from his face. All the assurances he had received from the shipyard foremen, from his own people, and from the supervisor of shipbuilding's office had been lies. He had to admit that if he had thought about what was happening, an alignment in those circumstances had been foolish—and now every man on *Argonne* was going to pay for *his* mistake. Perhaps the hardest thing was admitting that McCloud knew more about his specialty than he did.

All he could think to say was, "Captain, I'm sorry!"

He turned to leave, with the full realization that nothing could be done about *Argonne*'s abysmal gunnery performance. Williamson knew that McCloud could and should ruin his career, if they survived. That price was small in comparison to the way he felt now. He had let everyone down, not the least being the Captain. If things went badly for *Argonne* with the Germans, he hoped that he would die in the engagement.

"Wait, Chuck."

Williamson stopped and faced McCloud.

"Everyone makes mistakes, some bigger, some smaller," the Captain said. "What is important now is not the mistake, after it has occurred, but how we deal with it. Tell me, were the six-inch and five-inch batteries also aligned at the same time?"

Commander Williamson was grateful for the subject change and the opportunity to give some good news. "No, sir; their alignment was well within specifications, as verified on the shakedown cruise."

"Good. How many smoke projectiles do you have on board?"

"I have about two hundred five-inch and maybe a hundred six-inch. Why do you ask, Captain?'

"Chuck, set up a meeting with Commanders Grabowski, Roberts, Scott, and Blankenship; Lieutenant Commanders Burdick and Becker; and yourself, in my sea cabin, as soon as you can." As an afterthought, McCloud added, "Have your smoke projectiles distributed evenly among all the mounts and six-inch turrets."

Williamson, his self-confidence still badly shaken, left to do as ordered.

—　—

Admiral Hamilton was in a conundrum. His search had not located Schröder's main force. His scout planes would soon be returning, low on fuel, losing contact with the unimportant scouts they had found. His combat air patrol F4Fs, also low on fuel, needed to land soon. Filling his flight decks currently were all his attack planes spotted for launch. If he chose to wait for better information, he had to "break the spot"— sending them all below to land his fighters and scouts. It would be a huge risk to have the fully armed and fueled aircraft inside the closed hangars of his *Brandywine*-class carriers.

He turned to his chief of staff. "Henry, I think we are damned if we launch and damned if we don't."

Burke nodded in agreement. "Admiral, if I was Schröder, the only thing I know is that there was a radio transmission from four hundred miles to the west of where we are now. If the Germans have a spy in Norfolk, they could put that together with our sailing and decide the radio transmission was from Task Force Forty-Eight."

"If you were Schröder, what would you do? How would you set up your scouting and reconnaissance?"

"I would set out a scouting line, Admiral, just as Schröder has done. What I don't understand is the absence of any air recon. We should have seen the Luftwaffe, the floatplanes from his battle cruisers, or his Stukas."

Hamilton felt irritation rising within. He wanted ideas and Burke was only giving him what he already knew.

"Yes, Henry, but if you were Schröder, would you be farther to the east or the west of the scouting line we discovered?"

"Schröder's mission is the convoys, Admiral. The convoys should be farther from the Spanish coast to minimize the Luftwaffe's chance of detecting them. That should mean that Schröder would be to the west to maximize his chances of detecting his prize. I believe the two missing cruisers are to the west and we can find his fleet behind the two western cruisers."

Finally, some logical sense.

"Very well, Henry, pick a spot based on the DRs and launch the strike. Turn Admiral Calhoun's squadrons and increase their speed to thirty-two knots for an interception." As an afterthought, he added, "I hope you are right."

— —

The weather was improving near Task Force Forty-Eight. An occasional patch of blue sky peeked through the dissipating cloud layer. Though the northeastern sky was still overcast, the afternoon looked promising. *Sabine*'s signal light, a precursor of increased activity, clattered away, pointed at *Raritan*. Answering with long dashes followed, as *Raritan* acknowledged the orders to launch the deck load strike at Schröder. Multicolored signal flags soared to the blocks of the carrier's signal halyards. The signal flags of the other ships in Admiral Hamilton's carrier force rose to the dip, fluttering expectantly in the clean air. Moments later, blocks squealed as signalman "two-blocked" them, signaling readiness to execute the orders.

In their ready rooms, the pilots listened intently to the expected location of the enemy, the wind, weather, and the all-important "point option." The two carrier-air-group commanders cycled through each briefing to provide the coordination instructions on how each squadron's attack should support the overall plan. Intelligence officers showed photos of overhead and silhouette views of the German ships, additional recognition training to prevent a repeat of the mistakes that the black-shoes had made earlier in the morning. Shortly, too soon for some, the loudspeakers blared out, "Pilots, man your planes!"

On the flight decks, each plane captain assisted his pilot into the cockpit, briefing him on the aircraft's status and then turning over his pride and joy to the pilot—each wondering if they would get it back. Once the pilot was strapped in and satisfied, the plane captains climbed down to the deck, standing by to start engines, with a fire extinguisher ready for emergencies. High in the carrier's starboard-side superstructure, the "air boss" watched closely as the last plane captain climbed down, signifying all were now ready. The air boss grabbed a microphone and the flight-deck announcing system boomed "Start engines" over the noise of the wind and the rush of the sea past the huge hulls. Coughing to life with a puff of blue-gray smoke, each engine warmed and then slowed to an idle.

Raritan's signal light flashed the message that all was ready. *Sabine*, too, was ready, and the signal flags fell from her halyards, turning the carrier force into the wind. They also ordered speed increased to twenty-five knots, providing plenty of margin for the reduced wind speed. The aircraft design, deck spot, and loading all assumed a minimum thirty knots "wind across the deck." It did not matter whether Mother Nature or the carrier's main engines provided that wind, but it was imperative for successful launches.

The white flag with the red-diamond "Fox" soared on *Sabine*'s and *Raritan*'s port and starboard yardarms. The two flight-deck officers began their choreographed routine with the plane handlers. As the aircraft took to the air, one by one they turned to the left, climbing to join the growing groups of planes. First sections, then divisions, and finally whole squadrons formed together in this counterclockwise circling formation. When the last squadron, the torpedo bombers, joined, the air-group commanders took their place in the lead, setting off toward their rendezvous with Schröder's force—with destiny.

No sooner had the last aircraft left than the flight-deck elevators cycled again, raising eight F4F Wildcats for positioning, fueling, and arming. The eight pilots, dejected at their assignment to stay behind, buckled into the cockpits. Air bosses quickly started and warmed engines for the replacement combat air patrol. Without the carriers having changed course or speed, they roared off at the urging of flight-deck officers, formed into divisions of four, and climbed away for an altitude advantage.

Now it was time to recover the waiting Wildcats from the morning launch. They formed up into a counterclockwise, slowly circling group. At about thirty-second intervals, one of the F4Fs would break from the group and line up on the axis of the carrier. That pilot would lower his landing gear, his aircraft wobbling as he cranked down the wheels, and then he would lower his tail-hook and flaps. He'd look for and find the landing signal officer—LSO—at the aft port corner of the flight deck. Watching the LSO continuously, except for an occasional scan of his instruments, the pilot would follow the LSO's instructions, adjusting his speed or flight path as ordered. Finally, if the LSO thought that the landing would be safe, he gave the signal to cut the engine and glide to a touchdown. If he did not, the LSO would wave his signal paddles rapidly above his head, ordering the pilot to increase power and go around for another try.

There was one last obstacle to success. The tail-hook had to engage one of the steel cables stretched across the after end of the flight deck. After a safe landing, plane handlers coaxed each plane to a safe position forward and ordered the engine stopped. Only then could the pilot exit, turn the aircraft over to his plane captain with any gripes about what needed repair, and lay below to the ready room for debriefing on his flight. Once all the aircraft were on board, plane pushers started repositioning the fighters to the aft end of the flight deck, where the fuelers refilled the gas tanks, readying them as reinforcements for the CAP.

No sooner had the last plane landed than Admiral Hamilton ordered a course change to 340 degrees. The launch and recovery had taken him well to the east of Admiral Calhoun. He needed to stay closer, for the safety of his carriers with enemy battle cruisers in the vicinity.

— —

Vizeadmiral Klaus Schröder was surprised at himself. He found his thoughts increasingly turning toward his son Eric. He had no idea why. Why was Klaus thinking about him now? Was it another omen?

There were more immediate concerns. *Erfurt, Chemnitz,* and *Zirndorf* had also reported that dive-bombers were shadowing them. The Americans had found four of his scout cruisers, and *Gneisenau* had seen one other plane, low on the horizon, just beneath the clouds. Had the Americans found him? Would the American admiral launch an attack believing he knew enough for it to be a success?

It had been the same in the Imperial Navy of the first war: you never knew enough to be sure. The difference between great officers and lesser ones always came down to playing the odds. He could wait no longer. He had to trust his instincts. He called his flag lieutenant and issued the orders. Shortly afterward, the four battle cruisers increased speed to the southwest and began readying Arado 196s to catapult for a search centered in that direction. Turning into the wind, *Graf Zeppelin* and *Anton Fokker* began launching Messerschmitt fighters. All twenty-one Bf 109s safely left each of the carriers. Schröder had decided to keep one full staffel above his carriers and send the other ahead thirty kilometers toward the center of his scouting line. If the Americans launched an attack, these pilots would see it first. He had absolute faith in his combat veterans.

In France, the first of the four-engine Condors rose into the air to begin its ten-hour search mission to the west. Others quickly followed, until a fan developed to the southwest. Luftflotte 3 had finally received reports of clearing weather from Spain.

— —

The department heads had gathered with Sheppard in his sea cabin. He would have preferred his stateroom to have more space to spread out, but though it was tight, this would have to do. To make a smooth, hard surface, Sheppard had borrowed the serving tray that Jefferson had kindly used to bring a hot lunch. He had also taken an old chart from the conning station quartermaster and was using the back as a large piece of blank paper. With care, Sheppard began to draw from memory the armor scheme of *Argonne* and the column of the four German battle cruisers.

"Gentleman, I've called this counsel to resolve a problem of our own making. Commander Williamson and his people have thoroughly investigated the causes for the large pattern sizes we observed this morning." It seemed like days ago to Sheppard. He was so tired. "The results of their findings are technical, and I would not expect any of you, with the possible exception of Mister Becker, to understand," Sheppard said, flashing a smile at his resident genius.

As Sheppard had hoped, there were a few smiles and a chuckle from the doctor.

"Fundamentally, our main battery is very inaccurate. In all honesty, we cannot expect any more than three shells of a broadside to land near enough to a target at long range to have any chance of a hit. Unfortunately, we don't even know which three of our guns may be shooting accurately. We are going to have to fight this battle without the expectation of being able to penetrate the heavy armor of our enemy."

With the exception of Williamson, everyone looked stunned.

"Gentlemen, I share your concerns, but I think there is a way we can still carry out our mission and live to tell about it. First, let me say that each of you will have a critical role to play, and coordination of activity will be the key. Jonathan," he said, turning to Becker, "you will play the most important role in that effort. You're going to be the quarterback. Your air picture will be critical to our success as well as integrating it with the surface picture. Bronco, rather than Chuck and his people being our primary weapon system, your squadron will now have that responsibility. You are our halfback, and I am going to launch your whole squadron as quickly as we can when the battle appears imminent. You will have the ball, but you can't break through the line until the rest of us have made our blocks."

Sheppard talked for almost an hour, covering his plan and everyone's part. As he progressed, the department heads began to smile. They, too, recognized that it was just crazy enough that it might work.

"Well, gentlemen, that is it," Sheppard concluded. "I hope each of you has gotten to know me well enough to recognize that I value your input and, at this time, your criticism. If any of you see a way to improve on this plan, please speak up."

The men looked at one another. Finally, the most junior officer, Becker, spoke. "Captain, I think it will work, and I for one can't see a way to improve it."

"Thank you, Jonathan. I am certain we will not have to wait long to find out."

When the others departed, Doctor Blankenship stayed behind. "Captain, can I ask why you included me in this discussion? After all, I am a noncombatant."

"Hugh," Sheppard said, and then he paused. "I don't think the others understand what a smoke shell will do to wounded personnel lying in the open. I know you realize what white phosphorous is and what will happen to personnel showered by those pellets. I glossed over it during my presentation, but now, with you …"

Doctor Blankenship's face went pale. "My God, Captain! Do you know the hell you're going to unleash on those men?'

"Unlike the others, I do, and I will have to deal with the results of my actions before God and man. You, on the other hand, may have to deal with what I assume will be numerous German casualties we might later rescue."

Not wishing a discussion, Sheppard turned his back to his ship's medical officer and stepped back onto the conning station, where he could listen to the air-to-air radio network.

CHAPTER 10

ENGAGE

Argonne's signal lamp was clattering out a long message to Admiral Calhoun. Sheppard was trying to inform him of the alignment problem with his eighteen-inch guns and the hopelessness of any attempt to correct it at sea. It would not be well received. Ray Calhoun had a temper, and the odds of successfully completing Calhoun's mission had no doubt just become sixteen to one in Calhoun's eyes. In Sheppard's mind, he had done everything that needed to be done. Though there were culpable people on *Argonne,* they had demonstrated the best of intentions. As far as Sheppard was concerned, relief for cause and court-martial proceedings would be counterproductive.

It did not take long for a reply to come; it was in the form of an order. Sheppard had no option but to answer. Calhoun's message read simply: "Report the names and service numbers of the responsible officers!"

Calhoun wanted scapegoats. Sheppard was not going to give him any. He took a signal pad and wrote a quick response.

—-—

Six decks below Captain McCloud, Chief Evan Bryce had been watching his signalmen transmit and receive the messages. The scuttlebutt of what had happened and how the Captain had handled it already had flown throughout the ship. Chief Bryce knew, or at least thought he knew, what had happened to *Argonne*'s guns and who had been involved. When the answering message to Admiral Calhoun came back from the conning station, Bryce had another reason to respect his Captain. He decided that he would send this flashing-light signal himself. No snot-nosed lieutenant or wet-behind-the-ears signalman would ever read it, and that admiral would know firsthand exactly what *Argonne*'s crew thought of their Captain. As he started sending, the signal light didn't sound like a clattering old Model T; it was more like a machine gun, with staccato bursts. There were no long dashes of acknowledgment for any word until Bryce had repeated them more than a dozen times. Bryce only hoped the fucking admiral was trying to read it.

When the whole message was finally receipted for, it read simply: "Sheppard Jackson McCloud six-nine-one-seven-seven-five."

No more messages came from *Belleau Wood*.

New scuttlebutt flashed through *Argonne*.

— —

High above the sea, Commander Patrick "Irish" Hernandez had to make some decisions. As the *Raritan*'s carrier-air-group commander, he had led his three attack squadrons and fighters to the designated coordinates and found … nothing. The cloud layer had descended during the flight, limiting his range of visibility. If *Sabine*'s scouts had been unable to find Schröder, he did not feel his chances were much better. His torpedo planes had only about thirty minutes of fuel left before they needed to turn back. The last thing he wanted was to return to *Raritan* with all the heavy ordnance still suspended beneath his bombers. Accidents were known to happen in hard landings. He didn't want to do the enemy's task for them and take out his own flight deck. He cupped the microphone for the radio with his left hand.

"This is Irish. Bomber Ten and three sections of Torpedo Ten, attack the southern cruiser we passed. Scouting Ten and the rest of Torpedo Ten, follow me against the northwest cruiser. Squadron leaders acknowledge."

— —

"Bombing Ten, roger."

"Torpedo Ten, roger, sections one, two, and three follow me. Sections four, five, and six, follow Irish."

"Scouting Ten, roger."

Sheppard was enjoying the new lash-up that allowed him to listen in on the air-to-air network in the secondary conning station. Suddenly, the 21JS phone talker working with the Sugar George radar operator sang out with what was the first indication of the enemy's proximity. "Sugar King radar reports many bogies bearing zero-five-five, range six-zero miles."

Sheppard turned to his officer of the deck and shouted, "Man battle stations!"

This time, the sense of urgency was heightened by the strange time of day for the call. With renewed purpose, sailors ran in the familiar counterclockwise rotation. The repair parties threw open the equipment lockers and laid out tools, portable pumps, hoses, and firefighting equipment, knowing full well that now they might need them. Sailors donned breathing apparatuses and tested them but left the masks loose for the moment. Sheppard directed that all boilers be lit and the engineering plant split into four distinct parts. That way, any sudden casualty caused by enemy fire would only affect one shaft.

Shortly—in fact, the fastest Sheppard had ever timed—the report from Art Roberts arrived: "Battle stations manned and ready; condition zebra set throughout the ship; answering bells on all main engines; boilers one, four, five, six, nine, twelve, fifteen, and sixteen on service."

Now it was Sheppard's turn again. "Action starboard, air attack!"

The coordination between Becker in CIC and Williamson in the top level of the armored command tower was getting better and better as Mark 37 directors within Sheppard's field of view immediately slewed to face zero-five-five, the invisible beams of their Mark 4 radars reaching out to find targets. Sheppard made a conscious decision to not send Bronco and his squadron aloft yet. Before committing the Kingfishers to the fight, he wanted to wait and gain contact on the German surface ships. For now, he had to risk them being damaged by a strafing attack or a lucky bomb hit in order to preserve his primary strike's limited fuel supply.

— —

Commander Robert "Hawk" Talbot had reached a different conclusion than his fellow carrier-air-group commander, Irish. Over the years, he had learned to follow his instincts—the instincts of his ancestors. He was willing to try to find Schröder's battle cruisers and carriers, even if he only had one bombing squadron armed with semi-armor-piercing bombs for dive-bombing when he made contact. "This is Hawk—follow me!" he yelled.

Sabine's air group started an expanding-square search to the east. After ten minutes, Hawk turned his squadrons to the north. It wasn't long before they made contact. Hawk, as expected, was the first to see the Germans. He had always attributed his keen eyesight to the Indian side of his heritage; after all, he counted the great warrior chief Tecumseh as one of his ancestors. Unfortunately, the Germans he spotted were not seamen. They were airmen.

— —

Major Willy Kohlbert was an ace three times over, with seventeen air-to-air kills; he was part of the elite of the Luftwaffe trained to fly from aircraft carriers and attack ships at sea. As commander of *Graf Zeppelin*'s *Tragergruppe* (Carrier Air Group) he flew with his *stab schwarm* (headquarters flight) of Bf 109s and two *schwarmen* of four fighters each above the clouds. Circling well behind the cruisers, he kept a lookout for search planes or the American attack aircraft. His real goal, though, was to act as surprise reinforcements to the three other schwarmen below the clouds. Those twelve fighters would likely make the first interception of the Americans, once spotted. They would engage any escorting fighters and, if possible, make a pass at the bombers. It wasn't really important if they were successful in gaining bomber kills. What was important was that once they had engaged the fighters, they would notify him of the optimum time to initiate his surprise reinforcement. When they called, Kohlbert would lead the rest of the *jagdestaffel* (fighter squadron) in a diving attack through the clouds. Once the formation of the deadlier dive-bombers had been broken up, his formation would continue its dive against the slower torpedo bombers.

"Stupid Americans—they publish their doctrine in open sources," Kohlbert said under his breath.

If the American fighters broke off and tried to intercept his diving schwarmen, the initial group would follow them down, reengaging the fighters with a tactical advantage. This was a tactic that had worked many times against the English, until they learned to position an escort of fighters both below and above the clouds. The difficulty with his plan was in coordinating the two groups. Kohlbert's jagdestaffel had frequently practiced flying timed turns at steady speeds to keep the circling groups synchronized. An occasional peek above the thinning clouds by one of the lower schwarmen was all that they needed to keep one group positioned correctly above the other.

— —

"This is Hawk. Escort, engage one-oh-nines eleven o'clock level!"

Hawk watched as the Wildcats raced to intercept. It would boil down to the longer-range four .50-caliber Browning machine guns of the F4F-3s against the shorter-range armament of the Bf 109s.

"Three … two … one … now," Hawk whispered to himself as his Wildcats charged.

As if on cue, rivers of tracers poured from their wings, the sound of machine guns lost in the roar of wind passing his open canopy. Whose nerves were better? Who would break off first, losing the advantage with a rapidly expanding target? Hawk knew he had discussed this very type of engagement with his fighter pilots many times—and now they did not disappoint him.

As the twenty fighters passed each other, three Wildcats began smoking. Hawk watched two of them fall, gliding down with propellers frozen. Only one Bf 109 burst into flames, with one other smoking heavily, but Hawk's keen eyesight detected the telltale spray of coolant, and he knew the radiators of two others had suffered critical damage. American and German aircraft simultaneously turned to reengage. Now the vastly greater experience of the German pilots showed as a classic dogfight began, with the Americans outnumbered eight to five. It was not long before Hawk watched two more Wildcats fall in flames, with their pilots seeking safety in their parachutes. Only one additional German fell. The three surviving F4F-3s sought a respite in the embrace of the cloud cover.

Fighting Squadron Eleven had lost five Wildcats, but five Krauts would never make it back to their carrier either. Hawk also suspected the seven survivors had expended their entire store of 20 mm cannon shells before they turned to engage his passing Dauntlesses. That would make it a fair fight, with the twin .30-caliber Brownings of the Dauntless gunners against the two 7.9 millimeters of the Germans.

"Close up!" Hawk shouted. "The Gerries will go for any stragglers first."

If he kept his squadrons tightly packed, the eighteen Dauntless gunners defending against the seven attacking Germans stood a good chance. Despite their experience, the Germans had not faced the deadly twin Brownings of the SBD-3s before.

Hawk's gunner reported two additional Bf 109s shot down, and two more suffered the telltale spray of coolant. It had cost Bombing Eleven three dive-bombers.

"Close up, maintain formation!"

Hawk looked over his bombing squadron. Of the fifteen remaining aircrew, one gunner was slumped over his machine guns, though his pilot appeared to have escaped serious injury.

Hawk was feeling good about what he saw of the engagement in his SBD-3 off to the side of his air group with the two wingmen of his command element. At least, that was until ten 109s dove out of the clouds, catching the remaining dive-bombers by surprise. Six more dive-bombers fell in flames or spun out of control with a dead pilot. It cost the Germans only one Messerschmitt. As the German fighters continued their dive, Hawk realized in horror that this last group of Germans was intent on attacking the far more vulnerable and valuable torpedo bombers.

— —

"Here they come!"

"Got the son of a bitch!"

"Cut the chatter!"

Sheppard recognized Hawk's voice.

"Eddie, break right—there's a Kraut on your tail!"

Rat-a-tat-tat! Ugh, ugh!

"Eddie, bail out, you're on fire!"

"Eddie … Eddie, do you read?"

"Skipper, there's one on your tail."

"I know, I know. Shut up!"

Rat-a-tat—tat! Thud, thud!

Those must have been the heavier 20 mm cannons on the German fighters hitting, Sheppard thought.

"Looks like the CO's okay; he's got a good chute!"

"I said cut the chatter!"

Hawk again. Sheppard could only guess at the terror in the young fighter pilots facing their first combat. Much of what came over the radio was unintelligible, as one pilot stepped on another. New voices joined in, alone in a cockpit with their fears and anxieties. It was no wonder that the need to reach out for the comradeship of their fellow pilots was overriding Hawk's orders.

Sheppard looked at his conning officer, helmsman, the two lee helmsmen, and the others around him. There was reassurance in the discipline and formality of the conn, the routine of reports, orders, and acknowledgments providing structure and solace that all was normal and secure—an illusion that he alone knew could be shattered in an instant. It had been the same on *Shenandoah* until a Jap shell had demonstrated his flawed decisions. His men had paid the price in blood. Sheppard shook his head. He had to regain his focus. These men were relying on him now—not the dead of *Shenandoah*.

Hawk was on the circuit again, encouraging his bombers to tighten up their formation, though Sheppard didn't understand why.

"Good shooting! That'll teach 'em to mess with the best!"

"Knock it off!"

"One-oh-nines, eight o'clock high!"

"Tom, bail out, bail out!"

"Fighters, reengage diving one-oh-nines!"

Hawk was calling again, but this time his voice sounded desperate. As good as it was to listen to what was happening, Sheppard could not understand as much as he wanted about the air battle over the horizon. Who was winning?

— —

What Kohlbert had not anticipated was the diving speed of the heavy Grumman aircraft. His remaining fighters of the first group were unable to catch them before they attacked the nine remaining Bf 109s of his own. It cost him two more Messerschmitts before the Wildcats zoom-climbed back to the sanctuary of the clouds, just ahead of the pursuing remnants of his first schwarmen. His seven remaining Bf 109s were no longer a cohesive unit. Elements had broken free as the .50-caliber tracer bullets had zipped past the cockpits of the German fighter pilots.

"Don't engage the fighters," Kohlbert ordered. "Leave them to the others. We must get the torpedo bombers."

The first diving attack had claimed six for the loss of only one Bf 109. Kohlbert and the five other fighter pilots made their second attack from below and claimed four more of the Douglas TBDs without loss. Looking over his shoulder, Kohlbert saw the remainder jettison their torpedoes and dive for the safety of a wave-skimming retreat.

Almost out of ammunition, he had accomplished his mission despite the high cost. He smiled, congratulating himself on his three kills. He was the only quadruple ace in the naval component of the Luftwaffe.

— —

Helpless, Sheppard had listened as *Sabine*'s carrier air group was shot to pieces by the German fighters. The only thing he could do was direct his officer of the deck to coordinate with CIC and mark the location of the air battle on the navigation chart. If they lived through the afternoon, he would send his Kingfishers to find any survivors.

As the quartermaster of the watch was plotting the position of the air battle, the bulkhead speaker above him blared, "This is Hawk! Four German battle cruisers and four destroyers, forty-four fifty-five north, nine fifty-six west. Attacking!"

Sheppard jumped out of his chair and hurried to the quartermaster's small chart table. His quartermaster was already plotting the reported position, only forty miles to the northeast, but it was clear that Admiral Calhoun's force was headed in the wrong direction. Sheppard was grabbing for a signal pad to retransmit the report to *Belleau Wood* just as the signal flags were run up the halyards of *Belleau Wood*—ordering a column turn to an intercepting course. He could hear the squeal of the blocks as his own acknowledgment was run up, hardly pausing at the dip. The execute signal came an instant later. Raising his binoculars to scan the horizon, Sheppard also noticed the long dashes of *Sioux City*'s signal light receiving the admiral's instructions to take *Bellingham* and scout ahead of *Belleau Wood* and *Argonne*. Then it was *Colchester*'s turn to receive a similar message, but taking *Burlington* and scout to the east on the starboard bow of *Belleau Wood*.

"Smoke bearing three-three-five," reported his 1JS phone talker.

— —

Irish Hernandez had made contact with the two cruisers spotted earlier. Having heard the battle of Air Group Eleven, he anxiously scanned the skies for the anticipated German combat air patrol. But he saw … nothing. There were no defending fighters!

At ten miles, the ugly black splotches of antiaircraft shell bursts began to dot the sky. It was not long before Hernandez and his other dive-bombers were bouncing from the near misses. The Germans were using their long-range guns to target the dive-bombers.

Good, he thought. *At least my torpedo planes will get closer before the short-ranged flak weapons start knocking them down. Maybe the Gerries haven't spotted them yet.*

The first bomber, 10-B-13, began smoking and fell away from the formation. All of the pilots of the SBD-3s were having difficulty with the jostling caused by the flak bursts. 10-S-4 was the next Dauntless to fall. Hernandez held back the Devastators until they could divide into four roughly equal groups for a coordinated attack from both bows of each cruiser.

Despite the ferocity of the flak, the roar of the engine drowned out all but the closest bursting shells. Damage to the bomber and scout squadrons was beginning to accumulate. Hernandez could see smoke from some of the engines, and two Dauntlesses were falling behind the attack formations. Thirty-seven bombers reached the pushover point initiating their run, including his command element of three. Unfortunately, the cloud ceiling forced glide-bombing runs instead of the steeper and more lethal dives. Without a steep dive, the telescopic sights on the Dauntlesses were useless, blocked by the engines from a clear view of the targets as the SBDs reached the point to drop. Each pilot had to guess at the release points for the bombs. The results were disappointing.

As Hernandez pulled out of his glide and zoomed beyond the range of the 20 mm flak, he banked to observe the results. Only three hits occurred, though several near misses probably wrinkled the hull plating on both cruisers. A single thousand-pound bomb struck the main deck just forward of one cruiser's second funnel, penetrating before the fuse action was initiated. That cruiser was visibly slowing and listing, with smoke pouring from both funnels.

The other cruiser was farther away, but looked as if it had been hit twice. The first bomb did not threaten the ship, but her bow was bent to starboard, and she was settling forward. The second hit looked deadly. She was settling by the stern and rapidly slowing to a stop. Hernandez could see that her aft-most turret was set at a crazy angle, which explained the cruiser's dilemma. The five-hundred-pounder must have detonated right among her propeller shafts, opening her engineering spaces to sea. Without propulsion, she coasted to a stop twenty-five miles from the approaching American surface ships.

Slow and vulnerable, the Devastators began their approach. Hernandez cursed his timing as the TBDs had to endure the full weight of the remaining antiaircraft fire that the cruisers could muster. Six of the torpedo bombers splashed before they reached the release point for their torpedoes—one disappearing in a fireball when the four-hundred-pound torpedo warhead exploded. Twelve Mark 13 "fish" entered the water, aimed at the cruisers.

Unable to help, Hernandez watched the torpedo wakes. Six of the seven that shot at the first cruiser missed ahead, as his pilots misjudged the speed of the slowing cruisers. Three of the five directed at the other also missed. In disbelief, he watched as the three that looked like sure hits ran harmlessly under the keels of the two cruisers. At the cost of one-third of the TBDs, Torpedo Squadron Ten had achieved ... *nothing!*

— —

"Herr Admiral, *Chemnitz* and *Erfurt* have been attacked by three squadrons of bombers. Both are sinking and request assistance."

"Very well, Fritz, detach a destroyer for each from Eisner's battle cruisers to assist."

Schröder was thrilled with the results of the air battle between his Bf 109s and the American squadrons and additionally pleased that the Americans had wasted a full strike on his scouting line. However, the reports from the scout cruisers and *Graf Zeppelin*'s Messerschmitts indicated that five American squadrons had attacked his forces. No single carrier had five bomber and torpedo squadrons assigned. There had to be two American aircraft carriers in the vicinity; neither had been located. He had to find them before they found his carriers—if he were to strike before he was struck again.

His second problem was the fuel state of his fighters. *Graf Zeppelin*'s were very low on fuel and out of ammunition. *Anton Fokker*'s had not expended any ammunition but also needed fuel. These Messerschmitts, with barely two hours' endurance, were really not suited to carrier operations. Reluctantly, he decided to break the spot on his carriers' decks for launch, put the Ju 87s back in the hangars, and land his fighters.

Surely, as soon as they were on board, German forces would know the location of the American carriers. His Arado 196 floatplanes would not fail. It wouldn't take more than an hour to refuel and rearm the Messerschmitts. Then he could launch all his dive-bombers with an escort of five schwarmen of fighters. Forty-two Stuka dive-bombers would make short work of the American carriers.

— —

As *Argonne* changed course to the northeast, the gun directors tracked to the left, using invisible radar beams and maintaining contact on the four bogies detected, which appeared to be fanning out from a common point.

"Quartermaster, coordinate with CIC and plot the origin point of those air contacts!" Sheppard ordered.

Jonathan Becker called Sheppard on the 21MC to report that the closest bogie was sixteen miles and closing. Chuck Williamson was next, with a request for permission to open fire; he desired to engage the air contacts as soon as they were within range. Sheppard wanted to wait. There had been enough of shooting at friendly contacts today. He wanted a visual identification of the aircraft *before* he authorized Williamson to shoot. It wasn't long in coming.

It seemed that John Hamblen was just as good at identifying aircraft, at least friendly, as he was with ships. Using his long glass again, he reported on the 1JC phones, "Bogies, hostile, twin-float seaplanes. No US or British scout-observation planes have twin floats."

Sheppard passed the order, "Commence firing," on the 21MC.

Chuck Williamson next spoke to his phone talker. "Sky One, control mounts five-oh-one, five-oh-two, and five-oh-four; Sky Three, control mounts five-oh-three, five-oh-five, and five-oh-seven; Sky Five, control mounts five-oh-nine, five-one-one, and five-one-three."

Sheppard watched as his five-inch mounts swung quickly to match the bearings of the directors as fire-control personnel deep inside *Argonne* threw "J" switches to align the designated gun mounts to the indicated directors. The long barrels of the five-inch/54-caliber guns rose forty-seven degrees to loft the shells out to their maximum range. "Load special antiaircraft common" was the next command from gunnery. Sheppard could only guess at the surprise of the five-inch gun mount crews when they got their first look at the radar fuses. Many questioning glances would surely be exchanged between gunners as the plastic-nosed projectiles rode the hoists to the mounts, were loaded, and then rammed into the gun breeches with a cartridge case behind.

Williamson had no sooner spoken the words, "Fire continuous, five rounds, commence firing," than eighteen five-inch guns cracked together. Now it was a race, with each gun's crew trying to reload and shoot faster than their mirrored opposites in each mount and each mount's crew trying to fire faster than all the others. Hot-case men grabbed the thirty-three-inch brass empty shell casings with thick asbestos gloves as the breech blocks dropped to eject the cases from the bores. The empty cases were tossed out the auxiliary ejection chute to land with a clatter on the decks behind the mounts. Staccato barks of the guns mixed with the clangs and bongs of brass powder cases hitting the decks and each other. In twenty-five seconds, the guns fell silent. Williamson passed, "Check fire; replace ammunition." Handling-room crews labored to refill the ready-use racks with ten new projectiles and powder cases that magically appeared one at a time from the top of the dredger hoists leading to the magazines on the fourth deck.

Ninety seventy-pound projectiles were spinning toward three different Arado 196 floatplanes at 2,700 feet per second initial velocity before the first one arrived. Just visible through his binoculars, Sheppard watched as shell after shell detonated. Three flaming meteors fell where once floatplanes had flown.

— —

The German battle cruisers were firing at Hawk Talbot and his remaining Dauntlesses. Approaching from the starboard side of the column formation, Hawk was facing forty-eight guns, all firing as fast as the gunners could reload. It wasn't long before the commanding officer of Bombing Squadron Ten, flying 11-B-1, fell out of formation, jettisoning his bomb and gliding to a water landing with a frozen engine. Another shell took the left wing off 11-B-9. Neither of the two-man crew was able to bail out before it hit the water.

Hawk's own 11-00 was next. A close shell burst with a deafening blast caused Hawk's SBD to jump.

"Hawk, we're on fire," yelled his radioman-gunner.

Hawk undid his harness, rolled his aircraft over to the left, and fell out, noticing that another SBD was also on fire and doing the same. Three of the four crewmen in the two planes, including Hawk, parachuted successfully to a water landing.

Every aircraft was damaged, but eight made it to the pushover point. Again, the cloud ceiling limited the SBD-3s to a shallow gliding attack. 11-B-3 staggered and fell out of control when the pilot died from a direct hit by a 3.7 cm shell. The gunner in 11-B-2 was killed by a shell burst above the aircraft that also wounded the squadron executive officer. Seven bombs were dropped. Five were aimed at the leading battle cruiser. Hawk saw one hit as he floated down in his parachute.

Two bombs were dropped on the other one, but Hawk could only see one explode in the water alongside. Of the seven remaining Dauntlesses, two more were shot down on their pullouts. Bitterly disappointed, Hawk could only disentangle himself from his parachute on landing, and inflate both his "Mae West" and raft, climbing into the latter. Would the Germans pick him up?

Weighing on his mind even more than trying to survive in the ocean was how much they had sacrificed to achieve so little—one hit for a full squadron!

— —

Sioux City was signaling, "Skunk, bearing zero-two-three, range seventeen miles." The light cruiser had discovered one of the drifting German scout cruisers. American and German warships were now in contact with each other.

As Sheppard watched, it took less than a minute before the signal lights of *Bellingham*, as well as *Sioux City*, were flashing acknowledgments to Admiral Calhoun's order to engage the German cruiser. Like hounds scenting a fox, the American cruisers turned to attack, twin puffs of black smoke showing their eagerness.

Three minutes later, the flash from the muzzles of their turrets sent twelve 130-pound projectiles each toward the German. It took almost twenty-four seconds for the rolling thunder to reach Sheppard on the conning station of *Argonne*. He raised his binoculars in the hope of seeing the light cruisers' target but only could see the multicolored forest of shell splashes rise above the horizon. The four turrets on each cruiser flashed and rumbled again. This time, the forest of splashes produced a rising column of smoke in addition to the spray. It must have been *Sioux City*'s hit, as her guns now began to fire continuously at a rate of eight rounds per minute. Shortly thereafter, *Bellingham*, too, went to rapid fire. In less than three minutes, however, both cruisers stopped shooting. *Sioux City*'s signal light began flashing a request to Admiral

Calhoun to dispatch a destroyer for the purpose of rescuing survivors, as both cruisers turned to regain station on *Belleau Wood*'s port bow.

Sheppard decided he could wait no longer to launch Bronco and the rest of his squadron.

"Officer of the Deck: Prepare to launch aircraft."

Art Roberts relayed the order to the men waiting, not very patiently, on the fantail. A few seconds later, the starter cartridges of the two Kingfishers fired, but only one engine caught and ran. A new starter cartridge in Mustang Zero-Five had to be loaded by the pilot. This time, Barry Jensen took his time with the starting procedure. When the new cartridge fired, Mustang Zero-Five's Pratt & Whitney engine caught, and both aircraft engines warmed.

Sheppard verified that everything was ready except for the report from his officer of the deck. Finally, it came.

"Launch aircraft," he ordered.

The catapult cartridges fired, sending two OS2U-5s shooting aloft.

"Prepare to launch aircraft!"

This time it took longer, much longer, since the armored hatch had to be slid forward and two Kingfishers hoisted to the cradles on the catapults, wings unfolded, depth charges hung, and the scout-observation planes fueled. Eventually they were ready, and two more Mustangs joined up with Bronco. The last four went much faster, as some of the work could be done in the hangar, and at last all eight Kingfishers were airborne. The huge armored hatch shut with a clang. The aircraft-and-boat crane was lowered and locked into place, clearing the stern arcs for turret III to fire aft.

— —

Admiral Hamilton was ready to turn the carriers into the wind. *Raritan*'s air group and the remnants of *Sabine*'s air group were circling his carriers, waiting to land. *Sabine*'s signalmen started running the admiral's orders up her halyards. Quickly acknowledged, the execute signal turned the carriers into the failing wind, and speed was raised to thirty knots. First off were the eight F4F-3s from each carrier as the replacement combat air patrol. It was then time to start landing aircraft. The remaining Devastators were lowest on fuel and thus had priority in landing. One from Torpedo Squadron Ten, with a wounded pilot, ignored a wave-off and crashed into *Raritan's* barrier. It took a full eight minutes to lift the injured pilot and dead gunner from the aircraft before it was unceremoniously pushed over the side. The remaining TBDs landed successfully.

Next, it was the turn of the F4Fs of Fighter Squadron Eleven to land on *Sabine*. As the three remaining Wildcats taxied forward from the arresting gear, each pilot extended one or two fingers, denoting the number of kills he had achieved. Then it was time for the dive-bombers. What had been joy turned quickly to sorrow. Only four of the bomber plane captains had an aircraft to greet. Seventeen SBD plane captains stood with the eleven TBD captains in a forlorn and poignant group, occasionally shading their eyes, scanning the sky and hoping against hope to see one more—theirs—limping home to the carrier. Alas, they would be bitterly disappointed that day. The eight F4Fs of the combat air patrol were the last to be waved aboard by the LSO.

Sabine finished recovering her few and was waiting for *Raritan* to finish recovering her many.

— —

Vizeadmiral Schröder suspected sabotage. What else could explain the disasters that had befallen three of his Arado 196 seaplanes? The French dockyard workers had been all over his battle cruisers in Brest. The only ship they had not worked on was *Scharnhorst*, and her aircraft was operating normally, currently scouting to the west-southwest. He held back the rest of the battle cruiser floatplanes until a complete inspection of every nut and bolt could be made, including draining the fuel tanks and inspecting their interiors for explosives. He needed those planes to find the convoys when his fleet was out of range of the Condors.

Erfurt's loss was regrettable, but her report of two light cruisers confirmed that his fleet was properly deployed for an interception of the Americans. Those two cruisers were undoubtedly the scouts for the two American *Antietam*-class ships. At any moment, his battle cruisers and destroyers should be making contact. The carriers would be close by, allowing him to launch dive-bombers as soon as they were ready.

He directed his flag lieutenant to turn the two carriers and four destroyers into the wind. Signal flags flew from his flagship's yardarm, and the carriers turned east into the light wind. Schröder enjoyed watching the Messerschmitts land. The first, of course, was Major Willy Kohlbert. Schröder sent his aide to request that the young major come to the flag bridge so that Schröder could personally congratulate him on becoming the highest-scoring ace in the fleet. This was going to be a great day for the Kriegsmarine.

He still needed to be careful. Though he was much more powerful than his enemy, the Americans still outnumbered him. Those two armored cruisers that *U-179* had reported might show up unexpectedly. His destroyer escort was no match for them.

Turning to his chief of staff, Schröder said, "Fritz, turn the carriers back toward Eisner. I want to stay within visual distance, for safety, as soon as the last one-oh-nine has landed."

Unless he had badly misjudged the relative positions of his forces, he calculated that about the time he sighted them his air strike would be ready. It also would not hurt that, being in visual range of the battle cruisers, he would get the credit for the victory.

— —

"Skunk bearing one-two-zero, range eighteen miles."

Sheppard wasn't sure what *Colchester* had detected. Could it be another one of the scout cruisers—perhaps one of the four that had been located earlier? He checked the quartermaster's DR of the last contact reports from Scouting Squadron Eleven. Yes, this contact should be the third cruiser of the scouting line. That left only one unaccounted for. It should be about twenty miles farther in the same direction. Through his binoculars, he saw *Colchester* sending the long dashes of an acknowledgment, followed by the familiar twin puffs of smoke from both her funnels and those of *Bellingham*. Admiral Calhoun was sending the right-wing cruisers to engage and sink this contact.

Sioux City's signal light demanded Sheppard's attention. "Smoke bearing zero-four-five!"

That had to be the German battle cruisers. All the pieces were falling into place, except for the location of the two German carriers. This, Sheppard remembered, was the way *Shenandoah*'s agony had started: a contact report from radar, the thrill of a lifetime of practice and preparation coming to fruition, and then the crash of the guns as his ship sought revenge for the Japanese attack. Would this end the same way? How many of his men would have to die today? Would he suffer in agony again for weeks as surgeons tried to repair a shattered limb—or worse? Sheppard said a quick prayer for his ship, his men, and himself.

He had to block those thoughts. He wished the waiting would end and that the Germans would come within range of his guns. He would be busy then, guessing on how to avoid the next salvo, directing his guns to accomplish his mission. Courage in battle was really only a product of training and staying busy. As long as you could keep your mind occupied with the problem of the moment, it was easy to be heroic.

— —

Raritan was signaling. Admiral Hamilton, standing on *Sabine*'s flag bridge, had been watching the circling fighters of her old combat air patrol and the few remaining SBDs of *Raritan*'s Air Group that had yet to land. There seemed to be more urgency in this message. "Skunks bearing zero-four-five and zero-one-five, range one-six miles!"

Hamilton knew that *Raritan*, like *Sabine*, lacked the new surface-search radar called Sugar George. He had to act quickly. *Raritan* needed another ten minutes to finish landing her aircraft. If he turned away now, he would lose eight Wildcats. If these contacts were German ships, their contact reports would be all the information that Schröder needed to launch an air strike and cripple or sink the American carriers. Hamilton would need every fighter he had to defend his fleet from the inevitable German air strike.

It was imperative to direct *Quincy* and *Bethlehem* to investigate and engage the contacts if they were enemy. Signal flags detaching the two armored cruisers flew up *Sabine*'s signal halyards. "Form column, investigate contact bearing zero-four-five!" The two cruisers would need destroyer support if Schröder's battle cruisers were in the vicinity. Hamilton's next signal was flashed to the squadron commander of DESRON 28, directing him to detach a division to screen and assist the armored cruisers.

Raritan was signaling again: "Contacts German cruisers!" As if to add punctuation, four columns of water rose beyond the carrier as the first German salvo landed short.

"What kind of cruisers?" Hamilton shouted to no one in particular.

Six more minutes, Admiral Hamilton thought. Six more minutes and he could turn his carriers away from the threat. His armored cruisers were increasing speed to close the Germans. Hamilton could see the guns of their forward turrets start to elevate. Once they started firing, perhaps it would distract the Germans and save *Raritan*. The one remaining thing he could do was direct his remaining destroyers to make smoke and charge the enemy. He had to save *Raritan* with her nearly full air group!

— —

Vizeadmiral Schröder could not be happier. *Karben* and *Schifferstadt* were both in contact with the American aircraft carriers. *Schifferstadt* was also engaging the closer one. He had been right in his estimate that there were two—both were of the *Brandywine* class, fifty-five thousand tons each. Their high, long funnels had made it easy to spot and identify them before the Americans reacted.

His last Messerschmitts were landing on *Anton Fokker*, and soon he would be able to ready his strike. It would take time. The shorter-endurance fighters would need to be launched last, thus maximizing the time they had for engaging the defending American Grummans. His flight-deck crews would have to work hard to bring the Stukas up from the hangars at the same time the Messerschmitts were stuck down. His fighters on *Graf Zeppelin* also needed rearming, and a few required repairs to combat damage. He would do without those five for now.

— —

John Hamblen's head poked out of the armored hatch on *Argonne's* forward Mark 38 director. Having the best view of anyone gave him a sense of responsibility and empowerment. Using the long glass, he saw the mastheads of first one and then all four German battle cruisers.

Funny, he thought to himself, *for the first time since leaving the Academy, I'm not nervous.* He knew what he had to do and was sure he could do it.

"Guns, Spot One," Hamblen said. "Four mastheads in sight; bearing zero-five-two; estimated range two-eight miles!"

He then turned the director toward the contacts, coaxing his trainer and pointer onto the leading target. If the worst happened, Hamblen hoped someone would find the letter he'd written to his father. He wished his father could know his own recognition of the wisdom of his advice. He wanted him to know what had transpired with the British and Captain McCloud's reaction. More than anything, he was determined not to let Captain McCloud down—to not betray the faith shown in him.

— —

Chuck Williamson began the litany of gunnery officers, using his 1JC phone talker. "Spot One, control Turrets I, II, and III. Turrets I, II, and III, load armor-piercing!"

Sheppard's phone talker kept him apprised of what was being said. It was time for him to designate a target. Using the 21MC, Sheppard passed. "Guns, target is second battle cruiser in the column."

Doctrine stated that ships should fire at their opposite numbers in the enemy line. Sheppard knew that *Belleau Wood* would shoot at the leading German. As long as the Americans were out of range of the German guns, it made sense to concentrate and try to eliminate one enemy. But since *Argonne* was shooting large patterns, she should let luck give her a chance in all directions from what she was aiming at. The clangs of shells being rammed home confirmed that Williamson was loading the guns.

The conning officer interrupted him. "Captain, flagship is signaling."

Sheppard raised his binoculars to read the flag hoist. "Zero-one-five corpen!"

A column turn to course zero-one-five degrees? What was Ray Calhoun thinking? All they had to do was execute a slight turn to starboard, and *Belleau Wood* and *Argonne* would accomplish the classic capping of the T, allowing all their turrets to fire at the Germans with the enemy only able to respond using his forward guns. Calhoun was condemning the two American battle cruisers to fight a passing action with the Germans headed southwest and the Americans, east by north.

More signals as *Belleau Wood* turned to the new course: "Prep speed four-five!"

Calhoun must be avoiding the TBS for fear that the Germans will listen in, Sheppard thought. At least Calhoun was going to go into battle at high speed. The signal light was now flashing: "Maintain open order; conform generally to my movements!"

Good, Sheppard thought, the admiral was at least going to let him chase salvos and act as he thought best. Being outnumbered as badly as they were, it would be a disaster if Sheppard and Bailey did not do everything they could to make the Germans miss. Finally, the command was given by flag hoist: "Commence firing!"

— ▬

Dolf Hamilton was beside himself. The German salvos were falling all around *Raritan*, the distant thunder of their guns an urgent reminder of the danger. Each time one landed, he counted the shell splashes and thanked God when he saw all four. The last two times, there had only been three, indicating that at least two German shells had hit home. Smoke was starting to rise as the last F4F landed on *Raritan*.

He grabbed the microphone for the TBS and ordered, "Immediate execute: emergency turn two-one-zero, speed three-eight!"

Turning away from the German cruisers and increasing speed to the maximum of his carriers was all he could do to help. With luck, *Raritan*'s damage would not be too severe.

Sabine heeled well to port as she turned at high speed to the right. How many aircraft would he lose from the sudden angle of the deck? Hamilton grabbed the windscreen as he lost his balance, transfixed at the sight of *Raritan*, smoking and heeling. Acting like an overgrown destroyer, she even had a bone in her teeth. *Raritan*'s turning hard to starboard caused the next two German salvos to fall well clear. On both carriers, the propeller wash from number four shaft passed directly through the number two propeller. The resulting vibration would put any rodeo bucking bronco to shame. The ships had been tested on sea trials after every overhaul, and this was not unanticipated by the designers of the carriers. Both had withstood the test well then, with no damage. But now it was too much for *Sabine*'s damaged stern.

— —

Konteradmiral Eisner stood on the flag bridge of *Scharnhorst*. The reports that had come in from the scout cruisers had been most satisfactory. *Erfurt*'s, particularly, convinced him that at any moment he should gain contact with American warships to the southwest. He wasn't sure whether he would initially have to face only light cruisers or the two *Antietam*-class battle cruisers. It really didn't matter to him. His squadron was more than powerful enough to sweep both forces aside. Once he dealt with the surface ships, he could turn to the south-southwest and cut off the American carriers from any escape.

Schröder might be the fleet commander, but he would be the hero, just as at Jutland. His father had died aboard Hipper's flagship, *Lutzow,* before she sank. Eisner knew his father had been proud of him as a boy, but the elder Eisner had never seen the real success he had achieved in the service. As the Kriegsmarine's youngest flag officer, he had the dream assignment: command of a battle cruiser squadron on independent operations. Now he was going to win a great victory, even if it was only against the Americans. He had hoped that it would be Force H under his guns. Exacting his revenge for his father's death on the English would be the highlight of his career.

Eisner was startled out of his daydreaming by the rumbling whoosh of heavy shells, followed by red-tinted, sky-high columns of water shooting up all around his squadron. He had no idea where they were coming from, until a lookout reported seeing a flash and smoke on a bearing of 235 degrees. Because his floatplanes had not finished their inspections yet, he felt blind and extremely vulnerable. Konteradmiral Eisner had to close his enemy to engage and do it quickly. Flags fluttered from *Scharnhorst*'s yardarms, ordering a speed increase to thirty-eight knots just as a green-tinted salvo arrived short of his flagship.

— —

Bronco and his radioman were spotting the fall of *Argonne*'s shells and had a priceless view of everything that was happening. According to doctrine, Bronco should have been passing corrections for *Argonne*'s salvos on the spotter network, but the reality was that the new Mark 8 main-battery fire-control radar was doing a better job. All Bronco had to do now was concentrate on staying out of range of the German antiaircraft guns and watch for German fighters. Accordingly, he hugged the bottom of the thinning cloud layer with his squadron, in readiness to climb and avoid any of the Messerschmitts that might try to claim some easy kills on the Kingfishers.

"Wow! Mister Burdick, will you look at that!"

Bronco had seen it. "Beautiful!"

The second German's hangar had erupted in a volcano of orange swirling flame, smoke, and aircraft parts in a sea of red splashes. Bronco wondered where *Belleau Wood*'s spotter aircraft were. Why hadn't they launched yet? It didn't seem to make any difference; her shooting was good. The green splashes were centered on the leading battle cruiser. As he watched, he counted the splashes of her salvo: six ... seven ... eight. A hit, but he couldn't see any effect.

"Okay, Mustangs, time to form divisions, echelon right second division above. We'll take our directions from Panther."

— —

Admiral Hamilton raised his binoculars. *Quincy* and *Bethlehem* were nearly to the horizon, firing broadsides as fast as they could. The closer German cruiser was ablaze from end to end, listing to port and down by the bow. Her stern belched a plume of yellow flame at least three stories high. Between the blasts of his armored cruisers' main batteries, he could hear secondary explosions from the German. There was no sign of the second contact, but his armored cruisers were altering course to close the unseen enemy.

It did not matter much, as Hamilton understood that Schröder knew where he was. The deadly Stukas would soon be winging their way from the two German carriers. Hamilton looked over at *Raritan*, smoke still pouring from her forward elevator. No more shells splashed in her vicinity. "Thank God for small favors," he said to no one in particular.

The real question, though, was whether she would be able to extinguish the hangar fire before her air group was rendered incapable of flying by the smoke and soot.

Then he noticed something else. "Lieutenant, did *Sabine*'s bridge acknowledge the order to come to course two-one-zero?"

As if in answer, the halyard blocks above him squealed. A quick glance confirmed his worst fear: *Sabine* was again disabled.

"Lieutenant, recall *Quincy* and *Bethlehem* as soon as they have dealt with the other scout."

Hamilton was going to need every screening vessel he had to fend off Schröder's air attack. He did not even have the ability to open the range.

— —

It wasn't long before Commander Radisson and the aft engineering repair party had made their way to the steering-gear flat. Just as they had the last time, they found the circuit breakers tripped to the two steering hydraulic motors. This time, resetting them didn't do any good, as they immediately tripped again. Radisson ordered his men to take local control and manually try to reposition the rudder. That, too, was unsuccessful. He decided that there was nothing more he could do until Captain Evans decided to slow down. Perhaps then the reduced stress from lower speed would allow him to move the rudder.

Regardless, this news and his assessment had to be delivered in person. Radisson began to formulate a plan as he made the long climb to *Sabine*'s bridge. It didn't surprise Radisson to see Admiral Hamilton waiting there with Captain Evans.

"Kenny, how bad is it?" the admiral asked.

"I don't know," was the only honest answer he could give. The weight of the world seemed to close in on him.

"What do you want to try, Kenny?" Captain Evans interjected.

"Well, Captain, I was thinking of connecting a hydraulic test pump to the rudder rams. When we slow, I'll raise the pressure until the rams move. If we can get the rudder away from hard over, maybe then we will be back to where we were."

"What is the risk?" Evans asked.

"If the rudder doesn't move, I could damage the piping or the rams, and short of a shipyard dry dock, that rudder will never move again."

"I see."

Solemnly, as if passing a sentence on every soul aboard, Captain Evans said, "All right, Kenny, set it up, and let me know when you are ready."

— —

Eisner could see the masts of the American battle cruisers through his spotting glass. They were drawing rapidly to the right and appeared to Eisner as being on a course of north. There were two things troubling him. The first was easily corrected. Eisner knew that Schröder was to the east-northeast of him. Were the American battle cruisers trying to outflank him and attack Schröder's carriers? If they were successful, his battle cruisers would not have air cover to destroy search planes or prevent attack from even the antiquated Swordfish of the Royal Navy's Fleet Air Arm. Those torpedo planes had managed to damage three of his four ships on their return to Brest. He would have to head off the American ships and fight on a parallel course.

He turned to his flag lieutenant and ordered a column course change to the north. The *Scharnhorst*'s captain also reported that the Americans were within range of his main-battery guns. In two and a half years of war, it had always given Eisner satisfaction when he could order the guns to start firing. This time was no different. As his flagship steadied on the new course, the first split salvo of four guns crashed out and turned the sea on *Scharnhorst*'s port side to froth. His squadron soon followed suit.

Eisner's second concern was more of a puzzle. His guns could outrange those of the *Antietam*-class ships, yet they had opened fire while still over the horizon. In fact, they had already gained two hits on his squadron. *Scharnhorst*'s was inconsequential, piercing the fo'castle and flooding some small spaces in the bow. His damage-control parties were shoring up the adjacent bulkheads. The hit on *Gneisenau* was more serious. All her floatplanes had been destroyed, and a significant fire was raging in her hangar. The fire was the real problem; it could spread to the secondary armament and ready-use ammunition storage. He gazed through his binoculars at the damage-control parties struggling with their hoses.

— ∙ —

Sheppard saw the German flagship's control tower and mast start to come together. She was turning. He checked the others. No, they were not. It was a column turn, which meant they would all pass through the same turning point. Sheppard jumped to the 21MC. "Guns, target the turning point; rapid fire!"

Chuck Williamson knew exactly what to do. He ordered Joe Archinbald in forward main-battery control to set target speed to zero, range and bearing to the leading German. He ordered all three turrets, "Continuous fire; master key!" With those commands, the automatic firing key was locked shut with the fire-control computer shooting the guns automatically as soon as the gun laying matched the computer's order.

All three turrets leapt into action. Each gun fired as quickly as ammunition was rammed into the chambers, the breeches closed, and the gun raised to the correct elevation. The instant a gun returned to battery from firing, the gun captain lowered it, racing through the reloading cycle like a bootlegger running from the law. Once the breech locked shut, he threw his gun-ready switch to "ready," and the breech end dropped into the gun pit as the muzzles elevated to fire again. With the exception of the loading cycle, *Argonne*'s main battery was in full automatic.

— —

Holding the stick with his knees, Bronco searched for *Colchester* and *Burlington* with his binoculars. He saw that they had closed on the contact to the south. Bronco guessed the range to the scout cruiser to be about fourteen miles. First *Colchester* and then her sister ship started shooting. By the third salvo, both had achieved straddles and went to continuous rapid fire. It was all one-sided, as the German 15 cm guns could not reach the American light cruisers. After that, it was just a question of time before another of Schröder's scouts became a defenseless, motionless, floating wreck. Once she had gone dead in the water, not appearing to be in danger of sinking immediately, the Americans turned to hustle back to the north. The sound of heavy guns required their attention.

Bronco figured that the light cruisers might need a vector. He radioed *Colchester*. "Bacon, this is Mustang Zero-One, recommend corpen zero-two-five to regain Buccaneer."

It made sense to Bronco to do whatever he could to help.

"This is Bacon, roger."

In the absence of orders to the contrary, the primary duty of light cruisers was to steam to the sound of the guns and scout the enemy.

Bronco watched as the two cruisers heeled sequentially, white bones in their teeth reaching for their main decks. His vector was a hunch.

— —

"All stop!"

Commander Radisson knew that the order meant *Quincy* and *Bethlehem* had made short work of the other scout cruiser and that Admiral Hamilton had dispatched two of DESRON 28's destroyers to pick up survivors as the armored cruisers turned to close on the carriers.

Radisson had not wasted the time while *Sabine* circled at high speed to avoid any German gunfire. He had sent his chief machinist's mate to set up a test pump capable of going up to the designed rupture point of the rudder hydraulic piping. He knew that the rudder had to be brought back closer to amidships for there to be any hope of controlling *Sabine*'s course using the engines. It would not even be possible to tow the stricken carrier with the rudder hard over. *Sabine* would yaw even at three knots and break the tow wire. The only hope was to move the rudder.

As *Sabine* slowed, Radisson began to apply pressure through the test fittings in the rudder hydraulic lines. With pressure on the aft side of the port hydraulic ram and the forward side of the starboard ram, he vented off the forward port and aft starboard supply lines. If the rudder was going to move at all, this should do it. He really did not have a choice; he had to risk a rupture. He ordered every man out of the rudder flat as the pressure from the test rig climbed above the maximum operating point of the system. His chief machinist's mate, Rufus Jones, refused to leave.

The two men silently prayed as the pressure approached the maximum designed pressure of the system. The rudder did not budge. Radisson and Jones looked at each other solemnly and kept the test rig pumping.

— —

Bronco and Petty Officer Miller in Mustang Zero-One watched transfixed as the red-tinted columns of water rose one after the other in what appeared to be one continuous mountain of rising and falling bloody water and pink mist.

"Mister Burdick, holy cow, will you look at that!" Miller called on the intercom.

Bronco was enthralled by his own spectacle of *Argonne*'s starboard side continuously wrapped in gun smoke, punctuated by balls of flame unevenly spaced in time but with all nine guns firing twice a minute. He could even hear the rolling continuous thunder of her firing above the wind roaring past his cockpit.

"Miller, you don't see this every day."

The second German entered the water columns. Miller let out another whoop, and said, "Yeah, look at that turret!"

The battle cruiser's forward turret had stopped turning, with one gun partially raised and the other muzzle falling to the fo'castle deck, indicative that an eighteen-inch shell had penetrated the barbette and exploded in the machinery space. Then there was another hit. The aft main-battery director sailed overboard. She had been hurt and lost a quarter of her offensive capability. As Miller reported what he saw, Bronco kept up a running commentary for the benefit of everyone listening in on the spotter network.

Miller did not see the first hit, but the third German battle cruiser stopped shooting for almost two minutes. Bronco saw the anomaly, but both he and Miller were at a loss to explain what had happened.

Then Bronco saw the second hit. The hangar erupted in smoke and flame as a shell passed through it. A third hit came in quick succession. Bronco could only guess at the cause when black soot burst from her stack, but it was enough to prove the shell had hit home in her engineering spaces. Soon she was losing speed, and the formation became ragged.

The last battle cruiser saw what had occurred to her sister ships in the deadly red columns and tried to turn early. *Argonne*'s large salvos still managed to catch her, but only with one hit. The armor-piercing projectile landed on the quarterdeck, causing a white splash when it detonated. The last ship was essentially intact but nearly collided with her sister ship as the latter slowed.

— —

The damage reports were coming in: *Scharnhorst* had been hit twice, but neither was significant. *Gneisenau* had lost turret Anton and a director. It was *Yorck* that had been hurt the worst: she'd lost her main fire-control computer and a quarter of her boiler power. If Eisner wanted to keep his four battle cruisers together, his maximum speed could now be only thirty-five knots. At least *Blucher* had avoided that hell of red splashes.

Eisner wondered which of those two ships was shooting the red-dyed salvos. That was the one he should be concentrating on. She was the greatest threat to his force. It might be the second ship in the column, but that was illogical. The best-trained and most proficient ship always led, carrying the commanding admiral. Should he change target assignments? Should he deviate from doctrine?

"Herr Admiral, mastheads bearing zero-six-eight."

That was probably Schröder hustling to share the glory. Better to follow the doctrine under his watchful eyes.

— —

As the German column reformed, 45 cm main-battery salvos continued firing in revenge. Three were concentrating on *Belleau Wood,* with only one shooting at *Argonne*. White, yellow, and green salvos straddled Bailey's battle cruiser as both Americans raced north at forty-five knots. Sheppard could not believe that Bailey was not altering course to throw off the German gunnery. Even with the high speed, a steady course let the Germans take target practice. He watched in disgust at Bailey's incompetence, as a German salvo of white splashes landed. The armored hatch on *Belleau Wood*'s hangar rose, twisting in the air to a height of over a hundred feet. The hangar became a cauldron of flame. *Belleau Wood* must have had most of her Kingfishers fully armed and fueled. Shredded by the shell's explosion, they must have ignited.

As Sheppard watched, secondary explosions confirmed his worst fears: Bailey's pride and connections in Washington had just cost the lives of probably a hundred men.

— —

The commanding officer of *Fellbach* was determined not to share the fate of *Karben* or *Schifferstadt*.

"Weber, take binoculars and a signalman to the masthead. You will be our eyes. These Americans seem to know our location before we sight them."

"Jawohl, Herr Kapitän!"

"Keep a sharp eye out for the American carriers. Their high funnels should be easy to spot."

The captain was determined *Fellbach* would keep up a steady stream of reports to Schröder on the two *Brandywine*-class aircraft carriers.

As the reports came in, though, the captain was puzzled. Why was one circling and the other now stopped? Had she been damaged by *Schifferstadt* before her sinking?

— —

Vizeadmiral Schröder knew the position and movements of all the Americans. Smiling, he also suspected that they did not know his carriers' location. One of the American carriers had been crippled by his scout cruisers before they were sunk. *Foolish Americans! They should scuttle that ship and get on with searching for me!* If the Americans were foolish, that Eisner was an imbecile. Four of Germany's battle cruisers were under his command, and he could not quickly eliminate two *Antietam*-class ships inferior to his in every category. It had to be Eisner's incompetence. There was no other explanation.

Now Schröder would have to rescue him with his Stukas before the situation deteriorated further. He directed his flag lieutenant to signal *Anton Fokker*, asking how many Ju 87s were ready to launch immediately. Schröder would proceed to *Graf Zeppelin*'s bridge to ask Captain Becker the same question. Leaving for the bridge, he decided not even to wait for the answer, instead directing his chief of staff to turn both carriers into the breeze and increase speed to thirty-two knots for sufficient wind over the deck. The Americans and British really had a better idea for aircraft carriers. He needed more wind over the deck to launch the Stukas with full bomb loads from his shorter flight deck than their full-length designs required.

As the two German carriers heeled away from their turns, Schröder got his answers. *Fokker* had eight ready while his flagship had twelve. In less than a minute, the flag hoist soared on his flagship to launch aircraft. All of the Junkers' Jumo 211 engines roared to life, warming quickly. Admiral Schröder watched as the first of *Graf Zeppelin*'s twelve Ju 87Cs gained air speed and lifted off with five-hundred-kilogram bombs to attack the American battle cruisers. Like many sailors, he was entranced by the drama of aircraft operation. Schröder would redeem the situation that Eisner had created.

— —

Every time one of the blue-dyed salvos landed in *Argonne*'s vicinity, Sheppard altered course. Sometimes he turned his ship toward the center of the salvo; other times he turned away, left, or right. The direction was based on his intuition as much as the silver dollar he was tossing and catching each time. Whichever way the ship turned, he stopped the inboard shaft on the outside of the turn to prevent excessive vibration. To maintain speed, he had to run the other engines at their maximum power, but so far it had been worth it. *Argonne* had not yet been hit.

Belleau Wood had. Evidently, Kevin Bailey did not know what to do when faced with three different-colored salvos falling around his ship. Sheppard watched as Bailey maneuvered, but the course changes did not follow any one color, as they should have. Bailey was also not trailing a shaft, either, as Sheppard was.

"My God, you can actually see her masts shake!" Sheppard said under his breath.

A white salvo straddled *Belleau Wood*, but only six columns of water rose—before, there had been eight. Thick black smoke poured from the base of her aft funnel. *Belleau Wood* was losing speed. Sheppard had to do something to save *Argonne*'s sister ship.

CHAPTER 11

DECISIONS

Chief Machinist's Mate Rufus Jones screamed in pain as a piece of hydraulic pipe tore through his left arm just above the elbow and another nicked his forehead. Blood trickled down his face and oozed between the fingers of his right hand as he grasped the wound. His face contorted in agony, not only from the injuries but also the sting of the hydraulic oil.

"I ... I guess that's all we can do for the ole girl," he muttered.

Kenny Radisson nodded. *Sabine*'s rudder had not moved. Radisson shut down the pump and called to his men to take the chief to sickbay. He would give the bad news personally to Captain Evans.

Radisson made the long climb up to *Sabine*'s bridge. A piece of the ruptured hydraulic pipe had nicked his own scalp, but he hadn't noticed the blood. While ducking under piping in the rudder flat, he had also painfully bruised his shoulder. His uniform, soaked in hydraulic oil, was holed and torn. As he climbed, dripping oil in a trail of despair, he had to be careful not to slip on the steel ladders. He must be quite the sight, he thought, with one arm limp at his side. Soon enough, Captain Evans thought so. He took one look at Radisson and sent for a flight surgeon.

"Captain, I'm sorry," Radisson said. "We have tried everything we could think of to free the rudder. I'm afraid our last effort actually made things worse by rupturing a pipe in the rudder hydraulic piping."

"Is there anything you could do if you had more time?"

Gazing at the deck, dejected, Radisson continued, "Time isn't the problem, sir. We just don't have the equipment to disconnect the crosshead and rams. Even if we did, I can't say that it would make any difference."

"How did this happen?"

"There must have been more damage outboard from the torpedo explosion than we suspected. Steaming at high speed probably aggravated it."

Evans's shoulders slumped. Radisson recognized that his Captain was squarely facing the possibility of the worst thing any captain could do. "Kenny, what do you need to fix it?"

"We need to dry dock *Sabine* in a shipyard. Sir, I know your next question, and the answer is there aren't any close. The ones in Gibraltar are still too small. There was one in Alexandria, but that has been lost. That leaves England, but to get there, we have to get past the entire Luftwaffe. Even moving the ship is now something that will be very difficult. We can try it with the engines. Using different combinations of thrusts from the shafts might let us move more or less straight."

"Thank you, Cheng. The flight surgeon is here. I want that head wound looked after. I'll work with the navigator, and we'll try moving her with the engines as you suggested."

— —

Rupert Wythe-Jones had not had more than four hours' sleep when he called his crew and the other standby crew together for a preflight briefing. Air Commodore Blackstone had been most insistent on maintaining contact with Schröder *at all costs*. Wythe-Jones knew what that meant. The air commodore would sit in his headquarters while expecting Rupert and his men to pay any price necessary to stay in touch with the German carriers and battle cruisers, even if it meant running out of fuel or being shot down by German fighters.

The staff meteorologist gave them the unpleasant news of thinning cloud cover near Cape Finisterre. It would probably be completely gone by the time they arrived in Schröder's vicinity. "Unpleasant" was too mild a description, though; the mission was now bloody dangerous. There was a high probability of German fighters lurking overhead, vectored by Seetakt radar, and no place to hide.

The briefing was almost over when an elderly man in a naval uniform moved the overcoat covering his lap and sleeves, revealing the broad stripe of an admiral with four thinner stripes above. Wythe-Jones and everyone else jumped to their feet. Evidently, Admiral of the Fleet Sir Dudley Pound, First Sea Lord of the Admiralty, had been there the whole time.

"Gentleman, I am aware of your orders to maintain contact at all costs. Indeed, I originated them. Your Sunderlands are the best-equipped aircraft we have to accomplish this mission. There are currently three convoys within three hundred miles of Schröder's force. At this stage of the war, every convoy is vital. Our allies, the Americans, are engaged in a battle with Schröder's fleet as we speak, but frankly, I am not confident of the outcome. Every aircraft we have with sufficient range to reach Schröder will participate in an all-out attack tonight. You will have to guide them to the Germans. It is not an understatement to say the fate of the Empire hangs in the balance. *Godspeed!*"

— —

Hit again and again, *Belleau Wood* desperately needed help. The smoke from her fires was almost completely obscuring her from Sheppard's view. And Ray Calhoun was strangely silent. Sheppard went to the 21MC. "Engineer, Captain, give me everything you have got! Make smoke."

Huge clouds of soot-laden smoke began to pour from *Argonne*'s funnels. Designed to shield the *Belleau Wood* from optical instruments, it would accomplish nothing against the fire-control radars on the German battle cruisers. They would still get an accurate range through the smoke, but the bearing accuracy would be poor. That was what Sheppard was counting on.

Without orders from Calhoun, Sheppard would have to take control. He called the signal bridge on the 21MC. "Make to DESRON 30: 'Request torpedo attack on German battle line.'"

Sheppard was not confident that they would accomplish much, but he had to try everything he could to save *Belleau Wood*. At the least, the American destroyers should make the Germans open the range, further degrading their gunfire accuracy.

No longer concerned about unlocated German forces, Sheppard signaled *Sioux City* and *Bellingham* to support DESRON 30 in their torpedo attack. He suspected the German destroyers would attack the American destroyers as soon as it was obvious a torpedo attack was developing. The two light cruisers should make short work of the smaller German ships.

— —

Konteradmiral Eisner was becoming more confident. The leading American battle cruiser was slowing and smoking heavily. A huge fire was burning near her stern with occasional secondary explosions. The green-tinted salvos were more ragged, so he guessed there must be a problem with her fire control. Though accurate, the salvo size of the red ones was not improving, either.

Thank God for small favors, he thought. *That ship must be new and not properly disciplined, but she has a good captain. I need to be careful of her before I destroy him.*

Eisner did not think he needed to worry much more about damage to his ships. If he could concentrate his fire for a little while longer on the leading ship, he would finish her off and then be able to bring the full weight of his four battle cruisers against that last *Antietam*-class ship.

Eisner was glad he had turned north, as these Americans were steaming away from their carriers and the two supporting armored cruisers. He didn't think their guns presented a threat, but they would have forced him to divide his fire.

Child's play, he thought. *When I finish off the battle cruisers, I can race south and sink the carriers.*

Though unfortunate, the damage to his ships thus far would not prevent him from continuing with the mission against the convoys. He could even dispatch *Yorck* back to France for repairs and be little worse off than he had been a week ago.

— —

Kevin Bailey did not know what he was doing. Deep down, that truth had penetrated his consciousness. However successful his career had been in Washington, it had not prepared him to deal with the situation he now faced. Bailey could not anticipate the effects of his previous decisions once the battle started. As the commanding officer of *Belleau Wood*, he had wanted to keep his Kingfishers ready for launch while in the hangar. He had personally ordered them to remain fueled and stocked with ammunition. But stacking bombs and depth charges in places most convenient for loading, rather than keeping them in the security of the armored magazines, had set up the ideal conditions for disaster. His scout-observation squadron commander had protested, but Bailey had been determined to show Admiral Calhoun that he could launch aircraft faster than *Argonne*. Calhoun already knew that *Belleau Wood*'s gunnery was infinitely better than McCloud's. Kevin would prove that Hamilton's praise of Sheppard was misplaced. It was *he* that deserved the accolades, not that New York City street thug.

However, *Belleau Wood*, now crippled, drifting to a stop, and at the mercy of the Germans, continued to suffer because of Bailey's action— or, rather, inaction. He should have kept maneuvering to avoid the German fall of shot, taking advantage of the new Ford fire-control system's ability to keep the guns on target.

A shell from the third white salvo had pierced his hangar. It had failed to penetrate the armored deck that the fueled and armed Kingfishers rested on, only creasing open the armor between adjacent plates. As it ricocheted off, the shell had sliced through a Kingfisher.

Still within the hangar, it had detonated, destroying all the aircraft and boats and setting the paint, wood from the boats and gasoline afire. The burning aviation gasoline flowed through the cracked armor into the rudder machinery flat. Ablaze, with electrical leads melted, the machinery stopped answering the orders from the helmsman in the command tower.

As the inferno spread, the depth charges stowed in the hangar detonated at random intervals, each explosion contributing to the destruction not only of the hangar but also the rudder machinery and the adjacent berthing spaces. Eventually, the explosions breached the hull. Seawater came flooding in, finally slowing the destruction as *Belleau Wood* settled by the stern.

As the damage reports flowed in, Bailey retreated to a corner of the armored command tower. "What should I do?" he whispered to himself.

"Captain, the aft engineering uptakes have been destroyed, answering bells on two main engines!"

"What?"

"Sir, Admiral Calhoun has been badly wounded on his way to the bridge and been taken to sickbay!"

"How?"

Why couldn't he just focus on one problem at a time—think it through, get recommendations, solve that before moving on to the next?

"Damage control reports the forward uptakes have been hit. Aft boiler group evacuated, most personnel dead. Three taken to sickbay."

"What ... should ... I do?" he asked of no one in particular, chin down, shoulders slumped, eyes searching the faces of those around him.

— —

As Vizeadmiral Schröder watched the third Stuka trundle down *Graf Zeppelin*'s flight deck, he smiled. Soon, this strike would solve Eisner's problem; he would still have all his fighters and remaining dive-bombers to attack the American carriers. With one already crippled, the rest of his Ju 87s would be more than enough to cripple, if not sink, the lone survivor.

The loss of four of his scout cruisers was regrettable, but he would still be able to accomplish his mission. The Condors had finally left their bases; this was what he desperately needed—reconnaissance! Soon, he would know the location of every convoy in the eastern North Atlantic. Once they had been located, the floatplanes on the battle cruisers and the aircraft on his carriers would suffice to maintain contact. His heavy ships would intercept, beginning the slaughter.

Schröder, though, had failed to realize one real problem. Just as the admiral and Captain Becker were watching the German dive-bombers launch and circle the carriers as they formed up, so too were most of the German sailors. It was always hard to look at nothing when there was something going on nearby. Perhaps it was the hope not to miss an accident or just the novelty of aircraft flying nearby. Whatever the reason, the German lookouts responsible for detecting surface contacts were not doing their assigned task with sufficient discipline.

— —

Sheppard cringed as each salvo fell around *Belleau Wood*. Each was now producing more hits. He knew—or, rather, hoped—that the armored deck had deflected them from entering the "vitals" of the engineering spaces and magazines. As *Argonne* raced to her aid, Sheppard raised his binoculars to survey the damage.

Many of her antiaircraft guns lay in ruins. Their crews were probably dead or injured. Some gun directors uselessly served as tombs for the dead and dying inside them. Thick black smoke boiled from her superstructure. Sheppard guessed that all her uptakes had been destroyed and the boiler room crews incapacitated—probably dead. Without steam, she was limited to only the six diesel generators that she should have running deep in her auxiliary machinery spaces, enough for perhaps one main-battery turret to function. *Belleau Wood* was on fire, virtually defenseless, and continually being pounded by the Germans when Sheppard's smoke screen finally gave her a momentary respite.

Sheppard knew that the Germans would close the range. They needed to be less than twenty thousand yards away if their 45 cm shells had any hope of penetrating the sloped armor of the main belt. Even his planned attack would not stop them. He had to consider abandoning *Belleau Wood* and Admiral Calhoun to their fate. His mission was to stop Schröder, not to save a sister ship.

— —

Konteradmiral Eisner had ordered a simultaneous turn toward the Americans. As the range decreased, he finally got a good look at the battle cruiser that had taken over the lead of the enemy formation. This was no *Antietam*-class ship. There were medium-caliber turrets adjacent the bridge and eleven antiaircraft mounts visible on her starboard side, not the eight mounts that his reference books showed for American Civil-War-class battle cruisers. These were much larger and more powerful ships: *Santiago*-class ships. No wonder that they had given his squadron difficulty.

Well, it would not matter. Clearly, one was defeated already from the weight of his four ships. The other must surely also sink under the guns of *Scharnhorst, Gneisenau, Blucher,* and *Yorck*. He had closed the range to twenty kilometers. The smoke screen that the American had laid was dissipating. It was time to turn back into a column on a course of north. He could then use his broadsides to make short work of the Americans.

— —

Schröder watched his ninth Stuka leave the end of *Graf Zeppelin*'s flight deck and clear the bow. These dive-bombers epitomized birds of prey hunting their next meal of ships. He could see the face of the gunner before him. A good young German, determined to make the Fatherland proud of his actions today.

How well things are going, Schröder thought. He had still not been located and was about to unleash his most powerful weapon.

Every Stuka he had could drop its five-hundred-kilogram bomb within twenty-five meters of the aim point. No ship was safe from the Stukas' onslaught. He felt so proud of these winged warriors.

Thus, when the ninth Stuka ran into a column of water 120 meters tall and crashed, Schröder couldn't fathom why.

The four columns of shell splashes finally registered, not only in Schröder's mind but also in the minds of the derelict surface lookouts. They all stared through their binoculars and saw the two block-like shapes that had closed on the formation from the east. The image danced in the field of view of his Zeiss binoculars. Schröder could not believe it. *Force H cannot be here!*

It was impossible for them to go from the western Mediterranean to the southern Bay of Biscay in a day. What was it that the Italians were reporting, then? Their fears?

Regardless of how it had happened, Schröder needed his battle cruisers to protect the German aircraft carriers now. The Americans could wait!

— —

Ever since he had finished coordinating with the American admiral on those two battle cruisers, Admiral Sir Bruce Hardy had been racing north-northeast just outside visual range of the Spanish coast at the best speed his museum pieces could maintain. Helped immensely by the steady flow of contact reports from Four-One-Five Squadron, he had watched the developing situation as the Americans gained contact, engaging Schröder's forces. It had been a bloody shame that their air strike had gone awry.

Hardy had made a conscious decision to not break radio silence and relay the contact reports directly to the Americans on the frequency he had arranged with the American Admiral Calhoun. He had felt that maintaining the element of surprise was the only way he stood a chance of getting at Schröder's carriers without having to face the far superior *Scharnhorst*-class capital ships. If he ever came within range of their 45 cm guns, he would lose his ships. Those German battle cruisers were faster than *Renown* and *Repulse* by over ten knots; as well, they outranged their fifteen-inch guns by five miles.

So Sir Bruce had turned Force H to the west when he achieved a position directly upwind of Schröder's carriers. The Germans would have to come to him if they wanted to launch a strike at the Americans. When the German carriers turned into the wind to launch, the two groups of ships were closing at a combined speed of sixty knots. With a closing range rate of two thousand yards per minute, Hardy had decided to start shooting at the earliest possible moment. If Schröder did not run, removing the threat of more aircraft launches, Hardy's ships would make short work of the thin-skinned German aircraft carriers.

Hardy knew that the two US battle cruisers were engaging the four Germans, but he could not understand why the American carriers had not launched a follow-up attack now that they knew for sure where the German heavy forces were. He was getting frequent reports of aircraft to the southwest, near the extreme range of his Type 281 radar. Those aircraft were most likely a combat air patrol orbiting near the American carriers.

The British admiral had heard the reports of the first radar returns as the aircraft were climbing away from *Graf Zeppelin*. Hardy had to detach *Ark Royal* and *Leonidas* with four destroyers for flight operations. He had no option but to split his small force. In case Schröder redirected his dive-bombers at *Renown* and *Repulse,* he wanted a combat air patrol of his own.

— —

Sheppard needed to reverse course and lay a new smoke screen to cover *Belleau Wood*. The Germans had closed inside her immunity zone, where their 45 cm shells could penetrate her side armor, with potentially catastrophic results—*Argonne*'s, too, for that matter. He directed his conning officer to come right with full rudder, slowing the number two shaft.

As *Argonne* started her turn, a German 45 cm armor-piercing shell struck the command tower.

Kaa-lang!

Sheppard had heard that sound before, amid the spray of sparks and molten meteors. He stood transfixed. He stared at the twisted steel that had once been his bridge—sharp edges askew, plating bent at random angles and blackened. Wiring from cable runs whipped in the wind. Shattered glass rose and fell, catching the sun in a kaleidoscope of reflections and twinkling snow.

Sheppard had been there. He could see again the blood and gore—the men and bodies of men, *his men*, some moving in agony, many not. It was as if he were in the command tower right this moment. He had failed again. Again his men had died; again others were screaming in agony, soon—but not soon enough—to die. Other men lay maimed and broken, to return home shattered in body and mind. Why hadn't that shell hit him? Why couldn't he be among the dead? Why did he have to suffer this agony? *Why, God?*

He could smell the explosion, the scorched paint, hot metal, and blood. Images of *Shenandoah's* sickbay danced in his mind—the stack of lifeless limbs his surgeons had severed, and his chief medical officer, spattered in blood, trying to reassure him that his own leg was not in the pile.

If he had not turned, they, his men—no, they had names, they were his friends—would still be alive. Art Roberts, Chuck Williamson—dead. Sheppard could see Rachel and Kristen standing in the doorways of their homes in Norfolk when the Western Union telegrams arrived, standard trite phrases expressing regret and condolence, and Chuck's fatherless children arriving home from school to news that would change their lives forever. It was his fault—all his fault. Sheppard sought the solace of his chair, slumping into it with head lowered and eyes downcast, searching for answers to the unanswerable questions.

— —

Vizeadmiral Schröder had managed to execute an "emergency battle turn away." The tactic had been used by Reinhard Sheer at Jutland to save the High Seas Fleet from annihilation; Schröder now used it to save his carriers. He fired off a plain-language message to Eisner, ordering him to come east at maximum speed. He tried to recall his Stukas and redirect them from the Americans to the British battle cruisers now chasing him. Only *Graf Zeppelin*'s dive-bombers answered his frantic signaling to return and attack the British. *Anton Fokker*'s were already climbing to the west and out of signaling range.

Vizeadmiral Schröder brought his carriers to their maximum speed of thirty-three knots. Given time, he would outrun the British, but every turn that his two captains made chasing salvos slowed their ships. It was a question of running straight to open the range or zigzagging to force misses. Schröder decided to let them continue maneuvering.

Major Willy Kohlbert stood off to the side of the flag bridge, awaiting the admiral's attention.

"Yes, Major?" Schröder said, feeling somewhat annoyed that the fighter pilot would disturb him at this time.

"Herr Admiral, the lookouts did not spot the *Ark Royal* or the cruiser that left Gibraltar yesterday. I fear that they may be launching aircraft to attack us."

"Unfortunate, but what can we do about it? I can't turn back into the wind to launch your fighters."

"No, Herr Admiral, but I checked, and if we stay at this speed and have no more than four aircraft on the flight deck, I think we can launch the Messerschmitts with the current wind over the deck."

"Good, Willy, very good. I will direct the *Fokker* to do likewise. Get your three best pilots and prepare to take off."

Schröder issued the necessary orders to *Graf Zeppelin*'s captain. He would have to steer a straight course for two minutes to launch the fighters, but if he could prevent an air attack on his carriers, it would be worth it.

— —

Raritan's signal light was flashing. Dolf Hamilton needed some good news. It was clear that *Sabine*'s fight was over. If there were any likelihood of Schröder's ships finding him, he would have to abandon and scuttle her. Hamilton could not afford to keep all the others fixed in one place, hoping for a miracle, if Jake Evans was not able to control the course of his ship. Calhoun, cleverly, was leading them away to the north. That would give him more time.

At least there was some good news. *Raritan* was reporting that all fires were out. The message continued that she had suffered twelve dead and seventeen injured from the four 5.9-inch shells that had exploded. One had detonated in a machine shop, another in the spare-engine storage compartment. The one that caused the fire had exploded in the forward port corner of the hangar. The last had decimated the aft engineering repair party, causing most of the casualties. The hangar fire had proven stubborn, finally succumbing to a combination of the fire curtains and hoses manned by the forward hangar-repair party. That was the good news. Four aircraft, all F4Fs, had been destroyed by the shell explosion or resulting fire. Many of the other aircraft in the hangar had been soaked in seawater. It would be at least sixteen hours before they were flyable. It would also be an hour before *Raritan* was ready to resume flight operations.

All the usable aircraft that Hamilton had now consisted of the sixteen Wildcats he had in the air. Between the inoperable *Sabine* and the soaked *Raritan*, there was not a single attack plane he could send off against Schröder.

— —

"Captain, Guns."

Silence.

"Captain, Guns!"

Again, silence.

"Captain! Guns!"

Sheppard blinked; the 21MC was shouting at him. How could that be? Chuck was dead, wasn't he?

"Guns, Captain," Sheppard answered, still confused.

"Captain, Guns: the enemy is starting another column maneuver away. I have ordered main-battery plot to set target speed zero and put the turrets in rapid fire."

Shaking his head, Sheppard finally returned to reality. "Chuck, you're alive!"

"Uh … yes, sir?"

Recovering his composure, Sheppard said, "Guns, report your condition in the command tower!"

"Captain, we took a ricochet off the forward face of the command tower. The shell never detonated. Some of the younger men are a little shaken, but no casualties." As if it were an afterthought, he added, "Captain, thank God you turned when you did, or we would have been hit square."

"Very well. Officer of the Deck, report your status!"

"Captain, we're fine, but the bridge has been remodeled. The German shell passed right through it from starboard to port, bouncing off the command tower."

Sheppard shook his head again to clear away the demons of his own imagination. Why were the German battle cruisers suddenly turning away just at the moment when they should be closing to destroy *Belleau Wood*? He had to start trusting his instincts again. His turn had actually saved his men.

— —

In company with *Leonidas*, *Ark Royal* had turned into the wind, quickly launching twelve Fulmar fighters. Hardly a match for Bf 109s, with a top speed of only 280 mph and a climb rate of twelve hundred feet per minute, the Fulmar—actually an adaptation of an RAF light bomber— was nevertheless the only thing the Fleet Air Arm had. As the fighters climbed away from the carrier, both she and the light cruiser turned back to the west at the maximum speed that *Ark Royal* could muster. *Ark Royal*'s captain did not want to get too far from the protective guns of the British heavy ships.

The carrier's fighter-direction officer began to coax the Fulmars onto the German dive-bombers. It wasn't long before they tally-hoed the Ju 87s and began their attack. In the hands of a skilled pilot, even the two-seat Fulmars could be effective. Having to fight for two years with inferior equipment made the surviving FAA pilots skilled, if nothing else. As they attacked from below and behind, it was not long before all eight of the Stukas were smoking, flaming, or limping damaged back in the direction of their carriers, jettisoned bombs exploding in the sea.

Admiral Hardy had been contemplating a strike by his Swordfish torpedo bombers, attempting to slow the German carriers for the guns of *Renown* and *Repulse*, when his Type 281 radar operator reported additional air contacts. Hardy decided that those contacts were probably fighters. They must be very good pilots to have accomplished the downwind launch he had forced on Schröder. If those fighter pilots were that good, it would be suicide for the Swordfish crews to attack. Hardy decided not to try, for the sake of his men. He would have to damage those two carriers with gunfire alone before they reached the safety of the German battle cruisers' guns.

— —

"Flagship is signaling, Captain," Sheppard's conning officer said as he was studying the shell splashes at the German turning point.

Sheppard turned and walked to the other side of the conning station platform. He missed some of the message, but what he read explained the absence of direction from Ray Calhoun: "Injured, Captain Bailey incapacitated. What are your intentions? Captain Jensen sends."

It could only mean that Ray Calhoun was badly hurt and unable to continue controlling his ships. Harvey Jensen, Ray Calhoun's chief of staff, was passing control of the battle cruisers, light cruisers, and Destroyer Squadron Thirty formally to him.

Sheppard grabbed a signal pad and started scribbling "To *Belleau Wood*: 'Report your status.'" If he was in command of both battle cruisers, he needed more information.

No sooner had the signalman arrived than Sheppard handed him the new message. Within a minute, *Argonne*'s signal light was clattering. Sheppard wrote additional signals: "To DESRON 30: 'Recall torpedo attack.'" With the German's turn-away, his destroyers faced a long stern chase; they would likely be destroyed long before they got out ahead of the racing Germans. They needed to be well ahead of their targets for their Mark 15 torpedoes to have any chance of hitting.

Belleau Wood's reply arrived. "Boiler uptakes and intakes destroyed, ship aft of frame 310 on fire, spaces aft of frame 304 flooded, hundreds dead, 476 wounded, in no immediate danger of sinking. Need firefighting assistance."

Sheppard grabbed the message pad again and wrote, "To *Sioux City, Bellingham*: 'Close *Belleau Wood* and render assistance.'"

He had the information he needed. *Belleau Wood* was only in danger if Schröder's battle cruisers came back to finish her off. There was also a danger of the Germans ordering submarines to close and sink her. Sheppard flashed one more message to the destroyer squadron commander: "Detach a division to provide antisubmarine patrol in vicinity of *Belleau Wood*; with remaining force, follow me!"

That was when Jonathan Becker called up to report eight bogies closing from the east, range fourteen miles. Then came one more message flashing from *Belleau Wood*'s signal light: "Guard 2716 kilocycles for coordination with …" He could not make out the rest because of smoke. *Coordination with whom—Admiral Hamilton?* Sheppard had no idea.

— —

Konteradmiral Eisner saw the eight Stukas passing overhead en route to the American battle cruiser, black antiaircraft bursts starting among them. Their attack should be sufficient to at least slow the American and let him deal with the Brits who were threatening Schröder. How quickly that weakling had called for help after letting the British sneak up on him! Germany would see who the hero in this battle was.

Eisner raised his binoculars to study each of his ships as they reached the turning point.

That enemy battle cruiser may not be able to hit a target, Eisner thought, *but her captain is seizing every tactical opening and making the most of his poor gunnery.*

Once again, Eisner's squadron endured the crimson forest of shell splashes. Since putting the leading enemy out of action, *Scharnhorst* had received only one more hit, which did nothing but destroy one of his 10.5 cm twin mounts as it continued below decks, detonating in a berthing space. Turrets Anton, Bruno, and Caesar were firing steadily. Only Dora, hit earlier with a heavy shell from the other ship, was out of action.

Now it was *Gneisenau's* turn to enter the red columns of shell splashes. There was a flash of a hit on her forward command tower! Another hit ricocheted off Turret Dora without significant effect. Her signal light began flashing. The calamitous hit on the command tower had killed the captain and everyone else inside the structure. The ship's executive officer was now directing her from the after conning station. That was unfortunate. Schieffer had been a promising officer. That remaining American was lucky.

Yorck and *Blucher* turned early, slowing to maintain interval. *A good move*, Eisner thought, though Schröder would never have approved. At least *Blucher* avoided the area of destruction, but *Yorck* did not.

Emerging, her signal light reported that Caesar's barbette had been hit; damage was being assessed before firing could continue. Eisner vowed not to make another column turn until that remaining American battle cruiser shared her sister ship's fate.

— —

Anton Fokker's Ju 87s were closing directly at *Argonne*. Jonathan Becker had alerted Chuck Williamson as soon as the first aircraft had risen above the radar horizon. As each rose, Williamson had assigned one of his Mark 37 directors to track it. When some headed east, he dropped them to concentrate on the westbound threat. His litany aligned every five-inch mount that would bear while the aircraft were still at eighteen miles.

At fourteen, *Argonne* commenced rapid fire. The Ju 87 pilots might have been the best the Luftwaffe had for attacking ships, but unfortunately they had no experience with the American long-range five-inch/54-caliber guns. Chuck Williamson's first salvo of twenty-two special antiaircraft common projectiles destroyed three of the eight. Immediate jinking and side-slipping threw off the aim of subsequent salvos—but also spread the formation. As Williamson watched from the command tower periscope, two more Stukas became flaming wrecks before they reached the pushover point where they started their dives. The famous Stuka howl soon filled the ears of the *Argonne*'s 40 mm and 20 mm gunners.

— —

Boatswain's Mate Second Class Cruz was not satisfied to be just the captain's coxswain. He took it upon himself to see to the personal safety of the man he credited with giving him a better path to follow in life. When first reporting aboard *Argonne,* he had made it a point not only to see Commander Grabowski for assignment to Sheppard's gig but also to see Commander Williamson. Rebuffed by the gunnery officer, he next went to Chief Turret Captain Hancock with his request. Chief Hancock had listened and set out an extensive list of items that Cruz would have to complete. Cruz worked every spare minute he had, not going on liberty and cutting back on his sleep until he had completed the advancement courses and qualification requirements that *Argonne*'s senior chief had laid out for him. True to his word, soon after the *Argonne* got underway, Hancock went to the gunnery officer and intervened on Cruz's behalf.

Becoming the mount captain for the starboard 40 mm mount just aft of the bridge was not the end of his plan. With access to the largest pool of nonrated individuals on *Argonne* in the deck gang, Cruz had screened the personnel records of all the recent arrivals. He'd found the two individuals he was looking for in Seaman Second Class Osgood Thurman and Seaman Second Class Billy Bob Wainwright. Thurman was from Spruce Knob, West Virginia, and Wainwright was from Hector,

Arkansas. Both boys had learned to hunt with a .22-caliber single-shot Remington. To them, cartridges were expensive, and missing a pheasant or partridge after it flushed meant the family would not have any meat on the table that night. Of necessity, they were both crack shots.

Cruz drove them hard until they were ready to be the pointer and trainer on his quadruple 40 mm antiaircraft mount. Cruz also arranged to have all the members of his mount crew in the same watch section, practicing loading and tracking drills daily. Cruz drilled his men in changing barrels until they could accomplish the task on all four guns in fifteen minutes. Captain McCloud had seen them exercising on the mount, but the steel helmets had prevented him from seeing who was involved.

Anton Fokker's Stuka pilots would not know their names either, but with a steady stream of over 400 two-pound high-explosive projectiles coming up at them every minute, Osgood and Billy Bob were beginning to take a toll on them. No sooner had the first Ju 87C pushed over than Mount Four-zero-three put two high-explosive rounds into the Junkers' Jumo engine. One other projectile hit the left-wing root, and the dive-bomber, minus its left wing, spiraled out of control, hitting the water abreast the Number I turret.

The second bomber was closer when Osgood and Billy Bob hit the windshield with an explosive shell. The pilot died instantly, the gunner when the Ju 87 crashed on the port side twenty feet from the hull.

The Germans certainly had to be the best the Luftwaffe had to offer, Cruz figured. Despite seeing every other plane shot down, the last Ju 87 reached the drop point and released his semi-armor-piercing bomb. Cruz had thought through this possibility too, having eight clips of four armor-piercing shells each immediately available to the loaders. As soon as the bomb released, his loaders put those clips into the guns. Even though Osgood and Billy Bob hit the bomb twice with high-explosive shells before the AP rounds chambered, it did not detonate. The bomb case must have been too thick. Three more hit, as indicated by showers of sparks when the projectiles hit the steel casing and ricocheted off.

The crew of the last Junkers dive-bomber did not get to see the results of their bomb release. Other *Argonne* gunners made short work of the Ju 87 as it attempted to pull out of its dive. With flames sprouting from both wings, it carried both pilot and rear-seat gunner to an instant death, crashing off the battle cruiser's starboard bow.

The bomb hit the upper deck just aft of six-inch turret Number Six-Four. It penetrated the main deck, bounced off the armored deck, and came to rest in one of the crew's berthing spaces on the third deck—a dud.

Cruz looked up to see Captain McCloud leaning over the windscreen to look at the gun crew that had saved *Argonne* from more hits. Cruz looked back. Sheppard shook his head, smiled, and flashed a thumbs-up as Cruz noticed the loader on his number three gun looking up at the Captain, with Jefferson's unmistakable smile.

— —

Admiral Sir Bruce Hardy's cigar twitched in his mouth. Funny, he didn't remember lighting it, nor did he remember asking his flag lieutenant for one of his favorites—the ones Churchill had sent him on his posting to Force H. Everything depended on what happened in the next half hour. HMS *Renown* was shooting at her absolute maximum range—32,500 yards—and had not been able to get one hit on the leading German carrier. *Repulse*, following *Renown*, was shooting at the closer one, but her target was still 31,750 yards away. At those ranges, facing only four-round salvos, the Germans easily dodged all of the shells he sent their way. Hardy knew Schröder would rendezvous with his heavy gunfire support ships at some point, and Force H would be in serious difficulty. Despite extraordinary effort, he could not coax any more speed from his ancient ships to close the range. Sir Bruce had to face the possibility that his bold plan was not going to work. If he could not destroy or cripple the two carriers, Schröder would still be capable of destroying convoys.

"Flags; make to *Ark Royal*: 'Ready maximum strike of Swordfish with escorting Fulmars against retreating German carriers.'"

The young lieutenant hustled off to send the radio message that Hardy feared would condemn at least half of his air group to death.

— —

Vizeadmiral Schröder could see the masts of his battle cruisers coming to join him. At a closing rate of sixty-eight knots, it was only a matter of minutes until Eisner's ships would begin firing on Force H. Schröder decided to ready an air strike with his remaining Stukas and Bf 109s, trusting that his continued maneuvering would prevent a disastrous hit by Force H's museum pieces. At this point, he wasn't sure against whom he would send it. That decision would depend on *Fellbach* maintaining contact and also what Eisner achieved shooting at his antagonists. Schröder felt he had time on his side—about an hour until he would have to launch or risk having his pilots return after dusk. That gave him plenty of time to observe the results of his battle cruisers engaging Force H.

— —

Sheppard knew that he had to play the odds. If he tried his plan too soon, the Germans would still be in range of *Belleau Wood* and would most likely seek revenge on her. Yet the longer he waited, the more likely it was that *Argonne* might be hit and lose the speed that was critical to making the plan work. For the moment, he was still chasing salvos and laying smoke, working to a position directly astern of the German battle line. If he was successful in keeping that relative position, Schröder's battle cruisers not only would be limited to using only their aft turrets against him, but at shorter ranges the leading ships would have to risk hitting the ship astern, firing with the low-elevation angle of their guns. He would gain the unlikely advantage of an inverted crossing of Japanese Admiral Togo's famous T.

"Jaguar, Mustang Zero-One; two aircraft carriers bearing zero-nine-three, range two-one miles from you."

Bronco's report shocked Sheppard from his thoughts. At last! Now he knew where Schröder's carriers were.

"Mustang Zero-One, Jaguar; remain to west of Jaguar—enemy fighters," Jonathan Becker called out on the spotting network.

Knowing Bronco, the scout-observation squadron commander would try getting a better view and more information. Right now, that would be a disaster. Sheppard's Kingfishers needed to remain behind the shield of *Argonne*'s antiaircraft guns.

— —

Jake Evans had been trying for over an hour to get *Sabine* to move in a straight line. What he had found so far was that it was easy to twist his carrier to the heading that he wanted, but beyond that, the forces he needed to balance were complicated. He could not use the two inboard shafts. The propeller wash from either turning ahead had too great an effect on the heading, impinging directly on the hard-over rudder. He was currently trying to go ahead on the number three shaft and astern on the number four. As the carrier started to move forward, it was still a problem trying to balance the thrust of the port shaft with the changing headway.

Try as he might, every time *Sabine* started forward, she started turning right. Evans could not order engine speed changes fast enough to control the heading and move his aircraft carrier at anything other than a haphazard crawl.

— —

Sheppard was watching the German battle cruisers through his binoculars as they continued to send salvos from their aft turrets in his direction. Suddenly, the leading ship's forward turrets also fired. The guns were at their maximum elevation and pointed almost directly ahead of the ship. Whomever they were engaging must be about forty-three thousand yards from that leading battle cruiser.

Who would that be? Sheppard knew that Admiral Hamilton was well to the south. He had lost track of *Colchester* and *Burlington*; however, they could not be to the east of the Germans. They had to be somewhere between the southwest and east-southeast.

Sheppard stood and placed his left hand cupped to his mouth, lost in thought for a moment. Then the answer hit him like a lightning bolt—the Germans were shooting at the two British ships he had engaged this morning.

This morning ... It seemed like an eternity ago. Those ships must have worked their way to the east of Schröder's carriers and then run downwind until they'd found him.

Sheppard smiled, a twinkle in his eyes, and he dropped his hand. It all made sense. In an instant, he believed he knew where all his enemies and allies were.

That was why the German carriers had suddenly appeared! The Brits were chasing them. That also had to be the reason why Schröder's battle cruisers had turned away from *Belleau Wood* when they should have closed to finish her off. Schröder must have ordered them to go to the carriers' rescue.

Belleau Wood's last flashing light message now fit. Admiral Calhoun and the British admiral must have set up a radio circuit so that they could coordinate their actions. That was why Calhoun had sent them both north. It was to set up this situation. Sheppard now understood all the pieces of what had been happening.

Sheppard went to the 21MC. "Radio, Captain. Send the following message on 2716 kilocycles: 'To British admiral, are you under attack by German battle cruisers?'"

There was one other piece of information he needed. "1JC phone talker: 'Spot One, Captain. What is the maximum speed of a *Renown*-class battle cruiser?'"

John Hamblen might have been surprised at the question, but Sheppard quickly got his answer. "Thirty knots!"

Unless Sheppard slowed his enemy's heavy ships, those battle cruisers would make short work of the Brits.

"Combat, Captain; set up the attack!"

— —

The American message surprised Admiral Sir Bruce Hardy. His signalman brought it to him just after *Renown* and *Repulse* had executed a 180-degree turn. The first German salvo had landed short, but it was only a question of time before the Germans ran down and destroyed his two ships.

He composed an answer. "Admiral Calhoun, currently on course east at maximum speed. Schröder pursuing. Can you engage?"

If the Americans could distract Schröder's battle cruisers, perhaps he could escape to fight another day.

The answer he received two minutes later was the last thing he expected after seeing the two American warships this morning. Their size and power had convinced Hardy that they stood a chance of defeating the Germans. Clearly, something had gone wrong.

"Admiral Calhoun injured; *Belleau Wood* on fire and crippled. *Argonne* is currently engaging German battle cruisers from astern. Sheppard McCloud, Commanding Officer *Argonne*, sends."

Well, Hardy thought, *there's no relief to be had from the Americans.* His only hope was an attack by his Swordfish, which would send his aircrews to near-certain death.

Another messenger arrived. "Admiral, signal from the Americans." This one struck Hardy as unhinged. "Can you order your fighters to engage the German fighters and draw them off?"

What? Why would this man McCloud want him to engage the German fighters? What could that possibly accomplish? Surely, this captain must know that the problem was the battle cruisers. The fighters were not even a nuisance.

Why, Sir Bruce wondered, *should I commit my Fulmars against the superior Bf 109s?*

He thought for a moment. *What could this bloody colonial be up to? After all, didn't he try to kill me this morning? Is lunacy part of the American navy's requirement for command? Then again …*

Did this McCloud chap really have a plan that required the German fighters to be otherwise occupied?

Something told Hardy he should go with it. Was it the ghost of Calder, who had fought the French in these same waters over 136 years earlier? Hardy would never know, but he sent his flag lieutenant to radio the squadron leader of *Ark Royal*'s Fulmars.

— —

"Captain, Combat," the 21MC crackled. "Unknown group of aircraft to the east is now moving west. Based on speed, I think they are fighter aircraft."

Jonathan Becker had given Sheppard the best news he had received since they had joined battle with the Germans.

"Very well, Combat," Sheppard acknowledged and punched another button on the squawk box to connect to main control. "Engineering, stop smoke, blow tubes, give me everything you've got now!"

Over an hour of making smoke had fouled the boiler tubes with soot. Sending high-pressure steam through special "soot blowers" would remove it and improve the heat transfer for even more power.

Sheppard punched gunnery control on the 21MC. "Prepare to execute the plan using the port five-inch and six-inch battery. We'll fire at the German's last ship first and work up the column. I'll turn to port after the first two and use the starboard battery for the second and first ships in the German battle line."

He punched up CIC on the 21MC. "Combat, get the Kingfishers into position. We will need sixty seconds to change course between the second and third attacks."

Becker was quick with his acknowledgment.

Meanwhile, Chuck Williamson began issuing the orders needed to put the plan into action. "Sky One: track closest German battle cruiser, control all port five-inch mounts, master key, continuous aim. Sky Two: track third battle cruiser in column. Spot Three: control Turrets Six-Two and Six-Four, master key, continuous aim, track last German in column. Turrets Six-Two and Six-Four, load high-capacity contact fused, continuous fire. Spot Four: track third German ship in column. Port five-inch mounts, load fifteen rounds special antiaircraft common, then two rounds smoke; on my command, continuous fire."

Everything was in readiness. *Argonne* would erupt in five-inch and six-inch fire as soon as Bronco was in position. As *Argonne*'s speed climbed—forty-six, then forty-seven knots—her wake reached above the height of the main deck, and her bow wave rose and curled as far aft as the Number I main-battery turret. The antiaircraft gun crews in the open had to huddle against the wind. The German salvos began landing consistently astern. Sheppard wondered if their fire-control computers could not follow a surface ship steaming as fast as *Argonne*.

— —

Vizeadmiral Schröder lowered his binoculars, puzzled. What was that crazy American up to? Soon his battle cruisers would be able to reengage with full broadsides now that the cowardly Brits were fleeing—no longer a threat to his carriers. *Scharnhorst* and the others would make short work of those British relics and then could devote their full attention to that impudent American. He was actually closing the range.

What a fool.

His deck crews were bringing up the strike group's Ju 87s. Next, the remaining Messerschmitts would join the deck spot. In ten minutes, engines would be started and warmed, and he should be ready to launch.

Schröder turned to the *Graf Zeppelin*'s captain. "Becker, you look worried. What's wrong?"

"It is nothing, Herr Admiral."

"Tell me!"

"Admiral, it is my brother. He went to America many years ago, and he has a son, Jonathan, in the navy, an officer I think. It just struck me as ironic, that's all."

"Becker, don't give it another thought. We have more important work to do."

Schröder thought of his own son on *Scharnhorst*. She had suffered damage. He could see her blackened guns through his binoculars. Had his captain been wise enough to order the antiaircraft gunners below? Was Eric well?

— —

Sheppard had left the gunnery-control button pushed in on the 21MC squawk box. He was relying on the considerable abilities of his operations officer to do the motion analysis, geometry, and trigonometry in his head, while looking at the air and surface plots in CIC.

The spotting network was active now with Jonathan Becker's directions to Bronco's squadron. "On my mark, divisions turn away in sequence to course zero-eight-nine. Mark ... mark ... mark ... mark. Descend to two-five-zero feet. Make speed one-three-five knots."

It's time. Everything's in place—if only the British fighters can keep the 109s off the Kingfishers, Sheppard thought.

"Guns shoot," Jonathan called out when Bronco had reached the designated range to the last German battle cruiser's stern.

On the 1JC phone, Williamson immediately ordered, "Fire continuous, commence, commence, commence."

As her six-inch and five-inch guns leapt into action, *Argonne*'s port side erupted in flashes and smoke, commencing their rain of ruin en route to the Germans. The crack of the guns instantaneously followed. Again and again they fired, some sooner than others, until individual blasts were lost in the din of continuous, ear-splitting noise. The acrid smell of burned smokeless powder filled the air. Individual mounts were lost in the growing pall of blue-tinged smoke. As quickly as the noise had erupted, an eerie silence returned, exaggerated by ears deafened by the din. In just over a minute, the guns stopped shooting, having sent all seventeen shells from each gun on their murderous way.

Jonathan Becker spoke again. "Attack at five-zero feet; target is turret three; drop point when barbette width matches the tapes on your windshields. Remember, your head must be against the armored headrest."

"Check fire," Williamson ordered. "Sky Two: control all port five-inch mounts."

Sheppard could see each mount jerk to the right as the J switches rotated in the number one antiaircraft plotting room.

"Sky One: track second cruiser in enemy column. Spot Four: control Turrets Six-Two and Six-Four. All guns ten rounds, then two rounds of smoke."

Williamson's orders were setting up the same rain of steel for the third ship, but not as long, because Bronco's squadron would be closer.

Sheppard hardened his heart and mind to what he would see. The radar-fused seventy-pound antiaircraft projectiles began detonating above the German antiaircraft gunners. The shields that were part of most mounts only stopped bullets or shrapnel from shells coming from horizontal directions. The deadly spray of steel shards from Sheppard's exploding shells arrived from above. There was no protection for the crews.

Sheppard watched the detonations of six-inch shells on impact adding to the destruction of decks, bulkheads, ammunition lockers—and men. As Bronco and his wingman approached, there was no reply from the German guns. Unfortunately, the other German battle cruisers could engage the vulnerable Kingfishers as they approached their sister ship low and fast.

When the last two shells from each gun burst, dense white trails of smoke followed behind each piece of burning white phosphorous, masking Bronco and Barry Jensen from the leading German ships. Sheppard had told himself a thousand times that there was no way to prevent what also was happening. To allow Bronco and his wingman to reach the drop point, it was imperative to mask their approach from the ships that could still shoot. That meant the smoke. Tragically, the burning white phosphorous would also land on the decks of the German ships. Sheppard wasn't concerned about starting fires. No, it was the wounded men who lay everywhere. The white phosphorous kept burning after it landed, setting their clothing aflame, searing their flesh, and burning into bone. There was no way to put it out. The very helmets designed to protect from head injuries only prolonged the agony of being burned alive.

Those German gunners who could still move flung themselves overboard, trying to escape the phosphorous hell. Every man in the open on that last battle cruiser was now dead or wishing he was.

"Fire continuous, commence, commence, commence!" Now the shells would be flying over the heads of his scout-observation planes. Keeping them at low altitude was critical to prevent the radar fuses from killing his men too.

Sheppard gritted his teeth. His batteries lit up again, dealing death and destruction on the antiaircraft gunners of the next German ship. No sooner had the smoke shells burst than Bronco approached the drop point against the last German in the column. Shielded from the view of the leading two German ships by the smoke enveloping the third, Bronco did not have any German gunfire to disturb his aim.

— —

The Kingfisher approached at almost 160 miles per hour, near its maximum speed. After Bronco had analyzed Barry Jensen's attack on the German U-boat back near the mouth of the Chesapeake, he realized Barry had not missed his drop point: the Mark 17 depth bombs had skipped off the water's surface, travelling a hundred yards farther before sinking and detonating. Now his squadron was going to do the same thing deliberately, hence the high approach speed.

Bronco dropped right where he wanted, about one hundred yards from the port quarter of the German. His two depth bombs skipped off the water and sailed through the air until they hit the side of the battle cruiser. Had the fuse been located in the nose of the weapon, the impact with the hull would crush it—a dud. But it was not. Located halfway back on the bomb, the Mark 224 fuse survived the impact intact. Both of Bronco's bombs sank against his target, sucked by her wash to remain close to the hull.

Bronco didn't know, but the two propellers and one rudder on each side of the German ship's stern provided three equally good targets.

The barbette provided a great aiming point and rangefinder with Becker's taped windshield bomb sight. Bronco used them to perfection. In the period it took the depth bombs to sink the preset depth of twenty-five feet of the fuse, his target could not move outside the destructive pressure pulse when the 224 pounds of TNT exploded. Bronco's right bomb blew the propeller off the inboard port shaft, bending the tail shaft in the process. His left bomb bent the outboard shaft, breaking the strut supporting it. As the shafts rotated, they tore open all the seals in the shaft alley and engineering bulkheads to the forward port engine room.

Barry Jensen was not as accurate as Bronco. His bombs destroyed the inboard starboard shaft and the starboard rudder. The last German slowed. With only one remaining propeller shaft operable, and the rudder on the opposite side, she was barely able to make ten knots and couldn't really turn to starboard.

Bronco let out a whoop as he flew across the quarterdeck just ahead of Jensen's crossing, banking hard to stay in the area masked by smoke and low enough to avoid *Argonne*'s fire. It had worked! Bronco looked at *Argonne*, prouder than hell of his ship and her Captain. She was beginning her turn to bring the starboard guns to bear on the remaining Germans. *Argonne* looked like a destroyer as she heeled to starboard and the bone in her teeth rose to break over her main deck.

But he saw something else: the turn had slowed *Argonne*, and a 45 cm shell found her just forward of the armored hatch for the hangar, but there was no fire and no explosions. Bronco understood now why McCloud had ordered him to remove all the paint. Empty of aircraft, with all equipment stowed, *Argonne* did not share her sister's fate.

Using Sky One, Spot Three, and the starboard batteries, *Argonne* laid waste to the antiaircraft capabilities of the second ship and then the lead. The deadly shrapnel cut down the men—gunners, pointers, trainers, and ammunition passers. Gruesome, agonizing death followed the fallen as the smoke screen and its burning white phosphorous followed, masking the Kingfishers' approach to the next German.

Bronco watched the twin columns of water rise, port and starboard, on each ship in sequence—some a little forward getting both screws, some aft getting a propeller and rudder.

— —

Sheppard watched as Chuck Williamson shifted his target one last time to decimate the leader, preventing her antiaircraft batteries from interfering in the depth-charge attack on number two. He had come to realize that since only a few destroyers remained with the German battle cruiser squadron, his last salvoes of white phosphorous were most likely unnecessary. Sheppard thought about stopping the smoke shells before firing, stopping his gunnery officer from executing the last phase of the plan. Scout Observation Squadron Sixty-Eight probably did not need the smoke at this point. There were only two destroyers well ahead of the German flagship. Their 5.9 cm main guns were for surface actions only, and the remaining AA guns were too far to interfere effectively. Sheppard decided against changing the plan at the last minute—*"Order, counterorder, disorder"*—rang in his head. If even one battle cruiser escaped, the English convoys were at risk.

Again, almost every man in the open on the leading German would suffer in agony. Since the white phosphorous winging its way to that last cruiser was probably unnecessary, would history judge him a war criminal for inflicting horrific casualties and unimaginable suffering on the Germans now lying wounded on the decks of the leading battle cruiser? The lucky ones died quickly; some—facelessly unknown to Sheppard, including Oberleutnant zur See Eric Schröder—did not.

— —

Vizeadmiral Schröder watched the American's attack on his battle line, first with curiosity and then with horror as the twin columns of water rose both port and starboard at each ship's stern. Immediately, he directed Kapitän Becker to recall his fighters and attack the American floatplanes that appeared to be doing the real damage. What was causing those antiaircraft bursts appearing above his ships? Why were his ships not knocking the floatplanes down? They should be easy targets. He directed his flag lieutenant to send a message to Konteradmiral Eisner, demanding an explanation on why his ships had not destroyed those floatplanes.

At least his Bf 109s were returning. They had shot down six Brits for the cost of two. Well, they might be out of cannon shells, but floatplanes would be easy kills.

Kingfishers, he thought. That was what the Americans called them. He swore they were not going to escape unscathed.

— —

Sheppard was again laying a smoke screen, but this time it was to cover his own withdrawal. The German gunfire was haphazard. He suspected that his five- and six-inch shells had also caused significant damage to gun directors, rangefinders, and radar antennas. He had done everything he could to the Germans. *Argonne* had expended all of her five-inch smoke shells, and he needed to keep what was left of the radar-fused antiaircraft shells for their designed purpose. There was nothing he could do to stop Schröder's inevitable counterattack using his remaining dive-bombers.

He watched his forward main-deck repair party already at work trying to patch the hole created by the German bomb. Other men, whom Sheppard couldn't recognize, were clearing away spent cartridge cases from his mounts, ensuring unrestricted movement if another action developed.

Sheppard stumbled as he tried to rise out of his chair. Yawning and stretching gave him a momentary respite from the blackness trying to force sleep on his exhausted body. Everything ached. But he had more to do.

Turning to Petty Office Bergman, he ordered, "Boatswain, pipe the word."

"s^s-s-ssssssss, ₛs^sssssssssss" echoed in every manned space.

"This is the Captain. Today, Admiral Hamilton's task force engaged a superior German task force. Though *Belleau Wood* was badly damaged, with the help of British Force H, the Germans have been defeated. Well done!"

Sheppard released the key of the 1MC microphone, settling into his conning station chair, and returning to his thoughts of the death and agony he had inflicted. There was nothing else for him to concentrate on.

— —

Admiral Sir Bruce Hardy breathed a sigh of relief when he noticed that the Germans had stopped shooting at *Renown* and *Repulse*. Whatever the American had tried must have at least delayed the inevitable, shifting their attention away from Force H. It wasn't long before *Renown*'s Type 284 radar was reporting that the range to the leading German battle cruiser was opening. They were slowing! The American had somehow saved Force H.

Hardy's joy was short-lived, though. *Renown*'s air-search radar was reporting additional air contacts rising from Schröder's carriers. They appeared to be circling as they formed up for a strike. Hardy needed to get *Ark Royal* turned back into the wind and additional fighters launched. Evidently, Schröder had not yet given up.

— —

Bronco had stayed close to the German forces until his squadron completed their attacks. Now, he and wingman Barry Jensen were the tail-end Charlie as the squadron made its way back to the cover of *Argonne*'s guns. Bronco was the first to notice the two Messerschmitts diving at them to attack.

This scenario was one he had often war-gamed with his pilots. Both Bronco and Barry immediately dove down to hug the waves, gaining air speed in the process. With the Kingfishers mere feet off the ocean, they were much more difficult targets for a diving fighter. The two radiomen unlimbered their single Browning .30-caliber machine guns and waited for the German fighters to get within range.

The Germans split—the element leader was coming after Bronco and the other aiming for his wingman.

Bronco and Barry watched closely as they approached in their dives. The two American pilots had one more trick. They chopped the throttles on the Kingfishers to slow their aircraft. The Germans now had to make their dives steeper to keep the Americans in their gun sights. Just at the moment that Bronco thought the Germans would be in range, he set the Kingfisher down on the ocean, instantly dropping his speed another twenty miles per hour.

The Germans had a choice: steepen their dives further and risk crashing, or break off the attack and pull out of the dive sharply, losing air speed in the process. The fighter aiming for Barry chose the former— and crashed in a fountain of spray. The leader chose the latter.

As the fighter leader pulled out of his dive, Bronco gunned his engine, lifting the floatplane's nose, and fired a long burst with his fixed .30-caliber machine gun. Bronco's aim was perfect. His bullets hit the Messerschmitt, and the telltale spray of radiator coolant mixed with oil confirmed that Bronco had inflicted lethal damage. The Daimler-Benz DB601N engine smoked, coughed, and stopped. There was nothing that pilot could do except glide to a ditching a few thousand yards ahead of Bronco.

Bronco had seen numerous flags on the side of the fighter when it passed. He saw his enemy climb out of his doomed aircraft and jump into the sea. The German had an inflatable life vest but no raft. Knowing he had shot down an ace, Bronco decided to slow and rescue the pilot. Cautioning Miller to be ready for tricks, Bronco taxied up to the sinking Bf 109. Radioman Miller helped the pilot onto the float and assisted him into the middle of the Kingfisher, by the fuel tank.

The German, seemingly stunned by the realization that an American floatplane had shot him down, offered no resistance. He sat quietly while Miller put a cloth helmet on his head and plugged the cable into a jack on the side of the Kingfisher.

With Miller secure in the rear seat, Bronco took off and headed back to *Argonne*. Bronco had to ask, "Who are you?"

Dejectedly, the pilot answered, "Major Wilhelm Fredrick Kohlbert, Luftwaffe."

"Are you injured?"

"No, just sore from the shoulder straps on landing." Then, "Who are you?"

"Lieutenant Commander Bronco Billy Burdick, United States Navy."

The only thing Willy could say in answer was, "Congratulations."

Bronco was left wondering whether this qualified as an air-to-air kill, since he'd bounced on another wave after shooting.

— —

For the second time that day, *Graf Zeppelin*'s surface lookouts failed in their duty. This time, the results were far more severe. *Colchester* and *Burlington*, closing the sounds of the guns and following Bronco's vector, spotted the two German carriers as they were launching their strike groups. Knowing that time was of the essence, the commanding officer of *Colchester* turned his two cruisers into a line-ahead parallel to the Germans. He directed *Burlington* to shoot at the left-hand carrier while he took the right.

Both light cruisers went to continuous rapid fire, sending almost a hundred rounds per minute at each of the German aircraft carriers. Correcting on the fly, the two gunnery officers soon began to hit the vulnerable *Graf Zeppelin* and *Anton Fokker*—though not in time to catch all the Stukas before their launch.

Shortly, the two carriers turned to the north, seeking shelter behind the heavy guns of the German battle cruisers. The smoke from the burning aircraft on their flight decks added to the smoke that the German admiral had ordered, providing an effective mask to the optical sights on the light cruisers.

Realizing that they had done what they could, *Colchester* and *Burlington* turned away, laying smoke. Soon enveloped by the sooty black clouds, the two light cruisers escaped just as the first 45 cm salvos began to fall in their vicinity.

— —

Vizeadmiral Schröder realized he was beaten. As the crews of *Graf Zeppelin* and *Anton Fokker* battled the fires and secondary explosions on their flight decks, he decided to close Eisner's force and retreat back to France. To accomplish a safe withdrawal, he had to get past the English aircraft carrier to his east. Accordingly, he ordered all his airborne aircraft to head in that direction, find the carrier, attack it, and then land in Spain. Schröder knew that the Spanish would keep the aircraft for their own use and make a show of interning the crews, only to quietly return them to the French frontier at the earliest possible time. Without a flight deck for them to land on, he was going to lose the planes anyway. This way, the crews would not need to risk a water landing.

Suddenly, another idea struck him.

— —

Sheppard was grateful he could finally order, "Cease firing!"

As he approached *Belleau Wood*, he raised his binoculars to survey the damage to his sister ship. Her topsides were a shambles. Many of her five-inch mounts and six-inch turrets only resembled a junkyard, with gun barrels pointed at odd angles. Her forward main-battery turret had a prominent splash mark where a German shell had hit the faceplate and exploded without penetrating the armor. The Number III turret had a crease in the roof where another shell had impacted but failed to penetrate the thinner horizontal armor. She had settled by the stern with a list to starboard, but at least *Sioux City* and *Bellingham* had managed to put out the fires. He could see that the two cruisers were transferring some of *Belleau Wood*'s wounded sailors for treatment on the light cruisers.

Now that they were out of range, he had time to plan his next move. The only ship he had that could tow *Belleau Wood* was *Argonne*. Without his sister ship, any action in daylight was foolish, but the destroyers might be effective by themselves after dark. He signaled the commodore of Destroyer Squadron Thirty. "Prepare for night torpedo attack on retreating German forces."

In less than two minutes, he received an answer. "Unable to perform requested attack; fuel state critical!"

Well, that was that. All he could do was "suggest" to the British admiral that his destroyers perform the attack. At least the Brits were in a better position to intercept the Germans.

— —

Admiral Sir Bruce Hardy was both pleased and alarmed when the German strike group passed *Renown* and *Repulse*—pleased in that the ships in his vicinity were not going to be attacked, but alarmed that the Stukas were going after his one remaining effective weapon against the German heavy ships, *Ark Royal*.

Hardy had done everything he could. His Fulmars would engage the Germans as soon as they reached the altitude of the Germans, but they would be at a tactical disadvantage. He watched, anxious, as sixteen aircraft smoked, flamed, or just fell out of the sky. The ugly dark splotches of *Ark Royal*'s antiaircraft fire soon began to appear on the horizon. Soon, he could also see smoke rising. Sir Bruce feared the worst.

The report, relayed by a destroyer, confirmed his worst fear. *Ark Royal* had been hit twice. She'd launched her last aircraft, at least until repairs could be made in Gibraltar. The good news was that after the Germans left, she could still land the few remaining airborne Fulmars.

Now without air cover, though, Hardy needed to get out of range of the Luftwaffe before dawn. His yeoman of signals was trying to get his attention.

"Signal from the Americans, suh."

Hardy opened it and read, "*Belleau Wood* badly damaged and crippled; unable to steam. *Argonne* will tow *Belleau Wood* clear. German battle cruisers crippled and slowed. Both German carriers are on fire. Recommend night torpedo attack by your destroyers to finish off Schröder. Captain McCloud sends."

Hardy needed to let England know the good news.

"Flags, make to Admiralty: 'I have the honor to report a great victory; Schröder's fleet has been crippled and neutralized.'"

To send off even half of his destroyers with *Ark Royal* damaged was a great risk. The Admiralty should concur if the need to further damage or sink some of Schröder's force warranted the risk to Force H. He dashed off a quick signal with the proposed attack after dark on this moonless night. His flag lieutenant took it immediately to the radio room for encoding and transmission.

— —

Squadron Leader Wythe-Jones was still flying his lazy figure-eight pattern about forty miles to the north of Schröder's heavy ships when he noticed a change in their course. Instead of heading due east, they were now on course one-zero-five degrees true. Why?

Wythe-Jones turned over the controls to his copilot and went aft to the small chart table where his navigator was doing his best to keep up with their location. He took the parallel rulers and moved a direction of one-zero-five from the compass rose to Schröder's current location. Even allowing for his navigation errors, the line went directly to the mouth of Ria da Coruña, Spain.

Wythe-Jones sent another message, reporting Schröder's new course and speed decrease to ten knots.

— —

It was sunset when an anxious Admiral Hardy received a message reply from the Admiralty. "Break off attack! Do not enter Spanish territorial waters; Gibraltar too important. Pass to Americans. Admiral of the Fleet Pound sends."

CHAPTER 12

HOMECOMING

Sheppard was somewhat chagrined when he read Admiral Hardy's message. Schröder was going to escape with his ships to fight another day. There was nothing more he could do. Now, priorities dictated recovering his aircraft and the two floatplanes that *Belleau Wood* had launched. The weather continued to moderate, obviating the need to create a "slick" for the Kingfishers to land. It only took a few minutes to set the aircraft-and-boat crane back up and put the landing mat astern.

As the first to launch, Bronco was the first to land. No sooner had Mustang Zero-One been set in a trolley on the catapult than the waiting airedales began refueling the Kingfisher. Bronco climbed out and delivered his prisoner to the grinning Major Jenkins and his marines. Burdick left to report to Sheppard on the details of their attack, but first he directed one of his aviation boatswain's mates to paint a German flag under the broken submarine by his cockpit canopy. He doubted that there were many Kingfisher pilots who could claim an air-to-air kill—even if arguably he hadn't been airborne.

Soon, too soon for Bronco, he and Barry Jensen were fired off to search for survivors. Other Kingfishers quickly followed, including *Belleau Wood*'s two that were airborne at the time of her devastation. One by one they began to return, some flying with one survivor, others taxiing with more.

Sheppard needed to use the remaining daylight to fuel escorts. *Belleau Wood*'s tow would have to wait until tomorrow morning. It was only a few minutes before Commander Destroyer Squadron Thirty was alongside to starboard and another of his ships to port. Line-throwing guns shot messenger lines, and sequentially heavier lines were hauled by sailors until finally the fueling hoses were passed. It took less than ten minutes before *Argonne* was pumping black oil to the destroyers.

Sheppard took the opportunity to exchange views of the battle with the destroyer squadron commander, shouting through bullhorns, with the two ships steaming on parallel courses only a hundred feet apart. Sheppard was impressed with his crew for the performance they were putting on in this three-ring circus—fueling destroyers to port and starboard while recovering and launching aircraft astern. He doubted any other battle cruiser could match this feat, and he vowed to make sure the Navy gave them the recognition they deserved.

Before long, the two destroyers with full fuel tanks broke away from *Argonne* to be replaced by two more. Sheppard directed one of the first fueled destroyers to search the area of the attack on the German battle line in the little remaining daylight.

From somewhere, Chief Walter Bledsoe had come up with two extra trolleys for the catapults. When *Belleau Wood*'s and all of Scout-Observation Squadron Sixty-Eight's aircraft were finally hoisted aboard, they were stowed on the catapults forward of the two that belonged to *Argonne*. By the time the last two destroyers broke from *Argonne* with filled fuel tanks, the sun had already set, its afterglow bathing an ocean suddenly serene.

How quickly the sea covered the dead.

Argonne, accompanied by the four destroyers still needing fuel, then left the area to rendezvous with Admiral Hamilton.

Argonne's carpenters and deck gang would need to work through the night to ready the gear necessary for the tow.

— —

As dusk had settled on the sea, *Fellbach* had continued to watch the American aircraft carriers. Her captain had heard nothing from Vizeadmiral Schröder for hours, and it was clear that there would be no attack by German aircraft. In the absence of orders, *Fellbach*'s commanding officer decided to take matters into his own hands, to exploit the advantage of a moonless night and subterfuge.

At a slow speed, to avoid creating a bow wave or noticeable wake, *Fellbach* closed on the slowly moving American carrier. *Quincy* first noticed the contact on her SC radar but was confused by the navigation lights of a Spanish trawler. The contact closed to about 13,500 yards before extinguishing lights and turning away suddenly, prompting *Quincy* to believe it was German.

As she turned, the *Fellbach*'s captain ordered, "Torpedoes *los!*"

— —

Admiral Hamilton, determined not to be shadowed during the night, grabbed the TBS and ordered, "*Quincy, Bethlehem,* investigate skunk bearing zero-three-zero."

Before they could challenge the intruder, two torpedoes slammed into *Sabine*'s starboard side. Hamilton again picked himself up from the heaving deck as the water column of a hit amidships showered down. A second water column rose aft. *Sabine*'s hull whipped and groaned in agony.

Reluctantly, Admiral Hamilton decided he would have to scuttle his flagship in the morning, when he could get the crew safely off in daylight. Engine room number three was flooding, removing all hope of controlling *Sabine*'s heading. *Fellbach*, though, did not enjoy her success for long. *Quincy* and *Bethlehem* loosed a barrage of star shells, removing the blanket of darkness in the scout cruiser's vicinity, followed by rapid-fire salvos of ten-inch projectiles, *Fellbach* quickly slowed, settled, and capsized. The detached destroyer reported few survivors found in the black night.

— —

It was shortly before dawn when Vizeadmiral Schröder's crippled ships dropped anchor in Bahia A Coruña. A launch from the Spanish naval base at Ferrol putted self-importantly to *Graf Zeppelin*, bringing a very official Capitan de Navio of the Spanish Navy. The capitan quickly informed Schröder of the specifics of the Laws of War, Hague Convention XIII, of October 18, 1907, and suggested that no more than three of his ships be dispersed to each of the harbors surrounding the bay. He also insisted to Schröder that a group of Spanish naval engineers would board his damaged warships to determine repairs needed to render them seaworthy. With a wink, he asked if German officers would be so kind as to assist the Spanish in this effort. As he left, it was clear to Schröder that he could stay as long as he needed and the Spanish would cite the various articles of the Hague Convention, deflecting diplomatic notes of the English if they complained. As the sun climbed, Schröder would have to get on with the business of burying his dead ashore.

— —

Sheppard spent most of the night writing a detailed report of the battle from his perspective. His men had won a great victory. He might be excused for his action in bombarding the wounded on that last German battle cruiser with white phosphorous. But, if he didn't report it … would anyone other than the Germans know? Did it matter that he hadn't intended to cause the German wounded to suffer? He was not a lawyer, but he was familiar with the general provisions of the various Hague Conventions—"The Law of Armed Conflict."

There was a growing knot in his stomach. He couldn't even lean back in the chair of his sea cabin to think this through. If he said nothing and the Germans complained, would his superiors call him to account or dismiss the propaganda as an excuse for the German defeat? If they said nothing, could he live with his action? What would his men think? Would any of them wonder, should they read the requirements of the convention?

How did it go? *"It is especially forbidden to employ arms, projectiles, or material calculated to cause unnecessary suffering."* Strong wording.

Did it matter that he had known it would cause suffering, but the military necessity had been to make smoke? But that had only applied to the other three German battle cruisers. The last attack, on the leading German, had not needed smoke. He had known that before Williamson began the bombardment of that last German. He and he alone had decided to let the attack continue rather than change the orders. Williamson had not even questioned the plan. None of them had. Did that make all of his department heads complicit? He hadn't thought it through. Many more men had died than necessary. Sheppard alone was responsible.

"Always tell the truth!" The words echoed in his head.

It might be the end of his career, but his men deserved to go forward untainted by his war crime. As he sat writing, the words flowed out as he took responsibility for his action.

Then he wrote a letter to Evelyn. He needed to let her know about his actions and that there might be consequences, even if the Germans did not complain. He knew she would support him regardless, but he hoped that explaining it to her would help within her circle of friends.

Sheppard fully expected a court-martial. If the United States did not convene one, every American soldier would risk the same treatment at the hands of the Germans. He would have to be pilloried in the press. That would be the hardest thing for Evelyn to endure. Show trial or not, he would certainly lose his command and perhaps even be drummed out of the service. Would that be God's punishment for his actions? After all, Roosevelt could not afford to cede the moral high ground to Hitler.

— —

Admiral Hamilton had been up most of the night, reviewing his staff's work in drafting an overall report of the battle. He knew there were many lessons to be gleaned from what had happened, and Dolf was anxious to start the process as soon as he could. He also had to get the staff ready to transfer to the *Raritan*. That would mostly be Henry Burke's responsibility, but there were a million things to check.

As dawn broke, he was heartened to see *Argonne* about five thousand yards away from *Sabine,* with four destroyers. Surprised to see four Kingfishers stored on her catapults, he looked at the squadron markings through his binoculars. When he realized that two belonged to *Belleau Wood,* Hamilton surmised that the extent of her damage must have been more severe than he had originally thought. Even *Argonne* showed visible scars from the battle as he examined her bridge and port quarter.

One hell of a fight, he thought.

It was a miracle that Sheppard had managed to cripple the Germans.

Hamilton needed to let *Argonne* know the situation on *Sabine.* The carrier was unmanageable after the German scout cruiser attack. With the Luftwaffe still a threat, abandonment and scuttling was the only alternative to unacceptable risk for the rest of the task force. Admiral Hamilton called his communications officer to send his intentions to *Argonne,* requesting her assistance in receiving the majority of *Sabine*'s large crew. One of the saddest moments in the life of any sailor was when he left his ship prior to scuttling her—like deserting a faithful old friend just when she needed you the most.

Standing on *Sabine*'s bridge with Evans and Radisson, Hamilton was no different from any other sailor today as he began to read a flashing-light message from *Argonne*: "Admiral, with all due respect, if you have decided to scuttle *Sabine* anyway, why not try to blast the rudder off with torpedoes first?"

As the three read the message, they turned and looked at each other. It might just work, but how would they know?

No one ever figured out who authorized the reply to *Argonne* from *Sabine*; the signalmen seemed to have lost the message pad with the releasing signature. The answer read simply, "Thanks, we'll try it."

——

With the coming of dawn, Klaus Schröder began to see the dimensions of the disaster that had struck his battle cruisers: red stains and the hundreds and hundreds of white-shrouded corpses lining the main decks of each of his battle cruisers. Interspersed were bodies shrouded with the German naval ensign. Those must have been officers. Suddenly seized with anxiety for his son, he sent a message to *Scharnhorst* asking for his status.

An insensitive watch officer, sleepless and overwhelmed with the death and destruction that he had been forced to deal with all night, replied that the shrapnel from antiaircraft rounds had cut down Eric Schröder with wounds to his arms and gashes to his legs. The smoke shells had peppered him with white phosphorous on his chest and abdomen. A medical party had managed to carry him, screaming in pain, to the battle dressing station as the phosphorous burned deeper into his chest. Eric had died two hours later in excruciating pain.

It was too much for Vizeadmiral Schröder to bear. His eldest son had died a hideous death at the hands of this American. So many of his men had shared Eric's fate; was there no God of mercy to grant warriors a quick death? Schröder stood on *Graf Zeppelin*'s flag bridge, the blackened wreckage of his Stukas littering the flight deck, with tears running down his cheeks, cursing.

"Damn God! How could a loving Christ allow this to happen?" Children were not supposed to die before their parents.

"Unlike those godless Nazis, haven't I been faithful?"

He swallowed hard.

"I swear before the Almighty and every god of war, I will find the man responsible for this horror and take my revenge!"

— —

While the preparations were being made for the torpedoing of *Sabine*, Sheppard ordered the remaining destroyers of DESRON 30 refueled. After the first two destroyers finished fueling, he reversed course, steaming slowly back toward *Sabine*. *Argonne* was close enough that he could see a column of water and spray rise at her stern, quickly followed by another. Sheppard silently prayed that it would work since the shooting destroyer was a mere 750 yards from *Sabine*. This was going to be a long war; every carrier would be badly needed. It would take less than a year to repair *Sabine,* but it would take three or longer to build a replacement.

— —

No sooner had the vibration and hull whipping of the last explosion died away than Radisson led his machinist's mates back into the *Sabine*'s three remaining operable engine rooms. The damage-control assistant led repair parties to shore bulkheads and stop leaks from newly flooded compartments aft. Not unexpectedly, the shaft seals were damaged, and the shaft alleys for propellers one and two could not be dewatered. Radisson started turning the main engines on those two shafts as soon as the DCA reported that the new packing was ready.

Gratified that at least the shafts were turning on the jacking gear, Radisson worried that the thrust bearings again had been damaged, but there were no more spare parts. When the main engines were warm, Captain Evans granted the request to test them.

The test of the main engines was successful only in showing that the rotors were not bowed. *Sabine* now needed to actually answer bells to investigate how badly the thrust bearings might have been wiped, shafts misaligned, or propellers damaged. The Captain and Radisson had decided that if they could go ahead with one-third revolutions on either number one or number two main engines without the stern swinging rapidly to port, then they could assume that the torpedoes had removed the rudder.

Sabine did not steam straight ahead. Nor did she start turning rapidly. There was a heavy, slow vibration aft, indicating bent propeller blades or shafts, but both officers knew they could save *Sabine,* even if she had settled eight feet by the stern from the flooding.

— —

As soon as he saw *Sabine* begin to move in an apparently straight line, Sheppard asked Admiral Hamilton's permission to detach *Argonne,* with three of DESRON 30's destroyers, to return to *Belleau Wood.* He would need at least several hours of daylight to rig the tow and start the crippled battle cruiser moving toward home. When Admiral Hamilton approved, Sheppard turned *Argonne* back to the north with his destroyers, increasing speed to thirty-five knots. Sheppard was satisfied that he had not lost another day in the tow of *Belleau Wood* and rescuing the carrier's crew; however, the officers and men of *Sabine* were thinking they would never forget the man who had saved their friend and home.

— —

Admiral Sir Bruce Hardy was the first to reach a friendly port. Nursing *Ark Royal*, Force H pulled back into Gibraltar late in the afternoon of the next day. Hardy knew the German spies were watching, and he needed to convince them that *Ark Royal* was still fully functional. With canvas and paint, her crew had made the flight deck appear undamaged. Sir Bruce also ordered that every intact aircraft be placed on the flight deck. The normal British practice had been to keep them in the hangars, with the flight deck holding only the planes that would not fit after the two hangars reached capacity. To all external appearances, HMS *Ark Royal* looked like a fully functioning unit.

The minute *Renown* tied up alongside the mole, she sent ashore the admiral's report of the action. Encoded and transmitted, that report was the first detailed account of what had happened at sea to reach the Admiralty. No sooner had it arrived and the decoding started than the British prime minister arrived at White Hall to read the message text personally. Hardy had lavished praise on the Americans, making it clear that *Argonne* and her attached light cruisers were responsible for crippling the German battle cruisers and carriers of Schröder's fleet.

This was just what Churchill wanted; it would cement the Allied relationship as well as give beleaguered British citizens a solid victory to celebrate. Working with the Admiralty staff, the prime minister and first sea lord decided on a draft communiqué. Not included was Hardy's report of methods used in securing the victory or the damage suffered by Allied forces. The prime minister decided that the United States should have a naval hero, and he personally directed that both *Argonne* and Sheppard McCloud be included by name in the account. Dudley Pound suggested, and the prime minister approved, in the information provided separately to a few trusted reporters, that they allude to a "new Beatty"—in reference to the dashing, handsome leader of the British battle cruisers of the first war. With the subject of heroes open for discussion, they also decided to call Hardy the "new Nelson" for a spectacular victory against overwhelming odds. It seemed appropriate in view of the fact that Sir Bruce's great-great-grandfather had been Nelson's flag captain at Trafalgar.

Neither McCloud nor Hardy was consulted on their wishes, nor would either know the purely political motives that drove the decisions.

— —

Sheppard had not actually towed a ship before, but he understood the theory. The real problem to overcome was not one of horsepower but of the sea itself. Tying two ships together—each with a displacement of over 130,000 tons—created a system akin to two automobiles connected by a piece of fishing line. If you applied gentle force the towed car would move, but a sharp jerk and the line would break. The sea put forces—huge, independent forces—on each ship. The only way to keep the towline from parting was to make it heavy. The main problem was that almost nothing was heavy enough. The other problem was that the towed ship did not have any brakes. If the lead ship tried to slow, nothing would keep the towed ship from colliding with her.

While *Argonne* was still racing back to *Belleau Wood*, both crews made preparations, having to ready the towing bridle and anchor chains. The tow cable was arranged on the *Argonne*'s main deck, forward of the hangar hatch, so that it could be smoothly paid out to *Belleau Wood* without any kinks.

To prevent the tow cable from riding on any sharp edges, wooden bridges and a saddle were constructed. The saddle at the very stern prevented the tow wire from chafing on the gunwale where it left *Argonne*. Aboard *Belleau Wood*, the crew would have to connect it to one of her anchor chains. She would actually pay out her chain almost six hundred feet before *Argonne* started to move ever so slowly away from her in starting the tow.

As Sheppard had anticipated, it took the better part of six hours to get everything in readiness. He went dead slow ahead on number two main engine for only a few minutes, just enough for the tow cable left on deck to start paying out. He arranged for a watch officer on *Belleau Wood* to signal the angle that her chain was making to the vertical as the best indication of the stress on the tow.

The system worked well, and Sheppard was able gradually to build up speed to almost seven knots before sunset.

Throughout the day, *Colchester's* and *Burlington's* Kingfishers searched for survivors. Many of the aviators were rescued, having been supported by their small yellow life rafts; they were both American and German, including Commander Robert "Hawk" Talbot. The destroyer sent to scour the location of the attack on the German battle cruisers was not as successful, recovering only a handful of prisoners who were alive but badly burned.

— —

It was sunset before Vizeadmiral Schröder finished burying almost four thousand sailors from his fleet, well away from the prying eyes of the Spanish press. For almost an hour, on the *Scharnhorst*, he had stared at the corpse of his son, memorizing every wound and burn that had claimed his life. Schröder thought about sending Eric home to Kiel, but knew his son would not have wanted any special favors. He would have preferred to rest with his men for eternity, in spite of his mother's wishes. Schröder would arrange for his wife to visit Eric's grave sometime later in the summer.

When he returned to *Graf Zeppelin*, he found a terse message waiting for him from Großadmiral Raeder, ordering him to sail in the morning and return to Brest. Until he reached French waters, Schröder was to remain in Spanish territorial seas, exercising his "right of innocent passage." Schröder knew, even if the message did not say it, that the moment he docked in Brest, Raeder expected him to travel to Berlin and officially explain his actions. It would not be a pleasant encounter.

— —

The next morning, the two elements of Task Force Forty-Eight rendezvoused. Sheppard and Admiral Hamilton discussed by flashing light the best route to take back to the East Coast, eventually deciding on a southern path to avoid any late-spring storms in the North Atlantic. They would also be as far as possible from any patrolling German U-boats.

Sheppard called Commanders Grabowski, Roberts, and Williamson, and Lieutenant Hamblen for a quick meeting in his sea cabin.

"Gentlemen," Sheppard said. "I've decided that since Art knows more about *Argonne*'s handling characteristics than I do, I am going to designate him as my command duty officer. He will supervise the tow of *Belleau Wood* and act in my stead with respect to operating *Argonne*. Art, I expect you to use your judgment on what I need to know and what can wait.

"Gentlemen, that leaves the position of navigator open until we get back to port. Lieutenant Hamblen, you will fill that position. You will act for Commander Roberts in all matters required of the navigator. Chuck, I will leave it to you to reassign one of your junior officers to John's duties as main battery fire-control officer. Are there any questions?"

Hearing none, Sheppard ended the meeting, with Roberts and John Hamblen remaining on the conning station while Sheppard, Ted Grabowski, and Chuck Williamson went below. Sheppard asked Ted to accompany him to his stateroom.

When they arrived, Sheppard turned to Ted and said, "Do you think it will work?"

"If that doesn't get Art Roberts thinking about the thrill of command, I don't know what will. I was watching Hamblen when you told everyone that he would be the acting navigator. I swear his feet rose off the deck."

Sheppard smiled and nodded.

"Captain, if you don't mind me asking, what will you be doing on the trip back, besides catching up on your sleep?"

"I am going to be writing special fitness reports and award recommendations. Please send in Petty Officer Brewster on your way out, and give me your recommendations on both subjects as soon as you can."

— —

In Great Britain, the morning newspapers were full of the story of the battle off Cape Vilan. The radio reporters hailed it as a great victory that ensured the survival of the Empire. Admiral Hardy's photograph was prominently shown on the front page of every paper and he was described as the architect of the victory. "Brilliant Victory at Sea," read the banner headline of the *Times*. "Admiral Sir Bruce Hardy Follows in Ancestor's Footsteps," read the *Daily Mail*. Just as the prime minister had planned, Hardy was compared to Nelson; the victory over the only German fleet free to raid convoys in the Atlantic compared to the elimination of the Danish fleet at Copenhagen. There were several spontaneous celebrations by crowds in Trafalgar Square and elsewhere.

The Associated Press and United Press International flashed the story around the Allied world. The morning newspapers in the United States only had time to carry the wire stories, but even at that, a huge throng of reporters gathered at Main Navy in Washington by the Reflecting Pool, clamoring for details. There were precious few that the US Navy could provide other than official photos of Sheppard and the previous action of *Shenandoah* in the Pacific. That story was retold with fresh details that had been deemed declassifiable.

President Roosevelt saw the importance of the news coverage to the public as the first solid victory following the debacles at Pearl Harbor and the Philippines. Evelyn McCloud was flown to Washington for a well-publicized luncheon with the First Lady. Additional photos of Sheppard recovering in Balboa Naval Hospital after *Shenandoah*'s return, with Evelyn by his side, were released to the press. Reporters ambushed

Captain Chris Baer of the *Shenandoah* outside the Long Beach Naval Shipyard for a fresh perspective on the action off Hawaii. The details of Sheppard being carried by his loyal crew to the battle dressing station sparked another feeding frenzy as the Navy tried to locate the sailors involved to provide the press access for interviews.

Three days later, when the destroyer arrived with the mail and reports, the Navy released additional details of the Battle of Cape Vilan, as it was now named. Senator Russell of Georgia introduced a bill for Sheppard's immediate promotion to rear admiral. After the fanfare had died down, the senator was quietly informed that the bill should be withdrawn until the President determined whether Sheppard was going to be court-martialed as a war criminal.

— —

Squadron Leader Wythe-Jones was on routine patrol at the end of a long night in the Bay of Biscay when his radar operator reported a small blip twenty-five miles away.

Probably a U-boat, he thought. He turned the Sunderland to investigate in the light of a clear dawn and had depth bombs loaded on the drop points. Wythe-Jones was surprised that the U-boat made no attempt to crash-dive as he approached for his attack. His bow machine gunner strafed as the Sunderland roared in, the four Pegasus radials screaming in protest.

Three ... two ... one ... drop, he thought as the depth bombs fell away.

Banking sharply to throw off the U-boat's pathetic antiaircraft fire, Rupert saw that his drop had been perfect. Twin water columns rose, bracketing the submarine aft of her conning tower. The boat began circling and settling by the stern. Her aft ballast tanks must have been holed.

The longer he watched, now out of range, the more she settled. Men began to jump from her bridge. The bow began to rise. Bubbles and froth marked a desperate attempt to blow the ballast tanks as more men escaped.

Wythe-Jones circled the sinking submarine closer and noticed men struggling to stay afloat in the unforgiving sea. Assessing that the ocean was calm enough for him to attempt a landing, he flew downwind, circled, and attempted a landing to rescue the surviving Germans. With a series of bone-jarring splashes, the Sunderland landed into the wind and taxied up to the spreading oil slick that marked the location of her kill.

The Sunderland's crew managed to haul two dozen soaked and demoralized German crew members of *U-179* on board, including Johann Schmitt and Wolfgang Brandt. No other swimmers were visible when Wythe-Jones took off and headed back to RAF Pembroke Dock.

— —

Klaus Schröder had been correct. It was a very unpleasant meeting with Großadmiral Raeder. Reichsmarschall Göering had felt the need to also attend.

"How could you be so stupid in employing my aircraft?" Göering thundered, his powder-blue uniform heaving with his massive waist.

"Reichsmarschall," Schröder said. "We crippled three aircraft carriers and destroyed more aircraft than we lost."

"Lies! Our spies report *Ark Royal* intact."

Not surprised at the news, Schröder decided he could deflect some of the blame, at least.

"It was that incompetent Eisner who failed in only crippling one of the American battle cruisers and—"

"Crippling one American *Antietam*-class ship was no accomplishment!" Großadmiral Raeder said. "Your fleet had four superior battle cruisers."

"Admiral Raeder, Dönitz's submariners misinformed you," Schröder said, sensing a way to regain the upper hand. "Their guns had greater range; there were too many twin-gun mounts; and, finally, they sported additional triple turrets beneath the bridge. Those ships were *Santiago*-class battle cruisers, much more powerful than mine."

Raeder said nothing.

"I was fortunate to extract my fleet with the loss of only scout cruisers," Schröder added.

It was the only thing that saved him. Raeder had wondered about the Allied press reports that had talked of the battle cruiser's name being *Argonne*—a battle in the Great War. He knew the Americans were slaves to naming conventions and had suspected the *Argonne* was of a different class. The two senior officers were aware of the casualty totals that Schröder had reported.

"Reichsmarschall, Großadmiral," Schröder said, "My men were subjected to horrible deaths. My helpless wounded lying on deck were deliberately bombarded with white phosphorus shells. My men— including my own son—died in agony."

Both senior officers looked at him in shock.

"It was Sheppard McCloud, commanding *Argonne*, who did that to your men!" Admiral Raeder said, knowing the details of the international press reports.

Schröder stared at Raeder, mouth contorted into a thin straight line, eyes narrowed, fists balled. "So, that is the man that killed my son."

Schröder was dismissed while the leaders of the Kriegsmarine and Luftwaffe debated his fate. They sent for Joseph Goebbels. Together, the three crafted the propaganda release calling Sheppard McCloud a war criminal for inflicting unnecessary suffering and death. The release lauded the heroism of German sailors in the face of a vastly superior force, outnumbered by more than two to one. The Allied newspaper editors laughed at it and ran instead the leaked story of summary executions by the SS occurring in French shipyards. As is often the case, Schröder was hailed as a hero of the Third Reich and promoted to full admiral. There were only a few who knew the real reason—to put him on an equal footing with the Italian fleet commander.

— —

A few days later, Squadron Leader Wythe-Jones was sitting at his desk, working his way through the reams of RAF paperwork, when the telephone rang.

"Rupert, ol' boy, I thought I would ring you up with some good news."

It was Air Commodore Andrew Blackstone, Air Officer Commanding of Nineteen Group. A call from him was never good news.

"Sir," Wythe-Jones said, "I'm working on my overdues as we speak and should have them finished in a day or two."

Struck by déjà vu, Rupert laughed.

"Well, Rupert, I hardly think it is funny when you get an invitation from Buckingham Palace to present yourself to be knighted by the king. He seems to think you had something to do with the action off of Cape Vilan—accuracy of reports, timeliness of updates, and all that rubbish. Prime Minister and the Admiralty pushed it through—not something Coastal Command would ever advocate. By the way, I believe the king is also going to give you a DSC for your third U-boat kill."

Wythe-Jones said nothing, barely able to hold the phone to his ear in his shock.

"Well done, ol' chap. Please be on time in your number ones. Oh, and bring your wife. It would be a nice touch for the *Daily Mail*."

With that, the air commodore rang off, having neglected to inform Rupert *when* he was supposed to present himself at the palace.

— —

The German propaganda machine's attempt to brand Sheppard a war criminal killed every effort by those jealous of his success to have him court-martialed. Though President Roosevelt and his military chief of staff, Admiral Leahy, were never involved, the Washington whisper circuit would stop any attempt to promote Sheppard until the normal flag selection board. Despite their best efforts at letting the story die, Sheppard's actions in the battle kept coming back to haunt his detractors.

As soon as Task Force Forty-Eight came within range of continuous air patrols from the East Coast, *Raritan*, *Sabine*, *Quincy*, and *Bethlehem* left the two battle cruisers and steamed ahead to Norfolk at *Sabine's* best speed of sixteen knots. When the two carriers moored to the pier, crowds of sailors spontaneously cheered. Photos of the apparently undamaged *Raritan* were given to the press.

The Virginian-Pilot ran the photo with a banner headline: "Hero of Battle Saves Carrier." Admiral Hamilton was effusive in his praise of McCloud's tactical acumen in every interview. Picked up by the national press, the story helped balance news that Rommel had reached Tunisia and was advancing on Algeria with its prize of the large French sheltered at Mers el Kebir.

— ▪ —

The Navy decided that *Argonne* and *Belleau Wood* should go to Philadelphia, where a large graving dock was currently empty. That dock was orientated northwest-southeast, which Captain McCloud had requested, for some reason. *Argonne* would go directly into the dock for her relatively minor repairs while *Belleau Wood* off-loaded all her ammunition. It would take the better part of a year to repair *Belleau Wood*, but Kevin Bailey, still officially recovering from a concussion, would not see it. The Navy news release stated that he had been inadvertently leaning against the armor of the command tower when a German shell struck. The length of his recuperation made reassignment appropriate. His desk job in Washington as an assistant liaison officer to the United States Coast and Geodetic Survey surprised many, but none in the know.

Before crossing the hundred-fathom curve, *Argonne* passed the tow of *Belleau Wood* to a flotilla of fleet tugs at the entrance to the Delaware Bay. Proceeding up the Bay and then the River, Sheppard's crew removed the bridges, removed the saddle, and erected the aircraft-and-boat crane. The Kingfishers were flown off, with Bronco in the lead. They were the first to arrive at Philadelphia's Naval Air Station.

Bronco was mobbed by the press. *The Philadelphia Inquirer* ran photos of him with his white silk scarf and holding his aviator's helmet, under a banner headline: "Hero Aviator Cripples German Fleet." Bronco's catchy name and devastating good looks failed to sway every attempt he made to give the credit for the victory to McCloud alone. When it was learned that he was a fun-loving bachelor, rumors flew that the *Inquirer*'s photo of him was posted in every woman's dormitory at the University of Pennsylvania.

— ▪ —

G·

lrgonne approached the shipyard, another flotilla of tugs began
ı and pull her into position to enter dry dock number seven.
gs and a capstan line pulled *Argonne's* bow across the sill, the
ing officer became officially responsible for the ship's safety, and
ppard could finally relax. He was in his stateroom tending to award
ommendations when Jefferson appeared.

"This truly is a fine Navy day, Cap'n," Jefferson chirped.

"That it is, Petty Officer Jefferson, that it is," Sheppard replied,
somewhat puzzled, for it was getting on in the afternoon.

"No, Cap'n, it truly is! Brow is jus comin' down. There's some-un
'mportant to seez you."

Sheppard, expecting to greet an admiral as he followed Jefferson out into
the fading sunshine of a beautiful May afternoon, was glad he had his blues
on. He didn't remember whether he saluted the quarterdeck or the national
ensign at the stern as he left *Argonne*. All he remembered was Evelyn's face as
he limped to her as quickly as he could on his game leg. Reaching her, he lifted
her off her feet, embracing her lithe frame and giving her a passionate kiss that
was captured for eternity by a Navy photographer. The photo, expeditiously
provided to the press, received the title "A Hero's Homecoming."

— —

*She was happy. They were home and safe. She knew that whatever the
future might hold in this monstrous thing enveloping their world, this
war, he would see them through. Whatever her pain, he would comfort
her. Whatever their loss, they would have each other.*

*He had his friends about him, but their bond was stronger. She knew
the depth of his crew's loyalty, irrespective of whether he did or not. That
did not matter; her loyalty was greater. Even if she had to share her
beloved with this new one, he would always be the one, the only one for
her—this Shepherd!*

Philadelphia Naval Base

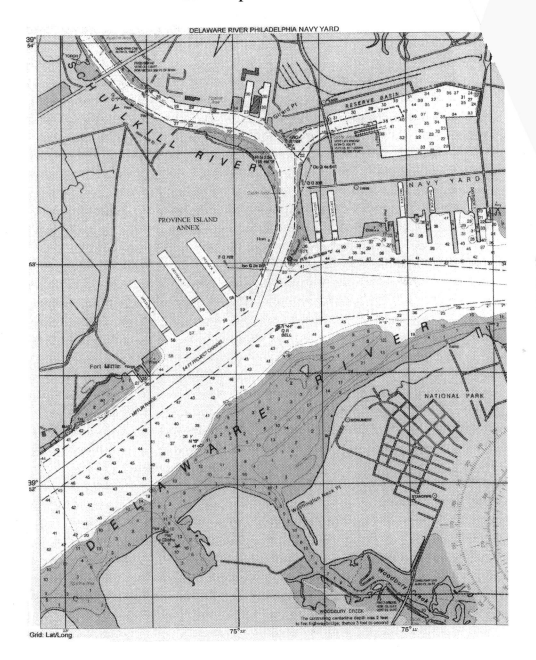